The Redundant Dragons

The Redundant Dragons

by

Elizabeth Ann Scarborough

Gypsy Shadow Publishing

The Redundant Dragons

by
Elizabeth Ann Scarborough

Gypsy Shadow Publishing, LLC.
Lockhart, TX
www.Gypsyshadow.com

Library of Congress Control Number: 2018965547

ebook ISBN: 978-1-61950-342-7
Print ISBN: 978-1-61950-343-4

Published in the United States of America

First eBook Edition: November 23, 2018
First Print Edition: November 27, 2018

Dedication

This book is dedicated to its Kickstarter backers, especially Anne Young and Stephanie Bonsanti, as well as to Nelson's Blood, my sea shanty group, who inspired the nautical bits.

Acknowledgements

I would like to thank my editors and publishers, Charlotte Holley and Denise Bartlett of Gypsy Shadow Publishing, cover artist Karen Gillmore, cheering squad and first beta readers Becky Kyle and Tania Opland who helped me navigate the story and suggested Malady should be a major player instead of a minor irritation. Thanks also to my final beta readers, Carolyn LaPlant, Becky Kyle (again), and Morgiana Halley.

What follows is a list of my Kickstarter backers for this book. Thank you.

Linda Cork, Joanne Forster, CE Murphy, Daniel Vinette, Anne Young, Wooster, Charlotte Holley and Denise Bartlett, Julia Bonser, Ruth J. Burroughs, Kristal Dalgetty, Jory Bernstein, Katherine Roe, Curtis Berry, Lis Halliday-Tyler, Susan Mandel, Corey Liss, Isaac 'Will it Work' Dansicker, Donna Bailly, Gail Sullivan, Jean-Marie Ward, Cynthia F. Shelley, Chad Bowden, Laurie Hicks, Gwen and Steven Yaple, Diana Rehfield, Gavran, Joella Berkner, Stella Sloop, Liv Margareth Alver, Daniella Gembala, Pyrrhalphis, Marti Wulfow Garner, Deborah Fishburn, Laurie Weaver, Katrina Oppermann, Sandy Hershelman, Daniel Pelletier, Becky Kyle, Victoria L. Sullivan, Jesse Fitzsimmons, Janice Ziv, Shala Kerrigan, Cat Allen, Barbara A Denz, Stephanie Bonsanti, Paul Bullard, Shannon Scollard, Tania Opland, Kirsten Pieper-Schulz, Amy Browning, Kal Powell, Carol Guess, Sandra Doherty, Vicky DiSanto, Thomas Bull, Katherine L. Mock, Esha, Christine Boyer Maj, Erica Hamerquist, Tom Linton, Greg Hallock, Elizabeth Sloan, Kathleen Lane, Traevynn, Jane Anderson, Marketa Zvelebil, Marilyn L. Alm, Jeanne Evans, Karen Gillmore, Jamie Cloud Eakin, Arnd Empting, Ted Briggs-Comstock, Virgina Korleski, Debby Rodrig, Carol Berry, Barbara Chandler-Young, Jinjer Stanton, Sarah Frazier, Karen Bull, Otomo, Lee Jackson, Kevin Andrew Murphy, and Lynn Garren.

Advanced Readers' Reviews

Clever, amusing, and inventive. Don't read it last thing before bed because you won't be able to stop. A considerable gallery of well-drawn characters. Verity is a splendid creation and very sound on dragons. And there are Ghost-Cats. What else could we want?
—Kerry Greenwood
Author of the Phryne Fisher detective novels (Miss Fisher's Murder Mysteries TV series) and *The Spotted Dog* in the Corinna Chapman series

The Redundant Dragons is a book chock full of quirky characters, effervescent dialogue and wicked humor. The story rockets from one character to another without a misstep. But underlying the fun there's a serious theme reflecting the best and worst in humanity (and dragonity) and a reminder of how easy it is to find oneself on the wrong side. Although this is the second in a series, I had no trouble following the plot. Now I MUST find the first, which I expect to enjoy just as much.
—Sharan Newman
Author of the Guinevere series and the Catherine LeVenseur Mystery series

Scarborough's Redundant Dragons is a wicked swirl of humor, fantasy and astute social commentary that moves along so fast you almost don't notice how deep it goes.
—Joyce Thompson
Author of *Bones, Sailing My Shoe to Timbuktu,* and the novelization of *Harry and the Hendersons*

Elizabeth Ann Scarborough does it again with another fantastic light-hearted fantasy where dragons aren't the villains, but likable heroes.
—Pamela K. Kinney
Author of *How the Vortex Changed my Life, Haunted Richmond* and *Haunted Virginia*

Elizabeth Ann Scarborough's new installment of the Songs from the Seashell Archives series slides through fantasy, literature, sci-fiction, and song as easily as one of her time-traveling characters slips through the ages. A reluctant queen, a pirate's curse, and a thunder of delinquent dragons are only the beginning in this fanciful tale. Oh, and ghost cats. We mustn't forget the ghost cats!
—Mollie Hunt
Author of The Crazy Cat Lady Cozy Mystery Series

Dragons, a bard, and witches, Oh yes! I made some new friends, and greeted some old ones. I even sang along with the bard. Elizabeth Ann Scarborough grabbed my attention with a Song of Sorcery and has kept it ever since.
—Elisa Ballou

I really couldn't put the book down. I had to know what was going to happen to the reluctant queen and her fanciful friends next!
—J. M. Jennings aka Billie Maverick
Author of *The Drenching*

Chapter 1: Dragons At Large

The controversial new queen watched from the battlements as the former drone dragons made their presumably joyous exodus from their workplace dungeons. More than one blinked nervously, poking its head out to look up and down the city streets. Then, claw by claw, each slunk out of its industrial den, abandoning the familiarity of the only home it had known for many years, if not its entire life.

'Hooray, the dragons are free at last!' thought the truth-and-justice side of Queen Verity, followed by the more realistic thought. 'Oh dear, the dragons are free. Now what?'

Malady Hyde, the queen's personal assistant, her predatory eye keen for signs of weakness in her monarch, swooped in to stand beside her. The crumbling gray stone of the castle's jagged roof had recently been reinforced with a lacework of wrought iron studded at intervals with the latest distant-viewing apparatuses.

"Just look at what you've done now!" Malady said. "Liberating dragons is all very well, but the next question is who will liberate us from the tyranny of dragons once they figure out that without the kibble, they have the upper claw."

Malady was a stranger to truth as Verity knew it, which made their relationship even more antagonistic than it would have been solely because of their differing worldviews, but in this case the queen very much feared that Malady had a point.

Verity had a feeling that the rest of the population of Queenston, whom she supposed she ought to think of as her subjects, were less than enthusiastic about the turn events had taken since she was recognized as the first royal to reign in four generations. Her feeling, as usual, was not wrong.

Verity knew she wasn't good at queening. Her mother had assumed that Verity's ability to tell the truth and be able to detect lies would be an asset in a leader. In fact, it made it almost impossible. The problem was that in politics, everyone was lying, all the time, in such tangled webs of interwoven falsehood that she couldn't say who was being untruthful about what since it all gave her an unbearable, raging headache. The pain had never been so bad in her life. Malady, appointed her assistant by the same troublesome mother who had appointed Verity queen, kept going to court in her stead, since lies were her native tongue.

In the politics of dragons, however, Malady was missing something. The dragons were no longer dependent on the kibble, but neither would they have anything else to eat for very long. The wild game was already much depleted in a matter of a few days, and the head of the Cattleperson's Association had begun complaining of livestock predation. "It's not like we're made of coos," were his exact words.

When Verity consulted dragon-wrangler Toby, and his dragon Taz about the matter, Taz flew off and conferred with some of the other dragons.

"They say that's too bad," Taz relayed via Toby. "But the humans made their living on dragon backs for long enough and it's no good complaining now that the tables are turned."

"Well, yes," Verity said. "I'd be the first to agree, except that humans have to eat, too, if they are to raise food for dragons. If dragons take whatever they like whenever, everyone will be starving very soon. I begin to appreciate the genius of the kibble."

Meanwhile dragons darkened the skies and crowded the streets. Actually, just one good-sized dragon was enough to crowd almost any street. Dragons lurked atop every building, like so much menacing architecture. Fire strobed overhead from dragons whose jobs had dictated timed releases of flame. Now that they were free, they couldn't quite kick the habit of firing according to their old schedules.

Horatio and Myrtle

"Why don't they go back where they came from?" complained Horatio the Hair, the Queenstreet barber, casting a glance of indignation not untinged with fear over his shoulder as he entered his shop. A grayish drake the size of a coach met his eye with a glare from a baleful yellow one.

"I'm afraid that's exactly what they're doing, but perhaps you'd like to be the first to suggest it to them?" his wife Myrtle, replied.

"The government should be doing something about this," he said.

"Perhaps that new lass, whatsername, the queen, will sort it out," Myrtle said soothingly.

He snorted. "From what I hear, she's to blame."

Her Majesty's Disability

Verity was of the same opinion. She was indeed to blame for the dragon situation. Toby, the dragon-wrangler, and his scaly partner, Taz, had instigated most of what he called a strike on the part of dragons suing for better food and working conditions. Even prior to that, they had, perhaps rather impulsively, destroyed most of the kibble formerly used to control the dragons through their diet, and disrupted the breeding program.

Verity's mother, who had missed being queen by a hundred years or so before insisting that the burden of the crown become Verity's, had also been responsible. But it was the queen's job to take the blame for unfortunate ramifications of events she set in motion. Someone better at the job could have made the consequences look like part of a plan. Verity not only lacked the talent for such pretense, but was constitutionally incapable of it, due to her curse.

Once her mother had forced everyone who was anyone in Queenston to acknowledge and honor the royal succession, she'd disappeared, off traveling, even time traveling, although Verity had not a clue what that actually involved, It had to be a real thing, or her curse would have let her know.

Nor was her father any help. Since his near-fatal accident, he had undergone a radical transformation involving a fish tail and a musical career, and thus far did not seem to remember who she was.

Her mother's old traveling companion, the family solicitor, N. Tod Belgaire, was out of the city supposedly locating an old history teacher to tutor Verity in the ways of royalty.

The country hadn't had one since her grandmother, Queen Bronwyn, sat upon the throne at the beginning of the Great War. Since that time, Argonia had become a commercial client nation of neighboring Frostingdung. Verity's return to the throne was supposed to break the chains of Frostingdung's economic hegemony over her land. The breaking of those chains, both real and metaphorical, was to begin with those that bound the dragons to industrial servitude.

It was a good plan, but she had failed to foresee that the solution to that problem could create many other, possibly worse ones.

Her views were not undisputedly popular and received no validation from anyone, least of all the Crown Council, particularly the members who had owned interests in kibble production.

"I do not know what to do," she confided finally to absolutely the worst person possible, Malady Hyde.

"Of course, you don't, you idiot, um, Your Majesty. You have no aptitude for this any more than you did for needlepoint when we took Introduction to Ladycraft at school."

Verity still had no idea what she had ever done to her mother, absent for the best part of her life, that her un-maternal maternal parent would foist Malady on her as an advisor.

"You don't think she'll give me good advice, surely?" she'd challenged her mother before they parted.

"No, but you'll know the difference and can just do the opposite from what she advises. I have my reasons."

That made sense, up to a point, but although she had never been wounded badly enough to know how it felt having salt poured into a wound, she suspected it must have been much like she felt about Malady.

The worst of it was, the advisers and nobles all listened to whatever Malady said and in general seemed to get on with her in a way they did not get on with their queen.

Verity's initial meeting with them had made that abundantly clear.

The Queen Game

She had tried to conform to what a queen was supposed to be according to the history books. She did her best to look the part, wearing the blue satin gown made for her by Madame Marsha. She'd straightened her spine, so she stood imposingly tall, her full height only a foot short of the massive oaken doors leading from the castle's entrance hall to the audience chamber and council room.

She'd settled the family tiara on her red-gold hair, which was plaited into a braided crown, making a cushion to support the tiara so it didn't dig into her skull.

She'd cleared her throat and said "Scat!" as she waded through the crowd of short shadowy figures slithering over her feet, between her and the door. The ghost cats could walk through walls, of course, as was the ghostly custom, but they preferred to wait to see if someone else, someone two-legged and solid, would open the door properly for them, as was the catly custom.

When no one else hastened to open it, as they really ought to for a queen (even if one doesn't respect the person, she'd always been taught, one must respect the rank). she did it herself and the shadows slithered into the room ahead of her.

At a great long table, nine prosperous looking men sat talking. The talking didn't stop when she walked into the room. At the elbow of each man sat a young woman, each more comely than the last, and each seated at her own little table, and on each of these nine tables clacked a substantial Smythe-Coronet typing machine.

This symmetry was broken only by the presence of an additional young woman, Malady (Verity had to hand it to her. She'd had to move fast to get to court and subvert everyone between the time Verity got off the train and the time she appeared at the door), whose brittle titter erupted when she stole a glance at her old schoolmate, now her queen.

"Excuse me, Uncle Oscar, Uncle Horace," the treacherous cow said, "there she is now. Are we supposed to bow or something?"

Verity tried out a royal glare. It was just the same as her usual one, which she actually didn't use a great deal.

"Malady, I wondered where you'd gone," she said. "I thought you were supposed to be my assistant?"

Not that Verity had ever imagined such an arrangement would work out. Her mother had used the dragon-calming kibble in baked goods that caused people to behave—quite temporarily—in ways so unlikely it would have seemed more likely if they'd turned into frogs.

She recognized three of these kibble-influenced people among the men seated at the table from the conclave at Fort Iceworm.

"I *am* assisting you, Bossy Boots," Malady retorted. "I was telling my dear uncles all about you and what we might expect from your reign."

Except for the table, the typing tables, and the chairs occupied by the men, their assistants, and Malady, it was Standing Room Only in the vast chamber. Verity had once toured the castle with one of her classes, shortly before her expulsion from that particular school. She seemed to recall there had been more chairs then.

"Looking for your throne, Majesty?" Sir Cuthbert, the head of the Crown Council, asked. "I fear it was in mothballs in the royal attic and it needs to be cleaned and reupholstered. There's a bench against that window over there." He swung his arm, flourishing the silken crimson sleeve of his robe of office.

A few of the ghost cats already reclined on the bench, while more stood in the window well, looking out the narrow, arched slit as the eye of something else, no doubt a curious dragon, looked in. Other ethereal felines sprawled across the middle of the conference table. One jumped onto the shoulder of a typist and peered over her shoulder as she pecked at her machine. The girl looked up from her machine and gave the feline apparition a startled glance. Verity recognized the typist. She started to say her name, "Fi—" But her former classmate, Fiona Featherstone, shook her head ever so slightly. She rolled her eyes then dipped her head to return to her typing machine. The cat rubbed itself through her cheek, sprawling across the keyboard so Fiona's fingers had to tap through the transparent form with every keystroke. Perhaps it tickled. Fiona Featherstone kept her head down.

Fiona had been in the first level at the second of the schools Verity had flunked out of, but Fiona left first. Verity hadn't known her well, but liked her. She didn't put on airs and was irreverent and outspoken. Verity was sorry to see her go.

At the schools they attended, one could get expelled for a variety of reasons, such as non-payment of fees or behavioral or social gaffes. The worst offenses involved boys and there had been some wild stories about Fiona after she left, though later Verity heard that Fiona's widowed father had died recently so her departure had to do with the financial offense and not with boys after all. Verity was glad to see she seemed to have landed on her feet.

At any rate, she didn't seem to want to be recognized, and Verity knew better than to ask Malady about her. Doing so would probably bring down some punishment on the poor girl's head, if not cause her to be dismissed.

Verity headed toward the bench, feeling eyes on her back and hearing snickers, only one of which sounded like Malady's. If they thought she was going to park herself clear over there while they conducted court business without her, they were very much mistaken. Because of her Frost Giant heritage (on her mother's side), Verity was not only quite tall for a girl, but very strong. Slinging the bench over her shoulder, scattering ghost cats, she carried it to the table, set it down, and tapped Sir Cuthbert's shoulder. He was seated at the head of the table.

"I believe you're in my chair," she said, and indicated the bench. "You may sit there."

He started to protest, then apparently thought better of it. Even had she not been the queen, she was bigger than he was.

The council sat as still as deer lacking sense enough to run away when a hunter drew a bead on them. Not that Verity wanted the council to run away. Not that she meant to frighten them. It was ridiculous to think of seasoned captains of state and commerce being intimidated by her, but if she was going to change things at all, she required their respect, or their willingness to listen at the very least. The problem was, other than a few monarchs she'd read about in history texts, she knew nothing about ruling. If her mother had actually stuck around back in the day when she would have been heir to the throne, for one thing, the Great War probably wouldn't have happened. On the other hand, since her mother did not become queen because she and Mr. Belgaire scampered off to experience life in other times, such as the current one, if she had become the queen,

Mother wouldn't have met father and Verity wouldn't have happened. As it was, Mother felt entitled to pass on the crown she'd never worn to her daughter, expecting Verity to do a job she herself had avoided.

Verity had returned to Queenston with all of the drag-on-kibble-drugged town leaders thinking the return of a Rowan to the mothballed Argonian throne was a good idea. Except everyone seemed to also be drugged into thinking that somehow or other her bloodline would fill Verity in on what queens did and how they behaved, and nobody seemed to want to insult her by telling her how.

The council members seemed to have gotten over any such reluctance.

"Now then," Verity said. "Why don't each of you introduce yourselves? I'll start. My name is Verity Brown, er—Regina. You, sir?"

The man she addressed said nothing, staring stubbornly ahead of him.

"Fine then, how about the next gentleman?"

More silence.

"Are you shy?" she asked, but she knew they were not. Malady made little noises behind her hand that sounded like suppressed giggles. Verity was being given the silent treatment. She had been snubbed and bullied often enough in school to recognize it. These august statesmen were just older, richer, plumper male versions of the mean girls who had made her academic career miserable. One of those girls had been Malady, who her misguided mother had appointed as her assistant. When Verity complained, Mother had put her finger on the side of her nose and said, "Keep your friends close and your enemies closer, so you'll have advance warning what they'll try to do to you next. Also," she said, "If necessary, you'll be close enough to slip a little something into their cup."

Verity cleared her throat and said, conversationally, "I only ask your names out of courtesy. You are eminent gentlemen currently of high position. Of course, I know your names. As you may have heard, I recently escaped from a dragon's den. Your attitude does not impress me."

"Ah, yes, the dragons," said Sir Cuthbert. "So you do intend to threaten us with them, so we do your bidding?"

"Of course not," she said, pleased to have found the topic that broke the silence. "There's no need for me to threaten you with them. They're capable of being quite threatening on their own. I thought we might discuss their position, however, and what to do..."

"To keep from being roasted in our beds?"

"No boiler room blowhard had better threaten my family," said Lord Weems, who was, Verity noted, young and clearly inexperienced in the ways of dragons. She had harbored a similar attitude before she met the dragon Vitia, having seen dragons only in menial positions until then.

"Perhaps it has escaped your attention what it is that they blow when blowing hard," Sir Cuthbert said. "These creatures can and do smelt iron more efficiently than a blast furnace." The very image appalled him enough that he buried his head in his hands for a moment before collecting himself. The anger and fear he focused on Verity when he looked up was not feigned. "Madame, what have you wrought?"

Verity said, "They were our allies. They did not deserve to be enslaved, have their wings clipped and their tails docked to fit the tasks we have for them."

"And the city doesn't deserve to be burnt to the ground because you favor wild and dangerous animals over your own people."

"All they want is to be fed and not be hunted."

The Lord Treasurer snorted. "You do know what their traditional cuisine is, do you not, Madame?" She had no time to answer before he did. "Us, that's what. Historically, dragons eat people. The development of the kibble kept their hunger at bay and their tempers placid, so their homicidal impulses could be moderated, and their temperaments rendered more biddable, but you and your friends have taken care of that. What did you think they were going to eat when you destroyed the food we'd trained them to rely on?"

"Animals, of course," she said. "Sheep and cattle and pigs and such. The farmers in other countries supply them to dragons to keep them peaceful."

"In Glassovia, you encountered three dragons, I believe?" Sir Cuthbert said. Verity nodded, and he gave her a withering look. "We have hundreds."

19

"There are many more than three dragons to feed here," Lord Oswald said. "Our breeding program was extremely successful."

Lord Remington-Sharpe looked up from inspecting his nails. He had been an acquaintance of her father, with an interest in both metallurgy and explosives. "Milords and Madame Queen, you are considering only the advantages of the dragons. Progress for man has not stood still while these beasts were in our employ. There are other means of controlling the dragon population—even convincing them to go back to work. They are not the only ones who can employ firepower."

Council

Following the queen's petulant departure, the council members continued consulting. Lord Remington-Sharp coughed into his fist. "She's worse than I feared."

"Won't do at all," Sir Horace agreed. "Not to the manor born, whatever her ancestry indicates. I can't believe the rest of you agreed to allowing her to assume the throne."

"Just because she assumes it, doesn't mean she can remain there," Sir Cuthbert said. "There are ways of dealing with undesirable queens."

"Marry her off to a distant king or princeling whose custom requires the wife live in his home."

"No treasure," Lord Murdo reminded them. "Therefore, no dowry. No dowry, no husband."

"Marriage would be one way, but there are others," Sir Cuthbert said.

"Find her guilty of some crime and execute her?"

"The circumstances of her ascension to the throne were rather casual," Lord Remington-Sharp said. "I don't think we need to stand on formality. I know someone..."

"What about the dragons?" Malady asked, twirling one of her golden curls around her finger. Supposedly her uncles had only her best interests at heart, but this talk of doing away with people made her nervous. "They seem to like her. And now that they're loose, might they not take revenge or something if she's not around to control them?"

"The wrangler boy does most of that..." Sir Horace said.

"But he's friends with her too. And he won't like it if she is dead." Why was she defending Verity, anyway? She was a scary tall gawk and prissy, too about what was true and what was not, which to Malady very much depended on what she wanted at the moment. The big prig, on the other hand, seemed to have no opinions to call her own. You could hardly talk to someone like that! In spite of her great height, she had no real regal presence the way Malady did. Her skin was too dark to remind anybody of milk or alabaster, and her hair was frizzy. She had no grace or daintiness. She could not possibly wear ruffles or the color pink.

"Who said anything about dead?" Remington-Sharpe said. "We must ask ourselves, 'what would Marquette do?' He would find a way to keep her alive and somewhat available, but unable to cause trouble."

"A sanitarium perhaps? Nice lunatic asylum with chains and padded walls. For her own protection, of course." Sir Cuthbert added, "There's an alienist giving lectures at the opera house. Perhaps she might be persuaded..."

"The boy or the dragons could easily free her from the madhouse if they got wind of it. And you know how hard it is to foment a decent intrigue in a small city like this. I have an idea," Sir Eustus said. "Since the dragons have stopped work, the ships that convert to sail are short-handed, I hear. Fiona, take a memo..."

Fiona Featherstone tried not to tremble as her keys clacked beneath her competent fingers. The fates they were dreaming up for her unwitting former classmate were very dire indeed. Personally, she much preferred a fate worse than death and moreover knew where to find one. It paid better too.

Chapter 2: Fiona

Two weeks after the dragon's 'coming out party,' as Captain Lewis put it, Verity was at Madame Marsha's salon in the former Brown family mansion, empty now that Verity's stepmother and associates were banished under threat of being eaten if they returned. She had put it to Madame Marsha that her old home might make a good premises for an upmarket design studio, seamstress/tailor shop and clothing boutique. Captain Lewis, an avid follower of fashion, was already there.

Verity told her friends how Malady had wound the privy council around her little finger to side against her.

"Well, most of them are Frostingdungian," Madame Marsha said, while stitching on a blue-green gown with a brocade panel embroidered with birds. "So she speaks their language and you don't."

"But that's not addressing the dragon in the drawing room," Captain Lewis said, eyebrows arched as he peeked over the top of his china cup. "Priorities, people. Verity, dearie, a good leader needs to do two critical things: establish priorities and delegate authority. Trust me, I've been a ship's captain for more years than you've been alive. As a matter of fact, I need to go be one again now. Farewell!"

Verity remembered the captain's words while walking back to the castle. She could have taken a coach, of course, but walking gave her a chance to monitor the positions of the dragons and also to look for Toby. She ought to have had a guard, if she'd been a proper queen, but she was not exactly sure whose side they were on.

The edifices of the city had aged greatly in the last few days. The weight of dragons on the rooftops crumbled brick and mortar, and dragons who did not flame regularly, on their unaccustomed raw diet, deposited streams of steaming sulfurous stinking scat all down the sides of the buildings.

The castle's turrets and towers now were embellished with dragons too, one particularly large specimen having wrapped itself around the privy tower. The courtyard was filled with four dragons diligently using their tails to whap a large ball back and forth. She guessed they might have worked in a textile mill where throwing a shuttle accurately was a useful skill. Between the whapping tails and the projectile, however, their activity made getting from the outer bailey to the great hall very tricky.

A series of menacing growls from above alarmed her until she smelled fresh sulfurous emissions and realized the growls were digestive rather than emotional.

With a sudden crash, a boar carcass dropped into the courtyard and the game of dragon volleyball was abandoned as all four players pounced on the prey, bashing heads and tangling tails.

"Oops," a voice said from a few feet above. "Sorry. It slipped."

The voice was Toby's, but all she saw was the soles of his boots on either side of Taz's now quite substantial neck, just in front of her wings. Her blood-stained talons spread as she soared in for a landing, well away from the happily lashing tails of the feeding dragons.

Toby scratched the base of Taz's ear. The first time Verity saw her, she was small enough to sit inside the mouth of a hot air balloon and use her breath to inflate it. Now she was large enough for Toby to ride and still a growing girl.

"How's she holding up?" Verity asked.

"She's worn out. Do you know there are 350 newly freed dragons now who haven't a clue how to feed or look after themselves?"

"Odd that they didn't just pick it up, as Taz did when she became hungry."

"Most of them had indoor jobs in cramped engine rooms. They never saw a prey animal from a distance. Taz was used to a healthier lifestyle, and she had me to help her. The others don't know how to be proper dragons. They've been thoroughly conditioned to be drones and drudges who do what they're told. I'm afraid now that nobody is in charge of them, they're an aimless lot."

Toby's eyes looked a bit sunken, with dark circles under them. His lips were parched, and his brown face wind scoured and ruddy. He seemed excited and determined on the course he and Taz had decided. He knew it was the right thing for him, but also knew there was a cost and had begun to see that it would be higher than he was prepared for.

"You think they might have been better off where they were?"

Toby stared at his boot.

"A lot of them don't have wings—were bred that way. No need for wings in a boiler room. More efficient to never have them in the first place. No. Not better off, but this is going to take some adjustment is all. They're living creatures, not automatons to have parts added or taken away as men wish."

"Certainly not, and people will realize that if they live through the times when the dragons figure out we humans never had any real power over them. That may get tricky."

"If there's trouble, people have only themselves to blame."

"I doubt that will be a lot of consolation," Verity said. "And, Toby, these days there are firearms—look what happened to the Dragon Vitia, and she was much bigger and fiercer than any of our town dragons. In the old days, when dragons were wild, humans had no firearms. The explosives weren't as powerful as they are now."

"No, but they had magic."

"True, but it had rules and had to involve spells and rituals and a lot more forethought than firing a weapon. It could only be used by magicians with talent and training, not by just anyone. If the dragons choose to be hostile, they would do great damage to begin with, but the people they didn't kill could wipe them from the world as if they had never been."

The dragons on the turrets impatiently huffed cinders, Taz nosed Toby in the back, and he remounted. "We have hungry dragons to feed, so we'd best get to it, Highness."

Before she could respond, they were airborne. They cleared the turret, just above the heads of three dragons poised there, looking upward, when suddenly the dragons in the courtyard and those on the turret seemed to come to a simultaneous decision. With wings flapping hurricane-force gusts the seven dragons took to the air as well.

For a moment, her heart lifted with them and she was happy for them, able to fly away and be themselves for a while. She would have liked to join them. Then, as it had so often done, the truth dragged her down again and she trudged into the castle where, after a short visit to her quarters, she would dutifully attend the council session for another lesson in queening.

But when she entered her chambers, the first thing she saw was a typed note propped against her pillow.

"Run," it said.

The Train

Typed. It had to have come from Fiona. Of all the people in the council chamber, she was the only one Verity might have counted as an ally. Besides, the ghost cats liked her. Fiona was in terrible trouble, Verity was sure. Where had she gone after leaving the note?

Tearing off her skirts and petticoats, Verity stood in her shirtwaist and trousers, which she chose to wear rather than knickers. Trading her dainty slippers for sturdy boots, she covered all with her shell-lined hooded cloak, containing the relevant stories from her Aunt Ephemera's archives and the dragon beads gathered from the Dragon Vitia's lair. She stuck the note in the little pocket Madame Marsha had put in the trousers.

Glancing out the narrow window, Verity saw someone running down the garden path, cape swirling in a satisfactorily dramatic fashion. She turned to run down the stairs. She would have preferred sliding down the banister, but that would attract unwanted attention.

The long-legged queen took the steps three at a time, and she was down the corridor, out the door and into the garden in probably less time than it had taken to write the note. The ghost cats swarmed ahead of her. At length, she spied the lone figure she'd seen from the window scurrying ahead of her.

"Fiona! Wait!" she cried.

The girl never hesitated, but kept running. Daylight fled rapidly this time of year and although she had seen her quarry through the castle window moments before, the shadows closed over the path. By the time she reached the drawbridge, Verity saw only a flicker of dark cloak by torchlight before losing her quarry to the shadows, but she continued her pursuit, glad the bridge was not yet raised for the night. She was so intent on catching up to a seeming ally that she was unaware of the many gleaming slitted eyes watching her from the battlements, though she was aware of their muttering.

The ghost cats took the lead, streaming together in a pale phosphorescent vaguely furry scarf toward the old cemetery outside the castle grounds, filled this night with stony moon shadows. The dead held no particular threat for Verity, and she followed the cats. She saw her former schoolmate standing watchfully among the stones.

"Fiona?" she asked from a few feet away, softly and calmly so as not to cause alarm. The woman's head lifted, and she turned to face Verity. "Wait a minute! A word, please."

Her quarry, huffing and puffing, gasped, "I—don't—think that's a—very good—idea. Clever of you to heed my note, but never mind me, just you keep on going. They have plans for you, you know, those lords of the council. Unsavory plans. I want no part of such doings, nor of the other things some of their lordships try to tell me are required of a typist. If I'm going to put up with that, I can make a better living of it at home."

"You're well out of here then. I had no expectation of undying loyalty from the lot at the castle, though they're a bit grimmer than I'd hoped. Thanks for the warning. But how did you come to be there?"

"After Papa died, my mother wasn't far behind him. They left me nothing but a pile of debt, though Papa did make provisions for the Sisters of Useful Commerce to take me in and teach me a trade, which as you can see, they did, teaching me to operate a typewriting machine. Unfortunately, I can no longer remain at the castle."

"Why not? I'd be glad of an ally."

"Lord Eustus has taken an interest in me. The last three girls he took an interest in ended up on the streets."

"Which one is that?"

"The scrawny one with the very bad breath and the wild eyes."

"Oh, him." Verity remembered a man who looked to be in his late seventies with eyes that seemed to be trying to burn through her clothing. She'd been too preoccupied to pay him much notice but come to think of it, he was creepy, repulsive and no doubt frightening to a smaller woman. Her fleeting impulse to pick him up by the scruff of the neck, using as few fingers as possible, and toss him into the moat had not been inappropriate. Next time, if there was one, she'd do just that and appoint a new minister in his place. "I might be able to protect you, but I agree it would be easier if you were elsewhere. I'll walk you to the train."

"Thanks."

"And as we walk, explain to me why you think I should run."

"They are planning to kill you, of course. I heard them. They didn't even bother to lower their voices. They're all in on it. They think they can make a puppet queen out of Malady Hyde. Why did you bring her with you, anyway?"

"It was my mother's idea."

"Mother's! Why?"

"I don't know. She said something about keeping your enemies close enough to slip something into their food or drink." Verity grimaced. "But she seems to have reckoned without the knife in my back. Bit of a mystery, my mother, and I begin to think that's a good thing."

The train depot took up an entire city block, only part of which was the ticket office and waiting area. The rest of the area was cross-hatched with tracks that ultimately carried passengers in three different directions with many feeder tracks leading to places like mines and large farming enterprises. Verity had ridden from the Queenston station, which was the farthest south, to the Ablemarlonian border and beyond, into Glassovia to the east and Fort Iceworm to the north. Fort Iceworm was home to the Seashell Archives and the archivist, Verity's Aunt Ephemera.

She supposed if her loyal council didn't kill her first, her reign would take her to the western coast as well. Her old school was there, but she hadn't been able to see much of the rest of the area, although she had once had a visit with another aunt who lived in a home built on the site of her famed great-great-great-Aunt Sybil's legendary ginger-bread cottage. Aunt Epiphany was some sort of doctor. Verity found her nowhere near as interesting as their mutual ancestress was supposed to have been, Great-Aunt Sybil, according to the shells, had possessed the gift of being able to tell people's fortunes. Not the future or the past, but what was happening with others at the present moment, which had all sorts of handy possibilities. When asked about her own gifts, Epiphany had answered truthfully but vaguely. "Insight, dear girl. I have great insight."

Verity's dragon bead and shell necklace rattled between her skin and her clothing. The ghost cat that had been fol-lowing Fiona mewed silently, put its paws on Verity's knee, and looked up at her as if to say, 'What are you waiting for?'

"Goodbye. Thank you for trying to help, but look to your own safety. I've typed some missives for their lordships that speak of their real plans for you." She shuddered. "I repeat, run. And now I must do the same. Come with me."

"They're not getting rid of me that easily," Verity said, wincing at the twist of pain above her right eye. Dumping the liveliest of the beads and shells into her hand, she hand-ed them to Fiona and thrust the necklace into her pants pocket. "These belong to you. Wear them. I don't know what kind of protection they'll give you, but it's inherited power and it ought to be good for something. The cat goes with them. You do see the cat?"

"Yes, of course. I can't seem to get rid of it. Better take it with you. It might get hurt."

"I doubt it. It's the ghost of a familiar to one of your magical ancestors. It should help protect you. Besides, I have plenty of others." She glanced down at the milling, mewling translucent clowder clustered around her trouser legs. "Good luck."

She watched from the shadows as Fiona swept into the station then, after only a few minutes, out again, whereup-on she ran to the platform for a train already beginning to huff and choo. She was no sooner aboard than the engine dragons whistled, and the train left the station.

Verity didn't want to return to the castle. Dressed as a boy, she had the freedom of the streets, or so she thought, and decided to go visit old friends at the dock, at the Changelings Cabaret. It was open quite late, and she hoped to find news of her father there. She hadn't had a real conversation with him since her return from the north. In fact, she'd believed him to be dead until Madame Louisa, the headliner (and owner) of the club (and Captain Lewis's alter ego) revealed to her that instead of dying when he fell from the burning hot air balloon, her father had been saved by mermaid kin and transformed into a merman. He seemed to remember nothing of his former life, however, and she was not entirely sure he remembered who she was.

The docks were busy with ships being loaded and unloaded, men coming and going.

Only one place was completely silent and dark, a hole in the fabric of activity. The Changelings Cabaret was closed, a sign nailed to the door. She turned to leave.

A cowl of foul-smelling fabric dropped over her head and was pressed against her nose and mouth with an overpowering sweet aroma. She wasn't aware of her knees buckling and her body wilting to the ground, her fall broken only by strong arms that grabbed her from either side as she was dragged like a drunkard onto a waiting ship.

Chapter 3: Malady Hyde,
Girl Regent and Almost-a-Princess

"Very well then, where is she?" Malady asked the unusually smug looking royal cabinet at the council meeting. "You lot did something with her, didn't you?"

She could have pretended, of course, probably should have, but it took her by surprise, and the sudden dearth of hulking great teenaged queens was not easy to overlook.

"Oh, my dear," said Sir Cuthbert, "you don't get quality leadership from any random place. We thought as our families have put so much work and expense into pulling this crippled country together, if there is to be a queen, she should be one of us. Even the raggle taggle Gypsy queen herself suggested you be next in line if her whopping daughter didn't work out, so we rather feel that with said daughter suddenly disappearing, you are to be regent until she returns, IF she returns. With our guidance of course. It's a statesmanlike compromise between what the local authority wants and what we, the allies and saviors of this dragon-ridden country need to make it work, don't you see? What say you, Niece?"

"It would be like being a princess, wouldn't it? I always thought I was excellent princess material with my looks and fashion sense."

It wasn't at all like that, and her uncles looked at her pityingly and questioned the wisdom of their choice for the first time. She caught their expressions but held her head up with defiant shallowness. She was used to the finer things in life or at least had always wanted to be, and if she couldn't get them in her present situation, where could she, pray?

Crimped

Verity came to, sputtering and cursing as cold water drenched her head and torso. She looked up into a hard red face scowling down at her against a backdrop of canvas and timber.

"Get to work, you, before I give you a taste of the cat!" He brandished a hydra-like version of a whip, with multiple lashes. He smacked it against the deck and it made a nasty noise.

"There's been some sort of mistake..." she said.

"Craven the Crimp don't make mistakes and 'tis a mistake on your part to say he does."

"I didn't mean..."

"What are you, stupid or just too drunk to follow orders?"

"I'm not drunk," she said. She started to say, 'I'm the queen,' but was pretty sure announcing her rank and gender was not a good idea.

Someone thrust a mop into her hand. At least she knew what to do with that, having earned many work details for bad behavior at her various schools and academies. Pretending to concentrate on the deck, she mopped her way over to the rail. She could still see land—barely, and three other ships. The most distant one looked familiar.

"What are you gawkin' at? Look lively!" the fellow with the 'cat' ordered, cracking it in the air so its knotted ends came dangerously close to her nose.

Without thinking, she snapped back, "Be careful with that thing. You almost put my eye out." Her curse was always worse when she was nervous. He lifted the whip to strike again and two burly fellows closed in on her. She vaulted over the rail with unaccustomed agility and struck the water ten feet from the hull. Beneath the water's surface, she heard no one and nothing. It seemed warmer underneath too. She wondered if she'd turn into a mermaid, as some people in her family, her father included, had done, but no, her legs operated separately. She knew she'd have to surface for breath soon, but she just kept swimming and swimming. When she finally surfaced, the sun sparkled on the water and only one ship danced on the horizon.

She swam with only her face above the swells, keeping the ship in sight.

She didn't know its name. Scraping her hair back from her face and with wet hands, wiping the water from her eyes, she tried to read the lettering on the hull. There seemed to be a lot of l's.

She hailed the ship, "Hello! Please let me board. It's wet out here!"

Her voice carried well, which was not always a blessing, but in this situation worked to her advantage. Three of the crew looked over the rail, followed, to her surprise and delight by Captain Lewis in full piratical regalia. "Eh? Who's that?"

"It's me, Captain! Verity Brown!" She felt it would have been rude to say she was currently, reluctantly also the queen. Captain Lewis did know that.

"Whatever are you doing out there, dearie?"

"Swimming, fortunately."

"Get a wiggle on, me hearties!" the captain said, turning to shout to the crew not already at the rail. "This be a rare fish indeed!"

Hands extended over the side. To Verity's amazement, she was able to spring from the water with a dolphin-like leap and grab the proffered hands, almost dragging her rescuers over with the momentum. She hadn't known she could leap like that. She also kept forgetting she was not a dainty girl.

When she was drying off with her back to the rail, Captain Lewis said, "Fancy meeting you out here. What brings you to cross our course?"

"Not my idea," she said. "I was kidnapped."

"Ah. So you weren't just in the neighborhood and thought you'd drop in, eh?"

"No."

"I'd offer to return you to port, but we are well underway to Crystal Bay, looking to return loaded, and there's fierce competition for cargo these days."

"I don't actually want to go back all that badly," she said. "No matter who my ancestors were, I am clearly not queen material."

"Are you not? I understand the job has its challenges, but queens don't get to run away, sweetie. It's not the done thing. It's shirking your responsibilities and all of that, as I'm sure your mother would tell you if she were here, or your father if he could."

"You mean my mother the time traveling Gypsy and my father the midlife merman who no longer recognizes me? Perhaps not. But I don't see either of them eager to put on a crown. Besides, it wasn't my idea to kidnap myself and put me on a ship."

"No. It could have been by chance. The crimps are doing a booming business with so many steam vessels converting to sail. It takes a much larger crew for a sailing vessel. The *Belle* is an older ship and has been equipped for both since steam became a possibility, so I thought we'd have a jump on the ships still converting and might beat them at picking up a cargo from Frostingdung."

"I get the feeling it was intentional that I was the target, that someone sicced them on to me, but possibly they didn't know who I was."

She shrugged the blanket back as the sun dried her hair and she grew warmer.

Captain Lewis said, "Perhaps it's just as well that your reign wasn't well established or widely proclaimed. Having the monarch go missing at a time like this what with the dragons free and the economy teetering is rather destabilizing to say the least."

"They had no queen before and they don't want one now," Verity said. "They'll be glad to think themselves rid of me. As for the dragons, Toby's managing that. He and Taz."

As they spoke, a white vapor boiled up from the sea, from which the swells had suddenly smoothed to a glassy calm. The vapor rose until it hung low over the water and slowly turned from totally misty to murky before it separated into individual cat-shaped fog forms. Each eye glinted with a mad gleam and was fixed on Verity.

"There you are. I wondered where you'd gone," Verity said to the spectral felines. "You were with me at the drawbridge, then poof!"

"I see the dead are still among us." Captain Lewis said, indicating the cats. The cats had been with her when the captain attended her mother's announcement at Fort Iceworm dropping Verity down the privy hole that was Argonian politics.

"They want to be reunited with the families of their murdered magicians," she said. "And I'm the only one who can do it, really. I don't suppose you'd like the other job? It comes with room and board."

"Thanks awfully, but between being absolute ultimate authority aboard this ship and Madame Louisa, diva of the Changelings Cabaret, I have quite enough to satisfy whatever appetite for power I might have. Any more, and I fear I'd suffer indigestion. But I suppose we could accompany you back to the castle and, armed with fiddles and banjos, defend you from your foes?"

She groaned. "Gags would be more helpful. Whoever kidnapped me actually did me a favor. The lying and manipulating in the council was so intense I could barely stand it. My head was about to explode. If I'm to actually achieve anything, I need real allies and advisers." She touched her necklace. "I think the beads will help me find them."

"Accessorization is so important," agreed Captain Lewis. "The right sword, seven league boots, cloak of invisibility, magician-finding dragon-manufactured beads..."

"I don't suppose you have any idea where I could start looking?"

"No. It would be too convenient, I suppose, if all of the known wizards lived on the coast. Have you spoken with your auntie the archivist about this?"

"If you mean Aunt Ephemera, well, no, not recently. But I did send her a message via Toby and Taz shortly before the dragons were released. She sent back a shell. Wait a minute. I have it here somewhere."

After a brief search of her damp clothing, she found it in her trouser pocket and handed it to Captain Lewis.

He inserted the shell into his left ear and heard Ephemera's response, "I'll send messages to my sisters, your other aunts on your father's side. There's Epiphany in the west on the border with Ablemarle and Eulalia in the east, at the Mermaid's Atoll."

"Not very specific," the captain said, trying to hand back the shell, "and I can't really help you with the one on the border."

"Fine. Keep listening."

Captain Lewis put the shell back in his ear and Ephemera's voice continued, "Neither one is much for drop-in visitors, but they might make an exception in your case. And I suppose you also should visit Erotica, further down on the southern coast. She's the closest and the least reclusive, but your dad didn't think she was a suitable influence for an impressionable girl. And it's a bit tricky getting there."

Captain Lewis did a double-take. "She's your auntie? Erotica Amora of the Sailor's Spa and Bawdy House?" The captain sounded impressed.

"You know her, then?"

"Everyone knows her, even though her—establishment—is rather isolated," Captain Lewis said. "Which is strange considering she's known to be a very—gregarious—lady."

"Very well, then. I'll start with her. Can you take me? I thought she might know some wizards or at least their families."

"I'm sure she will. She knows everybody—many of them quite well. The *Belle's Shell*, the crew and I are at your service. For a price, of course, and with one or two detours to deliver and take on cargo. Plus the passenger fare. That'll be two hundred twenty pounds."

"Are you giving me a discount because I swam part of the way?" Verity asked, patting her pockets again. "I think the men who got me the job on that other ship relieved me of my coin."

"You could work your passage. A strapping lass like yourself could have the sails aloft, furled and unfurled and all that sort of thing, with less bother than many a seaman, and I confess, we're short handed at the moment. A steamship doesn't require as large a crew as a sailing vessel, but now, what with the dragon quitting—not because we treated her badly, mind you, but in solidarity with the other dragons—it's back to sails for us. What say you?"

"I say just tell me what to do!"

"We must brave the trip round the Horn first of all. Are you ready for that?"

"It can't possibly be worse than queening."

Chapter 4: Meanwhile Back at the Castle

Dear Uncle Marq,

We have a big dragon problem here. The silly twit who has been put in charge of the whole country created the problem. Turns out she has some royal ancestors or something that supposedly qualify her, even though she has no interest in running things properly. She seems to have disappeared, no doubt with her tail between her legs, and left the country to me to mind. If she stays away any longer, I am a shoo-in for queen in her place.

Everything is in a dreadful uproar. As you may have heard, the lazy reptiles have stopped working and half the businesses are trying to persuade them to come back while the other half are looking for work-arounds using methods like the sensible ones you use in Frostingdung. The wretched beasts have destroyed the perfectly good food we used to feed them even though most of them have never had anything else until apparently some bright soul told them dragons only eat meat so—really, it's all too-too complicated. Now they are insisting on fresh meat and are eating up all of the other animals. They are pooing all over Queenston and turning it into a dragon privy.

Truly, Uncle Marq, it's all very irritating. This dragon business is seriously interfering with my social life. One of the beasts has even wrapped itself around the tower and peeks into my bedchamber. I haven't slept a wink in weeks!

As if that wasn't a big enough mess, it seems the treasury has gone missing, a little fact nobody mentioned before now, and I need to buy at least one new ballgown and some jewels suitable to my elevation in rank. I also need some ladies in waiting. All the best queens have them and even though it's not official yet, if I look the part and am well prepared ahead of time, perhaps nobody will even notice Verity's absence.

Your loving niece,
Mali

Dearest Mali,

While I am so sorry to learn of your predicament, I am overjoyed to learn of the opportunities offered by your current position.

How inconsiderate of the dragons to stage their rebellion just as you try to gather together the reins of your potential reign. But this too is an opportunity to modernize the city's industrial technology, so you need not rely on dangerous beasts. Several industries here in Frostingdung have installed clockwork devices in order to save on labor costs. That would put the dragons in their place, or rather, remove them from the places that have heretofore provided their livelihoods.

Had you written to me earlier regarding the upcoming ball, I would have been happy to provide you with a suitable wardrobe and a few baubles from the family jewels. As it is, I cannot possibly find a suitable courier in time to meet your needs.

Your affectionate Uncle Marq

Dear Uncle Marq,

Couldn't you just bring my things yourself? It would be so wonderful if you could come to attend the ball that will be given in my honor—or else. I know you are a very busy man, but you are my very favorite uncle and wisest advisor—the relatives on the council are useless.

If you could find a few more gowns, not quite as lovely as the one you bring for me, of course (cloth of gold looks fabulous with my golden curls), but pretty, bring them, too. I have several well-born former classmates who are princesses in their own insignificant lands and have asked them to attend me as my ladies in waiting. Verity was far too selfish to consider attendants. I know you understand how important appearances are and I would so love to see you. So do come. Please?

Your favorite niece, Mali

Devent the Dragon Bard

The young dragon known as 3336 spent the first day of the dragon liberation deepening the mineshaft where he had spent his entire life. When still a hatchling, his job had been to push ore cars from the depths of the mine to the open place above, where the ore was processed. The open place was brighter and had no walls. It was cooler and often the air moved, tickling the undersides of his scales. Still it was murky with dust and always looked blurred to the shaft worm, as 3336 was sometimes called. His eyes were weak from spending most of his life in darkness lit only by his own fire, the headlamps of miners, and smoky lanterns. But if his eyes were weak, his back, his neck and legs were strong and his flame steady and bright.

During recent years, his work consisted of loading ore into the cars, widening and deepening mineshafts, and sometimes opening a new vein, which he could do with less danger than explosives. The miners respected him, he was sure. If he had not felt loved in the time since his mother returned to the earth, he felt valued.

They'd like me if they knew me, he told himself. But they have to pay attention to work and they're shy.

Usually, he didn't surface until he emerged to feed at the trough of dragon kibble the miners filled every evening, when they took their own evening meal.

The other dragons, who seemed to know each other, tried to crowd him out of the trough as they'd done to that feeble little female dragon who came looking for work. If it hadn't been for the intervention of Auld Smelt, who pushed in between him and the others, he'd have gone hungry.

But now! To be free! He'd worked from the time he cracked the egg. His nursery rhymes were the dust-choked work songs of the miners set to the rhythms of pick and shovel, the clunk of the ore, the patter of gravel as it hit the ground.

He had never seen the sun or felt its warmth, because for most of the year it had gone to bed before he trudged aboveground behind the miners, pushing the day's last ore car with his head. He'd eat, then return to the shaft to sleep and await the arrival of the miners as they returned to work in the morning, which he recognized only because morning was when they came.

The routine never changed and from what most of the other mine dragons said, it never had changed for them in their long lives. Auld Smelt, who was born free and had been unemployed during his youth, said that his life fueling the steel furnace was easy compared to the Great War.

All the dragons looked up to Smelt. Even the humans respected his intense and steady flame, its necessity to their work and its carefully controlled application. They allowed as how Auld Smelt was something of an artist among dragons.

When 3336's mother died, Smelt had sent him stories to comfort him, for his mother had always told him stories too about the life she had known before the mines, and the lives of her grandparents and great grandparents. Dragons had very long memories, even though it took a lot of effort for her to recall what she'd heard. She wasn't sure she got the details right, the names of places or dragons or people, but the indistinct images she sent him told of a time before the darkness and the ore, a time when dragons flew.

That morning, he awoke as usual, and waited and waited, but the miners did not arrive. He worried, lonely and trying to imagine why they didn't come, and then he grew afraid. Bad things happened in the mines sometimes. As he climbed out of the shaft, he saw a brilliant light at the opening. The air was somewhat clearer than usual, and warmth wrapped his nose as he poked it out of the shaft. Through the haze, he spotted a yellow-orange ball in the sky. The camp was quiet. He heard a strange noise—a melodious trill—and realized with wonder that this must be the birdsong he'd heard the men speak of. He tried to answer it with a call of his own, and it stopped abruptly.

The men were gone now, and the other dragons were nowhere to be seen, all except Smelt, who lay on his belly beside the smelter he had fired for so many years. The young dragon stopped beside his friend, and Smelt opened one eye.

"Go. Go now before the men get over their fear and come back to kill the fearsome beasts."

"What fearsome beasts? What happened? Where is everyone?"

"They've all gone. That young female dragon that came here before, Taz, the one with the boy? She returned and burned up the kibble. The boy told the bosses it was making us sick and keeping us slaves. He said he and Taz were freeing all dragons by order of the new queen."

"So where did they go?"

"Wherever they wanted, I suppose." Smelt huffed an ashy sigh. "The men were scared though. They talked about what we would do to them once we knew we didn't have to do what they said anymore. They said we'd smoke them. So they left us."

"We should leave then?"

"I can't make it. Too old to walk, too earthbound to fly." He slowly turned his head and raised his back foot, the one chained to a thick iron stake.

"I'll free you! We'll see the world together. Go to those places in the stories you told me."

"It's not that easy, laddie. Leave me."

But 3336 was already busy trying to free his old friend. How could they have just left him? Wouldn't they miss him? He was the only one in the mine who remembered a life outside of it.

Smelt's stories and dreams told even more vivid tales to his friend down in the darkness of the mine, and surrounded him with a world of drama, death and fire, but also courage and camaraderie and something Smelt thought of as "honor." Those qualities were seen in men only when tunnels caved in and they had to free each other. Even then, it was inevitably the flame and tail of a dragon that cleared the way for the rescue of the trapped miners.

Smelt's knowledge was deeper than the mineshaft, deep as the core of the earth, and he still had much to teach. The dragon formerly known as 3336 wanted to know what it was, as if Smelt's previous life were one of his stories that needed an end. But now was not the time for the end. Now they would both leave the mine and see what lay beyond.

3336 reached down with his talons and easily broke the chain that confined his friend. Smelt's strength was all in his fire. The chains had chafed the scales off where they bound Smelt's leg. Very carefully, 3336 licked the wound, as he seemed to remember his mother doing with his injuries.

"Get up now, old friend. I want you to show me that battlefield you dream of, and where the ancient caverns were where your family once slept on treasure. Do you suppose we'll find treasure for hoards of our own?"

"Your belly just grumbled. Food first, treasure later," Smelt said. Slowly, creaking like a rusty gear, he hauled himself to his feet. A long stretch sent a ripple down his spinal ridges.

"How will we find food if it's all burned up?"

"We'll hunt."

3336 knew what hunting was—he'd seen it in Smelt's dreams, but he didn't know how to do it. The dragons in the dreams had wings and swooped down on their prey. 3336's wings were stumpy and most of the time hung at his sides since they were useless in the close confines of a mineshaft.

"Let's go!"

"I can't," the old dragon said, limping along beside his young friend. "They clipped my wings when I took this job."

"My wings don't work, either. So, what, we starve?"

"You have other things going for you—you're young and strong and fast, at least compared to me. I told you, leave me."

"I will not," 3336 said.

The older dragon grunted and limped forward with 3336 gently but sturdily supporting him. Step by cautious step, the two walked down the feeder track, toward the main railway and the outside world.

Beyond the mining compound, the air was clearer and brighter. Hills with sparse patches of grass surrounded the track. The further they walked, the thicker and greener the grass became. 3336 felt an exaltation surpassed only by the rumbling in his belly.

He gazed up the hillsides. He could see where wings would come in handy trying to find food.

Maybe if he took a flying leap? He released his hold on Auld Smelt, carefully gathered himself and sprang.

To his astonishment, the leap almost was a flying one. He had never had room to jump before, but his leg muscles were far more powerful than he realized from loading ore and pushing mining cars up the track. He sprang high into the air and landed atop the hill. The slopes beyond the track were stubbled with stumps that had once been a forest. Mining used up a lot of trees, apparently. That was too bad. He'd only seen trees in Smelt's dreams. He wanted to see them in real life. Snow sprinkled the ground and crowned the stumps. New growth burgeoned among them.

With each step further from the tracks, he could see more clearly. Standing atop a stump, he could see for a great distance. Here and there were small ponds of pooled water. Standing in the water in the farthest pond, facing away from him, was a large antlered animal that looked delicious. 3336 bounded over the stumps in five long jumps and with the last one, took down his prey as if he'd been doing it his entire life.

The return trip was a bit more problematic. The prey was larger than it looked from a distance and with it in his mouth, his most powerful leap only brought him and it out of the pool. That would never do. With a little cough, he produced a flame that somewhat over-cooked the beast, leaving the antlers. He ate half of it and carried the rest easily back to where Old Smelt lay dozing on the track.

Smelt awoke, accepting his share with a pleased hum. "I knew you had it in you, young'un," he said, expressing gas at both ends as he chomped and chewed. He had a funny way of eating, twisting his head to the side to finish his bite. Catching 3336's questioning look, he said. "Teeth. In the old days, we never thought much about teeth, but in the old days, you only fired up when hunting, cooking, maybe for warmth—for some purpose. I've been firing hour after hour, day after day, year after year. The sulfur in the

fumes takes a toll on the old dental stalactites and stalag-
mites, if you know what I mean."

3336 said nothing because he did not exactly understand, but that was all right. Everything felt better now that
they had eaten.

They reached the flat plains between the hills and the
distant mountains. The shining tracks stretched into the
distance in both directions. "They put people in the big ore
cars like the ones that come into the yard on the mine's
rail," Auld Smelt told him. "Except the cars carrying the
people have tops on them."

"Why?" 3336 asked. "It is not uphill all the way." The
only time the miners rode in the cars was when they were
weary at the end of a long shift.

"Yes, but your average human tires quickly, and on
the train they can go places, see more of the country—they
don't have wings and they're not very fast movers, humans,
as you may have noticed with the miners. They need something to move them around or there'd be too many all in one
place, and that would make them fight over whose hoard
was whose. You can see where that would be a problem."

"Was that why there was a Great War?"

"Partly, and partly I think it was just for fun because
they hadn't killed each other off in awhile. Humans like to
do that to thin the herds. Also, they make these tools to kill
with. See, without fire of their own, or serious teeth and
claws or tails to knock prey dead, they needed something
to help them hunt better and then, just so they didn't get
out of practice, they started hunting each other and using
the tools to kill. Poor things got frustrated because they had
tools and their prey had tools, so it was like dragons hunting dragons, if you take my meaning? So they had to build
better tools that would let them totally destroy the prey, but
then the prey got even better tools, and on and on. They
could all have used a good hibernation to sleep things off
but that is not the way of their kind."

"The miners slept sometimes."

"Not long enough, laddie. Not long enough."

Beyond the plain, white mountain tops blushed pink
briefly before the sky faded and darkened. "Ah, speaking
of hibernation, the Sky Dragon is firing one last flame before she takes her rest. It's she the men follow when they

rest. They don't seem to realize that as a celestial being, she doesn't need as much sleep as mere mortals. They're very fidgety, men."

"Are they?"

"Oh, yes. As long as they provided food, it didn't bother me as much, but now we're away from there and I remember they're always trying to 'improve' their surroundings, the earth, the sea, the sky. They want to own the world and are ever looking for ways to enlarge their hoards and test their firepower. See, not being able to make their own fire the natural way, they're afraid they'll forget how. In the old days, our ancestors had nothing to do with them except to eat one once in awhile. But then some of them made friends with some of us and that was the beginning of the end. Treacherous critters, men, and even if you find a good one, he's an exception and the others will overrule him in time and hunt you."

Along the track from the mine, a dozen or so black streaks seared the earth. At the long rail, the streaks turned sharply to the south, leaving little lines of flame still flickering between the scorched strips.

"Looks like the others headed for the capital," Smelt said with another grunt and an expulsion of gas. "Nothing for us there though, lad. What we need us is a nice deep cave high up in the mountains." The thought made him yawn.

3336 did not share his friend's desire for a cave. After spending most of his life in a mineshaft, he was dazzled by the sky and the vast spread of open land, both the flat bits and the pointy bits. He wondered aloud if the points were sharp.

Old Smelt snorted. "Only compared to you, lad! They have caves in them, them mountains. How sharp do you think they are really? The distance fools the eye."

"Let's find out!" said 3336, a giddy feeling sweeping through him knowing that nobody was going to send him down the shaft again. But then he began to worry about that. "What about the mine? Won't the men want us back when they return from the city?"

Smelt snorted again. "Fact is, we've been fired." He huffed a number of times, exhaling clouds of pungent smoke, and his young friend realized he was laughing at his little joke.

He sobered quickly as they crossed the tracks and headed in a northerly direction—or up the tracks. "You want to talk about fire? We're very close now to what was pretty much our last stand. Fire versus firepower, it was, and many a great dragon perished there that day. Without being able to go aloft, I'm not certain but I know it's around here somewhere. I feel it. It's burned into me bones, actually."

3336 hopped forward to explore, then back to the older dragon, needing to hop off some of his excitement at being free, breathing fresh air, hearing the wind whisper through the grass instead of the clunk of a shovel hitting rock. And now they were visiting one of the places the old one dreamed of often. Also, the same things were not happening today at the same time they always had every day for as long as he could remember. It was all new.

Auld Smelt's steps grew hesitant until finally he stopped and gazed reverently upon a field of wildflowers that lay not far from the railroad track.

"There it is, laddie, the site of our greatest glory, almost the end of our race, but the deciding battle of the Great War. Many a brave dragon warrior went down in flames that day."

"Why was that?" 3336 asked.

"To try to win, of course," Auld Smelt said with another snort, indicating he thought it a stupid question.

"Yes, but win what?"

"The battle, and ultimately the war!"

"Oh," he said, then, "Why were we in the war? What were dragons fighting about?"

"Oh, that. Well, to protect our hoards and to gorge on the flesh of the humans and horses who opposed our side's humans and their horses. It was all arranged ahead of time between our leaders."

"Did the dragons on the other side have humans, too?"

"There were no dragons on the other side."

"Then why did so many of us die?"

"Steel, laddie. Steel. And guns. We had no guns back then and the others did. Not very accurate, as such things go, but we dragons, back then when we were all wild, were big and easy to hit. That's one reason why when we went to work for the humans I decided to work in the mines where the steel could be made. The other good thing about an iron mine, you know what you're getting around so much iron. No tricky magic stuff there, no wizards shooting death rays at you, none of that stuff. Just the ore and the men and your own honest flame."

"Oh," 3336 said, less impressed with Smelt's approval of what they both already knew than with the story he had seemed about to launch into, the one concerning the war. "Were all of the other mine dragons in the battle too?"

Another snort from Smelt.

"They weren't even invented then."

"Invented? But how could they invent us? We're all dragons, same as you—" He had started off a little heated at the implication that he was other than what he'd always considered himself to be, but at Smelt's dubious expression, 3336's voice damped down to a whimper, "Aren't we?"

"For want of a better term, I suppose so, but most of the new ones were never wild dragons, proper dragons. A great many were messed about with by men before you ever were hatched."

"I don't recall anything about that," 3336 said. "What's the difference? We're not like their devices, unless Mother and I were both very much mistaken."

"No, but in my case, first there was me and who I was and then there was a job and I agreed to do it, using a skill I was already quite good at. In your case, in the case of most of the other mine-drakes, there was a job and they wanted a dragon to fill it, so they figured it out and how to make a dragon into what they wanted before putting him on the job. You never had any hopes, dreams or wishes before that, did you?"

3336 thought it over and said, "Well, maybe not at first, because there was never a choice, but I have a wish now."

"And that is?"

"To have a proper name, rather than a number."

"What sort of a name?" Smelt asked.

"Yes," the youngster said. "How did you guess?"

"Guess what?"

"Yes, how did you guess I want it to be that?"

"What?"

"Yes."

"Yes, what?"

3336 knew it was disrespectful, but he was getting hot under the collar he still wore, the one with his number on it. "Yes. Wat. What is so wrong with Wat?" and the moment he asked, he understood how Smelt had misunderstood. "I suppose Bill might be easier."

Smelt grunted. "The Dragon Bill. Bilious Bill they might call you."

"They don't call him that," 3336/Wat?/Bill? said.

"Who?"

"Bill, of course. Milton says old Bill is an artist with a pick. Milton is a good name too, don't you think?"

"Milton the Dragon, the Dragon Milton. Doesn't have much of a ring to it. You need a name that means something."

"Like Auld Smelt?"

"That's my *nom de flambeau,* so to speak. My work name. My real name is—uh—what was it? Been a long time since I used it. Wait. It'll come to me. It was a grand one, anyway, worthy of a dragon because it was bestowed by me dragon mum, who had a broader acquaintance of names than those found in a mining crew."

"People she ate? Like knights and such? The crew talk sometimes about how dragons used to eat people. They whisper and don't think I hear, because as they tell each other, they don't want me getting ideas beneath my station."

"Aye, that's true enough, but it was a long time ago, before the war. There's them as have said we ought never to have stopped."

"But it seems so rude! I would never have dreamed of so much as nibbling at Wat, Bill, Milton or even Harry, and I don't like him much."

"You'll understand when you're older," Smelt said.

"Speaking of eating...?"

"Yes, I know. I'm getting hungry again too, so we'd be better off not speaking of eating. Ah, did you catch that?"

"What?"

"Don't start that again. The way the wind is blowing, I catch the smell of fresh blood and raw flesh. Nothing like it. Give it a bit of char and it's tasty."

"But you said it was only before the war that we ate people."

"We never ate any people during the war. Only enemies. It's not like they were really people."

3336 frankly didn't understand the difference, but he kept quiet so as not to sound ignorant.

Smelt kept swiveling his head and sniffing every few steps.

"What is it?" 3336 asked.

"My nose isn't what it used to be but, by all the stones in my hoard, that is blood I smell."

Chapter 5: Up the Creek

To her relief, Verity found she made a much better sail-
or than a queen. She was good at hauling on the lines,
even climbing the mast. The physical work was terrifying at
times, but great fun once she got used to it. Her Frost Giant
heritage not only gave her height and strength, but also
granted her a tolerance for cold temperatures. She did not
get sick and she didn't mind the cold nighttime watches, or
the rough seas lifting the ship's bow and smacking it down
again in the water, 'shivering' the timbers of the ship. The
hardest thing was trying to learn what they called everything, but usually pointing sorted that out.

She no longer had trouble sleeping and was too tired
when she wasn't working to worry over cares she knew she
hadn't actually left on shore, though it felt like it.

During the first part of the voyage, when the seas were
calm, Captain Lewis displayed the flair for the dramatic
that caused Madame Louisa to be such a theatrical sensa-
tion at the cabaret. She told excellent stories, all of which
she claimed were absolutely true and most of which featured herself in a heroic role.

"Now then, lads, you've most of you been with me as
long as the *Belle* has been under steam on the trade route
between Queenston and Frostingdung. You may have noticed that on these runs we traverse the Gulf of Gremlins
from Queenston to Port Bintnar in West Frostingdung. In
the old days, before the *Belle* was fitted for steam, I dived
for salvage. Since we'll be sailing round the Horn this time,
and through the Strait, we'll be salvaging again. The waters
should be rich, as the Strait is known to be a graveyard for
sailors. Mighty warships have been lost without a trace in
those waters. Some say wrecked by the storms and rough
water where the North Sea meets the Gulf, some say they
were taken by monsters, some say lured onto the rocks and

pulled down below by merfolk. All anyone knows for sure is they sailed in but didn't sail out again."

"I never heard of no sailor's graveyard, Captain. I don't much like the sound of that," said the sailor who used to tend the steam engine while the ship was still dragon-driven, but now was a common sailor, and had almost as much to learn about it as Verity.

"Hasn't been much trouble of the sort since we've been under steam, has there, Mr. Gray?"

"No word that's come to me, Captain," the first mate responded. "Some say the curse that haunts the Strait doesn't like messing with the dragons in the engine room, but perhaps it's just run its course, as things sometimes do. The stories mostly date from those grim days just after the Great War. The spirits have probably quieted since then."

"We can hope that they will have realized they're no longer able to use whatever treasure might remain aboard the ships then," Captain Lewis said. "After all, we've got to eat, and they no longer have that problem."

The captain was accustomed to serving as tour guide for the paying passengers, of which there had been many during the recent years of flourishing trade between Frostingdung and Frostingdung-influenced Argonia. Oddly, Verity's lie detecting headaches did not trouble her, although the stories were far too outrageous to be true, weren't they?

"Off the port bow, you can just make out the coast of Outer Frostingdung, marking the entrance to the Frostingdung Strait, known to Frosty mariners as the Strait of Argonia. Have you been to Frostingdung before, Majesty?"

"Verity, please, "she said. "Just Verity."

Her ascension to the throne had been highly irregular and informal and possibly was not widely known throughout the country. Now that she considered it, being more or less incognito (since the captain and most of the crew were quite aware of who she was) was a good idea. Just as well not to advertise the crown that kept wanting to fall off her head.

Early the next morning, just before dawn, she climbed aloft with a spyglass to stand watch. She did not mind in the least. Her cabin was cramped and everything below decks was both cramped and smelly. She bumped her head on low beams and lanterns, but she didn't care. From the crow's nest she could watch the waves breaking across the bow, or stare into the ship's wake. Even the ghost cats liked life on shipboard. They blinked into visibility sitting in a line atop the yards, the horizontal timbers supporting the square sails. As the sun pinkened the sky, it shone through the hazy white cat bodies, giving them a blush and occasionally revealing the colors and patterns each might have worn in life.

All the cats were facing starboard, staring toward the coast of Suleskeria in Outer Frostingdung.

Shading her eyes against the blushing dawn, Verity stared in the same direction, blinked, then called out, "Captain, what is that blackish haze hanging over the coast? Is a huge storm coming? Ought we to batten down the hatches or furl the sails or some such nautical precaution?"

"No, lass. That's nothing. You've seen no real storm yet, although I reckon that you may before the day is done. But that, me dear, is no weather. 'Tis the famous Frostingdung Reek."

"What's that?"

"Frostingdung has not had the benefit of using dragons to fire their machinery and has instead relied on coal-fed steam engines. Behold, the veil of progress."

As they drew nearer the coast of Outer Frostingdung, the part known as Suleskeria, she beheld rocklike creatures that moved in a rather spasmodic fashion without changing their position in the water. They made a strangled sort of croaking sound.

She picked up the spyglass and held it up to her eye, focusing on the questionable rock creatures.

"My word! The rocks are swarming with seals! I've never seen so many all in one place."

The individual seals grew more distinct as the ship sailed nearer the Suleskeria coast, and their barks increased in number and volume.

Several of them began swimming toward the ship, perhaps looking for fishy handouts, Verity thought. They were so entertaining that she was unaware of what was going on behind her until she heard something large smack into the water. Staring over the rail, she saw a head surface and slice through the water in the direction of the rocks.

"Man overboard!" she called as she scrambled down the mast and raced sternward, hopping over coils of rope and other impediments. Then added, "But it might have been intentional!"

The group of seals that had been heading for the ship suddenly veered in the direction of the swimmer, barking excitedly.

She reached for the life preserver, but hesitated as the swimmer seemed to be doing quite well and would have needed to swim back to make use of the ring. She poised to toss it over the side, but the captain called back. "No need for that. It's just Mr. Gray taking a spot of shore leave while we're in the area. He likes to visit family when we're this near."

Mr. Gray was the first mate, a man of lively, graceful movements but few words. Even before she'd come aboard, she'd seen him playing washtub bass with the band that accompanied Madame Louisa when she sang at the Changelings Cabaret. As first mate, he worked hard and expected those under his command to do the same.

She returned to the helm and asked, "Does he always jump overboard and swim when he goes to visit relatives?"

"Aye. We can't sail too near their rocks and his kin are a bit leery of the rest of the crew."

As the seal welcoming party reached the rocks, some of their dozing friends and relations slid off into the water to join them. They frolicked and 'ork-ed' at each other in what seemed to be seal language for, 'About time you showed up! It's been far too long since you were here last...' It hadn't occurred to her that Mr. Gray was anything other than a human, but the denizens of the Changelings Cabaret did seem prone to having dual natures. The captain swore that when in the water, she became a mermaid thanks to a magical heritage she shared with Verity's family on her father's side. The club's bartender seemed normal unless the club was very busy and then all eight arms and hands were brought into play.

For this crew, it really wasn't at all odd that one of them was a selkie or seal-person. She hadn't met one before, but she had heard of them. She wondered how many other crewmembers also had dual natures—or perhaps more than two?

"So, do we drop anchor to wait for him?" she asked.

"Oh, no. He'll catch up in a bit. While he's there, he generally learns about the weather and waters through the Strait, which is apt to be treacherous. His relatives have connections all along the coast."

Selkies were a bit more magical than dragons, who were, after all, merely large animals equipped with extraordinary fire power. Mers were a hybrid, a characteristic that ran in families, hence the ability of her own father to turn into one and yes, that had to be magical, even in this day and age. None of this surprised Verity, especially now that she was surrounded by the ghosts of cats who had been watching and waiting for the delivery of the magicians, wizards, witches, sorcerers, and so forth, who had once been their companions. Even before she met them, before her father changed, before she'd lived among dragons, she was aware that, theoretically at least, magic existed. Vestiges of it were not uncommon in Queenston, even then. People who were not actually magicians, but were descended from a magical race (elves, trolls, fairies, that sort of thing) couldn't change what they were simply because their kind was no longer fashionable.

The night disappeared into dawn, and then the dawn disappeared, stalked and overtaken by billows of fog too thick to allow so much as a glimpse of the wheel.

The captain had an unusual reaction to that. All of a sudden, she sang a long, sustained, low note, then listened as it bounced back to her.

"Ah, good," Captain Lewis said and adjusted the wheel slightly.

"Were you going to sing the rest of that song?" Verity asked.

"Oh no, 'twas no song, that. I took a sounding to see how far we are from shore. Used to have the dragon moan to do the same deed, back when we had a working dragon in the engine room. I can also use the bell, but find my own pipes are more accurate and work as well. We're sailing into the narrowest bit of our passage now, where the North Sea meets the Sea of Glass with the Gremlin's Horn portside and the Suleskeria Peninsula just coming up starboard."

The captain, as watch officer, wore the boatswain's whistle on a cord and put lips to it to blow the shrill blasts to call all hands on deck.

The boatswain scrambled to the deck first and reclaimed the whistle, whereupon the captain ordered the sails to be reefed. Verity had learned a great deal, but still didn't know what half the things on the ship were called or were supposed to do. She wasn't alone. Many of the crew had signed on when the vessel was a steamer and had not yet fully adapted their skills for sail. Madame Marsha would have called reefing 'taking in a bit,' had it referred to a gown instead of a sail. It involved hooks and eyes and ties and things Verity was too inexperienced to operate.

At this point, she could hear everyone speaking plainly. Both sea and wind were calm, so calm the only sound from the sea was the light slap of water against the hull. When she looked up, a heavy curtain of fog swept over the ship, rapidly growing so thick she could no longer see the water.

Tiny pinpricks of brilliance pierced the gray pall. At first, she thought the brightness was the eyes of the ghost cats prowling around outside the ship, but it was soon clear that the stabs of light were not paired like eyes. Each grew to the size of a coin and swam into others to form shapes the size of clenched fists. The crew was so fascinated by them that nobody was looking where the ship was heading.

"What are they?" Verity asked, breaking the awed silence that had descended on the crew like the fog itself. Her voice sounded unnaturally loud in the stillness. Although the sails flapped, the water hissed against the hull, and the timbers creaked, no one seemed to hear her, and no one answered her question.

"Ought we not to pay more attention to steering the ship?" she asked, much louder than she needed to.

Everyone had stopped moving, even Captain Lewis. The only movement came from the dancing balls of light.

The seashells Verity wore around her neck rattled and the beads infused with magic from the walls of the Dragon Vitia's cave grew warm. Suddenly the ghost cats blinked back into view again and this time they were outside the ship, seemingly suspended over the water. They began chasing the lights, pouncing toward them—and through them, disrupting their choreography.

As if discouraged by the cats' interruption, the lights blinked out, cats in hot pursuit only to vanish without a glimmer of a whisker.

Well, cats were like that, ghost or otherwise.

But now the fog rolled back to reveal a face, hard and cracked, with sightless eyes, that pushed nose first through the thick gray damp to reveal a chest, arms crossed over it, and batwings. That was a little unusual, surely? The wings? Above the head, the end of a bowsprit drove toward them like a spear.

The bowsprit parted the fog to reveal a great sailing ship headed for them on a collision course.

The captain roused long enough to reach up and clang the ship's bell in warning.

"Bong! Bong! Bong!" another bell tolled from what seemed like the bottom of the sea.

Verity cringed, expecting to hear the splinter of deck and mast, perhaps cries of alarm from the other vessel. Relentlessly and without another sound, it bore down on them until its bow had somehow absorbed the bow of their own ship.

How could that be?

Someone yelled finally and ran for the rail to jump overboard, but the other ship kept absorbing theirs, first the bowsprit then figurehead, fo'c'sle, foremast and forward funnel. The mainmast and all its rigging were next, and the men who had climbed the rigging to adjust the sails. The other sailors on deck did not back away from the soundless collision but continued to stare, mesmerized.

Now the wheel disappeared, then Captain Lewis, who broke through the spell just before vanishing.

"Ahoy there!" the captain's voice cried from somewhere within the spectral hull. "Our vessels have become far too intimate! The *Belle* is not that kind of a ship!"

The phantom ship—for what else could it be? —continued devouring the *Belle*. As the ghostly bow crept over her, Verity tried to back away, but her feet held fast to the deck as firmly as if they'd been nailed there.

This kind of magic was too strong to be dispelled by a mere iron bracelet. The ghost ship was twice the size of the *Belle*, so Verity did not enter it at deck level but belowdecks, into the fo'c'sle's berthing deck. Instinctively she brushed at the spectral hammocks her head passed through. They hung, dripping seaweed, above cannons, their iron barrels encrusted with barnacles.

Then it was overtaken by the gun deck, and into the captain's quarters. Nary a soul was to be seen anywhere.

But as the phantom swallowed the *Belle*'s stern, the boatswain belatedly blew a series of blasts on his whistle and the crew leaped to life again, doing their best to follow the captain's orders and steer the ship out of the ghost's interior.

"Now you lot look lively?" Captain Lewis complained. Verity wondered herself. It was as if the ghost ship had waited until they were nightmarishly trapped before loosening them from its thrall. "This thing has no substance," said Bowen, the second mate/concertina player. "We must break free for I've heard of this before, and this ship's invisible masters aim to take us to the bottom when she returns to her watery grave."

"Is there nothing we can do?" Verity asked.

"You're the one with the magic jewelry, dearie," the captain said. "How about you do something?"

Even as they spoke, the sea slapped higher on the ghostly vessel's hull.

"It's not that kind of magic," Verity said. "Don't you have anything?"

"Well, there are them as say I've a magical singing voice," Captain Lewis replied, and after taking a deep breath, began to sing in a plaintive voice, "Pleeeease release us, let us go..."

Nothing at all happened with great speed.

But the captain was not only a charismatic leader, she was also the lead singer in the cabaret ensemble consisting of much of her crew. With none of their other efforts yielding results they joined in. "Don't take us to the ocean's floor. To wreck our ship would be a sin. Release us and let us sail again."

"Louder?" Verity suggested and joined the captain in a robust refrain that was surely heard all the way back to Queenston.

"I really, really hate to do this, but needs must," the captain said, and when she opened her mouth again, it was very hard to remember that she was at heart a lady. A huge booming baritone issued from her lips and she repeated, "Pleeeease release us (dammit) let us go!"

It was a noble sacrifice, but Verity felt there must surely be something she could do besides sing harmony. She slumped, discouraged, against the mast, realized the obvious course of action, and began climbing it.

"Up, up, aloft!" she cried, proud that she had remembered one word. "To the rigging and crow's nests and suchlike high places, me hearties!" Maybe if they climbed the rigging of their ship they could at least see how fast the phantom was taking them down. If the fog had lifted, they might see where they were.

"Aye!" the captain said, interrupting the baritone plaint long enough to cry, "Aloft! Step lively as you love your lives! Aloft!"

The boatswain's whistle shrilled a long blast, another, a low tone and a warble, followed by a final trill left hanging in the fog.

The entire crew swarmed up the rigging and hung there like floats in a fishnet. The *Belle*'s crew was fairly small—small rather than the dozens of people required to man (and woman) a larger vessel—such as the unmanned (and unwomaned) apparition surrounding the *Belle*. Just where was the crew or their remains? Didn't phantom ships have phantom crews? Not this one, apparently. Nary so much as a skull or a crossed bone.

Captain Lewis bellowed a song while climbing, the crew answering each verse with a chorus. Verity followed the soles of the boots above her—not the stylish ones with the high heels and gold embroidery but the sturdy ones with the extra pieces of hide sewn hair out to the soles to keep them from slipping.

Barely clearing the quarterdeck, the singing crew clung to their ropes. As their song died on their lips, their captor creaked and groaned like a spirit in torment.

Although the seas had been calm when the phantom overtook the *Belle*, waves they could not see now pounded a spectral hull while spray they could not feel hissed like a sea serpent beyond the unearthly barrier between them and the living sea.

Ghost cats swarmed up the masts, over the sailors and onto the spars. One phantom feline clung to the braid coiled atop Verity's head to keep her hair out of the way. Instead of her hair, she had to look past the swipe of a translucent tail.

The air shifted. Something was stirring among those wild waves.

It sounded as if the water had risen closer to her perch in the crow's nest. Was the ship sinking? With everything shrouded in fog and ectoplasmic hull, it was impossible to tell.

A blinding light broke through, flooding the ship. The fog cleared just enough to see that not only was the ghost ship slowly sinking, it had carried the *Belle* closer to the rocks of the Suleskerian coast.

The cook clung to the mast below her and called up. "What now, Cap'n? We seem to be caught between the rocks and a wet place."

The captain yelled into Verity's ear. "M'dear, we be bound for a watery grave. It's up to we two to save who we can, though our ship be lost. Captains usually go down with the ship, but if we're to spare the crew, we must go down before her. Are you with me?"

"M-me?"

The captain gave her a withering look. "Oh, please. Your father's a merman and you swim like a fish. Try to leap so that your dive will take you over the sides of both vessels."

What with one thing and another, Verity could hardly be any wetter and so she said, "Aye, aye, Cap'n."

The crow's nest, half a rum barrel, stopped at her knees, too high to permit her to dive from within it. She'd need to climb out onto the rigging, slick and icy cold as it was, if she could tell the real ropes from the ghostly ones. Hoisting a foot onto the edge of the barrel, she lunged for the yard.

The ship suddenly lurched and she fell back into the barrel and against the mast.

Ecstatic barking fractured the ragged fog.

A froth of seals, their heads so numerous and active they looked like furry gray bubbles, grinned triumphantly up at her from the fading phantom hull. The fog wisped it away to nothingness and the massed bodies of the seals glistened through the vanishing vessel's deck. The seals pushed against the hull of the *Belle*, their sleek backs and flippers undulating rhythmically as they shoved the living ship from the grasp of the dead.

One of the seals barked louder than the others. Above the sea and the rumble of distant thunder, as the sky flickered with lightning and the green flash of St. Elmo's fire, the seal said quite clearly and in a human tongue, "Heave, me beauties, heave!"

The voice was familiar.

It barked staccato commands, One bark, two, three, four and after the fifth bark, without so much as a pop of separation, the *Belle* rocked free, but free of what? The ghost ship was no more. The *Belle* wobbled drunkenly in the waves before righting herself.

The crew hit the *Belle*'s deck. The seals continued to push until she was well clear of the rocks.

Then it was back to work. Verity's shipmates setting to work hoisting, reefing, furling, unfurling, and other tasks with sails and ropes that she tried to keep straight. She was sure they'd be sailing away as fast and as far as they could get from the place where they had almost met a watery grave.

But Captain Lewis paused beside the boatswain. "It's her, Angus. Admiral Blood's famous vessel, the *SS Nice Try*. I feel it in me bones. I'm going overside to have a look below. Why would she haunt these waters, lest her corpse lies beneath?"

"You're thinking we may yet see a payday from this run, Captain?"

"I am. Lower me gig. I'm going to dive and search the bottom." With a wink at Verity, he said, "So, are you coming? You'll likely get no wetter than you are now."

The truth was, Verity felt a tiny bit hesitant about tackling the vessel that had almost killed them, although, of course, it hadn't. A chance to dive for sunken treasure and make the ghost ship give up her secrets was too good to pass up.

And the truth also seemed to be that her father's connection to the mer-creatures seemed to be hereditary in nature, at least according to Captain Lewis. Besides, when she swam to the *Belle* from the ship that had kidnapped her, she'd been none the worse for wear. Not even winded, to the best of her memory.

So she jumped in.

She beat the captain into the water, and heard the impact in the water when he went in. But when she shot to the surface again after her initial dive, a mermaid with the captain's face gave her a thumbs-up sign. Signaling for her to follow, the mermaid rolled into a dive.

Verity followed suit, diving deep as if she'd done so every day of her life. The water was cold but not unbearably so.

The seals had remained nearby and dived when she did.

Except for the disturbance caused by the *Belle* and her rescuers, the sea was calm and clear enough to see the captain's mermaid tail undulating beyond her and the seals chasing each other all the way down.

The rib cage of bent timbers enclosed the rest of what mortal material remained of the ghost ship. Barnacle-covered cannon still protruded from beneath the deck. The seals swam into a hole in the stern and out again. The mer-captain swam after them. Verity was about to follow when a pair of feline eyes glittered from between the planks in the bow. As she swam across the deck, a feline form rose from an open hatch, circled her, then returned to the hatch and sat there twitching its tail as if it expected to be fed. When Verity swam toward it, the cat ducked back into the hatch.

Being neither a ghost nor a sea-creature, Verity followed very carefully. What could be in the fo'c'sle that the cat found so fascinating? Nothing but rags of hammocks and broken sea chests of the type sailors used to hold their belongings while at sea.

The cat didn't leave her in doubt for long, but sat on one of these. When Verity opened the lid to inspect it, the cat put paws on the side of it and peered in, but the clothing and whatever else it may have held had long ago succumbed to the sea. All that remained was another little cask, sealed with tar but also covered with barnacles. The cat did not want her to leave it; that much was clear.

The cats were the spiritual remains of the familiars of wizards murdered by the craft of enemies. Verity was trying to find the descendants of those wizards, so possibly the cask interested the cat because it held some clues relating to the wizards. Tucking the cask under her arm, Verity propelled herself out of the hatch in time to see the captain swimming out of the hole with a larger chest, also heavily barnacled.

The mermaid/captain beckoned to her, and the two of them guided the chest to the surface.

With the help of a net and the crew, they hoisted the chest onto the captain's gig and back aboard the *Belle's Shell*.

By the time Verity had dried her hair and changed into borrowed dry clothing, Captain Lewis was no longer a mermaid, but any sorrow she might have felt because of that fact was overshadowed by excitement about the treasure chest. The little cask Verity had found was there too, a ghost cat's rear planted atop its lid as firmly as a phantom feline back end could be.

The seals grew bored and swam away, except for one that pulled himself up on the deck, water sluicing in sheets from his sides. He shook himself like a wet dog. When the shaking stopped, she saw that the newcomer was not a seal after all, but Mr. Gray, who looked to be quite bare except for the sealskin coat he clutched to his chest as he sprinted for the hatch.

He vanished down the hatch but was back up again wearing breeches and pulling on a shirt, before she had time to blink. The rest of the crew took no notice of the manner of his return, but the ghost cats slithered around his feet as if he were made of cat grass.

The captain called to her. "Come along, dearie, and let us see what we've found. This will teach the *Nice Try* to try and sink the *Belle*. We've robbed her of these and I'll wager there's more treasure yet in her hold. She was said to have sunk a transport ship carrying a roster of mighty wizards from the Southern Arm to Queenston, though no one knows who sank her exactly or what became of her passengers and crew."

"Whatever it was, Skipper," said Angus the boatswain. "Best to throw it back over the side before the *Try* comes looking for it and tries to sink us again. Mr. Gray's family has all gone home now."

"Aye. Although I be unaware of an old sailor's superstition against robbing a wreck that generates an eerie apparition, if there isn't one, there ought to be." This was from the sailor called Prof by the others because of his more or less erudite manner of speaking. He tried to fit in with the sailor's vernacular, substituting 'be' for 'am' and salting his speech with a few idioms, and although it didn't fool anyone, he was a good banjo player, so the rest of the crew forgave him his idiosyncrasies.

"Open it, Cap'n!" urged Mr. Funnel, the carpenter/surgeon who had been the engineer and dragon wrangler before the dragon went on strike with the others, rendering the engine room essentially useless, and reverting the *Belle* to her origins as a sailing ship.

Chapter 6: Treasure

Like the others, Verity had been fixed on the heavily barnacled chest, but when the ghost cats began surrounding it and sniffing at the edges of the lid, she watched them closely then said, "Let's see what's in there."

Captain Lewis tried to open it, but the lid didn't budge. Mr. Funnel offered a hammer and crowbar, but the lid remained firmly attached to the box.

Legs, the rigger, was also the bartender from Changelings Cabaret, and was as much octopus as it suited her to be in any given situation. She snaked out a tentacle and wrapped it around the chest.

"Oh dear. How disappointing. Well, then, I'll just take this down below and put it back where it belongs again, shall I?"

"Don't you dare!" the captain said, smacking lightly at the tentacle.

"But Captain, the ghost ship…"

"Had the unmitigated temerity to lay—hull—on the *Belle* and her crew. You all do remember who I am, don't you?"

"You're the captain, sir or ma'am, as you prefer."

"I am. And the captain is what on his ship?"

"Absolute authority—sir or ma'am, as you prefer."

"And don't you forget it," Captain Lewis said. "Get me a damn pry bar. Has it escaped everyone's attention that whenever the box moves, it jingles?"

With a lot of grunting, groaning, and a prodigious display of colorful language, the chest was at last forced open. The sight that met their eyes was almost too good to be true. It was filled with gold, silver and copper coins. The captain picked up handfuls and let them clink through her fingers. The crew crowded around and did the same before she pushed them aside and shut the lid.

"Well, me hearties. Cargo be damned. We're plenty wealthy enough now to pass it by and deliver Verity here to her aunt, who happens to be a great friend of sailing folk. You all know of the Sailor's Spa and Bawdy House?"

A cheer arose, loud enough to wake the dead, had there been any, in the wreck below.

"Now, stow this in my cabin and let's waggle our rudder and make way for Madame Erotica's."

The Hunter, the Traveler, and the Singer

The enticing smell of blood lured the dragons across the former battlefield, where wildflowers softened the contours of pox-like craters across the face of the earth.

A man stood outlined against the large carcass hanging from a tree. He carved a big piece of it off and spitted it over a fire.

3336 had no frame of reference to inform him as to what kind of a beast the meat had belonged to, but he didn't need to know that. His stomach rumbled, and sparks glittered in his nostrils. It was food, enough food for him and Smelt both.

And this man had better not try to stop them.

Auld Smelt followed, wobbling along behind him.

The young dragon growled menacingly, a growl intended to convey, "Hello, man. As you can tell, we are dragons, and we are very hungry, so you'd better forget that this is your kill and give it to us or we will be forced to use our fire in ways other than productive labor."

It was a menacing growl indeed. Very menacing. But the man looked up from turning his spit and grinned broadly, welcomingly.

"By the moon and stars, if it isn't a dragon! No—wait—there's another coming—a pair of dragons! Marvelous! I could use your help if you'd be so kind. I've no taste for raw elk. If you'd grant me the boon of a fire to cook a small portion of this for myself, you may have the rest if you like. Someone shot it—from the train, I suspect, and I was fortunate enough to happen on it as it died. But I couldn't pay the troll toll at the bridge, so my matches got wet in the crossing."

3336 looked to Smelt, who said, "You do it, laddie. My fire is trained to melt iron ore. I need to retrain it. I would incinerate our dinner were I to fire the meat."

After hearing about all the warrior dragons, 3336 really wanted to respond ferociously to the man, to show him that dragons were not just for cleaning up miners' messes, but he wouldn't have actually hurt him. There was no reason to do that. Unlike almost every human the young dragon had ever encountered, the man spoke respectfully, even deferentially.

He also seemed to understand dragon speech, for he cut off a hunk of the carcass and laid it on a rock, then backed away with a low bow and a graceful wave of his hand, involving a fascinating twirl of the wrist. Well, if he was even going to do tricks for his guests, he must be a good sort of man.

"If you could just char the hair off, please, great one?" the man asked.

3336 had in the course of his work used his flame for a number of delicate tasks inside the tunnel, where a blast such as Smelt routinely created would have charred all of his co-workers, seared off the hair as requested. Then using his claw, he flipped the haunch and with a low medium flame broiled the meat.

As the man ate, he said, "I was hoping by coming to the Battleground of the Blazing Bog I might meet one of your kind. I really need a dragon's response to my new song. It's—er—about dragons, you see."

Once more, even as he and Smelt made short work of the meal, 3336 noticed that every word the man spoke was clear and made perfect sense. Probably because as a mine dragon, he had listened to humans all day long and had learned to understand their speech, although mostly in a work context.

"We don't care about your song, man," he said, still not quite willing to give up his newfound ferocity. "We cared about the meat, and it was smart of you to give it to us willingly because—because otherwise we might have had to eat you."

He was rather proud of how tough and threatening he sounded, but then felt he should explain. "You see, all of the other dragons were loosed from the mine and they've all had first pick of the beasts around here and we were very hungry indeed."

"Yes, I suppose you would be," the man said. "But now that you've eaten your fill, I trust you are more content? Be my guests, do. Pull up a—well, I suppose you're used to sitting without pulling up anything, but make yourselves comfortable, and please, give a listen to my song. This is a time of great import in Argonian history and in dragon history, to be sure, and it is incumbent upon those of my profession to commemorate it accordingly."

"What do you think, boy?" Smelt asked.

"He doesn't seem to be armed," 3336 said. "There's just that box thingy."

The box thingy proved to have a sweet voice of its own, and as the man held it and stroked it so it accompanied him as he sang.

"Once upon a time in the days of 'ere
When people were feudal and dragons were rare
And fiery and fearsome when they went on a tear
They torched down the cities
And scorched the green fields
So the people were homeless
And the crops would not yield
Then warriors developed a fireproof shield
And scale piercing swords and really sharp spears
And dragons holed up in their caverns for years.
When they came out, there were less than before
Some befriended the humans
And helped them in war."

The man stopped and scratched his head. "I can't seem to come up with another verse."

Auld Smelt burped courteously in the direction of the fire, brightening it for a moment with his sparks. "This is a good place to sing about the Dragon Heroes of the Great Flame War. That field there is where we fought the Battle of Blazing Bog. Many a brave dragon died or was mortally wounded."

66

The man nodded. "That's why I came here. For inspiration."

"When the battles were fought, and the smoke had all
  cleared
The price of the winning was worse than they feared
For dragons, who once more went hungry again
When they tried to find food
People offered them chains
'Just work at these jobs
And get something to eat'
And they offered them kibble
Instead of good meat."

3336 said, "Wait a minute. I have trouble believing this part. You should explain why such brave heroes would settle for jobs in the mines and kibble when they were used to glory and flying wild and killing their own prey."

Auld Smelt shot a bolt of flame halfway across the clearing. "Because they were worn out, that's why. Weary, many of us—them—lame or maimed. Any food was welcome, and the livestock and wild things were consumed by the marching human armies. We thought they were playing some cruel joke when they offered us that kibble at first, but then were surprised to find how satisfying it was. It calmed the rumble in our guts and left us feeling peaceful—a feeling we weren't familiar with but oh, it was sweet. So when we tried to get more, and they said, 'Sure you can, old beasts, but first we need you to do these little things for us—' we didn't take much convincing."

"Brilliant!" the man exclaimed, pulling a feather from his hat and picking up a book to scribble in. "What was it like, being there, sir? I mean, your dragonness? I mean..."

"Smelt will do me fine," Auld Smelt told him. "What was it like? Not nearly so quiet as it is now, and you couldn't see the stars for the flames slashing the night like the aurora gone rogue." He licked his muzzle. "No darkness, then, and the air reeked of blood and seared flesh, soldier flesh, horse flesh, dragon flesh. Our side had a unicorn standing by over in the shadow of the hills to heal the injured, but I heard halfway through the battle its horn went transparent, all the magic drained away, and it died of exhaustion."

"Ah, I need to put that imagery in somewhere. Excellent detail. Thank you, Smelt."

He rearranged the verses, adding the detail, strummed through it a couple of times, then added some flourishes on the strings of the instrument and began to sing.

Halfway through the song, something strange happened. Smelt leaned away from 3336 with a wild look in his eyes. Even the man noticed and stilled his strings.

"What is it?" 3336 asked. "Smelt, what's wrong."

"You," his old friend said. "What you're doing there. You've never done that before."

"I was..." 3336 started to say, "just listening."

"Singing," the man said. "He was singing. Weren't you?"

"Was I?" It seemed to 3336 that he was just enjoying the music. There wasn't a lot of music in the tunnels. Sometimes one man or another would start a song. Sometimes someone joined in, and on the ones the men called dirty, sometimes a whole shift would join in the choruses. But most of the miners didn't sing as sweetly as this man.

"I can't be sure because I've never heard a dragon sing before or even heard of it happening. Is your family musical?"

"No," 3336 said at the same time Smelt said, "Yes, his mother was."

"Was she?"

"Oh yes. Your mother could sing the mountains down and did so to bury invading troops back in the day. But she had lived with a female human and before the woman died of old age, the two of them toured the country, the woman singing and your mother accompanying her—because the humans didn't understand what she did as singing. I—admired her, you know."

"I wonder what it would sound like if you sang with your wings spread, or if you could get different effects by pumping them?" the man said.

3336 tried, and when the man made another little suggestion, tried again. The man was delighted, but no more than 3336 at finding a skill he didn't realize he possessed.

Sometime during the conversation Auld Smelt curled his tail around his nose and fell asleep.

When the man stopped singing, 3336 did not realize it for some time. His eyes were closed in sheer ecstasy. He loved this. He had been a quiet, modest, subdued creature all of his life, trying not to look big or fierce to the men who worked in his tunnel. He had no wish to frighten them.

But his tail lashed in time with his voice and whumped like a drum with the beat of his lyric, sung with throat and breath. He felt so wonderful when he sang, he could have sworn he felt his wings growing. The swish, swish of them added a treble percussion to the bass whump of his tail.

He thought he was still singing with the man and that the other voice he heard inside his head was the human's. He didn't realize that echoes existed even in these wide-open spaces. He was hearing his own mighty voice bouncing off the distant mountains!

When 3336 finally ran out of sound, Smelt, undisturbed, was still sleeping, but the man had set aside his stringed box and regarded him with something like fear, but not. "I'm astonished! You're amazing. Magnificent. I had no idea dragons were so musical."

"Nor did I!" 3336 said. "Why, if I had sung like this in the tunnel, it would have collapsed on top of me!"

The man placed his steepled fingers against his chest and bowed low, saying, "Fate has brought us together, my friend, for I, the great Casimir Cairngorm, troubadour and talent scout extraordinaire, am just the coach and teacher to help you realize your great potential. With whom have I the honor of sharing my meal and music?"

"I'm 3336 of Tunnel Twelve," the dragon replied. "You already met Auld Smelt."

"A number? A mere number is pitifully inadequate for a singular artist such as yourself."

"I'd prefer a name, and Smelt and I discussed it, but he didn't like any of the ones I came up with and actually, I didn't think they sounded right either."

"Naturally you must have a special name, a worthy name. A bard's name, but one suitable for a dragon. Hmmm, it's on the tip of my tongue. I know such a name, but I can't quite—Devent!"

"Excuse me?" 3336 said. In the tight tunnel, courtesy was very important to keep the workplace from becoming hostile.

"Devent! It means bard, so you will be Devent, the Dragon Bard. Frankly, at the moment you dragons need good press..."

"Good press?"

"Reputation! Words of praise sung in your honor throughout the land. With my help and guidance, you shall be an ambassador for dragonkind!"

"Me?"

"You indeed! With my help, of course."

"And Smelt's?"

"Most certainly, if Smelt will not be put out when you are suddenly a celebrity."

"Oh, I don't think he would be. Why should he?"

Their conversation was interrupted by the low moaning cries of the train dragons as the locomotive rumbled past on its way north from Queenston.

"Were the train dragons not freed when the rest of us were?" 3336—Devent—asked the man. "I thought all of us were on our own now."

"As it happens, the railroad dragons prefer their work to unemployment, and the railroads are happy to continue running uninterrupted," Casimir said. "Their dragons have always been well-treated and enjoy a certain esprit de corps with the other employees, engineers, conductors, brakemen, firemen/dragon wranglers and such. I suspect our splendid repast was probably shot by a railroad man hunting for the dragons' next meal."

"They travel," Devent said. "I want to do that too. Before now, I only saw Tunnel Twelve." The thought of what he had missed for so much of his life momentarily saddened him. "I want to sing more."

"Your wish is my command," Casimir Cairngorm said with another bow.

Smelt did not wake, and soon Casimir also slept, but though 3336 sang less loudly, he continued singing while he watched the moon travel across the sky and the stars twinkle brighter and brighter. He was amazed. He had never seen either, although he had heard of them.

When Smelt woke, he said, "We should find food," and Devent fell in beside him, walking in the direction of the Majestic Mountains, where Smelt had his hoard.

70

They had not gone far when the man called out to them, "Wait! Devent! What about your singing? Remember, you need my help. I will come with you."

Devent started to say that he could sing whenever he wanted by himself. He hadn't really believed Casimir when he spoke of singing before men and making them think better of dragons. That sounded very complicated for a newly freed tunnel dragon. There was so much to experience before he settled into one course or another. And he liked walking with Smelt.

The older dragon answered Casimir. "Come if you will for a little way, perhaps. But we are going where only dragons go."

"Meanwhile you'll meet other men. I could be useful to you as an interpreter."

"How did you come to speak Dragonish?" Smelt said, suspicious.

"I was brought up around dragons," he said. "Wild ones. Free."

Smelt whipped his head around to face Casimir. "Really, and where was that? You are not as old as I. When would you have had a chance to meet wild dragons?"

"Oh, here and there. A bard gets around, you know."

Smelt snorted and faced the mountains once more. "I did not know any were left."

Casimir didn't seem to hear. He'd begun to whistle as he walked, then, rather slyly, to sing—about the former 3336!

> "Devent the dragon flew over the hills
> Singing his ballad compelling
> I whistled as he sang
> Till the mountains rang.
> People watched as he flew past their
> Dwell-el-el-lings."

Chapter 7: Casimir, Agent of the Underground

The traveling had all sounded very nice, but the reality was less pleasant, a fact that did not surprise Smelt and was not too unexpected to Devent, but which seemed to astonish Casimir.

"It was only one little ewe!" he complained when they were finally able to slow their pace again, feeling sure they were out of rifle range of the shepherd whose wandering charge had been their dinner.

Smelt mumbled to Devent, "Once we find my hoard again, we'll have gold to pay for our food like humans do."

Casimir did not seem to have heard him, but strode ahead of them, his step enlivened by their brush with mortality.

Devent's stomach rumbled.

Casimir was also quite hungry. It had been a long time since they'd eaten the elk, and the ewe had been very small, especially split between two dragons and a man, and both game and farms with herd animals were scarce so close to the mountains. He at least could eat berries and some of the hard bread he carried in his pack, but such was not decent fare for dragons.

Casimir's Ulterior Motives

Casimir could not simply return to the time he came from and bag another elk as he had the first one, and haul it into the Faerie Knowe with him. This entire area was devoid of game. He had been advised to bring the elk by the lady called Romany, an expert on this time period.

Like Casimir, the Rani Romany was Xenobian Gypsy by blood, though half-caste. Her mother, Bronwyn of the house of Rowan, had been the last queen. Her father, a Gypsy boy named Jack who became King of Ablemarle, since on his father's side he was descended from a Gypsy lady and a previously enchanted bear who was until his transformation the Ablemarlonian crown prince. These lineages were a very important part of Casimir's work. He sang family trees as often as great deeds. People not only liked to know who they came from, it was often necessary in business transactions among his people. People also liked to know who they were dealing with, which clan, if there had been cursed people perhaps or nobility among the forebears.

He had been perfectly happy doing that when he met Romany again by the hillside. He did not recognize her as the one who had set him on his true path in the first place. He'd thought her a fan. He was a favorite among the ladies, even Gypsy ladies, who unlike settled ladies got to travel around and ought to have known that life as a free roaming musician's love was not exactly glamorous. In Romany's case, she had no expectations about his glamor since she had plenty of her own. The first time he'd met her, he was glumly pursuing another line of work when she accosted him begging for his wine and bread. Fortunately for him, he'd been brought up to be kind to old ladies like the one she appeared to be. Years had passed between parting ways with her and meeting this younger, prettier version.

"You know those songs where people go into Faerie Knowes and disappear for seven years and a day, Bard?" she'd asked him by way of an opening line.

"Which one did you have in mind?" he asked. "I know at least three and could fake two others."

"What if I told you the stories behind them were real except, instead of Faerieland, once you entered the Knowe, you were able to travel to another time."

"Which time?"

"Any time past or future."

"Sounds dangerous. You could end up in the middle of a battle or some bedchamber in a castle where you were not supposed to be."

"You can choose the place as well," she'd said. "Think of the people you'd meet, the songs you'd learn, the stories you could tell about such adventures."

"There's a catch, isn't there? I don't suppose I could come back here when I wanted, could I?"

"After the seven years and a day passed. You have to stick it out, but then you can return."

"I wouldn't be able to do it often. A person only has so many seven yearses in him."

"That's the best part. You won't have aged at all and can pop back through whenever you wish. You could, for instance, leave to follow Princess Bronwyn on her quest, the one where she met Prince Jack, and come back here when you were finished to tell us how it all went. The only thing you must remember when traveling in the past is that you are only an observer. You mustn't change things or now won't be the same now any longer."

"And I'd have to rewrite all the songs. I think I could handle that," he said. "As it is I travel where I will and go where I may so no one is ever exactly expecting me and I'm almost always surplus to their requirements, so I can slip to the side and watch, and note, and rhyme with no one the wiser. I often do now."

"Excellent," she said. "Then you qualify to be one of my operatives."

"Operatives? I thought I was supposed to be observing things that would further my own career."

"Oh, you are, but now and then I may ask you to do some little favor for me."

"How am I to do so without changing things?"

"I will instruct you when the time comes."

But once she showed him how it was done, and he became not just a Traveler but a Time Traveler, she let him go where he would and do as he pleased.

He learned the food to pack for his journeys, the clothing to wear to blend with the current populace, that he must always bring with him a measure of mead to calm his throat until he could find the local equivalent in the period where he found himself. He learned to play any number of instruments, and a great deal about what had preceded his time and the years that came after, and with this lore he wrote a thousand songs. He changed history only in that his name was sometimes whispered among musicians who came after and he was called the Master Minstrel. He had no problem with that.

Sometimes he encountered others of Rani Romany's operatives, all Gypsies like himself, and learned that often they were sent to spend seven years sometime, someplace, to insert themselves in one place to perform one task, after which they were free to do as they liked.

If the task were one that might cause them to be pursued, their entry time was planned so that they were able to leave once they'd accomplished their purpose, slipping away into the nearest Faerie Knowe.

At the campfire of one such band, once they knew that he knew who they were, and he realized they knew who he was, he heard some of their stories of their perilous missions. He asked them to explain to him how it was that they were permitted intervene in events that might change the past for some point in the future.

"We think of ourselves as instruments of fate, for so it must seem to those whose lives we change at a certain moment. To them, meeting us or one of us is an accident, a coincidence, a chance encounter that changes everything, but the Rani and her fox friend have lived far into the future and she has a plan for how it ought to be, and if that doesn't turn out so good, she comes up with another plan and we help with that one too. It's a great joke. We may seem completely expendable to the people we meet during these missions, but in fact, our presence helps bring about the most important things that happen to them."

Casimir puzzled over this for many miles and many years until after one seven-year journey he emerged from the Knowe back to his own time, back to a moment shortly after he met the Rani, and there she was.

He was about to ask her about the people she gave a purpose when she said, "Music and traveling come naturally to you. Have you ever taught music?"

"Oh yes, quite often," he assured her. "I teach lute and crumhorn, piccolo and pipes, harpsicord and harp alike."

"And lyrics? Singing?"

"Especially lyrics that tell stories to be sung, and the vocal skills to impart them. My students are much sought after in the great houses during all times and in all places throughout Argonia and the continent."

"Excellent," she had said. "How do you feel about dragons?"

Chapter 8: Horn Haven

A chattering, gaudily but not too heavily dressed delegation of females met the *Belle*'s longboats as the crew landed.

"Hello, me darlings," cried a voluptuous lady wearing a fur coat over her negligee. "Which of you is my true love, eh?"

"You there, handsome." A raven-haired beauty in tiers of pink, yellow and red taffeta, pulled at second mate Bretwen Bowen's arm. Her voice was as low and sultry as she could manage, what with the wind whining down from the glacier-studded mountains. "Where've you been all my life?" Something about that voice was vaguely familiar too, but Verity didn't see how that could be since she'd never been here before.

She tried to walk apart from the crew and their new friends, as her head had started throbbing when the amorous banter and bargaining began. A lot of reciprocal lying was involved. She knew—or thought she knew—that the business about true loves and so forth was just a commercial courtship sales pitch, not to be taken seriously by anyone, but the chatter stimulated an ache along her eyebrows that slightly nauseated her.

She was still dressed as a man, albeit one much bedecked with shells, an oilskin hat pulled down over her coiled braid. Sailors spent long hours alone though and rigged themselves out in all sorts of individually accessorized apparel. Angus had a fascinating array of self-inflicted tattoos. Legs liked to do scrimshaw in her spare time and found interesting ways to display it on her person and appendages. Shells were fairly conservative, as such things went. At least two of the other sailors had collections they wore as necklaces and bracelets, but unlike Verity's, theirs didn't contain the voices of murdered magicians.

A purple-haired woman sidled up to her. "Who are you, then, my sweetie? Strapping lad like you is a bit large for a cabin boy."

"I'm a girl, actually," Verity said. "I'm looking for a relative of mine, an aunt named Erotica Amora."

The woman chuckled. "You're in luck. We're just headed back to our mutual rooming house. Madame Erotica is our landlady, you might say. Also our business manager, talent agent, and the Human Resources Department."

Verity nodded and tried to smile, but the woman's euphemistic job description of her aunt, the brothel keeper, did not help her rising gorge. Not that she was any more of a prude about naked stuff than anyone else. It was just that lying seemed to be an integral part of any conversations surrounding the transactions being negotiated all around her. When her classmates spoke of lewd doings, real and imagined, it hadn't bothered her. For the most part their discussions had been frank, if a bit exploratory since only one or two had any idea what it was really all about. But somehow, this was different. The honest crew of sailors and musicians, with whom she had trusted her life, were making extraordinary promises and telling incredible lies to these painted ladies who gave as good as they got in the lying department.

Her colorful companion had momentarily turned from her to try to snag a crewmember. She clutched a posy of little yellow flowers in one hand, and now Verity noticed that the other women did as well. The crew seemed to have all found other escorts, while the woman with a scarlet mouth and purple eyelids satisfied her curiosity about Verity.

"How far gone are you?" the woman asked. "Might be you don't have to stay the whole time."

"What do you mean?"

"Just that there's some of us knows a thing or two about that—" she made a bump over her belly with her hand "—kind of thing."

At first Verity was a little confused, and then she understood. A young woman seeking out an aunt in a remote place? Most likely with child.

"Oh, it's nothing like that," Verity assured her. She started to explain about the magicians and the dragon crisis, but before she could the woman cast her a side-eyed suspicious look.

"You're not looking for Madame to give you a berth here, are you, just because you're related? You look a bit of a gawk right now, but there's homelier than you been put right with their hair done, a little paint, a flashy frock. Oh, yes, with your youth and all, you'd be popular." She glared over at the young woman who gripped the second mate's arm as the two briskly strolled up the hill ahead of them.

Her voice had taken on a hostile edge, and Verity felt she could ill afford to lose a possible ally.

"No, no, it's to do with another matter altogether... family business. Not that kind of family business, but another issue my aunt's sister, my other aunt, thought she might be able to advise me about..."

But the other woman was no longer listening and instead was sizing her up in a different way. "Well, then, if you ain't sellin' and you ain't buyin'—unless you prefer your own sort?"

Meaning other women, Verity surmised.

"No, no, nothing to do with this side of my aunt's—enterprises," she said. "I just need to meet with her and discuss an entirely different subject with her. Mostly because she is familiar with this area of the country, and I'm looking for the relatives of someone who might have lived here."

"But you don't mean to stay here?"

Before the woman could continue, the boatswain and two of the other men and their companions caught up with her. The boatswain put a comradely arm around Verity's shoulders and said to the other two.

"Let's personally escort our young mate to see her auntie, in case there's a friends and family discount!" he said.

Horn Haven was a grubby little town built between the harbor and the mountains. The Sailor's Spa and Brothel looked like a compact version of a manor house. The crew seemed collectively excited to be there.

"This is a long way from Queenston for such an establishment, isn't it?" Verity asked the first mate.

"No, it's the perfect location actually. This way Madame avoids city taxes and has a steady clientele. Any ship coming round the Horn is likely to need to hole up here for awhile for repairs, and the crews need some relaxation and comfort-like, while they're in port."

Verity considered this and found it to be a well-thought-out arrangement. "Umm," she said, nodding.

When she walked into the mansion with her crew of apparent swains, (though truthfully the term could only be applied correctly to the boatswain) the men already in the parlor, apparently from some other ship, did not mistake her for the cabin boy. One whistled so shrilly she thought he must be a boatswain, too. "Fresh talent, lads! Where'd you come from, sweetheart?"

"Fine strapping lass, that. Come sit on my knee, love. You won't break me, I promise."

"You louts got no idea how to woo a lady," a third soul, snaggle-toothed and leering, said. He held up a dirty leather pouch and jingled it. "Hey, my henny, just got paid."

She wasn't exactly sure what he expected her to do about it, but she didn't want to find out.

She looked around for her shipmates. They had quickly become otherwise occupied, getting drinks and being fawned over by the ladies. The young woman with Bretwen Bowen sat down at the pianoforte to play while he brought forth his mouth harp, and the other men and their new friends were gathering round as well.

"I've come to visit my aunt," she announced to the room in general, hoping her relative would appear and relieve her of the necessity of perhaps damaging a few of the customers.

"Hoo-hoo. Going into the family business, are you?" a voice behind her inquired, followed by a hand on her posterior. She didn't even think about it when she whirled around and socked him on the jaw. He staggered back and fell to the laughter of the others. Rubbing his jaw, he gazed at her so foolishly she thought she'd hit him harder than she intended.

"I think I'm in love, boys."

Captain Lewis stood, fingers still on the keys, and looked as if he were about to intervene, perhaps—if he really had to, when a short buxom woman clad in brown velvet swanned into the room. Her dress almost exactly matched her chestnut hair, which was dressed atop her head in a complicated confection of curls. She carried a red feathered fan and snapped it shut.

"What's all the commotion?" she asked, then saw Verity. "And who are you, Miss? We have no openings at the moment."

This made the men laugh for some reason.

"I am your niece," she told her. "Er—your brother's daughter. Is there somewhere we could speak privately?" Stepping closer, she said in a lower tone, "Aunt Ephemera said I should seek your advice."

"Step into my office," Erotica said. "Gentlemen, the primrose ritual will commence directly. Meanwhile, drink up and get acquainted."

Erotica's office wasn't a large one, but it was filled with bookshelves, a writing desk, and a fainting couch. A large table draped with a silken shawl embroidered with yellow flowers dominated most of the space. It stood on a thick rug in turkey red. The books, to Verity's surprise, were bound in paintings, not in leather. They did not entirely fill the shelves. The two shelves at waist height were filled with an assortment of crystals, candles, and cobalt blue, brown, and green bottles. Verity could not see what they contained. The walk-in fireplace in the room held a large pot hanging from a hook inside the cavernous opening. Something musky and slightly sweet smelling bubbled in the cauldron.

Verity sniffed.

Aunt Erotica said, "I'll leave the recipe for you in my will. It's my world-famous love elixir and massage oil."

"Very kind," Verity murmured, referring to the promised legacy.

"So, what brings you to my establishment? I assume you're not looking for a job."

"No, thank you. I already have a job that, believe it or not, I feel even more unqualified for than I would be to work here, but that's not really why I'm here either. I have more of a task to perform than a job." She explained as succinctly as she could about the dragon-torched beads formed from the crystal deposits on cavern walls impregnated with magic purloined from magic practitioners murdered during the Great War. "So Aunt Ephemera suggested you might know where I could find one or more of the heirs of the late magicians, so I could return their ancestors'—er—spiritual belongings to them?"

"Possibly. Can you tell me who you're looking for?"

"I wish I could. That would make my job a lot easier."

"After all these years, it's surely not that urgent."

"Well, it wouldn't be except for the dragons."

"Dragons? We don't really use them much out here except for the occasional steamer, and lately we've been seeing more sails than smoke."

Verity explained as well as she could about the dragon difficulties Queenston and the more inland parts of the country were experiencing.

Erotica interrupted her before she'd got to the part where the dragons were building-sitting, imitating gargoyles.

An hourglass whose bottom was full of sand gave a little chime as the last of the sand drained from the top. "Elixir's done. I can use your help now."

She whisked the shawl from the table and at her direction Verity lugged the heavy bubbling pot off the fire and set it down on the scarred and stained wooden surface. Erotica arranged blue bottles with their tops off in lines down the length of the table.

"Is this elixir an aphrodisiac?" Verity asked, being proud of herself for remembering the word. The other crewmembers had mangled it pretty well, discussing their plans for shore leave at this establishment.

"No place in the world has girls make you feel as good as hers," Bretwen Bowen had said. He was from Horn country and knew the establishment even before he went to sea at the age of fifteen.

"Aren't you a clever girl?" her aunt said, beaming through the steam of the musky-sweet liquid. "It is, though not in the usual way."

Verity wasn't sure what the usual way was.

"Your ordinary aphrodisiac works exclusively on the nether regions. My potion appeals to the whole client, particularly the brain, heart, and sensory receptors. After a little trip to my place, the boys don't rightly mind if they drown rounding the Horn on the return trip, because they've already been to paradise."

"That sounds almost scientific," Verity said. "All but the last bit."

"Oh, it is! When my granny, Goodie Longlove, handed it down to me, it was called a love potion, but I analyzed it scientifically and found out it has all sorts of endwarfins in it."

"Endwarfins?"

"Why do you think dwarves can delve in the mines so tirelessly and enjoy it? Endwarfins! Makes them feel like they can go at it in the dark for months on end!"

"Is it dangerous? I mean, could it poison the people who take it?" No matter how enthused her shipmates had sounded about this place, she didn't want to be a party to them taking anything that would harm them.

"It is certainly likely to disturb their peace of mind. But other than spoiling them for all other establishments, no, not really. They may be melancholy for awhile but eventually, I'm told, the sea air disperses the lingering sense of loss. Usually the lovelorn letters delivered by carrier gull stop coming a fortnight or so after the ships sail."

She poured some into a crystal decanter. "Let's take some out into the parlor and add a little something to the drinks. There's still some of the last batch in the massage oils."

She opened the door and they went behind the bar where Erotica began mixing drinks with the elixir.

The captain and the black-haired woman played a duet while Bretwen Bowen hung over the back of the piano, apparently anticipating another sort of duet. The men who'd been there when the *Belle*'s crew arrived were entertaining Legs, who had one of hers wrapped around each. The ends of the tentacles made little stroking gestures on the men's cheeks or snuggled into their ears unless they tried to move. Then the suckers came into play.

Verity trailed behind her aunt, "Lovelorn? Why? Isn't this—aren't these liaisons—er—commercial?"

"Not entirely," Erotica said. "There's an extra dimension with the elixir." She poured and handed a glass to Mr. Bowen with a benign dimpled smile.

Verity's curse prompted her to tell him, "That's been drugged."

"I know," he said cheerfully, and drained the glass. "Bottoms up!"

"And to you, my sweet," said the black-haired woman, doing the same, and glaring defiantly at Verity with a look that plainly said, 'Interfering priggish cow.'

Verity saw through the makeup and recognized her in that instant, and she must have done the same because her eyes widened, and she stifled a squeak.

"Fiona?" Verity asked the typist and former classmate she had seen off at the train station.

"My—Verity?" she asked, before catching herself and saying, "Fawn, actually, Madame."

Erotica took Verity by the elbow and led her away. "Let's keep you from making trouble, shall we?"

"I didn't mean to," Verity said, lowering her voice when her aunt squeezed her arm. "But I know her. We were in school together, and she worked at the palace. She warned me."

"It's her professional name," Erotica said. "All of my ladies use them. It saves awkwardness with former clients later, or perhaps family or old friends. How long is your ship in port?" Still pouring elixir into opened bottles with her free hand, she drew Verity back to the office.

"I'm not sure, really. The captain wants to pick up cargo in Frostingdung, but was happy enough to detour to bring me here." She didn't mention finding the treasure, although it was the reason the captain and crew were more relaxed about reaching Frostingdung in time to pick up a cargo. The captain had sworn everyone to secrecy and gave the crew just enough coin to enjoy their shore leave. The fewer people who knew about the treasure the better until they could cash it in or hide it somewhere safe. At the moment it rested in the captain's walk-in closet, with a collection of Madame Louisa's shawls, garter belts, boas, and stockings concealing the chest by making it resemble a pile of fripperies. With her shoes stacked on top, it was invisible. No one would suspect. No other captains had walk-in closets, and hers was cleverly disguised with a sign declaring it, 'Captain's Bog.'

It wasn't that Verity didn't trust her aunt, but she did not know her and was incapable of lying to her. The secret was not hers to tell. No one need suspect the treasure until the crew paid their bills in gold coin, and swiftly set sail thereafter.

She shifted the topic, subtly, she thought. "I hope once they're ready to leave here they might take me to my father's other sister. The one who lives up the coast near Mermaid's Atoll?"

"Eulalia? That could be a bit hazardous for Captain Louisa and her crew," Erotica said, rubbing her chin carefully so as not to gouge herself with her long red nails.

Verity cocked an eyebrow.

"You do know your Aunt Eulalia is a mermaid?" Erotica asked.

"I do now. There seems to be a lot of that going around. So she's the mermaid of Mermaid's Atoll?"

"The only one now. She had a partner, but she died a few years ago. Got caught in a net. Sister has it in for fishermen now."

"How much mer do we have in our family anyway? Are you—?"

"Heavens no. I've never even liked swimming. Wreaks havoc with my hairdo. I will, however, send a message to Eulalia to tell her you are here and encourage her to forego her revenge singing long enough to come and visit."

"How?"

"Haven't you heard of sending a message in a bottle?"

"Well, yes, but that seems a random way to organize a family reunion."

"I give it a little guidance. A recipe for a love potion isn't the only thing left me by my Granny."

"You didn't all have the same one?"

"We all had the same mother. Other than that, it's complicated. Mother didn't want Dad to know, but the neighbors reported the selkie who shed his skin at the door while our father was at sea. When the next two babies—Eulalia and your dad—arrived, it was obvious. One strain of selkies can actually convert to merfolk, and Mum's suitor was that kind. Eulalia had a birth enhancement, the doctor told her—fins, gills and a tail. Your dad's was only apparent if he spent too long in the water. Ephemera, Epiphany and I—well, honestly, we were never sure about Epiphany, but she's a Pisces so even with Dad being at home around the time Mom conceived—well, you never know. That selkie— Uncle Flip, we called him—was one slick fellow."

"What did your father do? I mean, with the selkie and all."

"He knew mother had 'certain needs.' She was a passionate lady, and selkies can sense that kind of thing from out in the water. Dad was away from home for months at a time, even years, and when he was home, the last thing he wanted to do with Mom was fight. Besides, folk do say that having a selkie on board or as a friend of the family brings a sailor good luck. He badly wanted a son, so he never quite got around to asking about your dad.

"Eulalia—well, she wasn't exactly just one of us kids because she had to be in a saltwater tub in the yard until we could haul her and it down to the water.

"One of his shipmates told us later that Dad would get everybody to plug their ears before they got close to the Atoll; then he'd take a longboat and row out there to make sure she was doing well, take her a gift or two from some foreign port, like he did the rest of us. Dad was a kind man, and he didn't like the idea of Eulalia out there all alone. He said a lonely mermaid was a particularly dangerous mermaid. I think he wasn't sure who he felt most protective of, Eulalia or the other seamen. He had a lot of friends on other ships.

"Anyway, he was very glad when, last time he rowed out there, she introduced him to Meranda. He died not long after in a big storm."

"But you think she'll come back here to visit?"

"I can't be sure. She hasn't been back since Meranda was killed. But there are all those wrecks up that way since then. She's getting revenge, but I think she's also lonely. We'll see."

She wrapped herself in a big brown wool shawl and pulled an oilskin coat over it, tying a cap of the same material under her chin, covering her coiffure.

Verity, still dressed in her shipboard clothing, trudged and sploshed beside her in the half-frozen mud as the two of them walked down to the seashore.

Erotica had written a note and just before tucking it in the bottle, asked Verity if she had anything to say. "Just that I really want to meet her."

"Very well," Erotica said, and corked the bottle and flung it into the water. It landed in the shallows beside the harbor mouth. Erotica muttered a few words and the bottle ceased bobbing and began cutting its way through the water.

"So that's magic?"

"No, it's the underwater delivery service." Erotica said sarcastically. "Of course it's magic, girl. What else would it be? Magic's been all around you at least since you arrived here. And didn't I hear something about you and some dragons?"

"That's different. Dragons are just animals."

"Who happen to breathe fire."

"There are scientific explanations for that," Verity argued, then changed the subject. "How long will it take for her to receive it?"

"A few days. And if she comes here, a few more. Anywhere between a week and a fortnight."

The ghost cats, who had been absent or invisible since her aunt began distributing the potion, ran down the hill on paws either still invisible or hidden in the scrub grasses.

"Missed me?" Verity asked them. The cats swarmed her and her aunt, who did not notice them.

Once back in the parlor, Erotica walked over to a plate-sized gong on the bar and struck it. Just one 'bong' and the women disengaged themselves from conversations or other forms of communication and formed a circle.

"Now then, have you girls given each of the gents his posy?"

"Aye, Madame," they replied as meekly as schoolgirls, and with a similar amount of giggling.

Erotica clapped her hands twice and said in a flirtatious tone, "Gentlemen, your attention please. Now begins what you've all been waiting for—the dance of love! Form a circle and begin to turn clockwise. The girls will circle around you turning widdershins. As the girl you want to give your flower to passes, tuck it in her bosom."

This they did until three of the most attractive girls had collected quite lush floral trim to their décolletages. Then the girl with the most flowers asked each of the men who had presented her with one, three questions:

1. What would you be willing to do for my favors and half my father's kingdom?

A. Scale a wall of thorns.
B. Climb a glass mountain or
C. Discover how I wear out my dancing slippers so quickly?

2. If you were a frog, how would you persuade me to kiss you and turn you into a handsome seaman? And

3. How would you rescue me from
A. A dragon
B. An evil wicked knight who wanted to do truly nasty things to me or
C. A horrid brothel, not a nice place like this one?"

The men answered with patience that amazed Verity. The little ceremony actually did seem to whet their appetites rather than diminish them.

The man with the answers the girl liked best received her hand to hold as a promissory token of the rest, while they toasted each other with an elixir-laden drink before disappearing up the stairs.

It was purely subjective, since it seemed to Verity that the prettiest girl actually just chose the best looking among the sailors whether or not he could answer her questions with more than a stammer and a blush.

As the selection process continued, more drink was taken, more flowers were dispersed and tucked. Probably because of the drink, the girls who received the last of the droopy primroses were as avidly sought by the remaining customers as their more attractive sisters had been before them, and soon everyone felt they had won a prize. The parlor emptied. Soon the entire house, sturdy brick edifice though it was, was thumping and bumping.

"I thought the men would be asking the questions, and not nearly such romantic ones," Verity told Erotica. "The men who met us when we arrived didn't strike me as sentimental."

"You'd be surprised. A lot of that posturing is for the benefit of the other men. It's not uncommon for a client to want simply to talk to a woman, although for those who might want to limit themselves to talk because of physical limitations, the elixir can restore some of their vigor. Of course, there's always the deranged ones who want to slap the girls around, but once they take the potion, it takes the wind out of their sails."

"I had no idea there was so much to your business. Not that I've given it a lot of thought, but just because I've mostly been to girls' schools doesn't mean I haven't heard things."

"Nothing makes members of the opposite sex as intriguing as being cut off from them," Erotica said with an amused twist of her mouth and a raised eyebrow.

Verity nodded. "And, I confess I believed that the sort of—um—arrangement between ladies who worked in these places and their clients was rather more temporary than the relationships you describe; but then, I've never heard of a formula like yours. Interesting, though a bit beside the point for my current mission."

"Well, dear, you never know what will come in handy. I won't live forever, and your current line of work doesn't offer nearly as much security as this one. A girl can always use something to fall back on—especially if she makes the choice while she's still young and in demand. We can offer a certain amount of on-the-job training, though my sisters would be cross with me if they knew I suggested it to you. And I don't, really, not seriously, although you'd be surprised how many society ladies had their humble beginnings in places not nearly as posh as this one."

"Like Fiona? I mean Fawn, as she wants to be called here. I accompanied her to the train station after she warned me of how hazardous the castle had become for my health."

"She's a good girl, Fiona."

"Yes, she and I were in school together briefly. She was always quite decent to me, unlike some of the others. They were brutal to her when her parents were killed. Good thing for her she had to leave. I didn't know her well. I was surprised to see her at the castle."

"More surprised to see her here, I'll wager," Erotica said. "She's a clever one though and has made herself very useful with the books and such. I've ordered a typewriting machine from Queenston. Might as well take advantage of all the assets a girl has to offer."

Verity studied the rows of glass bottles, frowning. Whatever her aunt said, she didn't much like seeing her friend from the castle and former classmate in a 'house of ill repute.' Wasn't she humiliated to be here?

Erotica changed the subject. "Several of your lads are a bit—unconventional, physically. But the elixir won't harm them and since its benefits are emotional as well as bodily, they should derive satisfaction even if we don't have, say, another octopus to entertain them."

Verity grinned. "Legs seems to be doing fine without one. She's not entirely an octopus all the time."

The walls and ceiling thumped and thudded. Erotica led Verity through the office to a small but comfortably furnished room with a single bed. "You should be comfortable in here, dear, while waiting for your ship to leave again. Unless there's something else you need? I confess I have to wonder why Ephemera thought you should visit me. I doubt she just wanted me to give you a seminar on how to run a brothel."

"I'm searching for surviving remnants of the old magical families in this part of the country."

"Other than you, me, and Captain Louisa? There was a mage around here, back in the day. I don't know much about him except that he's been presumed dead for a great long time, but he was said to be very powerful in his day, back during the Great War. He disappeared before the end of it though."

"Tell me about him, if you would, please, while I lay these out on the bed." She spilled out the beads and shells, the shells that told songs or stories relating to different wizards each strung with the bead that resonated most strongly with that wizard's magic.

Erotica shrugged and turned away.

"Sorry, my dear. You'll have to talk to someone who pays attention to such things. I've a business to run."

An earth colored bead with linear blue and red spirals, wrought in a much more subdued pattern than the others, began to spin. Eight of the smaller shells that held shorter, more portable spoken and sung tales from the Archives, repeatedly jumped up and down on the blanket. Verity scooped them up and held the first shell to her ear. In a gossipy but authoritative voice, the first shell began speaking. It sounded like an excerpt from a history lesson, just a little, she thought.

"An avid gardener, Adaham Warlock was noted for his ability to gather and hold energy gleaned from the ground, plants, water and sunlight. He was fond of planting, fertilizing, watering, and weeding but not much for harvesting. His energies were always held in check, waiting for just the right time to bloom."

The second shell proclaimed in a rather nasal female voice, "Oh, good with plants, 'e were, but not so much with people. Time was I'd have married him in a heartbeat. Thought he was the perfect man, so smart, so learned, handsome he was and strong too, from all that weedin', no doubt. He seemed real down-to-earth too, sensible but with an earthy, lusty humor, you know. But alas, turns out he had feet of clay, preferrin' women he made up himself to the real thing..."

Verity wondered what on—earth—that meant. Obviously, this part of her collection knew of the local wizard.

The last one was the most poignant. It was the voice of one of the few remaining witches who remembered the lost wizards.

So these unremarkable remarks were supposed to hold clues to unlock the magic in the bead, according to Ephemera? Verity wished the descendants the very best of luck with that.

She stepped into the office again and asked, "Can you at least show me on a map where he was supposed to live and recommend the best way to get there?"

"There isn't really a good way, except on horseback, and some places on foot. The Heart Hills lie between here and there and they're a good deal steeper than the name suggests. At one time it looked as if the railroad would come past there almost to our door, but the company decided expanding east was more important than toward the Horn, as they didn't figure many sailors, fishers and the assorted folk needed to support them would provide as much commerce as Brazoria and Glassovia."

Erotica, rummaged in a desk drawer, extracted a map, and handed it to her before disappearing into the parlor again. The tinkling sound of the pianoforte and laughter penetrated the door.

Once Erotica left, the ghost cats made themselves at home on the map, the table, the fainting couch and other surfaces. Verity stuck the beads and shells in a little pouch and spread the map out on the table where she'd helped Erotica with the love elixir.

Studying a map through the haze of feline ectoplasm was unproductive until, as if a breeze had blown them away, the cats crowding the table evaporated.

Before Verity's sigh of relief escaped her lips, screams erupted from the upper regions of the house, accompanied by hearty swearing.

Chapter 9: Feet of Clay

The cats had found a target.

Verity poked her head out of the office in time to see Bretwen Bowen, his feet bare and his undone trousers flapping at the waist, running down the stairs followed by Fiona, now perilously robed in a loose garment with leaves embroidered in vinelike patterns all over it. They were being chased by three of the ghost cats, a faded gray tabby, a very pale black, and a diluted ginger, all trying to trip them. Fortunately for the pair, the cats were too insubstantial to present actual obstacles.

"Brown, call off your beasts!" Mr. Bowen called to her in the loudest voice she'd ever heard him use.

"They're not mine," she called back, turning to pick up a broom she'd noticed propped in a corner beside what she assumed was a water closet. "They don't obey me or anybody else, as far as I can tell." She intercepted her crewmate, Fiona, and the cats, and brushed right through the gray and the black with the broom.

They gave her reproachful glances that clearly said, "Really?"

"There's one on my head," Bowen said, swiping both hands through the ginger one as it clung to his skull and tried to lick him between the eyes. "Get it off."

"You can see them?" she asked.

"I can feel this one!" he said.

"Stop clawing my gown!" Fiona told the cats, slapping at her skirt in an attempt to disperse them.

Mr. Bowen, still swiping at his head, told her, "I'll make it up to you, darlin', I will, as soon as she," he swiped his head in Verity's direction while his cat chapeau, she could have sworn, grinned at her, "rids us of them."

Verity shrugged, "Sorry, Mate, they may be ghosts, but they're cats and neither you nor I will make them go where they don't want to go. I don't suppose you have relatives from this area, do you, Mr. Bowen?"

"I do, as a matter of fact."

"I'm guessing then that the cats are wanting introductions."

Cousin Clodagh

The cats hadn't bothered Mr. Bowen while on shipboard, nor had they previously paid much mind to Fiona, but suddenly the phantasmal felines haunted both of them with such relentless pestering that both parties agreed to go with Verity.

"What is it the kitties know about you two that I don't?"

"Er—well—" Fiona began, when the three of them were tucked away in Aunt Erotica's business drawing room, tastefully decorated with red brocade wall coverings and gold painted babies with wings and archery equipment. "I suppose you're wondering how I came to be here."

"It had crossed my mind," Verity said. "I wondered if one of my royal cabinet might have gotten you in a family way." Which was a polite way of asking if she were pregnant.

"No, though not for want of trying. But actually, I grew up around here. My mother worked here before she met my father and became the lady of the manor. We have a castle-y sort of house back in the Horn Heart, but since my parents died it's gone to ruin. I thought the job at the palace would help me get it in shape to either live there or sell, but repairs are very expensive. This job is the quickest way to earn a new roof and modern plumbing I know of."

"Besides, you saw me around sometimes when we were younger and liked the cut o' me jib, didn't you, Lady?" Bowen asked, teasing.

"That and your modest demeanor," Fiona agreed.

"So you come from this area too, Mr. Bowen?" Verity asked. It was hardly surprising that one of the crew and one from the palace might be from this place. Argonia was a large land; except for Queenston, it was not heavily populated. The few habitable places held small families or small communities, in some cases business interests, but sooner or later, the people from those places ended up in Queenston, at least once, at least for a short time.

"Aye. This was my Da's homeport 'til he stopped coming home at all. Lost at sea, we figured, Ma and me. Now she's gone too, him returned to the water and she to the soil so I haven't been back until this trip. I've got only one odd cousin remaining somewhere in the Horn Heart."

"The cats seem inclined to go there," she said, and explained about the beads, shells and cats. Before she was halfway through her explanation, they both agreed to go with her and by the end of the following day, their rented horses were picking their way along snow-choked mountain trails.

The ghost cats seemed somewhat mollified to be moving in what they appeared to consider the right direction, but nonetheless they continued to make general nuisances of themselves, weaving through the horses' hooves, sitting between their ears, and trotting off the trail to sit in mid-air and stare at the travelers.

"Tell me more about this relative of yours," Verity said.

Bowen scratched his chin, recently relieved of the brushy beard he'd sported on shipboard. "My cousin Clodagh. Bit of an embarrassment to the family, what's left of it. Daft as a brush. Supposed to be the offspring of the wizard who was skipper of all wizardly things around here."

"But people say that wizards are a thing of the past," Verity said, wondering if that opinion was quite as widespread as she'd supposed it to be. Perhaps magic was not quite so out of fashion here as in the city?

"Officially, Missy, but wizards don't care about official."

"Really?"

"One of my great-aunties married one, and I could tell you stories..."

"Oh, I wish you would!" Verity said.

"Well, I could if I remembered half of them. I left home and shipped aboard a freighter when I was fifteen, after my poor widowed mam remarried a scoundrel who had no use for an extra mouth to feed. She it was who knew of the cousin, but when I was small, I had a granny on her side of the family too, and she always told me when I got dirty or muddy that I reminded her of great-uncle Adaham.

She never said why actually. Just give me these side-eyed knowin' looks and nodded to herself."

Verity wondered why the cats hadn't bullied him before if he was one of the people they were looking for. Did they realize he was of no use to them on shipboard?

"That's funny," Fiona said. "I've a daft cousin of the same name who lives out here, too." She and Bowen exchanged an alarmed look, and both said, "Ewwww." A mutual cousin, however distant, was not quite distant enough for the activity that had brought them together.

"How so?" Verity asked.

"I'm told she lives alone in a cottage outside the village. She's not a blood cousin, of course, but I suspect I've run out of that kind."

When at last they beheld the village and ventured into it, they found that their mutual Cousin Clodagh was held in less than high esteem. People spat over their shoulders or wrinkled their noses before speaking about her.

"Her's peculiar," the blacksmith confided. "Comes from magical doings, her does. Not that her's the sparkly type."

"No?" Verity asked. "What type is she, then?"

The blacksmith grinned, his teeth white as bleached bones against his sooty, sweaty face. "The earthy type, I'd say, Missy. Very down-to-earth is our Clodagh. Takes after the old wizard, they do say, him that disappeared at the end of the Great War. Made her first, though. And here her stays, lookin' no older now than she did when I were a lad."

The blacksmith directed them to the edge of town where foothills backed up against the mountains on the opposite side of the basin cupped in the heart of the peninsula called the Horn.

They were still a quarter of a mile from the entrance when the ghost cats streaked off and disappeared into the hill.

The heiress apparent to great wizardry emerged from the interior of the hill looking as if she were carrying a large portion of it in the form of stacks of plates held by each hand, cups dangling from her fingers by their handles, and a pyramid of bowls on her head. They rattled with a deeper and more resonant rattle than the shells.

"Cousin Clodagh?" Fiona said. "You may not remember me, but I used to live nearby as a girl. This is our cousin Bowen. You won't know him. He's never lived here, but him and his crew are moored up at our place in the port. This is Miss Verity, a friend of his."

"Perhaps your cousin would like to relieve herself of her wares before we talk, Fiona," Verity suggested, while Clodagh stared wordlessly at them.

Without acknowledgment or invitation from Clodagh, they followed her into a mud brick house, where she proceeded to divest herself of the pottery. Fiona stepped forward, taking a stack of plates from the woman, and plucking cups from her fingers. Verity followed suit by removing the bowls from her head, revealing plastered looking ditchwater-brown hair. It was dim inside the house, but Clodagh's appearance was remarkable, though her features were somewhat blunted, and she was uniformly brown. The Brown side of Verity's family had a penchant for the color, but no one Verity had ever heard of was brown in the way Clodagh was. Brown as mud, as dirt, as clay.

"You'll have to do the talkin', dearie," Fiona told Verity. "Clodagh's mute, aren't you, love?"

Verity looked reproachfully at Fiona. She might have thought that worth mentioning at some previous point in their journey.

Clodagh evidently remembered Fiona, but looked askance at Verity and Bowen, plainly waiting for them to state their business and leave. She wasn't exactly unfriendly. She left no impression of a personality at all, actually. Verity had never encountered anyone like her. She sensed something was quite wrong with her, apart from her inability to speak, but since she did not know what that was, and everyone seemed agreed that she was Adaham Warlock's heir, Verity took the bead and the string of shells from her pocket.

"Mistress Clodagh, some time ago I was captured by dragons—well, I won't go into that—and subsequently found a cave in swampland that proved to be both crime scene and final resting place of your kinsman, Adaham Warlock. As a result of these experiences, I have with me a bead that contains some of the remnants of the Wizard

Warlock's magic. I've been entrusted with the task of returning his legacy to you, and..."

Clodagh stuck out her hand. Verity dropped the bead and the shells into it. Clodagh dropped the shells into a pocket and stuck the bead in her mouth.

Then she said, "How good of you to come so far to bring this to me. I have not until now had need of food or drink, but perhaps you would be my guests at our little inn? I need to deliver some of these dishes to them and feel sure that they would be glad to barter a few plates and bowls for our meals."

"I guess you weren't joking about that bead being magic!" Fiona said with a low whistle.

At the one small table the inn offered its customers, Clodagh treated them to food and drink and explained. "Had you not brought my master's magic home to me, I would have remained a mute brute forever, without purpose or guidance. I have lived so long among humans that it has long been a matter of wonder to me that I am not one—and how I am not one. The bead informs me that I am a creature of clay—a golem, but by its power, I am now a truly living creature."

"I knew you were old, but I thought you were one of our ancestors somehow or other, even though you're a cousin," Bowen said.

"In truth, I am no cousin to either of you, and am blood kin only because my maker's blood, blood he shared with your line, was used in my creation. I was a golem, a magically mechanized servant, if you will. I served my master while he was here and his family when he was gone. Since his wife died some years before he made me, when I appeared most folk thought he had taken me as his second wife, but that was not the case."

"The shells tell us a little about the wizard," Verity said. "Could you perhaps tell us more?"

That proved to be the wrong thing to ask, as the former golem, who had heard speech and ideas expressed all around her for generations, could not stop talking once she started.

She talked until the innkeeper moved them out, and long after Verity, Fiona and Bowen fell asleep from the exhaustion of their trip, she continued talking. Just before she lost consciousness, Verity had enough presence of mind to hand her unrecorded shells and urge her to speak into them, recording her information for the Seashell Archives.

The Golem's Story

"I have sometimes heard foolish women say that they live for a man and for him alone, as if it was a good thing or a noble thing. They have no idea what they're talking about. I was made to live for one man and him alone, to do his bidding, to do his work, to protect him and his family, by a human woman. No thought was given to me, to what I wanted or needed. I was expected to have no desires or needs, except to serve."

"I'm sure you were very good at it," Bowen said, not a bit helpfully. Verity felt Clodagh bridle.

"What was it that you wanted?" Verity asked.

"What all the others had from him—if not love, affection—or at least, appreciation. I tried to tell him not to go to that so-called conference, the one he never returned from, but although he knew how to tell me what he needed from me, he didn't seem to understand what I needed from him when I needed him to do it. He ignored my pleading as if I were a broom or a mop."

"Oh, my dear," Fiona said sympathetically. "You mustn't take it personal, like. They are all like that with us, even if we talk."

"Hey!" Bowen protested.

"It's true. Even with Mistress Erotica's elixir, it still never occurs to them to wonder what they might do for us other than pay—and payment should be enough."

"I never was paid," Clodagh said. "Never until now, when you brought me this bead, girl."

"I'm—er—glad it's what you needed. And perhaps what the wizard needed." She noticed that one of the ghost cats had curled up in Clodagh's lap where she sat on the earthen floor that matched the rest of her so well.

"Does my speech sound stiff—rusty, perhaps?" Clodagh asked. "I'm surprised to find I have a voice at all."

"It's a good voice," Verity assured her. "A bit deep as a lady's voice goes, throaty, perhaps that is from the disuse, but not unpleasing. I wonder—can you sing?"

"How would she know?" Fiona demanded. "We just now heard her first words ever. You heard her say as clear as I did."

"True," Verity said. "But singing is very important in record-keeping and spell casting and you might do well to try it."

"You can do it, cousin," Bowen said encouragingly. "Everyone in our crew of uneducated louts sings. It's easy. Here, I'll start one:

"Wind or steam, sail or fire
"Sail or fire, wind or steam,
"Dragon boiled, or tempest tossed
Our ship will ply the seas."

"Deep inside the *Belle*'s own shell
The dragon made a living hell

To haul our cargo for to sell
And keep us sailors well."

Clodagh caught the second chorus and sang along like a schoolgirl repeating something she had learned by rote, her tone flat and monotonous.

Her voice gained inflection as she continued, however, and her blunted features sharpened and became more distinct, radiating new spirit, as if she'd swallowed a sprite rather than a bead.

Verity and Fiona joined Bowen in coaxing the mud girl to sing, and even sang with her until they grew weary and sleepy, but Clodagh sang on.

The mud-girl was newly infused with life—magical life at that—so why wouldn't she feel like singing?

Fiona and Bowen, accustomed to the thumpings and bumpings of the bawdy house on Fiona's part and the ship-board noises on Bowen's, soon fell asleep, but Verity lay awake, hearing a babble of voices outside the hut. Lifting the blanket covering the entrance, she saw a small crowd gathered by the noise of Clodagh's song. Their faces, lit by a full moon, reflected consternation and also fear.

"Oh, really!" she said, stepping out to join them. "Her singing isn't that bad and she's improving."

The blacksmith regarded Verity without sympathy. "You're to blame, giving that fancy bauble to a walking mud pie!" he said.

"How do you know what I did?" Verity asked.

"Village this size? You hear everything. Why didn't you give it to one of Warlock's human heirs instead of that thing?"

"I was following directions," Verity said, meaning the ghost cats, the warming of the bead and the rattling of the shells. "He wanted her to have the bead."

The blacksmith snorted, "Says you. There's those of us related to him by his first wife, you know."

"Blood relation?" she asked.

"Yes!" he said belligerently, which set off her alarm bells and an impending headache.

"No you're not. What was it? You were children by the first marriage of his first wife? Because you're no blood kin of his or I'd have known."

"That thing cannot be called kin to anyone human," he said.

"She can be, and she is. She says his blood was in her making. So back off."

"We can just dissolve her, you know. She can't stand a good downpour and even if she's got a tongue on her now, she's still mud-born and can go back to mud with a good dousing."

"If the bead isn't intended for you, it will do you no good," she said, though she had not known it before she did.

"Himself won't know. Him's long dead," the innkeeper's wife said.

"You don't know that," Verity said. "Wizards have their ways, or so I'm told. I suggest you disperse. We know the bead allows her to speak, but that was a very powerful wizard you had here. Don't you suppose the magic in his bead may give her other powers as well?"

After some muttering and growling, they did leave, but she could feel eyes on the entrance of the hut anyway.

She woke her companions and said, "We have to go. Now."

Clodagh continued to sing, but Verity pulled at her arm. "Come on. You need to come with us before they harm you and take the bead away."

Surprisingly, Clodagh stopped singing and said, "Wait," before resuming her song at a lower volume. Then digging her blunt brown fingers into the cracks between the mud bricks in the back wall of her hut, she pulled out enough of the wall to pass through, and for the others to pass through too. "I must fetch Kiln first. I'll not leave him here for them to kill to spite me."

They followed her through the back wall, out the edge of the village and to the cave where they'd first seen her emerge. A glow came from within. Between it and the will o'wisp-like shapes of ghost cats, they found their way in after her. Clodagh strode toward a bend in the cave wall beyond her potting table where slabs of clay and coils of clay lay and a wheel waiting for clay stood.

Verity had her own bead that gave her certain powers, from the days she had spent training the young dragons who helped form beads from the magic once sprayed over the walls of their mother's lair. So she heard what was unsaid, or at least one side of the conversation, and was not surprised when Clodagh reemerged with her hand protectively on the head of a dragon the size of a small pony.

"Strangers, this is Kiln. Kiln, these folk are to be our new companions."

Now that she could talk, Clodagh's mouth had become something of a perpetual motion machine. "I have known Kiln longer than any being here. He worked with Wizard Warlock before I was made. When the wizard took his last journey, Kiln and I waited together for him, looking for him to return. When he did not, and the village began to decline, we went into business together, me fashioning the clay, Kiln firing it."

The three ghost cats that had come with Verity, Bowen, and Fiona now sat on Clodagh's shoulder, the dragon's back and the top of his head. Unlike Bowen, Kiln did not seem to mind.

The villagers did not challenge the travelers as they departed. They paid little attention to Kiln, such a small inoffensive dragon. Since he was associated with Clodagh, the village seemed glad to see the back of him.

As the travelers mounted the trail to the pass, the dragon flew away.

"I suppose he's happy to have his freedom now?" Fiona ventured, interrupting a string of gossip Clodagh was sharing about the blacksmith and the innkeeper's second girl.

"Oh no, he's just hunting," she said, "But that second girl just had a babe and the poor little thing was born all muscley..."

"Has Kiln had the trouble adjusting his diet since the kibble was destroyed?" Verity asked.

"Since what was destroyed?" Clodagh asked, in mid-description of the muscley child's birth. Verity suspected that if Clodagh had remained in the village, they'd have wanted rid of her for reasons other than envy.

"The kibble. What working dragons have been eating since the Great War."

"Not Kiln. We heard something about that kind of food, but it sounded a very odd diet for dragons and nobody bothered. We've plenty of game here and he pays his way for it. Since I have not needed material goods, the villagers and other customers often give us farm animals for him to eat and when business is slow, he hunts."

By the time Kiln returned from his hunt, they were picking their way along a ledge. Kiln positively frisked ahead of them, melting the snow and ice from their path, much improving their journey. And when the melt turned back to ice, it would make the way much harder traveling for any who might want to follow.

Chapter 10: The Hoard

Auld Smelt made no secret of his dislike and distrust of Casimir. "He'd never make it in the mines," the old dragon told the younger one, now calling himself Devent. "Too soft and scrawny."

"I don't think he would have liked mining," Devent agreed. "It would be pretty hard on his voice."

Smelt snorted. "It would have been too much like work. So look, are you coming with me to winter in my lair or will you be goin' with him?"

"I have more to learn about singing," Devent said. "I thought all three of us could..."

"Think again," Smelt said, sounding harder than the steel he'd once smelted. "That human is getting nowhere near my hoard. Come with me or go with him, I don't care."

Devent huffed out a small cloud of ashes. Auld Smelt was like a grandfather to him, had he known what a grandfather was. Returning to Casimir, he said, "Smelt will not finish his journey while you are with us. I don't think I should try to be a singer after all. I cannot abandon him."

Casimir said, "Don't dragons usually go to their lairs to hibernate?"

"I don't know for sure. I have heard it said though..."

"So go with him to his lair and wait 'til the old boy goes to sleep, then come back. That way he will have your company while he needs it and his privacy while he slumbers. Then you can return here, and I'll continue to tutor you in the art of the troubadour."

Devent thought it over and decided that was a very good way to do everything he wanted. "You may have a long wait," he said. "But if that doesn't bother you, as soon as Smelt goes dormant, I'll return."

"I don't mind as long as I have my instrument with me," Casimir assured him. "I shall occupy myself in practice and evaluating how I may best combine our skills to illuminate your talent."

"I may be gone for some time," Devent told him.

Casimir smiled, as if amused by Devent's caution. "As it happens, my dear dragon prodigy, time is something of which I have a sufficiency beyond what you might expect."

Smelt by that time was deep enough into the forested foothills that Devent had lost sight of the tip of his tail. So he simply grunted agreeably and in a couple of bounds was within the trees, where he could no longer see the minstrel but could smell the gas from Smelt's last meal. One more long hop and he was alongside the older dragon. He noticed as he hopped that he was able to achieve some elevation and remain aloft for a moment or two before landing in what he thought was a graceful stance, on back legs and the broad part of his tail. Were his wings a bit wider now?

"Where is your lair?" he asked Smelt.

"At the top of the pass, of course, overlooking the sea."

"Is it far?"

"Not if we stop talking and keep walking."

Secrecy was not the only reason they'd been wise not to bring Casimir. Distance that could be covered in a short time by dragons, even flight-impaired dragons, would have taken the swiftest human much longer, if he could have made it up the stony steep slopes at all.

Just ahead of them, atop the next perpendicular upheaval of the forest floor, the remains of a moss-obscured stone staircase curved up the mountain.

Devent gave his wings a trial flap and jumped. After two tries, he had successfully flown to the bottom of the staircase. Smelt lumbered determinedly forward, but turned to his right and with a slight hop climbed first one moss covered stair, then another. Devent had ignored stairs in his eagerness to reach the lair. Recent days had been so full of new wonders and discoveries, he couldn't wait to see what would come next.

Smelt had known exactly where the stairs were and kept climbing as the steps crested the hill where Devent waited, then wound up to the next level.

Devent burned away some of the low wet moss and lichens and Smelt turned back and roared at him. "Stop that!"

"I just thought the footing would be better if I cleaned off the steps for you."

"It would, but it would also point like an arrow to my lair. You might as well put out a big sign that says, This Way to the Dragon's Hoard!"

As Smelt grumbled and huffed, Devent continued frisking upward.

"Oh, look at this!" he cried, stopping to peer at a small round creature with prickles all over its back. "Are these good to eat?"

Smelt's eyes looked down at the top of the forest canopy below them and upward to the mountain ridge that jutted above them.

Devent lifted the small creature. It squeaked, doubled its size by bristling, and trembled in a heartbreaking way, staring into Devent's fangs with terrified little round eyes. The young dragon gently returned it to the ground. The utter destruction of the creature's entire world wouldn't make a decent bite for Devent.

The spiky thing hurried off to hide in some greenery. Devent heard a different bird song than those he had noticed before. He craned his neck, then rose toward it, hardly realizing he was actually flying until Smelt grumbled and the voice faded with distance.

Looking down, Devent was amazed at how high he was—above the tallest craggy vestige of the ruined castle—and how far below him his friend was. He folded his wings a trifle and sank back to the mountainside.

"Nobody likes a showoff, boy," Smelt said. "Besides, you overshot the entrance."

As much as he enjoyed looking at the world around him, after living his life in the darkness underground, Devent's vision was not particularly acute. He saw a rocky prominence above them, while the rock wall alongside him was interspersed with crevices and crannies of greenery with small pockets of wildflowers.

He shot a questioning glance at Smelt. The stair his friend occupied was many steps below the yawning arch that had once provided access to the fortress. But although the stairs were carved from the same rock as the cliff-face, they were sculpted into a long gentle crescent. Suddenly Smelt leaned to the side and poked his head into the moss and brush clad surface supporting the steps above him. That section of cliff face swung inward, followed closely by Smelt. Devent rushed in just before the stone slab swung shut again.

Malady Hyde Rules!

"Are you an idiot? Because I'm pretty sure I made myself clear. Death to all vagrant dragons but a conditional amnesty for those who return to their employment."

"But, ma'am," Toby, the Dragon Czar, interrupted, "how are you going to feed them?"

"We've done it before and we can do it again," she said. "Don't trouble me with details. They left their employment and have been hanging around making trouble for some time now. They should expect a little inconvenience, but I won't have them killed if they return to making themselves useful. Now you make yourself useful and summon the seamstress and the printer. I want my flyers sent out to all corners of the realm. The True Queen Has Revealed Herself and she is ME!" Her flourish of the slightly moth-eaten ermine trimmed cloak was spoiled when it caught on the spear held by a stone heraldic lion, but the effect was nevertheless dramatic.

She was disappointed that nobody had yet located the crown jewels or the crown itself. Regency didn't actually entitle her to wear it, but that didn't mean she couldn't try it on. Nor could anyone recall what had become of the royal treasury. The current treasury, from the taxes the various industries had paid last quarter, was in a bank vault somewhere, she was told, but nobody could tell her where exactly. For that reason, her uncles said they thought a grand ball was probably out of the question, so rather than have princes from neighboring countries over to vie for her hand, they wanted her to settle for a tea party with her male cousins. The Miragenian side of the family considered cousins the only proper marriage partners anyway. It kept the money in the family.

It was helpful that Argonia had done without royals for several generations and that Verity Brown's claim on it was bolstered only by rather weak hypnotic spells, now largely dissipated.

Fortunately, the creature had seemed to recognize true class when she saw it. At the same time she declared the very inelegant Verity to be queen, she'd appointed Malady to be her companion, assistant, and adviser. Verity had never specifically forbidden Malady to promote herself in her absence. And there was nothing in whatever the spell was that prohibited Malady from assuming her current role. She was obviously much more suited for it than the lumbering, awkward, obnoxious giantess, especially when the giantess in question had virtually begged Malady to relieve her of the burden of rule by running away. Had the big gawk not left, her head would have been less likely to be crowned than it would have been to be removed from her shoulders. The thing was, although Malady's uncles were under the hypnotic orders to accept Verity's rule, they were not bound to like it. They were much happier to have their beloved niece, cousin, granddaughter, sister, sister-in-law, etc. filling the post, figuring she would have to turn to them for the important decisions, like what to do about the dragon situation.

They totally failed to grasp the importance of ballgowns, however, or how critical it was for Malady to gain access to the crown jewels.

She was trying to explain this, yet again, to her Uncle Eustus who was being obtuse as he obsessed once again about the pesky dragons.

"Why not just kill all of them and import labor from Frostingdung?" Malady asked, exasperated. "Wouldn't it be cheaper? If her oversized highness happened to get killed at the same time, what's the difference?"

"Her mother might object to that," Eustus replied with a glance over his shoulder and a slight tremor in his voice.

"She's just a cheap flim flam artist," Malady said. "What could she do really? We ought to put the army to work and have them kill the dragons."

Uncle Eustus gave her a rather pitying and highly uncomfortable look. "You must learn not to underestimate people simply because you dislike them, Malady petal. They say that Lady Romany, if that is who the Gypsy woman truly is, is descended not only from royals but also from powerful witches. There are even those who claim she can travel in time."

"Preposterous!"

"Perhaps."

"What would be the point of that, anyway?"

"I can't claim to know what's in her mind, nor can anyone, but stories about her have been around for many generations longer than she could possibly have been here in a single lifetime. You need to sit still and pay attention to the council sessions, niece."

"You never let me say anything, anyway," she complained.

But if the time travel thing was true, then surely Romany would know exactly where the crown jewels were hidden. Malady set about her rule with a will, determined to choose a dragon exterminator who was also good at extracting valuable information from human captives.

"My dear, you are still learning. Governing countries is not all gowns and jewels, you know," one of the uncles said in an impertinently scolding fashion.

"Yes, but who cares about all that stuff? Not the people! They'll only be interested in what I wear to which event. It gives a little glamor to their dreary humdrum lives. Of course we have to deal with the whole dragon thing, but you lot have been creating the situation for years. I have every confidence that you'll be able to un-create it, given the proper motivation. Meanwhile I will keep the populace dazzled and distracted while inspiring all with my fabulous fashion sense."

"Be careful you don't glitter too much, niece," Eustus responded. Truly, Malady's unwillingness to focus on real issues secretly pleased him. She wouldn't interfere that way. On the other hand, business, with the dragons out of order, was not good and she had expensive tastes. And she was letting this regency thing go to her head, thinking she was in charge. The uncles discussed it.

"But you can't commit someone without an order from a qualified alienist!"

"As I like to plan ahead, I've sent for one." Uncle Horace told them.

They did not realize they were being observed at the time, nor that the watcher was accidentally endangering the very masonry of the tower by squeezing it in sympathy with and for Malady. Treasure and jewels were terribly important. Surely everybody knew that?

When the bills began arriving, the uncles convened a private conclave, to which Malady was not invited, being told it would be boring for her.

"The girl is getting ideas above her station," Finance Minister Uncle Murdo said. "Just because she's the Regent—goodness only knows why—doesn't make her Empress."

"It does rather work in our favor, though," said another uncle. "I admit I wondered what that Gypsy and her giant daughter had in mind when they appointed her. No love lost between our Malady and her old schoolmate, from what I've heard."

"Never mind them," Murdo replied. "If we don't curb the girl, she'll bankrupt the kingdom before we can persuade her to run it properly—that or the giant returns."

Uncle Malachy shrugged. "All of this sudden power seems to have driven her out of her mind. I agree with Horace. We should have an expert examine her and relegate her to a nice comfy sanitarium—there's a revolutionary clinic at Bluing Glacier, where they deep freeze the patients until they come to their senses."

"Does it work?"

"Who knows? They haven't thawed anyone out to learn if they've become sensible yet."

"Sounds ideal. Who shall we get? Alienists don't grow on trees, even these days."

"How about if we marry her off to some rich prince? Remember those contests kings used to have in the olden days when they'd offer the princess's hand as a prize to the winner? We could hold a contest to solve the dragon issue."

"What interest has a dragon in the princess's, I mean, the queen regent's hand? Oh! Oh, dear. You don't mean that really, Eustus? She's family!"

"The gown she's ordered for the ball welcoming the King of Ablemarle features golden thread, ten thousand pearls embroidered onto it with a design encrusted with colored precious gemstones. I can't think why she wants it. I understand it weighs 150 pounds, counting the bustle and train."

"I trust we cancelled the order!"

"Modified it. They can do wonderful things with colored glass these days. She won't know the difference. I've seen to it that her orders must go through me first. That should take care of that."

"If only it were so simple to take care of the dragon situation."

They'd convened in the same room where they met as a council. It was in the process of being decorated for the state ball. The great echoing room served various functions, with furnishings, tapestries, floor coverings and draperies changed to suit the occasion. Although the castle had many rooms, only some were large enough for state or public functions. The rest were too small, too drafty, or too decrepit and in need of renovation for receptions or government business.

That upstart, Verity Brown, would have been astonished at the swags of gilt-trimmed (if somewhat moth-eaten) velvet scalloping the walls and the brilliant sparkle of the crystal chandeliers. The most expensive decorative item, though, was the greenery. Huge flowering trees and bushes grown in a local glass house had been purchased at bargain prices since the dragon that had supplied the nursery with year-round warmth for the plants was now idle and brooding, like the rest of them. With the hypnotic spell of the dragon kibble eroded by time, none of the people truly thought of Verity as a queen any more than they thought of Malady Hyde as a royal of any description. But the thing was, the people did seem to like the idea of having a queen or maybe even a king—one person, anyway, on whom they could pin both the blame and their hopes.

As the day was chilly and the castle drafty, the council members had foregone their formal stations at the council table in favor of comfortable armchairs around the hearth. The chairs faced the fire, their high backs blocking the draft from the windows, so no one noticed the watchful slitted eyes staring in at them. Their discourse, amplified by drink, masked the subtle sound of slithering scales on stone as the watcher shifted position to peer into another window.

Chapter 11: The Lair is Where the Hoard Is

Devent followed Smelt into his lair. It smelled of musty, very old dragon, and earth and very faintly, of blood.

From the way Smelt talked about his hoard, Devent expected to see piles of glittering stones, but all that was to be seen was a single heap of metal with a jewel embedded in something here and there.

"Erm. Nice," he muttered, only half to Smelt, who he didn't suppose was listening.

"It's not!" Smelt said gruffly. "This is not my treasure. This looks to me like what's left of the old armory. The humans must have looted my hoard after I flew into battle for them. Ah well, war is expensive. Maybe when I wake up, I can weld this together into something useful. Sorry there's not enough for two beds, lad."

"No problem," Devent said quickly. He had no wish, after spending his life underground in a mine, to leave the sun and sky, the fresh air and the mountains and streams, for another subterranean enclosure. "I am not at all sleepy. I need to explore more. Sleep well. Er—when do you expect to be up again?"

"When the ice breaks on the river."

"I'll come and look for you then."

Smelt yawned. "Do that. Stay out of trouble. If possible."

"I'll do my best."

He continued through the cavern toward the light he could see at the far end and emerged among some tumbled stone that once had formed a tower. The mossy stones beneath his claws were still flat and even smooth in some places, though the moss, weeds, and roots had pushed them up in others. But most amazing was what lay beyond them. This castle was perched, not on a mountain where the other side led down another slope and to more foothills—no, it ended in a flat faced cliff and below, the roaring he had heard but not understood what he was hearing as they approached proved to be a vast steely wetness with dirty white undulations slapping the rocks beneath.

Watching the water, smelling its salty old-fishiness strong enough to rinse from his nostrils the scent of cinders that commonly obscured other smells, he heard the rumbling roar of the sea in motion and felt the wind trying to tear him from the cliff.

Malady's Ally

Malady began dreaming of treasure, following not a trail, but a tail, through the labyrinthine lower corridors of the castle to where she knew, somehow, she would find a glittering hoard.

Always when she awoke and tried to find the entrance to the place she'd dreamed, however, nothing about her surroundings looked familiar. Yet she knew it was here, in this castle, which her nightly searches took her. She flung open the door to her somewhat moth-ridden chambers and called her maid.

"Bring me the oldest map of this castle in existence."

The girl scuttled away. Or rather, waddled, Malady thought. She was at least a stone overweight, which suited Malady fine since it emphasized her own beauty even more. She had to dress herself while she waited, but she put on the oldest clothing she could find, the things she wore after school while at Our Lady of Perpetual Locomotion, when she wasn't in uniform. Since the sisters often assigned the girls to cleaning tasks after school, it consisted of a beige underdress with a skirt the color of grass stains with brown spots. Malady's blonde curls and peachy coloring made it look good, nevertheless, but it was certainly not her best. Which was fine. She had no intention of encountering anyone of importance while she searched anyway.

The stupid girl took forever to return—hours!

"How long did it take you to find an old map, anyway?"

"I'm sorry, milady, but the maps were very interesting, plus there were some fascinating papers about the construction of the castle and its uses in the early days."

Malady slapped her, leaving a red spot on her cheek. "Idiot! I sent you to fetch, not research."

She actually regretted the slap immediately. The uncles had warned her that her temper would not serve her well in diplomatic circles, but although she expected to apologize as tears ran down the girl's cheek, the tears were not forthcoming. Instead the impertinent drudge's mouth hardened, her chin jutted out, and her eyes blazed as she threw the rolled map at Malady, whirled, and stomped out of the chamber, declaring, "Next time find it yourself. I quit."

"No, wait! I..." It was too late though. The overly-sensitive twit was storming her way down the hall and the stairs to the grand entryway. Several minutes later the huge iron and timber grand entrance door slammed so hard the suits of armor on each side clattered and clanged. Bother! If the fool had to take her time doing that research, the least she could have done was given Malady the benefit of it. One never knew what might be helpful when chasing a dream.

"Oh, who needs her anyway!" Malady cried, and it was her turn to stomp her foot.

"Exactly, my dear princess," something said in her head, but not in her ears. "You have no need of her when you have me."

She looked around and saw nothing and no one, unless she counted the peeping tom dragon that liked to wind itself around various parts of the castle and observe nobility going about its business.

She was about to say something scathing when the slit-eyed dragon gave a sinuous slink that pulled its tail up even with its face. She recognized that tail. It was the one she had followed in her dreams.

"So you're the one who's been spying on me, invading my very thoughts! I should call the royal guard and have them pry you from your perch!"

"Oh, don't be that way, pretty, pretty princess," the dragon fairly cooed at her. "Say not that I have been spying, only admiring your beauty and fire. You are quite the spicy d—damsel."

Malady's eyes narrowed. "You were going to say 'dish' weren't you? You just want to get me alone so you can eat me."

"Hssst! Of course not. Dragons haven't eaten people for centuries and centuries. You know that, brilliant beauty that you are. I am simply cultivating your acquaintance as a fellow fan of the shiny, the sparkly, the glittering and bejeweled things in life. I know where all of the kingdom's most magnificent treasures are—many, most of them, would show off well against your tender alabaster flesh..."

"If you know where it is and want me to have it, bring it here!" she said. The description of her skin sounded just a bit too much like a menu item for her comfort.

With a scrape of scales on stone, the dragon disappeared. She'd thought as much. The stupid creature couldn't back up its lie and had thought it could trick her. If anyone was going to be tricked around here, it wasn't going to be Malady Hyde.

Regretfully, wistfully, she went about her duties that day—at least the ones that interested her, concerning the upcoming parties and balls. The uncles all wanted to be in charge of the boring political stuff anyway, so she let them do what they wanted to. She began to believe, by midday, that the visit with the dragon that morning had been another dream, like the ones in which she followed the tail down the corridors. She took a ride in the royal carriage to go talk to some downtrodden poor people and looked back at the castle but didn't see any dragon wrapped around any part of it, staring in windows. Most of the dragons at the castle were on the roof. They liked the crenelated parts. Yes, she surely had been imagining the flattering beast that thought her a princess.

That night she went to bed with a bitter feeling of being let down, somehow, by the position Verity had bequeathed her. She got to go gallivanting about the countryside while Malady was stuck dealing with a lot of cheapskate, if related, nobles in a drafty cold castle steeped in a miasma of dragon poo.

Hot Times at the Sailor's Spa and Brothel

Verity imagined that by the time her party returned to the Sailor's Spa and Brothel, most of the crew would be down at the dock, readying the *Belle's Shell* to sail again.

"Will you be needing a ride, Mistress Warlock?" Mr. Bowen asked Clodagh. "Perhaps up the coast or back to Queenston?"

"In a boat?" Clodagh asked, and though her features didn't change shape or position, her expression shifted to one of horror. "On the water? Oh no, that's not for the likes of me."

"We'd try not to let you drown," he promised her.

"I wouldn't drown, but I might dissolve and so far from shore, I'd never be able to re-sculpt myself in time," the mud-girl explained.

The little party had made a small campfire just below the timberline on the far side of the pass between Horn Haven and Horn Heart. Fiona was the only one who shivered. Bowen was used to the freezing spray. Verity's Frost Giant heritage protected her and although Clodagh looked a bit ice-rimed around the edges, she didn't appear uncomfortable.

"She'll be comfy enough with us," Fiona said, hugging a blanket closer around her and patting Clodagh on the shoulder. "She's an earthy sort of girl after all, aren't you, love?"

Clodagh giggled uncertainly, as if trying the noise out. "Fiona, you are making a joke. Wizard Warlock made jokes sometimes."

Verity stared into the fire, thinking it would not take long before the ship was loaded. The crew would be laughing and joking with each other until time to depart, while their erstwhile sweethearts among Erotica's staff would play their parts, standing tearfully on the dockside, wrapped in new shawls, sporting new combs and wearing the iconic lockets from Erotica's small gift shop—the broken token locket. Half of a heart pendant remained with the woman as evidence of her true but temporary devotion, while the other half would be worn by her seagoing 'beloved.'

Erotica had told her that sometimes as ships pulled away from the dock, her ladies were wont to skim folded paper 'doves' toward the ship. None came back to them though because, after a few longing last looks, the crews had to jump to the bosun's whistle, raising anchors, hauling on yards, and the intricate and labor-intensive business of putting out to sea again.

"Love notes?" Verity had asked her aunt.

"Of a sort," that lady had replied and opened one, smoothing it on her knee.

"For another good time, ask for your Sadie, room 423," the note read. Verity blushed as she read Sadie's catalog of her specialties.

Verity was unsure whether to stick with the *Belle* or continue her quest further inland. She'd know more once she'd spoken to her mermaid aunt, so hoped she might arrive before the *Belle* was ready to depart. It should prove an informative chat.

As they continued their journey the next day and were drawing close to Horn Haven, they heard a cannon roar.

"That's not good," Mr. Bowen said.

Grudge

"I'm sorry, I'm sorry, please forgive me! I didn't mean it!" Grudge cowered as her parents and brothers pummeled her with fists and clubs. Her whiskers were soaked with blood and tears and she couldn't see out of one eye.

"How could you? You're a disgrace to your race!"

"But it just popped out! I never saw one like that! I don't think she even heard me."

"Surely you could have thought of something better to say—or just kept your mouth shut."

Her youngest brother mocked, "'That's darling. Hand it over?' Grudge, if you hadn't added the last part you know we'd have to kill you for the honor of our race."

He sounded horrified. In his own way, Sneer was—well, not fond, exactly, but he growled at her less often than the others.

"And then you let her walk across the river instead of taking it from her!" her mother cried. "I could have forgiven anything if you hadn't done that."

"But it was too small for me, and it did look cute on her," Grudge said.

Her father turned purple, and not a shade that went well with the usual gray-green of his skin.

"The worst thing is that you denied that family an authentic bridge experience," her sister Supercilia said with a sob in her grunt, which managed to be shrill and nasal despite being, well, a grunt. She was very impressed by appearances, was 'Cilia. She punctuated her opinion with another kick to Grudge's back and a stomp on the hand shielding her head.

"I won't do it again," Grudge whimpered.

"You said that last time."

"Yeah, it's not like you've not been told before," Sneer said, gloating.

"I'll remember," she said. "The bruises will remind me."

"It's no good, girl," her father said. "Out with you. Go find your own bridge."

"Where?"

"Find it, I said. If you make a success of your enterprise, we might consider letting you visit again on holidays."

"Like Ringwormmass," her mother said. "Prove you can live up to your calling and you can come back and celebrate, can't she, Snark?"

"Over my dead body," her father said, pulling her up by the hair and booting her in the butt so she flopped into the stream. "Don't come back."

"That means he'll think about it, Grudge," her mother called as the current carried her downriver. There was nothing that way but the iron mine, so Grudge dragged herself out over the bank, shook herself like a dog, and began dripping back upstream and to the south, toward the mountains.

Nobody ever said being a troll was easy.

Durance the Vile

Malady woke from an unusually restful sleep, yawned, stretched and blinked. Sunlight blazed off something sitting in the three-foot deep windowsill of her chamber. The dragon's face no longer filled the window, fortunately. She was sure she wouldn't have slept a wink with the beast watching.

However, at some time during the night the beast, or part of it, had been there, judging by the shiny object, which proved to be a delicately wrought silver coronet inlaid with blue stones. She picked it up and turned it over in her hands, then carried it over to the full-length mirror in the center of her dressing table.

The blue did pick up the blue in her eyes, brightening what could sometimes be steely undertones that belied her sweet expressions when she was trying to wheedle something out of one of her admirers. And the silver did show up well against her golden locks. But sapphires were lesser stones and silver was not gold. If this was a gift from the dragon—and what else could it be? —what did he think she was, anyway? Some child to be fobbed off with cheap baubles?

When the dragon appeared behind her in the mirror, the wretched creature asked, "Do you like it?"

Before she could express her disappointment, the beast added, "There's more where that came from. I bestowed upon you a mere trifle compared to what I could give you. If I wanted to."

"It's very nice, Dragon. I can wear it in council chambers or during archery practice, but I had in mind something a bit more upmarket? Sapphires are such practical stones, but don't you feel they lack authority and grandeur? I was thinking gold with diamonds and emeralds. Perhaps in a matched parure of necklaces, bracelets, brooches, clips and earrings?"

"I seem to recall seeing something like that from time to time. For a very good friend, I could rummage around in my hoard and see if they turn up."

"Or I could help you," she said.

"Aren't you afraid I'd eat you?" the beast asked with a sly gleam in its eye.

"I thought you lot didn't do that sort of thing anymore."

"We haven't for years, but due to the current food shortage, the matter is open for renegotiation."

"Oh," she said. The truth was, she wasn't really accustomed to thinking of dragons as dangerous. They were big, of course, but so were carriages and trains. They were, or had been, simply part of what made things work, except of course, now they weren't. "But you wouldn't eat a friend, would you? Like me, for instance?"

"Of course not. Not if you were my friend, Princess Malady." She thought she heard him mutter under his breath "—unless I was very, very hungry."

"Er—what do I call you?" she asked, following her deportment instructor's cardinal rule of social intercourse, when in doubt, make small talk. "'Dragon' seems to be rather a general term these days, as it could apply to so many."

"Durance," the dragon replied, "the Vile."

"So, Durance, your lair is in the castle, I presume?" she asked, still conversationally, but now that she was trying to draw the beast out, her demeanor seemed to have become inappropriately coy.

"The castle that was," Durance said. "Many castles ago."

Malady was confused. So far as she knew, this was the only castle that had stood here. Ever. But history wasn't her best subject.

"I'm wondering why I can talk to you," she said. "You're not by any chance a handsome prince cursed into dragon form until a beautiful princess kisses you?"

A deep hissing sigh rattled the roof tiles. "Just wear the headpiece, will you? Didn't your mother ever tell you not to look a dragon's gift in his mouth?"

Malady blinked three times. "No."

"Well, don't."

"But I want to choose my things," she said stubbornly. She had begun to feel the dragon had gained the upper claw in their relationship, and she didn't like it.

"Consider me your stylist," the dragon said, and slithered down the stonework.

She wanted to stamp her foot and have a good pout and maybe tell the uncles to have the beast removed, except that Durance promised her even more wonderful things.

"My uncles think I spend too much on finery," she told Durance one day after a particularly trying interview on the Budget and the Economy. "But I haven't spent anything for weeks except on dresses. They think being a royal is all about boring stuff..."

"They are peasants. They plot against you. Did you know? I hear them through the council chamber windows. They have no respect for their betters."

Malady sniffed, offended. "They think they know better than I do because they are men and older, but I tell you, Durance, they have no class, no sense of occasion."

"And you do, pretty, pretty princess. It is your Faerie lineage, no doubt."

"Faerie lineage? What do you mean by that? Faeries aren't real and even if they were once in this country, I'm from Frostingdung and they have never been real there. I think."

"Believe what you will, but blood will tell," Durance said. "Do you think it a coincidence that you are the one who's been chosen? I am a castle dragon who has lived in the bowels of this palace for many generations. I certainly know a Faerie princess when I see one."

Malady was very disappointed in the uncles, though she expected a certain amount of plotting. She'd planned to play them off against Durance to ultimately force him to cough up the crown jewels and whatever else he had in his hoard. She'd considered the dragon untrustworthy, but if he was to be believed, her uncles were even more scale-brained than he was. Good thing she'd convinced Uncle Marquette, from her mama's side of the family, to come for a visit. He adored her. She was sure of it.

Chapter 12: The Fountain Pen Pirate

Marquette Fontaine did not aspire to be the scourge of the seas. He just wanted to own them, and more importantly, to own the land adjoining them. Beachfront and water view property were always good acquisitions. With the economies of both Frostingdung and Argonia in extreme flux, which naturally affected the economies of the adjoining countries, people on dry land were liquidating their assets for low, low prices. The Queenston Bank had enjoyed an unusual run of foreclosures on business properties now that the businesses were put out of business when their source of power was having a collective pout and had slithered away from its duty stations.

This presented no catastrophe to Marquette, who saw the circumstances only as a great opportunity to take advantage of the downturn. His agents were collecting properties not only in Queenston, but also all up and down the coasts. Though he usually preferred to rule what he thought of as his private empire from the comfort of his fashionable manor house in the town of Rosegilt, the largest city in Suleskeria Province, his niece's invitation to visit her in Queenston was too tempting.

Nubile young nieces in positions of power struck him as a versatile commodity. You could of course marry them off to someone more powerful, but then dowries might be involved, or you could seek to be the power behind the throne, which, with someone of Malady's temperament was a risky proposition indeed, or you could marry them yourself, especially after having fostered a warm if distant relationship beforehand. She was actually a niece by marriage—his first wife had been her mother's sister, though there was a tangle of family interconnections between them as well. The other uncles were not particularly clever fellows, old, dull, and unimaginative. He was certain he could take full advantage of the situation far more effectively than any of them, while maintaining the impression that he was only coming to help.

He had one of his ships loaded with Frostingdungian goods to replace those not currently being produced in Argonia, thanks to the dragons, or rather thanks to the absence of dragons in the work force. He also carried a map case full of his most recent acquisitions, including the holdings of a major shipping company whose properties included a number of small company port towns. He'd always had a horror of dragons in the past but recently had begun to feel quite fond of them.

His stateroom and an adjoining cabin were full of frills and trinkets of the sort Malady favored. Marquette had gone through three wives already, the latest meeting her timely demise only a few months ago. Malady was old enough for marriage, and as de facto regent of Argonia, was extremely eligible as well. He wanted to remind her of her fondness for her dear uncle—her fun uncle, before his brothers and cousins decided to marry her off to some minor noble in some obscure hole of a country. With her beauty and sense of occasion and his brains and business acumen, they would make quite the fashionable power couple.

He sighed. He knew he was fantasizing. Malady was a handful, spoilt and willful. Even with the training he was much too busy to give her, she was unlikely to cooperate with his plans without interference. He would end up either having to bribe her, bankrupting himself, or beat her into submission, which he had found in the past to be counterproductive.

Although the sea was calm with only the gentle rocking motion that made him sleepy, he had no wish to remain belowdecks where it was dark and not a little smelly. Besides, it was good for morale for the men to see their leader.

They greeted him with a salute. 'Cap'n,' each would mumble as he passed although in reality he was not the captain but the owner of the ship. But 'captain' was a rank these rough fellows respected. They called the man who ran the ship and saw that it got to where it was supposed to go with as few seagoing hazards as possible "skipper" or "skip," a title Marquette could live without. 'Captain' had dignity.

At a cry from the crow's nest he looked aloft to see the lookout gesturing leeward. The sun glinted off his spyglass as he raised it for another look.

"What is it, man?" Marquette called.

But the man now was staring fixedly at an object too far for Marquette to see without a glass.

Whatever they might think of him, Marquette was still young enough, slim enough, spry enough to climb with the best of them. He grabbed the ropes to climb, but the lookout was on his way down. "Mermaid, sir. I swear. I never heard of a ship spotted one swimming, but like a dolphin she was, or a seal, but her tail is all shiny scales, looked purple sometimes, green others."

Marquette grabbed the spyglass. "Where?"

The sailor swung his arm to the starboard bow, "About there, sir, close enough I could see her long green hair when she surfaced, but when she spotted us, she dove back down again."

"After her!" Marquette cried. Spying the skipper, he gave an order, "Get on it, man, and sharpish. We've a mermaid to catch!"

"Oh, I wouldn't do that, sir!" the lookout said.

"Why not, pray? Has it not occurred to any of you that such a creature could show us the location of any and all sunken treasure in her domain? It's said there's many a vast fortune down there."

"Aye, sir, so I've heard. But 'tis bad luck to catch a mermaid, sir. Them as tries it never makes it to port."

"If they don't make it to port, man, how would anyone know it had anything to do with a fish woman? I gave an order and I expect it to be followed. Skipper?"

"Aye, Milord, we'll give chase, but I fear we may have lost her."

"While your seamen stand around arguing with their betters. No wonder!" he said, but just then there was a yell from another sailor who spotted the creature and this time the ship was in position to give chase.

Hours later, weary from pacing the decks and straining his eyes to search for the mermaid, he decided there might be something to the superstition. They were far off course, and he was about to order that they forget the creature, correct their course and sail on to their original destination when the song began.

Sirens' Lips Sink Ships

Eulalia was peeved. Honestly, a girl couldn't go anywhere without some stupid ship following in her wake.

Typically, one did not lure ships from a swimming position. One sat upon conveniently located rocks and brandished comb and mirror while serenading sailors, the better to wreck ships.

She did not frequent these waters, however. On the way from her Atoll, she had caught up on the current gossip with the always well-informed schools of fish, the octopus and her seal cousins. Only pressing family matters were important enough for her to abandon her post and look where it had got her! When she couldn't lure ships to her, it seemed she had encountered them anyway. No time off, ever. No help for it.

Popping up long enough to confuse her pursuers, she hoped, she turned on her siren.

After the first eight bars, she dived deep and swam back under the ship and took a detour to the coast of Frostingdung where her distant selkie relatives welcomed her to their rocks and they had a good natter about a recent adventure full of juicy details.

What she did not reckon on was that the ship was already headed for the same ultimate destination as she. Giving chase to her had merely delayed it.

Leaving her friends, she swam beneath the rough water surrounding the Horn, surfacing only as she neared some sheltering rocks offshore from Horn Haven. She signaled her arrival to Erotica by blowing on a conch shell that could be heard for miles at sea.

It was also heard aboard Marquette Fontaine's ship, which crept up on her while she was under water and had a net waiting for her. Before she quite knew what happened she felt a weight drop on her head and shoulders and then she was suspended over the deck like a landed salmon, sailors laughing and gloating over her while she fumed.

"What are we to do with a woman who's all scales belowdecks, Captain?" One of them asked, poking her through the net so it swung to and fro in a way that was unharmonious with the movement of the waves. She spewed. He and the others laughed even harder. "A seasick mermaid! Well, I never!"

"Don't worry about that, brave boys," the overdressed merchant with the bright buttons and braid told her tormentors at large. "We're quite close to port. I want something else entirely from this one."

"You mean like treasure?"

Eulalia saw her opportunity. "I know where to find treasure. Let me go and I'll tell you." She didn't really care who had treasures. They were not the kind of treasure she was interested in. Once she was free, if this ship was on the sea, she'd see to it that the treasure was soon back on the ocean floor where it belonged.

"Tell me, and I'll let you go," he echoed, but as she should have known, he didn't, even after she gave him the details of the story she'd gathered from the seal people.

Marquette knew that the gods and all the fishes were on his side that day, because as he pulled into port, his ship slid neatly into the dock and moored next to none other than the reported treasure ship the fish woman had just named, the *Belle's Shell*, which was in the vulnerable position of being loaded at that point.

"We have our work cut out for us this day, boys," Marquette said, and gestured toward the smaller ship. "Take possession of yon ship and bring me the treasure. Which we'll divide evenly after tariffs, excise tax and other taxes, plus expenses are deducted."

He said the last line quietly, after the men had begun boarding the target ship.

Unexpected Guests

The sun bloodied the horizon as it sank into the sea. Along the trail, the trees snapped and shivered in the wind as Verity, Bowen, Fiona and Clodagh and Kiln descended the long hill leading into Horn Haven. The closer they drew, the darker it grew.

Down in the harbor, the *Belle* quaked in her berth while a second ship, outlined against the draining light, disgorged torch-bearing sailors? Pirates? brandishing weapons.

Mr. Bowen kicked his mount, but Verity restrained him by grabbing the reins. "Don't."

Fiona was not to be held back. "Another ship's come in! I don't believe Madame was expecting another for another two weeks. I'd best get back to work!"

"Fickle wench!" Bowen muttered under his breath, scowling as the *Belle* was overtaken.

Fiona paid him no mind and clucked at her mare to proceed.

He jerked the reins from Verity's hand. "We're needed," he said, and galloped down the hill.

Clodagh and Kiln held back, the three ghost cats that had attached themselves to her flickering between her and Verity. Her clay face was impassive, but her eyes were frightened.

"No need for you to come," Verity told her. "Unless Kiln..."

Clodagh shook her head and protectively put her arm around Kiln's neck. The dragon whimpered and buried his snout in the folds of her skirt.

"Very well, then," Verity said, and led her horse down the hill.

In the gathering gloom and groaning wind, no one paid them any attention. They approached Erotica's house from the rear. Fiona opened the back door and dashed inside, leaving it ajar. As Verity entered, she heard the other girl's footsteps pounding up the steps of the back staircase. Verity charged down the hall into the kitchen and parlor.

The Spa and Brothel staff, clad in loose silk robes, lacy underthings or even less, crowded against the windows, sharing a spyglass to watch the drama in the harbor.

"Who's that?" Verity asked the woman with the spyglass.

"Dunno, but they're attacking your ship."

Verity took the glass, trying to discover the identity of the attackers.

They swarmed the *Belle*'s decks, and though she couldn't hear everything that happened in the harbor, the invaders were plainly whooping and hollering, possibly emitting war cries. The *Belle*'s crew responded stolidly, and no doubt with cursing, but they had been plainly at a disadvantage and had been taken by surprise.

A cannon cracked. Flying streaks of charcoal cloud unmasked the moon to reveal the black flag flapping from the second ship's top mainsail. No sooner had the boom died away than they became aware of another sound, a high, wailing keen that seemed to come from everywhere.

Erotica came running into the room and snatched the glass from Verity. "Eulalia!" she said grimly, then handed it back. "On the strange ship."

Verity saw her this time, although she could scarcely make out what the pear-shaped bundle dangling from the yardarm was. It swung in and out of the shadows. But once she saw it, she knew it for the source of the keening that was louder than both battle and wind.

Erotica doused a candle and started balling up melted wax, handing a portion to each of the women. "Stop up your ears or it will drive you mad," she cautioned. "Sailors aren't the only ones who are susceptible."

The newcomers held members of the *Belle*'s crew at sword point on her deck. The crew liked to play at swashing and buckling, Verity knew, but they were far more adept with musical instruments than weapons, and in this case, the pirate attack was totally unexpected.

Legs the Rigger was clinging to the topmast by two tentacles, while the other appendages writhed in frustration as she reached for ropes that were out of range, trying to make her way back to the crow's nest.

The pirates rampaged on deck, breaking open flasks and kegs and some of the men's sea chests, including the ones containing the theatrical costumes.

One of the marauders climbed out of the hold brandishing an oddly shaped blanket. He held it above his torch, as if about to ignite it, and Mr. Gray, already under guard, screamed, "Nooo!"

Verity smelled Erotica's perfume as her aunt crowded in close to her. "Let me through," Verity said. "Mr. Gray is a selkie, and without that skin, he can never rejoin his family."

"He has to be alive first if he's to rejoin anyone," Erotica said. "How are you at throwing things?"

"Good, actually," Verity replied.

"Excellent. Throw these at the pirates." She pressed five stoppered glass vials into Verity's hand and closed her fingers over them, then shoved some of the staff aside to open the door. "Out you go. You too, Sadie, Selina, Fiona, and Foxy..."

Verity ran over the uneven ground, stumbling twice, but as soon as she was in range she flung the first vial at the pirate threatening to burn the seal skin.

The glass smashed against the deck, but startled the pirate into dropping his torch.

Reinforcements arrived as the other women caught up with Verity at the dock. The smoky torches sent shadows jigging across the deck, dock, and hulls of the ships.

Mr. Gray's tormentor bent swiftly to retrieve his torch.

"Hold your fire!" Verity cried, though she had a hard time making herself heard above Aunt Eulalia's siren song. "We need to get close enough to see the veins in their blood-shot eyes."

Devent Gets Professional Advice

For a very long time, Devent had lingered within the doorway of the ruined castle above Smelt's lair, half asleep, listening, feeling, hearing, even tasting the sea and the wind that seemed to drive it boiling beneath the rocky prominence that held him. A song threaded through his dreaming wakefulness. He thought at first it was one of his mother's songs, come back to him in a dream, but another part of him knew that it was not. It was a song he'd never heard before.

When he wakened, he thought perhaps Auld Smelt was making the song with his breathing as he slept. Devent crept back down the tunnel toward his friend's lair but there the song vanished in the snort and whistle of hearty dragon snores.

He didn't bother to creep as he returned to his previous vantage point, but as soon as he was out of earshot of Smelt's snores, the singing was again audible. This time he heard it in the roll of the waves and on the winds billowing around his cliff-top perch.

The song was unlike any Casimir had taught him. If it had words, he couldn't make them out and he knew the singer was quite some distance to the south of him. He needed to hear it more distinctly.

He rose and began walking and hopping down the coast, always within sight of the sea.

How long he travelled, listening for the song, he didn't know. It was different by night from the daytime melody. Devent thought it was probably a female voice, though he had never heard a female human sing. But this voice was more like his mother's than Casimir's, and yet, not at all like hers. It wove in and out, at times alluring, at times menacing, but always compelling. Oh, if only he could sing like that! The singer seemed to harmonize with herself in many different parts, making it difficult to follow the core melody. But he tried. The first time the voice stopped, he stopped and while he rested, attempted to sing what he'd been hearing. He had some parts right, or almost, but he thought he would need to multiply himself to come anywhere near the same complexity and depth. Despairing, he was about to turn back and was stopped from doing so only because he was lost. Well, that and he hoped the singing would resume, which it did, two nights later.

He resumed his journey and learned that when the voice stopped, it would continue further down the coast, so he kept on, trying to softly harmonize while the song was in the air, and when it ceased, to recall the melody as faithfully as he could. He traveled on as if the song were a rope towing him to it. Sometimes it slackened, but always it continued.

Until it didn't. Then he gave a thought to Casimir, who must be waiting for him with disappointment that he had not yet returned. But Casimir was both a singer and a traveler and if anyone should understand the compulsion to seek this song, it would be the minstrel.

By now he was well down the coast of Argonia, the mountain range along which he had been traveling almost at an end, while he felt sure peaks he saw in the distance belonged to a different range. He kept to the coast, fearing he had gone too far and had passed his singer days before.

His relief when he heard the voice again instantly dispelled. The song was not the same, nor was it properly a song any longer, but a scream, a cry of distress. The voice was as beautiful as before, but now it cracked on some notes, and sounded dry.

Below, on the edge of the water, torches flared, and men tried to hit each other with long pointy things. What were they doing, playing around, when the owner of the most beautiful voice he'd ever heard was in such distress? He didn't wonder if he could fly or not or if his wings would hold him. He jumped from the cliff, the wind caught his wings, and he was not only airborne: he was swooping!

Boarded

The pirate who stole Gray's skin had changed course and refrained from burning it, instead wrapping it around himself and capering across the deck beside the rail.

Then an unexpected dragon occurred, swooping down over the *Belle*'s deck and landing on the *Spread Sheet.*

Verity thought at first that the dragon was Kiln, who had finally decided to wade in on their side, But even in the choking smoke and flickering light, this dragon was clearly bigger than Kiln. He blocked her view of Eulalia's net. She saw a taloned foot raise and slash—the net hung torn and empty and a dragon rose over the smoke with what looked like a large fish in its talons, except the fish had arms and hands which held onto one of the feet.

"Hey, you! Dragon!" Verity called over the din, "That is not sea food! That is my auntie!"

The distraction the dragon provided allowed Mr. Gray the opportunity to snatch his pelt from the pirate, throw it on, and jump overboard after Eulalia.

"Where did the bloody dragon come from, anyway?" the apparent captain of the attacking ship demanded.

Verity didn't know, and she didn't like to leave her shipmates at the mercy of the invaders, but she was the only one on the scene who could converse with dragons. Except for Clodagh of course, but could she talk to all dragons or only Kiln?

There was no time to ponder, as Erotica appeared, panting and winded, beside her, and handed her a fist full of fresh vials. But now, in addition to the whine of the wind, the rumble and hiss of the sea, the clamor of clashing swords and shouting, the siren song had resumed—that was all right then, if Eulalia could still sing, the dragon hadn't eaten her. It was accompanied by a very peculiar melodic noise sung in the tongue of dragons, though Verity could not distinguish the words.

"It's no good," Verity shouted at Erotica. "We can't see to aim."

"Ahoy, Missus Brown!" Legs called from the crow's nest. Verity pitched the vials one by one to the octopus. One by one, a vial per each tentacle, Legs fired off all eight vials.

The fighting slowed as some of the pirates ceased bullying and started wooing crew members. Those who had been struck by the glass vials smacked the cutlass-bearing hands of those who had not. "Don't hurt him, you!"

Amid the pandemonium, a single blast from a blunderbuss halted the quarreling. "Avast, ye mutinous lubbers! Be it known that by order of this writ, I, Captain Marquette Fontaine, claim this ship and the town of Horn Haven with all of its goods and chattels as my property! All of you work for me now, so step lively and put my ship back in order before we repair to my Spa and Brothel to take our leisure."

"He can't do that, can he? Claim the *Belle* and the town and your establishment, too?"

"Relax, my dear," Erotica said, "We get this a lot actually. A professional hazard of dealing with pirates. Oh, yoohoo! Captain! Why don't you and your lads come ashore and join the girls for some rest and relaxation? We can discuss business in a more congenial atmosphere."

As the captain and crew of the pirate ship and their prisoners—or guests, as some preferred to call them—from the *Belle* came ashore, Erotica told Verity, "Go hide out somewhere, my dear, and make yourself scarce. I'm not sure the goodwill my elixir creates would extend to getting a pirate to bypass the possibility of a royal ransom, should he recognize you for who you are."

"I don't see how he'd do that unless someone tells him. Otherwise he'll think I'm a man. He's got our salvage."

The first of the *Belle*'s crew, accompanied by a short stocky pirate, walked down the ramp between the *Belle* and the dock.

"Ladies," said the pirate's prisoner, the ship's carpenter, called Chips, "this gentleman is new in town and seeking..." Erotica's girls surrounded him until he walked off with one holding each of his arms, the girls chatting about how it must be ever so stimulating to be a pirate. The love potion appeared to be indiscriminate about who gave or received affection from whom.

The next to walk down the dock was the best dressed of the lot, presumably the captain. Behind him, one of the *Belle*'s crew and a pirate supported the chest from the *Nice Try* between them.

"Which one of you is Madame Erotica?" he asked, looking from Captain Lewis, to the lady in question.

Verity's aunt wiggled her fingers at him in acknowledgement. "I am. Erotica Amora, proprietress of the Sailor's Spa and Brothel, at your service, handsome sir."

"I wish to retire to your salon, madame, and discuss business."

"Of course you do, dearie," Erotica said with a flutter of her lashes.

The weird duet still rode the roar of sea and wind, but the sound seemed to be everywhere.

As Verity stood listening, Mr. Gray in selkie form and Legs busied themselves at the hostile ship. Neither of them had been affected by the vials, Legs clinging to the topmast and Mr. Gray in his recovered selkie skin swimming offshore. She could not exactly see what they were doing but the *SS Spread Sheet* went drifting soon after they left.

The song stopped and was replaced by the very muted sound of conversation, which she could not quite make out. However, talking was easier to locate than the song. She pulled off her boots and socks and waded into the swelling waves. A swim was required.

The mermaid, looking rather rumpled in spite of being wet, still had dry patches and the marks of the net on her skin and scales. She sat on a rock combing her hair and reached down an arm to haul Verity up beside her.

"There you are, brother's daughter. You must listen to this dragon, he has a fabulous barrow-tone."

The dragon made a good facsimile of a courtly bow. "Thank you," he said. "Casimir says the same thing."

"Wait," Verity said. "Who is Casimir and who, for that matter, are you?"

"I am Devent, Dragon-bard in training, at your service, m'lady," he said, imitating his mentor. "And whom have I the honor of addressing?"

"I'm Verity, and as my aunt said, I'm the daughter of her brother."

Eulalia nodded vaguely. Her hair was striped with different colors all in a rather frizzy blonde. "Lovely to meet you, Verity. What's all this about you being a queen now?"

"That was my mother's idea," Verity told her. "I can't believe I wanted her back so much and now she acts as if I'm a chess piece—go here, go there, do this, do that. Right now I'm to find the descendants of the wizards who disappeared at the end of the Great War."

"That woman!" Eulalia said. "I told your father she wasn't good for the likes of us—dry behind the ears! You poor minnow, being used like that. You just do as you see fit, my darling, and if that woman wants something done, tell her to bloody well do it herself instead of scampering around on her big flat feet messing up Time."

"Have—er—have you spoken with my Dad lately?" Verity asked.

"Why would I?"

"Well, I just thought since he's a merman now, maybe..."

"Oh, is he? I didn't know. The sea is a big place, sweetie. Tell me how that happened. Last time I heard anything about him, he was into fire."

"My stepmother—his second wife—tried to kill us. Merfolk saved him, but I guess when he nearly drowned maybe it tipped the balance of his nature so that he was more mer than human by the time they were done. He doesn't really recognize me yet. Perhaps you could talk to him? I don't seem to have any trouble conversing with you."

"Might be he's still shocked from the injury. When did this all happen?"

Verity needed no further encouragement to launch into the tale of the last year of her life. When she'd finished an abbreviated version, she said, "Listen, Aunty, about the ships? I crewed on the *Belle's Shell* from Queenston to Aunt Erotica's place at Horn Haven. Could you, uh, do me a favor and NOT wreck them?"

Eulalia twisted back to give her a dirty look. "You sure know how to take the fun out of family reunions, wanting favors like that on such short acquaintance!"

"Maybe so, but they're friends. You'd like them if you got to know them. Most of them are singers and musicians too. Maybe you could learn new songs from each other or is your repertoire, um, magically regulated or something?"

Her aunt snorted seawater. "Not exactly. It's just that I have very little chance to learn new songs. I only meet ships and as soon as I perform for them, well, you know." She shrugged. "Not that I don't enjoy that part, of course. Most of us merfolk are of the opinion that the only good sailor is a dead sailor, but drowning is a real conversation stopper."

Since Eulalia hadn't asked and it hadn't come up in conversation so far, Verity said, "In case you're wondering why I came to see you—and Aunt Erotica for that matter—I'm under a geas of sorts to find the descendants of some of the great magicians who were murdered just before the end of the Great War. Would you happen to know or have heard of any still living near your Atoll?"

Eulalia made a clicking sound behind her pointed teeth. "Err, I have the same problem with the living on land as I do when they're on shipboard. They tend not to survive the introduction. But I have heard talk that the family that used to occupy Cliffslide Castle once had a wizard in the family. I couldn't tell you if that's true or just rumor though, because apparently the castle went under siege toward the end of the war and got razed. I believe the family moved inland after a son married into the Raspberry family from Little Darlingham."

For someone who didn't know much, Aunt Eulalia was very loquacious once she got started.

She said hospitably, "I suppose you and yon dragon are hungry by now, aren't you? I'm starved! You've made it pretty clear drowned sailor isn't to your taste—er—how about yours, Dragon? They keep pretty well wrapped in seaweed, where they're protected from the fish." With that, she dove into the sea, diving deep, and resurfacing ten or fifteen minutes later some distance away, diving again, and resurfacing near the rock with an armload of seaweed, which she handed Verity.

"Here. Hold this while I regain my perch, will you? Get it? Perch?"

"I do," Verity said with an accommodating smile and nod. "Perch is a fish and you're a mermaid. Very clever."

By that time Eulalia had regained her seat. "I'm famished. Dragon, you could try it if you like."

"But it's plants."

"So it is. But they're very nourishing, and I think you'll find them delicious."

They dined on seaweed in a companionable fashion. Verity was surprised to find that the seaweed was naturally salty and even while wet had a nice crunch to it.

"This would be nice with fish."

Steam rose from the sides of the dragon's mouth.

Eulalia looked pained. "Fish? I'm a vegetarian! I don't really eat the drowned sailors. This tasty seaweed is much better for you."

"But the dragon will need more than..." Verity started to say.

"The sea serpent who used to live in these waters got by just fine with a seaweed diet," Eulalia assured her. "It's very healthful. I don't see why a dragon can't do the same."

Devent continued nibbling, shortening the long tube of weed Eulalia extended to him from a pile beside her tail.

"It tastes kind of familiar, actually," he pronounced as he finished the first tube and reached for a second.

Verity had to agree with him when she chewed on a second strand. It did taste familiar. It reminded her a bit of the scones her mother had made from the treated dragon kibble.

"Now then, Dragon, I promised to teach you my song. All I ask is one teensy itty-bitty minnow-sized little favor in return," she said, but her voice turned from wheedling to hard with the next part. "Just go out to that ship whose master dared lay hands on me and burn it to charcoal, will you? Pleeeease?"

The dragon's spine ridges stood straight up, and his eyes got as wide as dragons' eyes could. "But, lady, I do not kill people."

"There are no people aboard now." Eulalia said.

"They've all gone up to Aunt Erotica's house," Verity said. "I hope they don't turn ugly. The *Belle*'s crew are actually cabaret performers—you'd like them, drag—Devent. The only swashbuckling they've done is onstage, I fear. And the new lot seems to be getting along with them now, but how long the potion will hold them before they turn ugly again I couldn't say."

Eulalia laughed. It wasn't a nice laugh and showed all of her pointed green teeth. "Don't worry about that, sweetie. Erotica has her little ways of dealing with men like that. All Devent will be doing is teaching them a lesson they need about sailing onto other peoples' seas and throwing nets over people and letting them dry out while they make rude remarks. Actually, one little ship isn't enough to make up for that but—"

"You must leave the *Belle's Shell* alone," Verity said quickly. "My friends could not easily replace her."

"Excuse me, ladies," the dragon said, took a leap and landed in the water, then breached like a whale, except he kept soaring upward instead of turning to splash back down into the sea.

Moments later the night grew brighter with the lurid blossom of flame halfway to the horizon. Loud booms shattered the air and offshoots of fire flashed through the night sky like comets in reverse. Huge waves washed up and around their rock, further soaking Verity's skin and clothing.

Aunt Eulalia clapped her webbed hands in delight. "That will show them to go around netting people!" she said.

But shouts and cries of dismay were coming from the shore, where several of the men had returned to watch their ship burn.

Eulalia grew nervous. "Sorry, Minnow, time for me to go. Tell the dragon I can't teach him my song after all. It's a siren's song, and I'd be betraying a trade secret to teach it to a dragon. I can't even teach it to you, and you're kin!" She was blathering, totally forgetting that she'd earlier said teaching another song to the dragon wouldn't present a problem. "Tell Sister sorry not to be able to visit but I must swim! Tata!" She leaped into the water and disappeared into a wave.

Verity was cold, wet and rather frightened of the men on shore, but wondered if she shouldn't be more afraid of a disappointed dragon.

He swam, jumped, dived and flew to the rocks, slithering smoothly up them to sit facing her. He looked quite pleased with himself, then looked around at rock and the surrounding water for the mermaid. Verity told him, "Some of the men came down to watch you burn their ship and they scared her away. She said to tell you she was sorry, but she decided she couldn't teach you her song after all. It's some sort of siren's secret, I take it."

He huffed water from his nostrils and mouth and shook his head as if to clear his ears. Tentatively, he trilled a note in an undragon-like fashion. His voice broke when he tried to sing a bit higher. "Hmm. Beyond my range, I think. It sounded so lovely when she sang it, but I don't think it would be suitable for me anyway. But look, there's still some seaweed! Pass me a piece?"

"That's very reasonable of you," Verity said through chattering teeth. She didn't really mind the cold, but freezing and wet with no way to get dry was another matter.

"I'm a down to earth sort of dragon," he replied. "Allow me." He blew a soft steady flame and she grew warmer.

"That's better," she said. "Thanks."

"I think we should get you back to the shore and you should go into your house with the other people." He sighed, and the warming flame fluttered. "Shame about the song though."

"What will you do now?" she asked, as he very carefully closed his talons around her, a terrifying process for most people, but she found she trusted his good intentions and thanks to her curse, her trust was seldom misplaced.

"Find Casimir," he said. "He's probably in the valley where I left him, working on new material. I can give you a lift if you like. I'm plenty strong enough now!"

"That would be very kind of you," she said, climbing up behind his ears. "Thanks for helping my aunt, even if she didn't keep her end of the bargain."

"Don't mention it," he said politely, though he still sounded disappointed. "Hold tight," he added, and she felt the muscles of his haunches bunch as he made one long leap for the shore, after which his wings helped them soar over the darkened sea to a hidden place, away from the docks, somewhat behind Erotica's house, keeping out of sight from the crew of the burning ship, who had begun trudging up to the house.

"Ta again," she told the dragon in a whisper as he set her down. "I can make it from here."

He inclined his head slightly before taking another long flying leap and disappearing into the night. She hurried through the back door of the house, and through the kitchen and into the back of Erotica's office.

Only the beaded curtain separated it from the parlor, where a heated but friendly discussion was taking place. Amazingly, Captain Lewis was saying, "Captain Marquette, we could give you passage back to Queenston. Only if you give up claim to our ship and to Madame Erotica's establishment. And relinquish our personal property, such as that old props chest your men took from my cabin."

"Of course," the other captain said in a rich, melodious voice. Verity hoped Captain Lewis wasn't falling for it. She couldn't imagine what had made him offer until, peeking through the curtains, she saw Erotica offering more no-doubt love potion-laced drinks to the crews, who appeared to be still extremely chummy. The sailors were sharing stories and trying to impress each other while the employees acted as barmaids.

The pirates were still in charge, but at least the vials of love potion had stopped the fighting. The stuff could be more useful than Verity had imagined, so while the ladies entertained the newcomers, Verity put a pot on to boil and with the dubious assistance of the ghost cats, followed her aunt's recipe, concocting another batch of the brew, adding it to the liquor with which the pirates were plied during the primrose ceremony.

When they had all been sated and were sleeping, tied to the posts of the beds "So they'll think they had fun they can't even recall," Fiona said, the staff relieved them of their weapons. Captain Fontaine was more resistant to the love potion, but even he was mellowed by it, and quite fatigued after his exertions, so his brace of pistols, cutlass and the deeds were removed from his clothing as well, as soon as he slept.

Erotica kept the pistols, but sold the other weapons and the chest back to Captain Lewis, after subtracting a commission from the chest.

So much for returning to Queenston on the *Belle*. Erotica hadn't mentioned it, but apparently the love potion made for loose lips. Verity had no desire to finish her voyage on the *Belle* with a crew of pirates as passengers. She grabbed her pack and slipped up the back stairs. She didn't have a suitable men's ensemble to change into, but she had an idea. Poking around the rooms where the women plied their trade, she found one with a still-sleeping customer in the bed, his clothing laid out on a chair. It wasn't terribly clean, and it stank a bit, but it was dry, and the double-breasted jacket would help her stay warm. Her borrowed oilskins were still on the *Belle*. Snatching the clothing, she slipped into an empty room and exchanged her wet clothes for his smelly ones.

Then it was back into the night and up the hill to the trail where she'd last seen Clodagh. She saw no sign of the mud witch or Kiln, but she did see the silhouette of a larger dragon.

Devent grinned a somewhat alarming grin and said, "Hello! I was hoping you'd change your mind and decide to join me. Do you want to hear a song?"

Chapter 14: Verity and Devent Off-Road Trip

They walked along companionably enough, considering that the dragon was multiple tail lengths ahead of her. This disparity in strides made talking difficult for her since even with her longer-than-average-for-a-girl legs, she couldn't keep up with his hops.

"I don't suppose you brought a map or a compass or anything like that?" she asked, and immediately felt silly since she knew dragons didn't bother with such items, even if they knew what they were.

"No, but a friend of mine and I stopped at a ruined castle on a high prominence, where I heard the siren's song. If we keep walking the ridges, we're sure to come upon it again."

Verity thought it a splendid idea. The stormy night had given way to a day calm and bright, the sun warm, and the view clear. After the freezing wet perch on the rocks in a storm in the dark, it felt wonderful to walk on the high mountain ridges and see so much land before her, instead of only the sea.

When a mountain sheep appeared on the opposite ridge, Devent decisively flapped his wings and hopped, flew. and pounced like a cat on the hapless animal.

Verity hadn't realized quite how hungry she was until she smelled the cooking meat. She would have preferred not to smell the innards roasting. She knew that proper hunters removed some of the organs, but she wasn't sure which ones, so she took slices that still had singed hair attached and ate around it.

Water was no problem. Melted snow pools were plentiful. Animals sloshed out of them and bounded away.

At night they sang. Verity felt an unaccustomed freedom traveling with Devent, because who was going to attack them? Devent was quite a well-grown dragon, with a strong voice and strengthening wings. Though Verity's feet were tired, her spirits were high going into their fourth night on the road.

Devent made a fire and they sat by it singing, their bellies full of another mountain sheep he had dispatched before the stars came out.

They sang together, and she felt they were becoming very good friends, better friends than she had ever been with a dragon—perhaps better friends than she had been with anyone. Dragons didn't judge. They seemed to demonstrate their estimation of your value by not eating you.

The ghost cats flickered in and out, sleeping on Devent's back or in the curl of his quite warm belly. Sometimes they disappeared altogether, and she wondered if they were visiting their fellows who now traveled with Clodagh, wherever she might be.

Verity tried teaching Devent some songs she knew that she thought might be suitable for his voice.

They talked as if they were two human friends or, as it probably seemed to Devent, two dragon friends. Devent had never known a human female before, much less a queen, as it turned out Verity was.

She was much more interested than he expected anyone to be in the life of a mine dragon, in his work and Auld Smelt's.

For Verity's part, she found Devent's stories fascinating. The contrast between his life before freedom and the lives of the Dragon Vitia and her young, as well as that Auld Smelt had described to the younger dragon of life as a warrior dragon, were compelling. With Devent's enthusiastic approval, she recorded the conversation in a shell.

The young dragon listened particularly closely when Verity described what it had been like living with the wild dragons. "That must have been wonderful!" Devent said, his eyes almost whirling in their sockets with awe.

"It was frightening at first," she said. "But once I figured out I was a nursemaid rather than a menu item, it was better."

"You were frightened?" Devent asked skeptically. "Of dragons?"

"I don't suppose you've ever looked in a mirror?" she asked.

"Am I scary-looking? Really?" He sounded thrilled. "The miners never seemed afraid of me. Nor the other dragons. Nor—anyone, really."

"Yes, but your actions were very limited then, weren't they? They were in control and now they're not. Nobody knows what to expect from you now, and you are very large and breathe fire in addition to having rather large fangs and claws. You can see how people might be wary."

"I suppose so. But you needn't be afraid of me, Miss— or is it Milady? I'll protect you, since I am apparently so fierce. Ferocity should be used to protect others, don't you think?"

"I think you have a very good attitude about the whole thing. And 'Verity' will do nicely, thanks."

"I get the impression from Smelt's songs that dragons used to be guardians before the war."

"Your friend sounds like a very fine dragon. I recall meeting a dragon who fired a smelter when I visited the mines with my father. He was highly thought of back then, I seem to recall."

"Yes, he was."

Devent thought, It's a shame he's sleeping now. He still remembers a lot from the olden days and might be able to help you with your magic-restoration work.

Devent imagined Smelt dreaming of old times as he snuggled his scales into his hoard of old armor. The thought made him lonely for his old friend. Diverting as his human companion could be, she was no dragon and he did not know her nearly as well or for as long as he had known Smelt, who was the closest he had to family.

The mountaintops and sea cliffs they traversed were often smothered with fog. Ghost cats threaded in and out of it in a constant game of hide-and-seek. Along the sea cliffs Verity had to constantly watch her footing for fear of tumbling off onto the rocks, but Devent periodically flamed a little to cut through the murk and that helped. The trip was long and wet and cold. but Verity, having been so recently at sea, considered it a minor nuisance.

"I can see why we have no active volcanoes here," she said. "They'd get rained to smoldering piles of ash in no time in this kind of weather." Then she explained what a volcano was.

Devent judged they still had some distance to go before they reached Smelt's castle ruins, However, his hops had become increasingly flight-like and Verity's legs were long and her pace fast. And suddenly, a familiar aged face loomed before them, the rest of Smelt shrouded in fog until he flicked some of it aside with the twitch of a wing.

"What are you doing up?" Devent asked. "I thought you were napping."

"Yes, well, I couldn't sleep. Too quiet. And that is a very lumpy hoard I was left with. Gold and jewels are much softer. What with everything, I seem to have developed insomnia."

Verity stepped forward and said, "Hello, Elder Smelt. I'm Verity Brown. Devent has been telling me a couple of the stories you told him. I think you might be able to help me with my quest."

The older dragon grunted, then stopped and turned to Devent, "She speaks Dragonish?"

Verity nodded, and Devent followed suit.

"A word, Devent?"

The older dragon walked, with a slight limp, a few paces away.

"You didn't tell her about my hoard, did you?"

"Not as such, no."

"What does that mean?"

"I told her you'd gone to hibernate in your lair, but I don't really recall if I specifically mentioned the hoard or not. You just did, though. It—forgive me, old friend, but the hoard didn't look like something val—something humans would value anyway. And she doesn't seem like the kind of girl..."

"How many human girls have you met, exactly?"

"Well, only her, but how different can they be from the men we worked beside? They're the same species, right?"

"How many female dragons have you met?"

"There was my mother..."

Smelt hrrumphed and sizzled around the nostrils. "They are different."

"Better? Like my mother?"

"So different I could not say if they are better or worse or if they are different from each other. But certainly they are different from males, in any species."

Devent hung his head. "I didn't know."

An ashy huff blackened the air momentarily, then Smelt said. "Of course not. You're naught but a wee lad. I can see I was shirking my duty trying to retire now. Two dragons awake are harder to feed than one, it's true, especially with the human along. You have no way of knowing but as princesses go, that one is hardly dainty."

"I heard that," Verity said. "Technically, I'm a queen of Frost Giant heritage, and I like to think as Frost Giants go, I'm dainty indeed."

The old dragon blew sparks of laughter. "A dainty Frost Giant! Good one, big girl!"

Verity scowled. She didn't especially like references to her size, even from those of a different species. "I have a name, you know. I am Verity Brown."

"Brown?" Smelt asked. "Like the famous witch Maggie Brown, friend of Grizel and Grimley? They were ancestors of mine."

"Maggie Brown was an ancestress of mine," she said, seizing the conversational opportunity. "I hope you will tell me more about your family and dragons before and during the Great War. You lot live to be a lot older than humans, and I'm looking for some people whose ancestors you might have known."

"Who were these ancestors? How might I have known them?"

She explained about the cave where the wizards were murdered and showed the dragons some of the magic beads from Vitia's hoard.

But as they talked they walked, so by sunset they had descended from the mountain ridge and were back in the valley. While Verity explained her mission to Smelt, his belly rumbled. He wouldn't have been hungry if he'd been hibernating but with wakening came appetite. Devent hopped back up over the mountains. The ghost cats had reappeared and were shimmering in a ghost-catly moonlit way around Verity when he returned. Smelt seemed very impressed by them.

"Here's some seaweed to eat until we find more game," Devent said.

"To tide me over, so to speak?" the old dragon said with a fangy grin and a raised eye ridge. To Verity, he said, "Great ones for joking like that were my grandparents."

Devent said he'd already eaten his share of the seaweed before he hopped back across the mountains and bade Smelt to eat his fill of the ruffly, salty and vaguely slimy green mass. "The mermaiden, Aunt Eulalia, assures me that sea serpents find this very sustaining."

"Aye, so I've been told. We always rather considered it snack food, but it does hit the spot." He chewed once, belched, and flamed, torching upward with all of the ferocious heat of his iron-smelting blasts. "Ah, that did hit the spot!"

A strong wind sliced through Verity's jacket, the peacoat she had traded her cloak for when leaving the Spa and Bawdy House. The woolen jacket had seemed far more practical, but now she wished she had the cloak to throw over the top of it. Better yet would have been the oilskins. The rain soaked through her jacket quickly with the force of the wind, which was so fierce it thrust her forward until she all but ran down the mountain, in danger of rolling down it like a loose wheel.

At the bottom of the hill she slammed into Devent's substantial back. "Hssst!" he said. "Be still. Do you hear it?"

"Hear what?" Other than her own breath and pulse pounding in her ears, she heard nothing.

"Sounds of battle," Devent said. "You stay here with Smelt. I will investigate."

"I can investigate as well as you can," she said.

"Not from the air, you can't," Devent said. "Please stay here and protect each other while I determine the cause of yon ruckus. Is that my master's voice I hear?" He cocked his head.

Smelt grumbled. "What master?"

"Casimir. I am still his apprentice and he is the master."

"Kowtowing to another human! You might as well be back in the mines," Smelt huffed and sparked.

"Not the master of me, the master of our mutual trade. And it sounds like he may require my help."

This time he didn't hop up from a dead stop but ran down the next hill and halfway down, spread his wings, leaped into the air, and soared.

Casimir meets Bobbinears, Spike Tail, and Chainy

Casimir had followed Devent and Smelt at a discreet distance, though his object was not so much to track them as to reach the lowest of the foothills between the valley and Smelt's old home, for his own reasons.

The dragons were halfway up the mountain by the time he reached the base of the first hill, where the stone staircase began. It might be both lucrative and instructive to see the inside of the dragon's lair, but it would undoubtedly be dangerous and besides, his ends would be better served by staying friendly with the young dragon and continuing to guide and educate him. It was not that he didn't have a greedy side—simply that he had learned in his travels that one could only take just so much with one. Information was much more portable than jewels and gold.

His back to the woods and meadow, he searched the hillside, looking for the portal, until he felt a chill at his back and shadows fell over the land. Then it was that he grew aware that the strong wind that seemed to have come up so suddenly was not natural.

"Game, at last!" cried a voice from above him.

"It's a man. Not allowed to eat 'em, men."

"Do you see anyone around to report it?"

"Well, no..."

"What would a man be doing way out here? They belong in cities, bossing other folk around. That's probably just some really delicious critter that resembles a man, sort of. We won't know until we taste 'im."

"That must be it! You're so smart about this stuff!"

"All together now. Dive for your dinner!"

Casimir, seeing no door in the hillside but death in the air, burst into song before, as might be, bursting into flame.

"Three dragons went hunting, sing toora li ay!
Three dragons went hunting one soft autumn day.

They spied a poor troubadour along their way.
'He'll make us a meal, let's eat him,' said they."

The rhyme came readily enough but didn't actually improve the situation. Perhaps a clever but baffling riddle? Those always worked in the stories.

The dragons had hesitated while he sang, no doubt hoping to hear complimentary lyrics about themselves. Now they renewed their assault on him in a gusty swoop and he was within their singeing range.

"Wait!" he cried.

"Why should we?" the large, noisy, puce and persimmon colored one demanded.

"It's the rules," he said. He didn't actually expect it to mean anything, but these dragons until lately had been drudges in mills and factories and other commercial concerns and would be used to rules and regulations, even if they didn't like them. "You have to answer this riddle."

"What's a riddle?"

"It's sort of a game," he said.

"The kind where we bite off your head and chase it around the meadow or the kind where we see how many bite-size pieces we can make of you before we start eating them?" demanded a grubby gray-to-charcoal shaded dragon with drawings etched into his scales and bobbins inserted into oversize holes poked in his ears and eye ridges. Textile mill dragon then, powering the looms.

"Er no—the kind where I say something like, 'You're the most fearsome thing I ever did see. If you aren't, may this mighty mountain swallow me.' It wasn't a riddle at all, and barely a rhyme, but it might summon the Lady to pluck him from this situation, so he hoped there were no literary critics nearby, and if there were, that the dragons might eat the critic instead of him.

"The answer to that riddle is that no hill needs to open and swallow you. The three of us will be glad to do that!" Bobbinears said.

Rani Romany

Casimir's back longed to feel the breeze of a doorway opening behind him. His eyes yearned to see his new student flying down to chase away the three hostiles blatantly minstrel-menacing. But the dragons, fangs dripping with poor dental hygiene, snapped their teeth and whirled their eyes and smacked their tails together, first fanning out to surround him, then flying in ever-tightening circles. He did what any champion bard would do and cowered and quaked.

He also struck a chord on his instrument and tried to sing but his mouth was dry, and his beautifully trained voice quavered.

Then from somewhere beyond the giddy whirl of dragons a voice like a rock slide yelled, "Oy! You there, in the sky! What do you think you're doin' then?"

The dragons pivoted so that their backs were to Casimir. They ought to have remained where they were. Each was smacked in the chest, one after the other, with a huge boulder. Had he not seen it for himself, Casimir would never have believed stones that size could achieve such altitude and velocity.

The dragons plummeted to the ground, groaning, and Casimir looked for an escape route, but had no more luck than before, and was still standing there surrounded by fallen foes when a lumpy figure in a gaily floral ensemble of pink, purple, and yellow flowered skirt and tunic strode into the glade, the sinewy gray muscles of her massive legs bulging as she ran.

"You! Human! Your life is mine now! I just saved you."

"Yes, yes indeed you did, Miss," he said. Even though he had heard foghorns with more of a feminine lilt to them, he knew somehow she was female, though with trolls it was always hard to tell. They all favored floral garments which they claimed was camouflage for mountain-meadow dwellers. "At least until these monsters recover their breath and then I suppose we will both be roasted."

"If they try anything, I will stomp them down until they can't produce a candle flame," she growled. "That's a nice box you got there... er, no, not really. It looks useless, but I might be able to make kindling from it."

She was gazing hungrily at his lute.

One of the dragons—not Bobbinears, the puce one, started to rise and the troll lifted her foot and stomped hard on his tail.

He screamed as if scalded. "You didn't have to do that!"
"No. I just wanted to," she said, smiling unpleasantly.
"What did we ever do to you?" Bobbinears whined.

With the troll commanding the dragons' attention, Casimir had time to notice details about his assailants. Bobbinears' wings were two different colors, an anemic pink closer to the wingtip and a dirty maroon closer to his body. Recent growth, perhaps?

The middle dragon, the one who was shades of gray, all of them dingy and unattractive, wore what must have been a hundred yards of black chain looped around his middle and more tightly, around his neck, digging into it just below his whiskers. Scales on either side were broken and serrated.

The third dragon lashed his tail dangerously. He was the most fearsome of all, as his massive tail from spine to triangular tip was heavily studded with spikes, pointy side out.

Casimir, who was a professional assessor of other peoples'—make that creatures'—state of mind, judged that despite the dragons' ferocious demeanor, they remained slaves in their own and perhaps each others' eyes, still expecting blows, abuse, and orders. Either that or they were just mean and had mutilated themselves to show how tough they were. Which would be bad. For him. If the troll proved to be even meaner, that might not be any better. For him.

Where was a hole in a hill when you really needed one?

Chapter 15: The Fourth Aunt

Dr. Epiphany Hexenbraun, Alienist

The woman stepped down from the southbound train from Ablemarle. The ride had been a long one, but any weariness she might have felt was disguised by her authoritative, somewhat dramatic manner and purposeful movements as she hailed a hansom cab to take her to the castle.

She wore spectacles on a chain that bounced them on her chest when she moved. She wore what could best be called robes rather than a gown—layers of long tweeds woven in subtle patterns of brown lit with red, orange and gold shifting with each step or rearrangement of her arms, upon each of which she wore a silver bracelet. Her hair was gathered into a loose braid three inches above her waist and pearly shell disks hung from her ears. They emphasized her face, but couldn't do much to enhance it. She was old, the hair striped in shades of gray, silver, and pewter, with an undertone of the brown it must have been in her youth. Her eyes, hooded by wrinkled lids, sparkled at her welcome committee as if they were funny.

"Greetings, eminent gentlemen. You sent for me? I understand you have a problem with some dissident dragons with which, perhaps, I might offer some assistance?"

"And you are?" Malachy Hyde demanded with a raised eyebrow and his haughtiest tone.

"Dr. E.E. Hexenbraun," she said, and from a pocket in her cloak extracted a stack of calling cards, handing one to each council member. Beside her name on the card it said, Alienist.

"Thank you, madame, but you are mistaken," Volodny Seik told her. "Dragons are not the problem. It is the sad case of our beloved niece for which we require professional scientific intervention and your signature on a commitment document."

"Ah, forgive the misconception, please, but I overheard you speaking of a contest for dragons and I simply had to commend you on your perspicacity at proposing such a solution."

"You think it's a good idea, then?" asked the Minister of Subject Pacification, not stopping to inquire how she could 'overhear' them while they were in council chambers in the middle of the castle. She might or might not have overheard, but in this he committed an oversight.

"I do, I do!" she said, her voice slightly tinged with an Ablemarlonian accent, making it sound a bit guttural. In truth she was Argonian born and bred and lived in a bungalow built on the long-dissolved foundation of rock candy where once lived her ancestor and predecessor who had the ability to see into the present even when it was not actually present. In a way, Dr. Epiphany Brown (her real name, in Argonian) had a similar talent.

She had been fetched back to Queenston by a mysterious attorney, a friend of her great-great-great-niece Romany, who asked her to come and lend the newly-appointed young queen Verity (another niece with another couple of 'greats' attached to the relationship) the benefit of her accumulated wisdom—and talent. Before she could buy her ticket, the summons from the council arrived. N. Tod Belgaire had told her about the dragons but at that time he had not known, apparently, that Verity had fled the capital leaving the royal assistant, Malady, as regent. That the council wished Malady gone was an even more recent development. She needed time to get the lay of the land, as it were.

"Dragons adore contests!" she declared.

"They do?"

"Oh, yah. Contests appeal to the competitive nature of the beasts so necessary in their makeup as apex predators."

"Are you an expert on dragons then, Madame?"

"Doctor," she corrected. "I have studied these creatures a great deal, yah. I have a few little ideas about your situation here."

The council tried in vain to get the doctor to offer her services out of a sense of patriotism, but she was having none of it. She was frequently in the service of the Able-marlonian government, which paid her well for her insights and advice, and although she had the Ablemarlonian King's permission to assist the rulers of her native land, she was under no obligation to do it for free.

She bargained and bartered with the council, who kept trying to return the conversation to committing the regent to the Queenston Asylum for the Magically Muddled, but the Minister of Finance's carriage horses had disappeared from their traces only two days before, so he advised his fellows the investment might be a bargain after all if following the woman's advice could produce results.

"Half now and half when the situation is mended," he said. "The dragon situation. The Malady situation, we will pay for when the girl is safely incarcerated."

Dr. Hexenbraun smiled enigmatically. If she came to the sort of understanding with the dragons that would solve the dragon issue, or even partially solve it, the council would be unwise to welsh on their agreement, since she would then have connections among the dragons. Of which there was no shortage, and scarcely any space between them. The city smelled so strongly of sulfur that people began to wear kerchiefs over the lower halves of their faces when they went out. Piles of fewmets made sidewalks and streets into obstacle courses and standing near anything tall exceptionally hazardous to one's health.

Some of the dragons seemed to find this amusing but others—most—were too hungry and too bewildered by the problems of unemployment to care about the human reactions.

But the worst of the situation to many Queenston residents was not simply the menacing dragons loitering and looming around the city. No, the worst was the silent factories where nothing was being produced, no flames erupted at timed intervals. No exports filled the docks waiting to be exported in exchange for imports, which also failed to fill the docks. The country was temporarily financially embarrassed and couldn't afford even more of a trade deficit.

"Yah, a contest, I think. But first, one for the humans. You have here the scientists and the metal smiths?"

"Yes."

"Hold your contest to see which of them can build the best and most functional artificial dragon to replace those no longer working."

"Make another dragon? Are you mad? The city is overrun with them!"

"Not the kind I have in mind. The superior, mechanical dragon. Show the creatures that they can be replaced. Perhaps that will encourage them to return to work, you see."

The ministers exchanged dubious glances but... "It could work."

While the preparations were underway for the contests, Malady was introduced to Dr. Hexenbraun as a court physician.

Her first meeting with the doctor was little more than an introduction. The peculiar woman had shaken her hand—not so much as a curtsey! —and said, "Good afternoon, young lady. I am to be your doctor. You must tell me all of your secrets, you see, and I will tell you what you think about them."

That sounded no end of daft to Malady, but once she started talking she found it quite a relief to talk to someone who was not a man, was not a competitor, since the doctor was neither young nor even especially attractive, and listened to her as if what she had to say was worth listening to.

By the second meeting, Malady was prepared to give her an earful. She wore one of the tiaras Durance had brought her.

Epiphany Hexenbraun was not slow on the uptake. "Lovely piece, my dear," she said.

"Thanks awfully," Malady replied, making a minute adjustment to its position on her hair, "The dragon brought it."

"The dragon?"

"Yes, I have an admirer who is a dragon. The uncles don't believe me, but these days, with the creatures fouling the entire city, I don't know why it would stretch their credulity. Except—" she said, chewing her lower lip, "it may not be the dragon part that they have trouble with. Maybe they just think nobody would like me well enough to bring me expensive gifts. They certainly haven't been very generous with them."

"But the dragon is?"

"Yes, he brings them to me from his hoard. He understands the value of the proper jewels to a royal ensemble. He insists that I am a real princess. Imagine! Little me!"

The doctor nodded appraisingly, casting her eagle eye over Malady's peaches and cream complexion, her butter-yellow shining curls, her glacial crevasse blue eyes, and the rest of it, finally searching her face and taking inventory of her features again. "Ya, well, he may be onto something, your dragon. They are very wise creatures, at least in their natural state. He may realize that you have been chosen to lead your country."

"He'd be wrong then, wouldn't he? Verity is the queen. I'm just the regent as it stands. She's the chosen one."

"There can be more than one," the doctor said. "And the way I hear it, you were chosen twice—once by Ro—Verity's mother, and once by her. A great honor, of course, but hardly all it's cracked up to be."

"Why wouldn't it be?" Malady asked.

"Oh, that depends on you, of course. Some people, if they're feeling that others think they're special, are burdened by the thought that there are expectations they must live up to."

"Not me," Malady said, only a little uneasy at the notion.

"You would know," the doctor said agreeably, then glanced at her wrist chronometer. "Lovely visit, my dear. Must dash now. Contest to observe."

John Henry as a Dragon

The engineers and the metal smiths competed to see who could construct the most realistic, functional, efficient dragon to fit into at least some of the places the street dragons had once filled.

The competition was held in what was left of the town square. The judges were the owners of the factories that had used dragons in their boiler rooms. Dr. Hexenbraun, sat cross-legged on the grass nearby, taking notes.

There were three entries. One of them used coal to stoke the fire in the dragon's metallic belly. One ingeniously used the same gas as was in the lamps and a third worked from the energy created by a wheel turned by medium sized dogs. The first two provided fumes and fire hazards and the last was hard on the dogs.

"None of these work as well as the real dragons," one of the judges lamented.

"Shhh, don't let them hear you say that," said the woolen mill owner.

But the party with the best interests of dragons at heart, Toby the dragon-wrangler, had heard and smiled a carefully concealed smile. He'd made himself scarce since Queen Verity left, knowing he'd find himself back in the dungeon again. He'd been there before and hadn't cared for it. He sat atop the back of the dragon he'd raised since fledglinghood, Taz. The odd-looking lady doctor had suggested to the officials that they allow him to be there unmolested, in preference to having every dragon in the area monitoring the proceedings.

One by one, the mechanicals attempted to perform some of the routine duties of the average industrial drudge dragon.

The coal-fueled model, which came with a chimney between its wings, was able to produce the bursts of flame—but only if someone shoveled coal into it at regular intervals. The resulting smoke choked the judges, the alienist, the cabinet member attending the contest, and its inventor/engineer team as well.

"That one seems very effective to me," said a manufacturer of bathtubs. "I'll take it. That will show the ungrateful beasts who used to work for me that they can be replaced!"

Muttering, low hisses and snarls spread through the crowd of loitering dragons. Toby cringed. He was still aboard Taz since he feared if he left her back in the presence of the so-called lawmakers he'd be arrested at once.

Taz had become very good at reading him by now and said, "Don't worry. The worst most of these has-beens can do is sit on someone and squash them. No food/no flame, you understand?"

Well, there was that. Toby had noticed that for all of the fears of the human denizens of the city, remarkably little torching of homes and businesses had occurred. He suspected a lot of what had happened had more to do with insurance claims than dragons.

Be that as it may, the demonstration did not play well to the dragons. Prior to walking out on their jobs, most of them hadn't met another outside of work unless the other had been in the same clutch or was otherwise related. Most had slept at night where they worked during the day and received their food there too. No wonder they had needed the pacifying ingredient in the mysterious coating that had been applied to the kibble. The work routine of the average dragon was enough to drive many men to violent spasms.

Now that they had nowhere to go but the roofs and streets of the city, the dragons were getting to know each other, comparing stories, and developing strategies Toby guessed the ruling class would find quite alarming if they'd understood what was being said.

This would have gone so much better the other way around, Toby thought. If only Verity had stayed in Queenston and remained queen while he and Taz went off to find the remains of the magical families, she might have been able to control this. She had a bead that let her talk to dragons, a result of her time caring for the get of the Glassovian Dragon Vitia.

The problem with that, the difficulty for both of them really, was that they got along with dragons, generally speaking, better than they did with people. Verity had her awkward curse that put her off a great many people and vice versa, while Toby simply didn't know all that many people, having spent so much of his life with Taz.

He suspected that if he did know more people, he'd still prefer dragons. On the whole, they seemed more trustworthy.

The people gathered for the competition were bundled into furs and heavy woolens, coats, cloaks, hats, large mittens, padded pants and boots. These were among the wealthier citizens, as the poor couldn't afford to buy such gear. This winter it would be in short supply in Queenston for a number of dragon-related reasons. The chief one was that all of the great houses, for many long years, had kept a dragon or two to provide heat for their homes. Now that the factories no longer had dragons on site (though they were very likely squatting on the roof) they also were great cold places. The businesses that depended on dragons to produce their goods had stopped work altogether. But dragons had been used to warm the factories too. Toby was sure he would be warm as long as he kept close to Taz. Her skin radiated welcome heat.

"I need a practical on-site demonstration," the bathtub manufacturer said. "My premises are adjacent to the square. Bring your beast and let's see what it can do."

"That collection of bolts and gears isn't going anywhere, Ezra," cried the mutton-chop whiskered purveyor of gas lamps.

But the inventor pulled a large key from his smock and inserted it into the dragon's side, just below the wire mesh wing. He wound it several times, and with a great deal of clanking and grinding, rattling and banging, the mechanical dragon lurched forward.

From the building's roof, a blue-scaled flesh-and blood-dragon watched with sorrow, disgust, and dismay as the clockwork beast entered through the double doors of his old home and workplace. He fluttered his stumpy blue wings slightly as he hopped down from the building to poke his head through the open doors. People curious to see the new mecho-drake in action clamored to get past his bulk, but he refused to move. At the instigation of the factory owner, the inventor herded the clattering collection of metallic remnants of horse-assisted carriages, gears, pullies, springs, and rivets forward to stand in front of the boiler.

"Fire," the factory owner commanded.

"Oh, he'll need fuel first," the inventor said. "Bring us ten pounds of coal for his firebox."

"Coal? But that will cost extra."

"Even mechanical beasts need fuel," the inventor told him. "There's no getting around it. You'll need to lay in a good supply of it—where your former employee's nest used to be is a good place for your coal bin, unless you want to provide it as accommodation for the stoker."

"Wait, I have to pay for the contraption, and coal and another worker as well?"

"If you want a working machine, yes."

The blue dragon watched as coal was brought in from the railyard. The trolley wheeled past him through the double doors and onto the factory floor. It took an hour, but none of the dragons was in any hurry. At last the coal was deposited in the blue dragon's old nest and to save time, the factory owner himself stoked the coal into the mechanical whereupon it creaked to life again.

"Fire," the inventor commanded, pulling a lever indicated by the engineer.

The robo-dragon's gears clashed, and its sides lit up with the fire in its belly, causing both inventor and businessman to stand back. The creature made a belching sound and coughed up flame that shot in a broken stream into the boiler's firebox. But once the flame was released, it went from kindle to dwindle in a few seconds and the water in the boiler never bubbled.

"Isn't that blue fellow one of the ones who ate some of your last caribou, Taz?" Taz had been running a dragon's soup kitchen with prey she'd caught herself.

Taz grunted that he was.

The blue dragon had entered the factory as unobtrusively as it was possible for him to do so. Funnily enough, with dragons being so numerous in the city, blending into his background was not as difficult as it might have been elsewhere.

The factory owner fed more coal into the shiny metal beast and it again let forth a short stream of fire.

Taz and Toby were now watching from the doorway. "Perhaps the castle should hold another contest to see who does the job better, a real dragon trained in its job or one of those metal things."

That was what he meant to say, but somewhere around the word 'contest,' the blue dragon decided he had had enough. Turning his head at just the right angle to avoid collateral damage, he loosed a great gout of flame on the metal creation. Its gears and pulleys, their noise melted into a gloopy drip, ceased any activity while the artificial beast was liquified into a mixture of metals pooling where once the clockwork beast had stood. The blue dragon strode in, lashing his tail and warning bystanders to stand back, turned the tail on the now-cooling puddle of metal and swept it away with one stroke. The coal had been used up in the two attempts to fire the boiler and the blue's bed was once more unoccupied. He settled down in it and pretended to go to sleep.

Later that day, the factory owner visited Toby and Taz at their favorite perch and asked that they help him negotiate a settlement with the blue dragon.

"Live food is more expensive than kibble, but Old Blue wants to return to his job, and I haven't the heart to refuse him."

The Traveler in the Knowe

As if the dragon gangsters didn't have enough trouble with the attacking troll, suddenly a bolt of fire struck from above, and a lordly Dragonish voice commanded, "My music tutor is not for eating! Cease tormenting him at once! And stand back from yon fair maiden, too."

The dragons looked at each other, confused.

"What fair maiden? And who are you to be pushing us around?"

The troll stopped in mid sword thrust and bellowed skyward. "Heeeey, who you callin' a fair maiden, Bub?"

"She's doing quite well on her own," Casimir said, his voice pitched to a more conversational tone aimed at the sky.

About that time, the hillside behind him yawned and he stepped backward, calling to his rescuer, "Come, Devent. Milady? Now. Stardom waits for no dragon."

Devent was torn about whether to go with the minstrel or to stand and fight. He didn't really know how to fight other dragons, only how to be beat up by them. Should he wait for Smelt and his new friend or follow his teacher? But if he did that, what about the warrior maiden who defended Casimir? Surely leaving her to fend for herself was not the right thing to do.

He compromised, catching the maiden's garment in his teeth and reeling her in, twirling like a dust devil, too quickly for her to scream. The other dragons were doing plenty of that as they saw the dragon-who-was-not one-of-them disappear into the hillside with both of the only meals they had found in many days. Though she was probably on the bitter side.

The hill was hollow inside, and to Devent's expert eye as a life-long tunneler, it was not a natural phenomenon, but a made one, though the making had happened long ago. The walls and ceiling were spiked with crystals but without opening to the light, it opened onto a forest. The tops of the closest trees disappeared into the distant darkness of the cavern's ceiling.

He had little time to take in the scenery, however. Before he could blink, a woman stood before them and even before she spoke, he knew she was not a natural woman. The blue light surrounding her was a dead giveaway.

"Who are these creatures and why have you brought them into the hollow hills?" the woman asked Casimir. "You've been warned not to reveal the secret to anyone."

"Sorry, my lady, but circumstances were extreme, I was beset by dragons."

"So you brought one with you?"

"Not this one. He is the singer I was sent to seek."

"And what is she?" the woman asked, gesturing toward the warrior maiden. "His roadie?"

"I'm Grudge," the maiden in question said. "But what's a roadie? Whatever it is, I'm sure it's ugly and stupid and ought to burst into flames and die so nobody has to talk about it anymore."

"Oh, a troll!" the woman said. "They only burst into flames during very avant-garde concerts."

"She defended me when the dragons attacked," Casimir said.

"He means the other dragons," Devent said. "Not me. We couldn't very well leave her out there to be slain."

"Hah!" Grudge said. "You were just trying to rescue them from me. I was doing fine 'til you practically tore my tunic off in front of everyone. What kind of perverted dragon are you, anyway? I am not that kind of a troll!"

"Hmmm," the woman said. "Nevertheless, Casimir Cairngorm, it's fortunate that you entered the hill when you did. The situation in Queenston grows more and more dire as the dragons there become increasingly hungry and disaffected. You and your singer must hasten to begin Devent's work among his kind."

"What work?" Devent asked. "Singing?"

"Yes, of course, singing but in your current state there is absolutely no reason for anyone to listen to you. You, my friend, lack the necessary star quality." She reached into a pouch with a golden tasseled drawstring. A wad of used tissues, a tube of something crimson, a small frog that seemed to have wandered in by mistake, and finally, some sparkly powder fell from the pouch to the cave floor. The woman's fingers now glistened with the powder. "Here we are. Bibbity Bobacadabra," she said and threw the powder directly at Devent.

Devent sneezed. "What's that for?"

"It's a glamor. It will give you charisma—that certain something that will make everyone admire you even before you sing. Very helpful."

"We actually need other dragons to like him," Casimir said. "They're his target audience."

Devent wasn't sure what that meant.

"What's he doing in here, then?" the Lady demanded, piqued at being corrected by the musician, "There are dragons outside. Go practice on them!"

"They are not friendly," Devent said. "And they're very rude."

"Probably from hunger." the Lady said. "It can make some folk very nasty. With the glamor, you should be able to make them forget their bellies as you fill their ears."

Devent could see the lady was a person of authority, but the other dragons were rather frightening.

"What do you think they would prefer, lady?" He asked and started a high song. "This one or," he continued, beginning a low sound, "This?"

Before he could begin the second song however, Casimir laid a hand on his claw.

Verity and Smelt

"Where did they go?" asked a female voice Casimir could not identify.

"My guess is the laddie found a mine shaft in this hill and wanted to explore," replied her companion in a rasp that could only belong to Auld Smelt. "Or that man he's been warbling with fell in and the young one followed to rescue him. Too bad the fight seems to be over. I'm a bit slow for fighting these days, but I could have roasted 'em."

"Big cowards," the female voice said.

"Nothing for it but to drill a hole in the hill if we can't find a shaft."

No sooner did those words penetrate the hill than the lady vanished, and the doorway reappeared.

Devent cocked his head in surprise.

"She's rather a private person," Casimir said of the lady.

Devent left the cave first, followed by the troll. The portal to the Knowe vanished, sealed behind Casimir before the newcomers could see it. It was a secret place, so secret even he hadn't been sure it was there before the lady opened it for him. He hoped when they came out the world wouldn't be seven years older. That could be annoying if one didn't expect it and it was supposed to have to do with extended sojourns in fairyland, not when one was only using it, preferably momentarily, to escape peril.

"Where you been, lad?" Smelt asked.

"Oh, a most wondrous place..." Devent began. Casimir put his finger to his lips, but the troll girl overrode Devent.

"It was awful. Tacky, underdeveloped, overly rocky, some ancient idiot's idea of a home. Stank of bear, I thought."

Toby's Betrayal

Toby had worked with dragons long enough to realize that not all of them were as brilliant as Taz, not as reasonable, not as cooperative. They had what the scientists called Scale-brains, which were about the lowest kind a creature could have, according to the people who rated such things.

At first, they had listened eagerly to Taz when she told them what to do to make their employers treat them with more respect and fairness, or how to seek their own fortunes in the outside world, but as food grew scarcer and the scales began to drape between their bones, they grew more restless, impatient and even angry. He despaired of being able to help them.

Taz was more distraught than he was. Her colors dimmed, and her spinal ridges drooped. Her fellows began turning away from her even when she brought them the odd chicken or seagull. Dragons were not hugely sociable in the wild, but worker dragons tended to gather at the watering pools to discuss affairs of importance to them. Taz had only him.

Marquette

While Marquette Fontaine hadn't made the grand entrance to Queenston he'd expected, having had to borrow cab fare to the castle from his host captain, he had wasted no time acquainting himself with the present situation and considering ways to turn it to his advantage. After intense private consultations with the male members of his extended family, he had reached a number of important decisions. The council members had a few half-conceived ideas about the dragon crisis, but no comprehensive plan. That was where he came in.

Malady, deluded child that she was, thought that he had come to bring her baubles and fripperies, but it was plain she had no idea of what to do with her position other than to increase her wardrobe and her prospects for displaying it. She might not be necessary after all. Pity. She was a pretty child and they had always gotten along. But her adoration of him seemed to have wavered somewhat recently.

He felt neglecting her too much might be disposing of a possible advantage, so now as he strode about the castle grounds, he had her in tow, chirping at him. He nodded and gave her his most charming smiles, but all he would need from her, if anything, was to give her official stamp of approval to the measures he would require as he began setting the realm in order. His order.

Malady pointed to a young man washing a dragon in the courtyard, and Marquette waved his arm in a friendly and only slightly lordly fashion and beckoned for the youth to join them.

"You're the fellow in charge of the dragons, my niece tells me," Marquette said, flashing what he thought of as his 'always-take-an-interest-in-my-people' smile.

"I am, sir. Toby," said the other with only a duck of his head to indicate deference. "Taz, my dragon, and I are trying to help them, yes—sir," he added because he could clearly see that Marquette was someone of importance.

But Marquette wasn't ready to pull rank. He deferred to Toby as an expert consultant, with seeming respect. He nodded and smiled and gave Toby his most compelling gaze as he nodded to convey his understanding that Toby and Taz were only trying to do what was best for the dragons.

Finally, he pronounced his solution to the quandary the lad described. "Well, then, it would be ever so helpful, it seems to me, if we could move them into one location we could make their headquarters—Dragon Central, if you will. Also, it would make it easier to bring them food and make sure each got some of it than as they are, spread out all over the cities. What would you say the main problems are in reintegrating them?"

"Food, sir. There are quite a lot of them, and Taz has been wearing her wings to nubs trying to hunt for them all."

Marquette nodded knowingly. "Well, of course. So close to the city, there can't be enough to feed all these dragons, which are probably the greatest concentration of them in the land."

"Exactly," Toby said, clearly glad that someone finally saw the problem wasn't just the dragons. "Because they were working in the factories, the breeders produced more dragons than Queenston can support under these circumstances."

"They need to be re-homed somewhere in the countryside, where there are more meat animals, more room to fly, that sort of thing. Is that about right?"

"Yes, sir. Exactly."

The man clapped Toby on the shoulder. "I'll get to work on that then, Toby. Between us, I think we can solve this problem."

"They're very hungry, sir. Taz has so far talked them out of doing anything violent, but as I said, she's almost worn out trying to feed them."

"Leave it to me, son. I have connections in the northern part of your country."

Toby was very relieved. It had been a great burden on him and especially on Taz to try to keep the unemployed dragons from doing anything foolish and giving some factions the excuse they needed to take deadly measures. Finally someone understood the problem and was ready to take measures to solve it.

Marquette returned the next day and instructed young Toby, saying, "It's all arranged. If you and your dragon friend will have the others gather in the enclosure that's being built on the edge of the city, a special train will carry those who can't fly North to the hunting grounds."

"That's wonderful, sir," Toby said.

"Happy to be of service," Marquette said with a mock bow.

Malady's Third Appointment (in which she anticipates Uncle Marq's Arrival)

Malady Hyde looked uncommonly sour as, forgetting the posture she had learned in post-graduate charm school, she slumped into a chair.

"Dear, dear, what is the matter, Your Highness? I thought you would be excited. In fact, I thought perhaps you would not come to our meeting today." Malady did not ask why she thought such things. She supposed it was because doctors were supposed to be omniscient but actually, Dr. Hexenbraun took her meals in the kitchen with the servants and so knew all that had once occurred, was currently occurring, and was anticipated to occur in the future.

"I was excited," Malady said. "But it's all wrong. Uncle Marquette finally arrived, you see, and he was supposed to bring me gowns and jewels appropriate to my new station. With him here, I thought I wouldn't need to see you again."

Dr. Hexenbraun clicked her teeth in a message that, while unclear, generally meant that she was sorry to hear that, or possibly that it was rude of Malady to say so. But she nodded encouragingly, which was just as well since Malady had paid no attention and was continuing in a voice rising to a wail.

"He's always been my confidante, you know, ever since I attended school in Frostingdung as a child. I even wrote to him about the dragon. But since he's been here he has all but ignored me! Instead, he has long boring conversations with my other uncles about politics and government and complaining about dragons. He should be taking me shopping! Especially when he had the nerve to show up without the things he promised to bring me. He claims he didn't forget. His ship sank, he said. My dresses and jewels and shoes and hats and everything were on it. You'd think he could have saved something, wouldn't you? But nooo...

I was so looking forward to his arrival, but he's so different this time, it's almost more fun to talk to the dragon. He at least appreciates the important things in life and likes to tell me about his hoard."

"Perhaps your uncle is feeling the guilt for disappointing you. And also, he may be shaken by having his ship sunk. Perhaps he is different because he knows he has nothing to offer you now..."

"Oh, I know, and he should, but it's how we were before that I want the most, though that doesn't let him off the hook to take me shopping for the kind of things he was supposed to bring!"

"You should tell him that it is your relationship with him that you value—I wouldn't mention the shopping just now. Perhaps he feels he is less important to you now that you are a lady of such rank, such power and authority?"

"Oh, I don't think so. I was counting on him to advise me how to manage some of it—particularly how to manage the other uncles so they weren't such sticks in the mud about my spending. But he seems to spend most of his time with them."

"Then perhaps he could be jealous of your relationship with this dragon, hmm?"

"Do you think so? Uncle Marq? Jealous of a dragon?" She giggled. "That would be priceless! But he doesn't need to worry. The dragon is—well—a dragon, and he—Uncle Marq—is family."

"Men can be most insecure. Perhaps you should tell him?"

"And lose the advantage? Really, Doctor H., don't you know anything? We have taken one walk in the city and he and the dragon boy were talking about what to do with them. I almost told him that since I met Durance. I've realized dragons are not all bad, after all, but they were chattering like old friends. Perhaps the next time Durance is curled around the privy tower I will chatter with him and ignore Uncle Marquette. That will teach him to ignore me!"

She flounced out, still giggling, while Dr. Hexenbraun shook her head slowly and replaced her spectacles on her nose.

Chapter 16: Malady and Durance

The sparkle, the glitter, the sheen, the shine, the opulence of crimson and purple velvet, all played hide and seek with the glow of dragon flame. Malady dove into the treasure chests head first, hands scooping.

When she stood up, her arms, ears, neck, head and hands laden with gorgeous jewels, she had no chance to admire them, as the room had fallen quite dark... and silent.

"Dragon? Where are you? I need some light here! And a looking glass—full length. Please?" she added as an afterthought. "Dragon? Dragon, come here at once and stop teasing me. I represent the crown in this country—I'm even wearing one."

The madder she became, the more unwise grew the threats she made if the dragon did not return. Which he did not. Malady tried to remember her way back, but kept bumping her shin on treasure boxes. Then her feet were caught and tangled and she jerked hard. The impediment broke, but she heard the distinct sound of pearls on stone. She was sure they were pearls because they rolled nicely and in a different way than she imagined diamonds would. Stepping forward, she slipped on them as they rolled where she wished to step, and she went down on her bottom. Fortunately, it was well padded by the opulent gown.

She burst into tears that were at first indignant, before she realized that she was somewhere far beneath the castle several stories down, she'd forgotten how many in her excitement to see the hoard. Why, oh why, hadn't she told anyone where she was going? Well, because she hadn't known herself, actually. Come to think of it, she still didn't know. And it was very dark. No windows under here, and she'd failed to realize how much she'd depended on the dragon flame to provide light. Possibly there were torches in wall sconces but what would she light them with? That dratted dragon!

After what seemed like hours and hours, her anger turned to fear, and cold too. She patted the piles of riches until her hands met the velvet garments she had seen briefly, before the dragon left. Wrapping them around her, she huddled amidst invisible treasures and longed for the dragon to return. At first. Then she started wondering if he'd just stepped out to fix himself some sort of sauce he thought would taste good with her.

How could she have been taken in by that story about how dragons didn't eat people anymore? They bloody well did! She was sure of it. How could she have believed his flattery? Oh, well, because he backed it up with presents, of course. Beautiful, valuable, glittery presents that were absolutely worthless in her current predicament.

"Dragon, you had better come back and lead me back to my chambers, or at least to the main part of the castle. My uncles and the servants will be missing me and coming to look for me with guns and pointy sharp things. They might torture you to say where you've hidden me."

From somewhere distant and echo-y came Dragonish laughter.

"Don't count on it, pretty, pretty princess. I have heard them talk. They will not know I led you away and if they did, they'd want to reward me. You are not actually very popular, you know."

"A lot you know! We're family! They adore me! They say I look just like my mother!"

"Yes, but what you have not heard because they do not say it until you leave the room, is that they didn't actually care for your mother all that much. Both of you would have made excellent dragons."

"Is that your dastardly plan, to turn me into a dragon so you can marry me and thus gain power and position in the country through my regency?"

Sparks flew finally and, though the image vanished almost before she saw it, she caught a glimpse of the dragon and a bearing on where he sat, laughing at her.

"Oh, please! Marry you? That would be bestiality, even if I turned you into a dragon, which I cannot do, by the way, because I don't have the power to shift the shapes of other beings."

"Yes, but it's what you want to do, isn't it? That's why you brought me presents and gave me compliments, to lure me down here to be your bride in an unnatural union."

"Er—no."

"What do you mean 'no?'" she asked, offended.

"If I take a bride as you call it, a mate, it would be one of my kind, foolish girl. And so I did many, many years ago. But she was killed in what men call the Great War before she could coil around our first clutch of eggs."

"Very sad, I'm sure," said Malady. "But nothing to do with me. I'm not a dragon."

The hiss and clink of scales sliding through jewels brought the dragon's eyes uncomfortably close to her. "Nooo," it said in its soft sibilant voice. "But you could be. You have all the right attitudes and instincts. Perhaps you're a halfling of some sort?"

"I most certainly am not!" she declared.

"Sssss... mmmmmm... well, you're very dragonlike in your fascination with jewels and gold, and I suspect will make a great hoard guardian, as I have been these many centuries. Now that dragons are out and about, I wish to renew my acquaintance with my kind. Still, the hoard must have a keeper. That is now you."

"You can't just leave me!" Malady said, her indignant command emerging as a squeak.

"I rather think I can. You just play with the treasure and I'll be back... or not, depending on what I find outside. Meanwhile, enjoy gloating over the hoard. Goodbye, Princess. Have a wonderful time."

Before he slithered away, Malady had the presence of mind to say, "At least leave me some light. If you want to torment me by ironically leaving me nothing but the jewels I admire, at least leave me a light to admire them by."

Durance the Vile mumbled to himself then finally said. "A candle, then."

"How about a torch?"

"You might be tempted to desert your post. Besides, candlelight is so flattering to jewels, don't you find?"

That was about all she could find by the single flame, and that would soon be gone. She wished she'd brought a snack or a jug of water. Surely the dragon must have a source of nourishment and moisture in here somewhere, if this was, as he claimed, his main den or lair or whatever.

She wanted to stamp and shout and throw things but for a time, she tiptoed around, carefully placing her candlestick on a flat smooth surface before moving anything else. Her eyes grew weary of reflected glory.

The entire chamber was eerily quiet except for the candle sputter, though somewhere far in the background was a distant roar that might have been the sea.

Despite her best efforts, she tripped over a long strand of pearls and fell, hitting her head on the stone wall, the pearls broke and rolled in a thousand directions.

She began gathering the pearls. She didn't see how the dragon could account for every piece of jewelry in the room, but he'd been down here a long time and she didn't want to risk his wrath if he did return and find something missing, even something so trivial as a pearl.

Rubbing her head with one hand, she tried to pick up yet another pearl with her other, but fumbled and it rolled away. She searched for it where it had rolled against the wall but found only a half pearl. A half pearl? She looked closer. It was caught under something. She flicked it and it rolled back but the secret door it had been caught under slid forward.

Aha! That dragon thought he was so smart. She had found her way out and when she got back to the main part of the castle, she'd order the dragon killed and the treasure—well, she'd decide what to do about the treasure later. Imagine that creature, squatting on the royal treasury and trying to turn her against her uncles!

Propping the secret panel open with a bejeweled sword, she gathered a tasteful assortment of necklaces, bracelets, earrings and both hands full of rings, stuffed her pockets with gold coin and loose gems, and, carrying her precious candlestick, slipped into the passage behind the door. Her candle held out for the first level but then died, and she was forced to feel her way up a step and a set of winding stairs. Two small beams of light ghosted through the darkness on the next level. They came from two cobweb-obscured holes that, once she'd run a finger over them and blew on them, fit her eyes as well as a pair of spectacles.

The passageway was illuminated dimly by the clouded light streaming into it from the eyeholes appearing every thirty feet or so along the corridor. She'd always thought there were far too many gloomy portraits of ugly grim looking ancestors hanging on every surface on every wall in the castle, especially on the interior walls. Where there were occupants in the rooms, she realized she would appear to be the Grand Duchess Morag or the High Sheriff of the Northern Icefields to them. Should they be so observant as to look into the eyes of the portrait, they'd be in for quite a shock. She wondered if some of the paintings were permanently affixed to the walls so the servants wouldn't catch on.

Perhaps no one had been in these passageways for a long time, but someone had at some time had need of the eyeholes.

She peered through them, and looked straight into the council chamber.

Uncle Marquette was addressing the council. He was speaking softly for some reason. Whispering. How inconsiderate of him. Who did he think would be listening anyway? One of the ancestral portraits?

Fortunately, she had excellent ears that were good for something other than to support earrings. She heard his plan, though not all of the details, and thought it by and large a good one, as long as they didn't try to take her dragon. After all, Durance was something of an old family retainer, wasn't he?

She shrugged it off as they began discussing how to finance the grand fair Uncle Marquette proposed. Budgets were so boring. She was itching—both literally from the dust and bugs and figuratively, from an urgent desire to examine her treasures in better light—to return to her chambers.

It came to her that where there were eyeholes there must also be doorways into the castle rooms from the passageway. Wasn't there something in the building codes requiring castles to have secret passages and hidden doors and such with adequate access from the royal chambers in case of emergency? It seemed that there must be. Not that she herself had grown up in a castle, but in her posh boarding schools she had met plenty of other girls privileged enough to have done so. She suspected some of them were not nobility or royalty, but probably the children of upper echelon servants, but nonetheless, they talked at times of playing in such places and, as she grew older and talked to more mature classmates, of using such secret places to meet secret friends (none of them dragons) for secret activities.

This would all have been so much easier if her candle had lasted longer. As it was, she was forced to feel along the walls for a telltale crack or gap in the stones. Her tender fingertips were as sore and bruised as they were after an afternoon of needlework by the time she finally located one. Too bad she couldn't trust a maid to keep her mouth shut after she'd cleaned up back here. But Malady vowed to always have a more reliable light source at least.

She found her own chambers at last and entered through the wall mirror she'd intended to replace because it was unflattering. Now she rather thought she might hang a tapestry over it.

She dumped her jewels on the bed and pulled the coverlet up over them, then inspected the portraits to see which ones might have spying eyes. These she covered with cloaks. No one but her had been in that passage for years, maybe decades, and she was certain that it was her secret, but in case it wasn't, she wanted her other secrets to remain secrets as well.

The Malady Mystery

Having failed to deliver the promised fripperies and foolishness to his fashionable niece, Marquette was unsurprised when she ceased to seek his company. She was a Hyde, after all, and although he was a wealthy man in his own land, he had arrived without his ship, cargo, or even a change of underwear. In the past, she had given him her undivided attention when they met during her breaks from school. Now, just when she had begun to be interesting, as soon as she learned he had not brought the gifts she requested, she cooled like an autumn evening. She wasn't exactly indifferent to his wishes, or an impediment, but neither was she an eager helpmate. The wench seemed distracted.

Malachy was much more receptive to Marquette's proposal for a solution to the surplus dragon dilemma.

His relatives on the council were willing to do just about anything to save the city's infrastructure, crumbling beneath the weight of the lazy beasts, and even the boy Toby, the liaison between the government and the monsters, had been amenable to Marquette's persuasions.

Of course, Marquette was very good at persuasion. He always sought to make his way seem like the most profitable, the most reasonable, and the most fun. He had obtained his present wealth and status by being Frostingdung's royal fixer.

He encountered no opposition from anyone in the city except the occasional aberrant dragon-loving former employer.

Marquette promised the council that he could solve the perplexing problem to everyone's benefit—even that of the dragons, in case their welfare concerned anyone.

After surveying the situation, talking to a few people, taking the lay of the land, Marquette addressed the council, all of them his dullard distant relatives. Malady was not present, though she should have been. He was disappointed in her to say the least. He had been determined to marry her, not only because it was convenient and advantageous to his advancement, but because he had always believed from the way she nodded and looked at him and came to him with her cute little problems that he had molded her mind into a lesser version of his own. Never mind, her absence was a minor issue.

"Cousins," he said, leaning confidentially across one end of the council table, "We whose families were the architects of the program to rehabilitate dragons following the war, who invented the kibble that allowed men and dragons to work together safely, are at another crux in the history of this client nation. Its people, in their backward way, have clung to these beasts as remnants of their glory days, now long past. But the time has come to break them of their dragon dependency. Dragons not subject to our control are far too dangerous for us to allow to exist. For a time, their flames provided cheap steam, but that time is now past.

"Because of the unnatural sentimental attachment some people still harbor for these beasts, the solution to this problem must take place far from the city and must address all aspects of this situation. People must be made to see the beasts not as the heroic protectors they were once considered, nor even as a means of inexpensive energy, since they are no longer inexpensive to use, but as the monsters they are."

"Can you not rebuild our kibble supply?" Cuthbert asked.

"Not fast enough to solve this problem. Besides, we may as well solve it rather than smooth over it with a temporary fix. The dragons have to go, and a new fuel source for the engines of industry must be created."

"Created from what?"

"From other monsters, dead ones," he said. "Their long-buried remains will provide a source of fuel far superior to any in use today, to provide the fire to drive the engines of all contemporary contraptions. Deposits exist in Frostingdung and according to our scientists, in Argonia as well. But to persuade people of the need to extract it, we must first exterminate the dragons in a graphic, dramatic fashion that the populace will never forget. Are you with me? All in favor say 'aye.'"

The 'ayes' were unanimous. Malachy Hyde had already found the perfect location for the fair he had in mind, quite near the former site of Malachy's Hide-in Valley Ranch. He already had a map. Transport was arranged. Word went out, proclamations were issued, the painting of enticing signs and banners occupied every artist in Queenston, broadsides were composed and issued, food obtained to lure the dragons, and more and more of them entered the enclosed area where they were rewarded with enticing bloody treats obtained from herdsmen and farmers throughout the land.

Between his organizational skills (which included a great deal of delegating the more onerous tasks to others, leaving him free to sell, sell, sell the project to all and sundry) and the council's thorough knowledge of the land, it came together rapidly.

Marquette did not concern himself with the details. He was the idea man, and the showman. And he planned to put on quite a show. There was only really one major obstacle, and that was the cost.

Malady's Fourth Appointment

Malady met Dr. Hexenbraun, as usual, in the castle's second drawing room. The first was for gentlemen to withdraw with their cigars, the second was for ladies to withdraw to get away from the gentlemen and their cigars. Malady debated about whether to show some of her new jewelry off, but then decided it was no good having it if she didn't and anyway, nobody knew what all she owned one way or the other. Dr. Hexenbraun was a stranger and none of the uncles—and apparently that included Marquette—had the vaguest idea what young ladies of fashion might have acquired. So she slipped on the blue tiara and a few little trinkets from the hoard she thought would look nice with it. It was very dressy for a doctor's appointment, but it wasn't as if anyone was letting her have any parties.

Dr. Hexenbraun was already seated in the drawing room, her back to the large bay windows looking out on the now-destroyed castle gardens. As Malady swept grandly into the room, her posture perfect—the better to display the tiara—the good doctor's left eyebrow raised.

"Good morning, Dr. H.," Malady said. While she had been reluctant to begin the appointments, she soon began to look forward to them. As no one had done anything about acceding to her request for ladies in waiting and her maid was of an inferior class, the alienist was the closest thing in the castle she had to a human friend. At school she had always been the head of a squad of the most attractive girls in her class, who made it their business to critique other less attractive students—for the sake of their own improvement, of course.

"Your Highness," the doctor said, bowing her head slightly in acknowledgment. "You are looking uncommonly shiny this afternoon."

Malady fluffed her curls around the tiara and patted the pearl-and-sapphire collar around her neck with a hand full of rings, including a stunning signet ring of carved lapis lazuli, flanked by star sapphires and bezeled with crystal-clear stones of a brighter hue. Earrings matching the collar cascaded to her shoulders. She didn't want her other arm to look naked, so she piled the matching bracelets on the slender wrist of that appendage. Fortunately she owned

175

a powder blue taffeta day dress, but to it she was able to add a white-fox lined blue velvet cloak—strictly for warmth.

"These old things?" she asked nonchalantly. "I had them lying around and thought I might as well put them to use."

"Striking," Dr. H. said. "And regal looking. In fact, your jewels are remarkably similar to the ones Queen Amberwine is wearing in the portrait on the wall above the buffet."

"What—what a coincidence!" Malady said, twisting to see. No wonder these things had looked a bit familiar. The beauty of the original Faerie queen of Argonia, whose hair, eyes and complexion resembled Malady's own, was so enhanced by the jewels they were no doubt made for her.

"Yes," the doctor said dryly, "Isn't it? Those jewels have a bit of history behind them. Before her ascension to the throne, according to reports from the popular press of the day, the queen wore only green, but King Roari liked her so much in blue he presented her with the jewels. I don't suppose you have had any more dreams about the dragon lately?"

"Not dreams, no," she replied at the same moment that Durance's scaly face appeared in the window behind the settee on which the doctor was seated. He winked at her and she made the teeniest gesture of greeting by wiggling the first two fingers of her right hand, the one with all the rings.

Dr. Hexenbraun twisted to look behind her and Durance slunk down so his face disappeared beneath the windowsill, but not before the door to the room opened. Malady supposed the maid had brought tea, although naturally she was not supposed to interrupt during the consultations.

"Just bring that little occasional table over here and set the tea things on it," Malady instructed, thinking the maid was behind her.

Dr. Hexenbraun turned back from the window. "How do you do, Lord Marquette. Do you require assistance?"

Cuthbert and Eustus were right behind him. "You're quite right, Marq. The girl is wearing part of the royal treasury," Eustus said. "I've seen the inventory."

"What I want to know, young lady, is where you got it," Cuthbert said.

"My jewels were a gift," she said.

"From whom?" Marquette asked.

"I'd rather not say," she replied. Out of the corner of her eye, she spied Durance slither across the windows, leaving a muddy streak across the expensive glass.

"I'm afraid we must insist, my dear," Marquette told her. "The country has projects that require funding, and the jewels will be a big help. Clever of you to find them."

"It wasn't me," she said. "I tell you, they were a gift."

"From...?" Marquette prompted.

"From the castle dragon, if you must know."

"I see," Marquette said. He plainly didn't.

"Just as I thought," said Eustus. "The child is delusional. Dragons that give crown jewels, of all things! Doctor, it's high time you signed that commitment order."

"And yet," the doctor said, "the jewels are real. And there are quite a few dragons in the vicinity, yah?"

"So does that mean you're not going to sign the papers to lock her up?" Eustus demanded.

"Yah, it means 'no, I will not.'"

"Maybe we ought to lock you up too, then," Cuthbert said.

Marquette said soothingly, "Now, now, gentlemen. No need for threats or for incarcerating our niece in a sanitarium. According to the doctor here, she is not crazy, but," he gave Malady a look that said clearly he was more saddened and disappointed than angry, "it seems she is a thief. When I spied her in her bejeweled splendor in the corridors earlier, I asked her maid to check her bedchamber."

"And?"

"Unfortunately, the entire treasury was not there. However, enough precious gems and crown jewels of great antiquity were in her possession to pay for our entire enterprise and a good portion of Argonia's national debt besides."

"I can't help it if I have good taste," Malady interjected in her own defense. "I had to carry those things a long way, so of course I only wanted the best pieces—and the most becoming, of course."

"We need not resort to sanitariums," Marquette continued, "When by all accounts there are perfectly good dungeons right here in Queenston Castle."

Malady opened her mouth. Dr. Hexenbraun stood. "No, no, you must not to that. Shame upon you for thinking to lock a girl of such tender years—and your orphaned relative at that—in a place so cold, so dirty and horrible."

"You've been there, Doctor?" Marquette asked.

"No, but such places are always cold, dirty and horrible..."

"What do you think, gentlemen? Shall we help the good doctor, who has not accomplished the task for which she was hired, expand her first-hand experience of what happens to thieves and liars—"

"The ones not in charge," Cuthbert put in.

"Oh, no, please do not! It is bad enough you would send a young girl to such a place, but I am older than you may realize. My arthritis! Oh no, you mustn't."

Malady wanted to say, "It's all right, Doctor. Durance will find us," but the doctor kept protesting loudly until the uncles' backs were turned and then she smiled brightly at Malady and wiggled her eyebrows as if to say, 'What fun, yah?'

"The dungeon it is, then," Eustus said, and called the guards.

The Dungeon

Midnight at Queenston Castle. The moon was irrelevant since it was invisible throughout most of the castle, especially the lower reaches. Nevertheless, the cold flagstones glowed with poison green light.

The job at hand was the sort Marquette would have preferred to leave to others, but this time he did not dare. He must capture the castle's beastie. His quarry was a slippery, stealthy sort, for centuries slinking through the subterranean circulatory system of the castle.

By necessity, the dungeon area was abysmally dank, furnished with objects sharp, slicing, squeezing or searing—why were so many words that sounded like hisses coming to mind in this place?

Marquette shifted his sitting position on the table portion of the rack, careful not to make a noise that would alert the women to his presence, in case Malady might somehow be able to warn the dragon of his presence. A selection of the most valiant guards was on the other side of the partially opened door, iron studded and heavy blackened oak, at the foot of the stone staircase descending from the castle's ground floor.

Tonight the castle was ringed with guards, equipped with weapons and parasols to deflect the dragon crap periodically plopping from the battlements. Marquette found it baffling that the city had not been completely buried in the sulfurous excrement decades ago. For creatures that famously had little to eat, the beasts certainly shat a lot.

He took a sip from his flask, feeling like some sort of romantic highwayman under such primitive circumstances, although if he really were a highwayman, he'd be behind the dungeon doors instead of on the outside of them, as he was, watching.

The guards outside would ensure that no creature could crash through the dungeon wall and pull out Malady as if she were a plum in a pie. Or, if it did come that way, at least there would be a lot of noise to serve as a warning. The ringing of steel, the crackle of flame, the screaming and whatnot, would give the rest of the guards ample notice for pursuit.

Not that he thought the dragon would come that way. From what little he had tricked out of Malady, despite its recent habit of curling around the towers to peer into windows, the beast was an ancient denizen of the depths below the castle. That was where it was likely to emerge.

The enforced quiet, coupled with the effects of the whiskey in his flask, combined to make Marquette drowsy. Twice he jerked awake after nodding off, but he was not the slightest bit tempted to lie down on the rack for a snooze.

When the crunching began, he took it at first for noise made by the guards at the dungeon's entrance, but it kept on and on, followed by clanging and crashing, smashing and splintering, all underlain by the susurration of scales on stone.

By the time the great head smashed against the door behind the rack, Marquette lurked (not cowered) behind the door, watching with the others as the serpentine dragon smashed in the cellblock wall. Malady, followed cautiously by Dr. Hexenbraun, climbed over the rubble as the dragon withdrew, and followed its massive head as it retreated the way it had come.

"Do we give chase, milord?" the captain of the guard asked.

"No, we do not give chase. We follow from a distance, all the way to the dragon's lair. Discreetly, you behind me. We do not want the dragon to know we are following it. You are all, I take it, armed with pikes, nets and the like?"

"Milord, we are."

"Then follow. We are giving them a good head start and will pursue them momentarily."

"Yes, milord. Do you not fear losing them?"

"I do not. They will be leaving a trail. Headlamps, men," Marquette said, speaking softly, pulling down the one he'd mounted on his own head when their vigil began.

He followed the glowing green path left by the dragon through the wreckage of the storerooms beyond the dungeon.

The storage area ended in an empty corridor with downward sloping flagstone floor and a vaulted ceiling. A wavy streak of the phosphorescent material was smeared down the length of the corridor.

Marquette smiled, waving the guard forward to follow the green glow through first a left bend in the tunnel, then into a spur on the right hand. Upon entering the second branch, they began to hear the rush of water, as from a small stream. Following the green trail, they heard the water more and more distinctly, and the atmosphere in the underground passages grew fresher.

With several more twists and quite a steep descent, they arrived at the stream. The banks and bed glowed, stained with the green phosphorous paint. There was no sign of the dragon, nor of Malady and the doctor.

Escape!

"Oh, no!" Malady moaned, pointing to what looked like green ichor leaving a trail in Durance's wake. "He's hurt! He must have been wounded when he tried to break us out."

"I'm right here, you know," Durance said. "I'll thank you, Princess, not to speak of me as if I cannot hear you. And I have not been wounded, thank you so much for your concern."

"What's the green stuff, then?" she demanded. "It's getting all over the hem of my gown."

Dr. H. dabbed her finger in it and held the glowing digit under her nose. "Phosphorous," she said. "Paint, I suspect."

"It glows, which is almost like shining," Durance said admiringly. "Pretty."

"They mean to track us with it, unless I am missing my guess, and I do not miss guesses," Dr. H. said.

"Get it off me!" Durance said.

He led them to the underground stream where they used their hands and skirts to clean his hide and their feet of the telltale green.

"Now we'll leave a wet trail instead of a green one," Malady said. "And my dress is completely spoilt."

"Hmmm, I propose to use another place of egress," Durance said, slithering more of himself into the streambed.

"There's another way out?" Malady asked.

"Of course. We are not far from the surface here. You can't imagine I eluded detection or pursuit for so long when the only exit is through the castle. Follow if you do not wish to return to the dungeon. The men will be in for a great disappointment if they think they can track me to my hoard."

The way was winding and wet. In the distance, they heard the muffled voices of their pursuers exclaiming—but they did not continue to follow as the dragon and former captives escaped, collecting mud and other slimier things as they went.

Malady found herself saying 'ewww' and 'ick' a lot. The water in the stream seemed clean, but the further they went, the fouler the air became, until it smelled as bad as the stench at the drawbridge.

The floor dipped again and the current increased in speed as the floor of the tunnel descended.

"Where are we going now?" the doctor asked. "Does this lead to a river, or will we emerge in a forest, perhaps?"

Malady was rather disappointed that Dr. H. and Durance the Vile seemed to understand each other perfectly well. She had been under the impression that Durance communicated only with her.

"After a short swim in the moat, yes," Durance said. "We continue our escape on the other side."

"You want us to swim the moat," Malady whined. "The privy tower empties into the moat!"

"Just a short swim," Durance promised.

"Absolutely not. There must be another way. What about those stairs we passed? I saw them before we got to the stream. Where do they lead?"

"Back into the castle, I suppose," Durance said in a bored voice. "Suit yourself. That passage is too narrow for me. I prefer the outside of the tower."

Dr. Hexenbraun said, "I do not relish a swim in the sewer either, child. But if we return to the castle proper, we will be taken again."

"I'm not stupid," Malady said. "I know a secret. Besides, I can't possibly go anywhere like this. I need to change my clothes and pack a few things."

"Foolish, foolish pretty princess," Durance said, and slid down the stream. They heard a splash as he hit the moat.

Malady shuddered and turned upstream.

The flight of stone stairs was just beyond the place where they had washed the paint from their feet and Durance's underside.

The phosphorescent glow had provided enough illumination for Malady to make out the steps on the way to the stream and she began climbing them without hesitation.

After a moment's pause, Dr. Hexenbraun followed.

The stairs opened onto a narrow corridor that offered some light from small holes in the inner wall, the doctor observed. Malady kept climbing, and, huffing and puffing, the alienist climbed after her. At the next landing, Malady stepped off into the corridor.

She stopped twice to peer through the sets of eye holes, the doctor discerned quickly. She had seen such arrangements in other castles. She was nevertheless surprised to see the girl pull open a bit of wall and slip into it. When the doctor reached the same spot, she stopped to avail herself of the holes in the wall for a preview of the room first.

Malady was already pulling gowns from the closet and stuffing underwear and toiletries in a trunk she apparently thought she would have servants to carry during the escape.

Dr. Hexenbraun was sorry she had not had the time or opportunity to introduce her patient to reality.

Malady's flurry of furious activity must have masked the footsteps outside her room, for suddenly the door from the hallway opened and Marquette Fontaine entered.

"Hello, my dear," he said as if Malady were exactly where he expected her to be. He chuckled in a disarmingly indulgent-uncle way—or it would have been disarming had Hexenbraun not already identified him as a manipulative sociopath. "Fancy meeting you here."

"I—um—was just throwing a few things in a case. I don't want to stay in the dungeon, but nor will I stay where I'm not wanted."

"That's a first for you, I'd say, dear girl. But you won't need all of those things where we're going. An appropriate costume will be provided."

Chapter 17: To the Dragon Hiring Fair

"This is Verity," Devent told Casimir and Grudge. "She's on a quest to restore magical traditions to the heirs of wizards who lived long ago. Isn't that exciting? I promised Smelt and I would help."

"Ah," Casimir said. "I believe I can be of assistance as well. I have long traveled these hills and valleys, seeking audiences and patronage, and have learned much of the history of Argonia's north eastern most regions."

"Perhaps you'll know where we should go next then," Verity said. Her beads and shells had begun rattling sometime during introductions. Five ghost cats wound among the human, troll, and dragon legs, as if twisting an invisible binding around the ankles of the non-cats.

Verity thought Casimir a very handsome man although his voice, rich and deep as some lovely dessert, might have given that impression more than his features, which weren't bad either. His skin was weathered and brown, but his eyes, not the skin around them but the eyes themselves, seemed far older than the rest of him. Curious.

"Get off me, you monsters!" Grudge fussed, brushing at ghost cats as if they were mosquitoes. Verity noticed that when the cats were present, mosquitoes weren't, which made a great advantage of being haunted.

"Hmm," Verity said. "They seem to like you."

"You're one bank short of a riverbed, lady. They do not like me. I am not the least bit likable and don't let me hear you say anything to the contrary! What do see-throughish cats know, anyway?"

"They've helped me identify the heirs of the murdered mages I'm seeking. I don't suppose you—?"

"I should say not! Off, you!" and she slapped wildly at her floral-patterned trousers, which provided camouflage among meadow flowers. The cat who had been there leaped to the top of her head instead.

"It was a long time ago, but there was Trouble the Thaumaturge," Grudge said, scratching her whiskers. "He was a troll mage who struck terror into travelers back before the Great War."

"Sounds promising," Verity said. "I know I have some shells somewhere in which the recorded voice is complaining about anything and everything. He doesn't seem to have taken part in the Great War though. He hated everyone on both sides equally.

One of Verity's dragon beads jumped up and down against her collarbone so hard she feared injury. She pulled the necklace off over her head and unstrung it. "Here," she told Grudge, capturing the lively bead and handing it to her. "A gift for fighting the brigand dragons that attacked Devent and Casimir."

"You surely don't mean to give me a gift!" Grudge scoffed.

"I do. I think it probably belongs to you."

"You're offering it to me as tribute, aren't you? So I don't hurt you or your friends because I am very fierce like that, you know."

"You and Devent both," Casimir said, sounding amused.

"So I heard. I suppose it is a kind of tribute—to your fighting skills, perhaps."

Grudge snatched it from her hand. "That's more like it. Don't try to take it back. I'm keeping it. As a matter of fact, hand over those other beads too."

She reached over and grabbed the necklace, which Verity had not yet returned to her own neck.

After a moment, the troll handed the necklace back. "Naww, keep it. Them don't feel right." She stared into the bead. "But this one—oh yeah. What does it do? Will it help me kill my brothers or do I have to do it the usual way?"

"I hope not!" Verity said. "I thought when I got these together with the correct people, they'd be able to figure out what they can do with the power inside them. The beads contain the combined remnants of magic splashed across the cave walls of a dragon's lair where I was—um—an au pair one winter. If it's got a lot of one wizard's magic, it seems to resonate the most with one of that mage's descendants."

"Blah blah blah. Bye. Thanks for the bauble. I'm going home to try it out now. Someone's going to be sorry they crossed me."

The ghost cat that had been on her head transformed into a live frog and hopped along after the troll until she picked it up and stuck it in her pocket.

Verity began to wonder if this business of reuniting magic with the families it came from was really a good idea after all, but she said, "Well, there's one more."

She turned to Casimir. "Suggestions?"

"There's a tower that used to be a little north of here, but I haven't been there in a great many years. Since the—uh—" He started to say, 'since the Great War' before he remembered he was not supposed to have been around then "—since the last time."

Casimir seemed to know where he was going, though Verity didn't see how. She supposed that since he was in a career involving a great deal of walking, he might be more acutely aware of landmarks than most people.

He didn't need one to find the road to the castle, however. The main road, a double rut made by the wheels of carts, wagons and carriages, met with a well-traveled track leading east. Along the way, they needed to step off into the tall grass while more carriages and wagons and three single steeds passed them, headed west toward the main road again.

To Verity's surprise, the travelers who passed were unanimously women, and unanimously they wore their hair in smart bobs or elaborate braids, loops, and towering confections of curls.

"Oh, she's done it again!" cooed one of three female occupants of a wagon drawn by two horses. She patted her hair and gazed into a hand mirror, turning her head from left to right and back again, admiring the braids entwined with ribbons and artfully looped over her ears.

"You'll be Queen of the Fair," one of her companions said dryly. "Or would be, if you were a dragon."

Casimir followed them, taking a few quick steps until he caught up with the wagon. "Excuse me, what fair?"

"The Dragon Hiring Fair," the woman with the mirror told him. "It's in aid of the unemployed dragons, to get them back to work for a wage this time, instead of just room and board. I don't know what dragons would spend wages on, but there'll be feasts and food booths and entertainments and a dance! You should take your dragons too!" she said, nodding at Devent and Smelt.

The wagon drove on and Casimir fell back. "Hmm, that's interesting."

"I can't believe the dolts on the council came up with that one," Verity said. "There'd be nothing in it for them, would there?" But her left eyebrow began to ping a slight bit.

Over the next hill they saw what Casimir sought, although he could scarcely believe it. "It's different," he said, sounding puzzled. "The staircase is new." A tall straight stone tower rose three stories above the road, which was now empty. Spiraling around the building to end in a little landing beneath the single window was a staircase, painted dark yellow.

A sign hanging above the window said, "Zeli's Zippy Golden Stair Hair Care, Fascinators and Millinery, No Appointment Necessary."

A young woman with a blonde ponytail and a cheery smile leaned out the window and waved. "Hello, strangers. I'm about to go off to the Fair, but you're just in time if you only need a shampoo or a bit of a trim."

The ghost cats bounded up the 'golden' stairs three steps at a leap. Another of her beads beat a tattoo over her right collar bone.

"Unusual looking establishment you have here," Verity called up to the woman.

"Yeah, my great-great-granny was a witch and a mad architect. They didn't let women study architecture back then, so she only ever learned how to build towers."

Casimir made a sweeping bow, indicating that she should climb the stairs ahead of him.

The woman kept talking while Verity sat on the sill and drew her legs in after her. "Her daughter, Rapunzel, (I'm named for her but Zeli suits me better than that awkward mouthful) had the stairs built. Her witch mother, Rampion, didn't want her to date until she was thirty-five. I think she hoped the girl would follow in her footsteps and stay single, so she made it so only fellows who could climb up her hair could get to her. If they didn't make it, or if she caught them, she plunged them into the blackberry patch below."

"Ouch."

"After Witch Rampion took a shine to one of the princes and persuaded him to forsake Rapunzel and marry her instead, as an alternative to the berry bushes, they left for his kingdom leaving poor Rapunzel stuck in the tower. However, the next prince was an uncommonly patient fellow and an able carpenter who built the staircase so they could court at leisure."

"Fancy a prince having a trade like that!" Verity said. "I'd always heard they were a pretty useless lot."

"Well, he wasn't actually a prince. He was an ophthalmologist who enjoyed carpentry in his spare time. He had been brought a number of patients who fell victim to the thorns and was curious to see the girl they blinded themselves for. He fell instantly in love, as did she, and they ran away to a nice one-level bungalow in Little Darlingham, where he had his practice. Rapunzel was the one who actually started the family hair care business. Rampion had cut her hair off in a fit of spite before running off with the previous prince, and Rapunzel saved her locks and made hairpieces for all occasions from them, while re-styling her cropped cut into a fashionable do. So. Now you know. Shall I do you? I can see you're dressed as a lad, but stuffing your hair under a hat gets uncomfortable, doesn't it? And makes it more likely your disguise will be penetrated?"

She held her hand out for Verity's cap, which had fallen off when she climbed through the window. She wanted to ask why the grandfather ophthalmologist/carpenter hadn't built a doorway while he was at it, but Zeli was patting a throne-like chair that backed up to a water basin.

She washed Verity's hair while chatting away about the family, her customers, and how excited she was to set up her booth at the Dragon Hiring Fair. "I was thinking I might get a very small one. I could train a very small dragon to be a hair dryer?"

Verity said. "I suppose, being small, she wouldn't eat as much either." She sat up and Rapunzel fluffed out her strawberry blonde bob, which now wanted to curl in a becoming but not especially feminine way around her head. "I have something..." she began, as the bead intended for the descendant at this address beat its tattoo against her skin.

"What do you want me to do with this?" Rapunzel asked, holding up the shorn sheaf of Verity's hair.

Before Verity could answer, she continued, "I could attach it to a headband, so you could just wear it when you want to dress up or look all girly? I do that for a lot of my customers, especially those who wish to chop off their hair so they can dress in men's array and follow their lovers across the sea or into battle or whatever."

"That would be splendid!" Verity said. She had no wish to dress like a boy all the time and her shorter locks might look a bit peculiar with one of Madame Marsha's lavish creations back in the city. "But first, I have a gift for you." She handed Rapunzel the bead before the hairdresser could launch into another story.

"A bead! How delightful! I have just the ribbon to string it on too."

"There are some shells that go with it. The voice is that of your ancestor before she was murdered with the other wizards back toward the end of the Great War."

"You can keep that. She wasn't really very nice and probably has nothing good to say. The family disowned her actually, but the bead is pretty."

"There's something else goes with it that neither of us have a choice about," Verity said, and as she stood, her place in the throne-like chair was occupied by what was at first a transparent cat, but re-formed with a longer muzzle, curly topknot and tail and other bits as an extremely groomed pink poodle.

"Wonderful," Zeli said, bending over to ruffle the dog's curls, receive licks on her cheeks, and welcome it with a few phrases of baby talk.

"How much do I owe you?" Verity asked.

"The bead and the dog are more than enough—aren't you my little doggie woggie?" Zeli said, then stood and added to Verity in a normal tone. "Are you going to the Fair?"

"I don't see how we can avoid it at this point."

"Good. I'll bring your hairpiece with me when I've had a chance to make it up. Now I have to rush. Robin and the children will be here soon. Oooh, they are going to love this little doggie!"

"You're married?"

"Oh yes, he's a doctor, you know, a tree surgeon. We're ever so happy. And my babies are dying to see the Dragon Fair."

A Fair to Die For

The main road between Kingston and Little Darlingham was bustling with both vehicles and pedestrians, and when a horse threw a shoe or a wagon wheel broke, traffic stopped while the problem was fixed and it could move again.

Verity would have thought that people who evidently were keen to attend a Dragon Fair would have been less leery of actual dragons, but their fellow pedestrians gave Devent and Smelt a wide berth.

The dragons couldn't help drooling at the sight of some of the carthorses. Verity told Smelt, "Don't even think about it. People get very attached to their horses."

"I don't see why," Devent said, almost whining. It had been quite some time since he and Smelt had eaten.

"They're useful," Verity said. "You just need to feed them and take care of them and they will provide you with faster transportation, save shoe-leather, and if need be, pull a plow or a wagon."

"Dragons have done more than that," Smelt said. "I worked for men for the last fifty years, and every other dragon I know has also worked for them."

"But not lately," Verity told him. "Most people have rather short memories, especially when it comes to remembering who they owe favors to."

Smelt cocked a brow ridge at her. "True, that is. Very true. You're unusually bright for a human."

"Not really. I just have to speak the truth. No choice." She paused then admitted, "It's a bloody nuisance, to tell you the... you know. I can never be clever or tricky or even lie to protect myself or spare someone's feelings. I was quite the most disliked girl in school. Any school."

"Glad to hear it, lass. Glad to hear it."

"That I was disliked?" Verity asked.

"That you can be trusted," the old dragon said. "Not many a human can be, I've learned. Not even me old tender at the mines, and I practically raised him from a pup since his dad was my tender before him and his dad before him."

"I haven't known any particular dragon that long. You were all busy working while I was in school. I think there were dragons in the furnace rooms at my schools but I'm not sure."

"I saw you once at the mine with your dad. You admired my work."

When a herd of sheep meandered across the road, blocking it, both dragons forgot themselves. Devent launched into the air and Smelt burped a campfire's worth of flame, then covered his mouth with his tail and looked as chagrined as his face allowed. The herd's dog sprang into action, snapping and barking at them and nipping at their tails. Verity said, "Perhaps we'd be better off following the train tracks."

"Perhaps so," Casimir said. "People on this road seem rather hostile and tense for some reason."

They lingered long enough for Verity to buy an unfortunate sheep from the herd's shepherd, so the dragons could feed.

Verity didn't even look at the sheep in question. Having enjoyed some pastries and cucumber sandwiches with the crusts cut off at Zeli's tower, she left the mutton to the dragons, although Casimir accepted a small portion. Devent burped this time. His flame had dwindled until now it was like one in a gas lamp. Smelt's gas came from the other end. The smell of burning wool followed their party for two of the many miles between the road and the tracks.

Closer to the tracks, another odor gusted toward them on the wind. The sickly-sweet stench of decaying flesh was tolerable from a distance, but became overpowering. Over the next swell in the spongy ground cover, they saw a mound lying a few feet from the tracks.

Casimir and Verity exchanged wary looks but Devent said, "I'll go see."

He hopped/flew across the distance, landing close to the object.

What is it?" Casimir called.

"Dragon," Devent said. "Dead one." Devent took a cautious hop toward the form and prodded it, then jumped back.

"Seems odd," Verity said. "How did it die out here in the middle of nowhere?"

"Fell off the train?" Casimir suggested. "Or perhaps was hit by it?"

They advanced slowly at first, but in this place the tracks ran through open country and none of them could spot any danger.

Devent turned away.

"What?" Casimir asked.

"He has no head," Devent said. "It's horrible."

Auld Smelt lumbered forward, Verity keeping pace.

The dragon lay on its side. Like many of the industrial dragons, this one lacked the variegated scales so useful in distinguishing one dragon from another. It was shades of gray, except for the gaping neck wound, blackened with swarming flies. For such a terrible gash, there was surprisingly little blood.

Smelt peered at the injury and hissed, saying, "At least he was dead before he lost his head. Otherwise there'd be more gore. It's a recent kill though."

"How can you tell?" Verity asked.

"I've seen many wounded and dead dragons in my time, though it was long ago," Smelt said. "This one is fairly fresh. A day or two at most."

"Disturbing," Casimir said, "And curious."

Verity inspected the visible parts of the corpse for an injury, but aside from lacking a head, the beast, from what she could see, was intact. It had no wings and its tail was foreshortened, a condition she recognized from touring the breeding farms once with her father and once on a field trip with her classmates at Our Lady of Perpetual Locomotion. "This seems to be one of the scientifically engineered ones, bred for his work, whatever that may have been."

"It ain't right," Smelt said. Verity nodded agreement.

"Wouldn't his wings have grown like mine did?" Devent wanted to know, experimentally fluttering his, which were not yet as wide as he was tall, but had been growing steadily since he left the mines.

"Probably not," Verity said. "He wasn't meant to have them. Father told me that they were bred to be unlike wild dragons insofar as they would be perfectly adapted to the way dragons have lived recently." She saw that his ribs stood out against his hide. "Oh, dear. I wonder if the kibble... if it was the only thing this one could eat."

They found one more body that day and another the next, both decapitated like the first. Verity very much hoped the beasts had not been slain, but without their heads there was no way to tell what had happened to them. It had to be awkward for whoever took them, trying to carry three dragon heads all over the countryside. Although the beasts were not as large as Smelt or even Devent, they were hardly diminutive. She said as much.

Casimir said, "They might be riding on the train. I suppose we'll know if we encounter them."

They made camp that night. One thing about traveling with dragons was there was no need to worry about campfires. Trees were few and far between, most of them having been sacrificed when the train tracks were laid. Trees in this part of the country were not large anyway, but peat was plentiful. Casimir and Verity dug up a few chunks and Smelt dried it with a few hot flameless breaths, before he and Devent set it alight.

Devent was unusually quiet. "Fretting over the dead fella, laddie?" Smelt asked.

"Well, yes, but also, I hate the idea that men caused him to be born disfigured, so they could make more use of him that way."

"I reckon they were scared of us and wanted to grow some that weren't wiiild," Smelt said with a fierce show of teeth.

"No doubt," Verity said. "I can't see them getting the dragon Vitia to fire a boiler."

She told them as much as she could what she had learned living in Vitia's lair and minding her twins while their mother hibernated. Smelt sighed with memories of his civilian youth, before he joined the war effort, and Devent listened eagerly, but with a distant look in his eye.

After minutes of mutual silence, he began to sing a mournful lament. It featured a lot of wailing, keening and sighing, and was short on actual words, but definitely got the meaning across.

"I call it 'Dirge for a Dead Dragon' in honor of the dragons who've died here lately," he said. "They never got a chance to fly in freedom like Vitia."

"Speaking of flying, lad, your wings seem bigger to me than they were when we left the mine," Smelt said.

Devent's eyes glowed.

By the following morning, his somber mood had given way to his customary optimism. He sang a soaring note and flew up after it. His wings were bigger and stronger, as Smelt said.

"Why not scout around while you're up there?" Verity called to him. "See what you can learn about why these dragons died. Someone will be sure to know something at the railroad."

Devent sailed off, flying with increasing boldness, trying a few tricks. As none of them resulted in him falling from the sky, he kept flying.

Verity and Smelt trudged on, the older dragon tiring quickly as they walked. "Hard to believe that I used to fly like that—better, truth be told."

"Tell me more about what it was like—the Battle of Blazing Bog," Verity said. "Were you very old at the time? Did the wizards and witches fight with you?"

"That wouldn't have been very smart of them," Smelt said. "Might've perished from friendly fire. Enough of us did. Hard to aim properly in all the smoke and darkness."

"The other side didn't have any dragons, did they?"

"No, no dragons, but plenty of firepower, even in those days."

"But if we had dragons and magic, why didn't we win?"

"Don't ask me, lass. 'Twas a human war. Besides, we didn't lose."

"No, I suppose not," she said. "We compromised. We did the sensible thing and sought advice from our allies."

Smelt shot her a side-eyed glance and blew cinders.

"Well, no," she said quickly, "It's not the same as winning. My dad said everyone had to make compromises..."

More cinders from Smelt. Verity decided the best thing to do was concentrate on walking, watching the grass wave, and feeling the wind blow. Walking through the springy muskeg was hard work.

Casimir hummed a little as he walked, his instrument jangling against his back when he had to hop over a tussock.

Verity had little trouble keeping up with the lame old dragon, although he seemed to gain energy as they traveled further.

They had made good progress and could see the glint of railroad tracks in the distance when Devent swooped in for a landing.

"The entire train is full of dragons on their way to the Fair!" he said, glowing with excitement. "I talked with some of them. They're riding for free!"

"This Fair sounds like quite an event. Zeli certainly thought so." Verity tried to imagine what dragons would do at the sort of village fete she'd seen in some of the towns near the various schools she'd attended, which was her only frame of reference. "Do you suppose there'll be pie-eating contests? Or maybe one to see who can blow the most impressive smoke rings?"

"Maybe," Devent said. "Mostly a Hiring Fair is about work. People who have jobs that can only be done by dragons will be there to select workers and moreover, negotiate contracts, which are apparently important to have."

"Hmm. I should think that will mean quite an improvement from the way things have been. Better working conditions, food and health care—I hope they'll remember to ask for hibernation leave and someone to look after the young."

"Surely the Fair people will have thought of all those things! The city dragons say Taz and her boy must have arranged it all. More dragons will come later, when the first have been hired. I wonder if anyone will need singers?"

"Or drillers," Smelt said, reminding him.

"I don't want to return to the mines," Devent said. "I love the sunlight. I love the rain. I love the snow. Casimir said you could always learn to play bass if you wanted to try your luck with me. He said musicians always need a good bass player."

Smelt snorted, the cinders flying from his nostrils threatening the tall dry grass on the southern side of the tundra.

A new era seemed to be opening for dragons. About time, Verity supposed. Toby and Taz were doing a wonderful job. Persuading people to hire the dragons, supposedly to pay them a wage to be workers rather than virtual slaves. It was a fantastic resolution for what had threatened to be a perilous problem. Why, she wondered, was her head suddenly throbbing?

"The Queenston dragons were all abuzz about the disappearance of the human queens, too," Devent went on. "They feared they might be blamed for it. The first queen just vanished the day she was to be crowned, they said, and she was the one who freed them, so that was a worry. She had had some kind of backup queen. Now it seems she has vanished as well."

Casimir cocked a questioning eyebrow at Verity. Did he know who she was? He certainly had a knowing look about him. If he brought it up, she'd have to admit it, of course. And she really would rather not, especially when they were going to a public event. It was very difficult to maintain the element of surprise when you couldn't lie about anything.

Devent decided to fly ahead of the rest of the party.

"Excellent," Casimir said. "Do a little advance promotion for your inevitable triumph at the Fair. Sing them a little song, maybe." He waved goodbye and, clumsily, Devent tipped a wing in acknowledgement as he flew on down the tracks.

They walked until they came to a feeder track where a handcar had been left. Verity had seen them operated once or twice, briefly, but Smelt had watched them used every day at the mines. He was too big to fit. With Verity on one handle and Casimir on the other, the device clanked down the tracks much faster than they could have walked. Smelt walked behind and made himself useful by burning up the piles of dragon dung stinking in the wake of the train. If he fell too far behind, the humans stopped and rested until he caught up.

Rowanwood Station

At the first train station they encountered, Verity and Casimir dismounted from the cart and joined Smelt on foot. Casimir shook out his hands and flexed his fingers. "I can't continue that infernal contraption," he said of the handcar. "As it is, I doubt I shall be able to play a note."

"I'm burned out," Smelt said in agreement. "I could use a small herd of cattle and another three or four months' nap."

The train Devent followed had already left Rowanwood Station and the stationmaster, holding his timepiece, waved at them as they walked into the station. "Won't be another northbound train for another twelve hours, if she's on time. Normally there's only the two runs a week, but they've pulled trains from all over for special shuttles to the Fair. You folks are welcome to visit our new Railway Cafe, in the shed round back. The wife baked her special raspberry pie and there's raspberry, rose hip, and blueberry tea as well, with salmon salad and zucchini sandwiches on her fresh sourdough bread. Lucky for you the last train mostly had dragons. If it had been people, there'd be nothing left, but dragons aren't much for fruit pies." He cast an apologetic glance in Smelt's direction. "Dragon food's been gone since a week ago last Monday, though we've been promised a herd of cattle and a flock of sheep from up north any day now."

Smelt steamed at the mouth, which was his way of drooling. He headed for the fields behind the stationmaster's house in case an unwary rabbit or some other game small enough to have been overlooked by the previous train passengers might come hopping by. The stationmaster's wife, coming out of her kitchen carrying a pie in each hand, called out to Verity and Casimir.

"I'll thank you to keep an eye on your animal. Fluffin and Rex are family, not food." A black and white spotted herd dog stuck close to her heels while a black cat sat just beyond the kitchen door, keeping an eye on proceedings.

The cafe boasted two tables made of old solid wagon wheels set atop a pile of sawn-off railroad ties. At each table was a bench like those found in the passenger cars aboard the trains, but cut in half so that each half faced the other, the cut end propped up with more railroad ties. The smell of the creosote preserving the ties added an unpleasant note to the delicious aroma of the pies.

Casimir, who had been unusually quiet for him (as Verity would have realized had she known him better), remarked on it.

"I suppose one gets used to it, living so close to the tracks," she said, between mouthfuls.

"Perhaps that's it," he said, and ate the pie, not so much because he could enjoy the flavor in spite of the reek of creosote, but because he was hungry. He looked around at the landscape surrounding the station. Although the muskeg had given way to fields surrounded by low bushes and tall grassland, it too was open and rolling as far as the foothills of the Majestic Mountains, the snow dusted tops of which saw-toothed across the eastern horizon.

"This used to be quite a forest, you know," he told her. "The king's men hunted it in the old days. See the foundation of the station? That looks as if it might be built from the masonry of the old hunting lodge."

Verity, who had learned quite a lot about Argonian history from perusing the archives at her Aunt Ephemera's mazelike home inside Wormroost Glacier, looked up from her pie to glance around her. "I would not have thought so. Where was the castle then?"

He finished chewing the last bite of pie and took a swallow of tepid tea before standing and indicating with a sweep of his arm a hill to the west of the station. "You can't see the castle ruin now. It was slighted during the Great War, but Rowan's Keep and the village surrounding it used to be on that very hill, among a thick stand of rowan trees."

"I've heard about it," she said. "But I never knew exactly where it was."

The stationmaster's wife, a plump lady whose fair hair was looped over the top of her ears, came to collect their payment for the food. Inside Verity's pocket, a bead inside the pouch began to vibrate, rattling against the shells containing the histories and last words of the slain wizards.

Three cats not Fluffins trailed behind the woman. The pathway paved with more railroad ties showed through their bodies.

"Excuse me, ma'am," Verity said. "Did you live around here before your marriage?"

"North of here," the woman said. "Up Little Darlingham way. My family's been there since before the war."

"Would you happen to know if any of your ancestors were said to be magical sorts? I've a good reason for asking," she added, in case the woman was one of those people who felt magic was something tacky that did not happen in respectable families.

"As a matter of fact, well, yes. A long time ago, one of my great-grandads was said to live in a little castle on an island in the middle of the Everclear branch of the Troutroute River. His name was Raspberry. I'm Pearly Raspberry-Smythe. They say the brambles completely covered the Raspberry Castle during the war, and my Gran who was one of his daughters slept through the whole shebang. These very pies are her recipe, according to me mum."

Verity fished the bouncing bead from the pouch along with the shells rattling in time with it. They stilled as she handed them to the woman, whose palm was open waiting for her coin.

"A gift for you," she told the woman, "your legacy."

"Very pretty, dearie," she said, trying to hand them back. "But I'll be needing proper coin for your food."

She looked pointedly at Casimir, who seemed to be inspecting a cloud.

Verity handed her one of the coins from the sunken treasure chest. It was gold and the woman bit it.

"Keep the change," Casimir said grandly. "Lady?" he added to Verity and offered her his fingertips, supposedly to help her rise.

"Be sure and listen to the shells," she called back as they walked away. "They'll explain anything—odd—that may happen. You might want to wear the bead around your neck at all times." *Or not,* she thought privately, since she had no idea what powers it conferred.

Back on the tracks, she and the minstrel exchanged weary glances and climbed back aboard the handcar. Smelt was right behind him, the dog unwisely snapping at his tail.

"No," Verity told him firmly, as he glared at the dog while his jaws began to glow.

"I wasn't going to," Smelt said, giving Verity a twinge behind her right eyebrow.

Pearly Raspberry-Smythe called the dog, who whined, but ran to the back of the station with a last bark to tell

Smelt that the station's guard dog still had his eye on the oversized interloper.

Casimir grumbled, "I hope once we get to this Fair I will be able to accompany Devent." He displayed the blisters on his palm.

Smelt climbed onto the tracks and gave the handcar a push with his nose that sent them clanking quickly past the station. "If it will get us out of here and somewhere that a fellow can find a decent meal, I'm driving. Sit still for a bit. I'll push."

Troll Bridge

Verity expected to see Grudge at the Troll Bridge and was interested to see if the female troll warrior had discovered which magical powers her ancestor's bead bequeathed her.

Grudge, however, was not at the bridge.

The other trolls, instead of lurking under the bridge and popping out to extort things from them as was bridge keeper custom, stepped timidly out from their lurk below the overpass, brandishing flyers. Perhaps their diffidence was because of Smelt, but it was definitely abnormal behavior.

"Taking your own dragon, are you, Missy?" asked the particularly slimy specimen who shoved a paper into her sore, red hand.

"Watch your handcar, Lady?" A smaller troll offered, sticking out its palm.

The river was bright and beckoned with shady banks and sparkling cool water that she could imagine pouring over her as she watched it.

"Thank you," she said politely, and didn't drop anything in the extended hand. Smelt waded into the water and smacked his tail in it, soaking her, making her laugh.

"Hey, you there, we has to drink from this river! You're mudding it up."

"Yeah, you commuters! Mudding the water for your elders and betters."

Smelt, revived by the water, was in quite a good mood, very playful for such a venerable elder. He gave what was for him a slight hop, scooped the water with what was left of his wings, which appeared to be larger than when Verity had first met him. He turned around so his back was to the bridge and smacked the water several more times with his tail.

Verity badly wanted to join him, but didn't trust the trolls not to run away with her pack, which contained items she needed.

After a bit she scooted higher on the bank. A sign was nailed to one of the sparse trees growing next to the water. Even at a glance she could tell it had more words on it than the one in Zeli's shop.

COME ONE COME ALL TO THE FIRST ANNUAL DRAGON FAIR. FUN FOR ALL SPECIES. JOBS FOR DRAGONS AND FREE FOOD!

Dragons: Get off the Northbound train at the Hydden Valley feeder track to proceed to the grounds for Dragons-only events and opportunities.

Humans: Continue to the Little Darlingham Station to enjoy spectacles and reenactments such as Dragons and Damsels! Monsters and Maidens! Visit our vendors' market for unique souvenirs and gifts. Ride in a dragon balloon! Join a treasure hunt for your own dragon hoard!

"There doesn't seem to be a list of attractions for the dragons," Verity said, flipping over the paper for the dripping Smelt to see.

"That could be because very few of us can read or write your lingo," the old dragon said with inescapable wisdom Verity did not quite believe covered the entire issue.

I wonder what Toby and Taz make of this, she mused to herself.

Smelt grunted sparks and ashes. "I wonder what's become of 33—the lad," he said. "Hope he hasn't lost his head."

The trolls were back under the bridge, preoccupied with throwing knives into the bank. Verity and Casimir climbed back onto the cart. "We could take over the pumping again," she told Smelt.

He leaned forward, lowering his head to push again. "It's not heavy and gives me sommat to do while I walk. You might as well save your strength. You may have need of it. I mislike the sound of this Fair."

Casimir grunted in assent. "I concur. The beheaded dragons are an ominous portent."

The sun was low in the sky by the time they left the river. Shortly after they left, the tracks began to vibrate, rattling against the handcar's wheels. Shimmering in the ever-decreasing distance, an engine barreled toward them, the drone of the engine dragons turned to a high-pitched moan, then a warning scream. Verity and Casimir leapt from the handcar and down the bank. The train roared by, barely missing the end of Smelt's tail as he rolled down the hill past them. He roared indignantly back at the engine dragons, snatching his tail up around his body. The handcar flew off the tracks to land in pieces at the bottom of the embankment. Casimir ducked as an iron handle flew past his head.

When the train had passed, they continued along the tracks, although no longer on them.

Relieved, Casimir and Verity trudged on in comfortable silence. Since the minstrel joined them, the silences had been fewer, at first, as he sought to entertain a new audience. Her winces and cringes every time he told one of his more colorful stories discouraged and puzzled him, and once Devent departed, to Verity's relief, he'd stopped trying. She was grateful for his presence, nonetheless, since she missed her father and found the company of an older man reassuring, as long as he was not actively trying to keep her company.

She scanned the tundra beside the tracks, looking for more headless dragons and some of the low life scum who were collecting the 'trophies.' She thought she saw two more in the distance, and shook her head, feeling sad and disgusted, but did not go to investigate further. She began to worry about Devent, who had not returned in a very long time.

If Smelt was concerned, he didn't mention it. On the other hand, he took a professional interest in the tracks, claiming that he recognized some of the steel he had once made in the manufacture of the gleaming rails. "I remember a bit coming out like this—can you see the blue-gray wave in the metal here, lass? That's fine sturdy stock, that is. You got to keep the heat even is the trick to it, you see."

Hours later, while she was gazing into the distance looking for Devent and Casimir was humming a tune he kept repeating bits of and revising, Smelt cried, "Oh! Oh! The tracks are rumbling again. Can you hear?"

Verity listened and after a beat said, incredulously. "That was quick. They must have put on even more special runs for this Fair. Didn't the stationmaster say there were two daily? This will be the third today."

Smelt surprised her by saying, "Let's flag 'er down. I've had me a hankerin' to ride one of them, see what the fuss is about. Probably won't find many more trains as accepts my kind for passengers after all this Fair business is over."

The train stopped, and the conductor leaned down from the platform to tell Casimir, "No room inside. This run is special for the Fairgoers, and it's crammed with people craving an outing. The dragon could ride on the roof if you like but..."

"I'll join him," Verity said and scrambled up the ladder, followed by Casimir.

Smelt mustered enough altitude from his regenerating wings to make it to the top of the car.

From their new vantage point, Verity could see the Majestic Mountains far in the distance. Small tributaries of the Majestic River flowed from both the mountaintops and the ice fields of the Wormroost glacier. Soon these sources would begin freezing again, after a brief spate of freedom. This far north, even the summer months were interrupted with occasional snowfalls.

Lulled by the rattling and rumbling beneath her, Verity was surprised an hour later when a gleaming apparition danced in the twilight. Flame spurted from it at regular intervals, and when the train's headlamps caught it, Verity hollered, "Look, it's a dragon automaton!" and pointed.

Smelt, who had been facing her, turned carefully on the curved surface of the train car and said, "Why, so it is, so it is indeed. Perhaps it is a child of mine, do you think, born of my steel?"

"It isn't alive," Verity told him. "It's a thing of science and technology, a machine. It only seems alive."

"Nonsense, lass," the old dragon told her. "Everything is alive until you kill it."

Verity was neither inclined nor compelled to dispute that. No splitting headaches. So it was either true or the old dragon believed it so profoundly that to him it was indisputable.

The train chugged to a halt and the conductor said, "Third class passengers and dragons are to disembark here. Third class passengers, your campsites are available on the far side of the tracks, around the pavilions previously erected for second-class passengers. Second-class passengers are invited to stay in the pavilions or proceed to the northern Fairgrounds for similar accommodations there. Dragons, please board the feeder car to take you into the southern Fairgrounds where your special events will take place." It was a mouthful, even for a practiced conductor. Smelt shifted uneasily but made no immediate move to disembark.

"What's the man jabberin' about?" he asked. "What's a special event?"

"Something they are making happen particularly for this occasion."

"What?"

"I don't know."

"Then I don't like the sound of that." Smelt said and Verity, no longer distracted by the wind and the rattle and clack of the train, found that she did not particularly like it, either. There was something wrong here—well, there were the beheaded dragons. Not a coincidence that both the Fair and the beheading of dragon corpses were occurring at the same time. "I didn't come for that. I thought we'd find the lad."

"We will," she said. "But..."

"Your dragon must get off here, lady," the conductor was saying to another passenger. He had removed his uniform jacket to show a waistcoat with a dragon patch on the shoulder.

"But I am a vendor and he is a part of my business," said a low earthy voice Verity recognized.

"Clodagh!" she said, and half climbed, half slid down the ladder and leapt off onto the platform. She landed with an 'oof' and buckling knees, alerting her that she'd been sitting in an awkward position far too long.

Clodagh bobbed a perfunctory curtsy. Kiln was hitched to a little wagon laden with the tools of their trade. They clattered as he twitched his tail.

"Milady," the former golem said to Verity. "Could you explain to this person why Kiln and I must go together?"

Verity told the conductor, "She is a potter and Kiln is her—well, kiln. He does not need a job. He seems perfectly happy working in tandem with this woman."

"All vendors belong at the northern Fairgrounds, but all dragons belong here," the man said stubbornly.

"Not this one," she said. "Better get back aboard, Clodagh."

"We'll walk," the earthen girl replied.

"We'll join you," Verity said, looking up, but Smelt was no longer atop the train car. "How did you learn about this?" she asked, sweeping her arm to encompass the Fair.

She, Clodagh and Kiln turned away from the man who was now busy directing other passengers to campsites.

"Everyone was talking about it. I traded some of my dishes for passage on the train from the southern arm through the Mountains of Morn to Queenston," she said. "I thought we would do well in the city, where no one knew my history, but then we heard of this Hiring Fair and it seemed a good place to sell our wares. Kiln has been uneasy. I wish we had not come."

"It sounded like fun, and a place to get answers," Verity said, agreeing. "But I know what you mean. There's something wrong." Almost without her noticing it, the beads around her neck had warmed and begun vibrating while those beads she carried in her pocket also vibrated and the shells on her shirt jerked on the threads that held them there. "There are others here with a claim on the powers of the beads," Verity said.

Something brushed her ankles and she looked down to see three ghost cats had returned. They had deserted her while she and Smelt rode atop the train. She supposed even ghostly cats did not care for too much wind in their ears, fur and whiskers.

Good. If the heirs to the wizards whose familiars the cats once belonged to were at the Fair, the cats would identify them for her and she could reunite them with their ancestral magic. Whatever this event meant for dragons, it seemed that it would be a boon to her mission.

All along the tracks, tents and pavilions offered shelter and the savory scents of cooked meats and baked bread, sweets, spicy dishes tempted them from their trek.

Suddenly above all the clamor and the chug of the train as it prepared to depart for the next stop, a familiar voice rang out, clear and melodic, but in the tongue of dragons.

"Gather ye dragons, be ye near or far
Come gather if by wing, by foot or railroad car
Come gather to this place, where your need will be met
At this wondrous festival no dragon will forget!"

"Laddie!" Smelt cried in a spew of sparks. He emerged from the far side of the train and at the sound of Devent's voice jumped up to the coupling and down beside Verity on the platform.

"No smoking on the platform," the conductor scolded Verity. "Tell your friend!"

But by then, Smelt was already headed down the feeder tracks. A large group of dragons had been grumbling among themselves, apparently unsure about whether or not to allow themselves to be funneled into their designated campground. They fell in behind him.

Verity stepped forward to follow, but a restraining hand pulled her back. "That's dragon country, that is. You don't want to go there."

"But I do," she said. "Some of my best friends are dragons."

"That doesn't mean that some of their acquaintances won't decide to barbecue you. We provide them with meat here, but some might see you in that light, if you take my meaning."

"I do, and I'll take my chances, "she said.

"We can't let you do that. Our liability won't allow it."

She wanted to say she was technically at least the queen and the only person who had to allow it, but she wasn't ready to get back to queening yet.

"You could hire me," she told him. "I speak a little of the dragon tongue. I could interpret for you."

"How are you with the other end?" Another man, this one wearing a gray and black striped coverall, asked. "There's plenty of dung to be shoveled."

She smiled. "I can take care of that." You didn't need to shovel it, if you reminded the dragon to incinerate it. She hadn't been looking for a job when she came to the Fair, but having one as a glorified dragon stable hand would provide cover, at least until she could get the lay of the land. So much travel had not exactly polished her appearance. If there was a pore on her body, a follicle on her scalp or a thread in her clothing that wasn't filthy, she would be very surprised. She could have competed with Clodagh for the title of 'Mud Girl.'

"You're hired. Report to the maintenance tent within the compound."

And with that, she followed the crowd to where young Devent was extolling the virtues of the wonderful event. The organizers ought actually to be paying him for advertising it.

Devent's new song was about the food he expected to find at the Fair. She chimed in with some of the treats she had enjoyed early in her life before she attended and was expelled from so many boarding schools.

"Whole beeves stuffed with hogs stuffed with luscious waterfowl stuffed with delicate fish!" Devent dreamed aloud.

"Candy floss on a paper cone, fried pastry dusted with sugar and cinnamon, cookies and candies, mutton sausage and tubers, winkles in the shell and fresh salted goobers..."

The dragons who had wings enthusiastically clapped them over their backs while those without stamped their feet until the very earth seemed to rumble beneath them.

Smelt could not, of course, show such a human expression as a smile, but Verity fancied she could see pleasure and approval on his saurian countenance.

She thought to bed down beside her dragon friends, but her new employers had other ideas.

"You can sleep when this is over," the man who was apparently her supervisor said. "You walk around the park picking up dragon crap. The grounds should be clean and inviting for opening day."

She yawned and nodded. She wanted to sleep, but this was an excellent opportunity to look around and see what this was truly about, because she knew the Hiring Fair excuse, while actually quite a good idea, was not the real reason for the Fair and its gathering of dragons.

Since the main site of the Fair had not yet opened, she had only the dragon meadow to clear of dung, which steamed in the chill of the night. Devent and Smelt accompanied her on her rounds, turning the piles into vapor with economical puffs of fiery breath.

It wasn't magic. It was a characteristic of beasts meant to be extremely large, able to fly and breathe fire. In their natural state the gas expelled from digestion was used as fuel for the fire, but once it was expelled as waste, a dragon could simply ignite it to clean a lair or hide a trail. Well, hide it if the pursuer was a near-sighted knight who might not notice a small amount of singed foliage once in awhile. She had learned this while living in the lair of the Dragon Vitia and her get. It seemed the dragons born and bred for industrial work had not had a chance to learn the basics of their species' hygiene.

Although the human side of the Fairgrounds bloomed with pavilions and bristled with stalls, the dragon side had fewer structures save for a long eastern wall between the Fairgrounds and the foothills. As it was well constructed of stone, she guessed it might have been there before the Fair was thought of, a relic of some old farmstead. Mostly the dragon side seemed to feature dozing dragons, weary from the long trip to the Fair, but not yet in natural hibernation mode. The working dragons had been trained into regular sleep periods like the humans, and she wondered how much of that conditioning held now that they had been unemployed for some time.

As she rolled her wheelbarrow and Devent hissed, flaming the smelly piles of poop into nothingness, up ahead of them two fires hardly bigger than candles flickered in the darkness, moving up and down, side to side, over and under one another.

"Babies," she told her companions. "Someone has brought her babies."

"Perhaps I could sing them a lullaby?" Devent suggested.

Smelt grunted. "Haven't seen any babies since you, laddie, were born one mornin' in the drizzling rain."

Verity smiled, "I spent most of last year raising a couple of sparks like that in their mother's cave while she hibernated. She had already toilet trained them, fortunately. I taught them some glass working skills to help them govern their flames. Maybe I could teach these young ones, too, if their mother allows? It would give them a marketable skill, especially if fairs like this catch on. Only problem would be—hmm, where to find some good bead making material? Vitia's cave had some magically infused crystal formations on the walls. But here on the grounds—"

Smelt snorted. "There's crystal in caves hereabouts, in the hills beyond yon wall. I could fetch you some for the young ones to learn with, if you like."

"Excellent!" Devent cried. Verity put her finger to her lips and he lowered his voice and looked around to see if his loudness had caused any damage. In the mines it might lead to a cave-in, but they were now in open meadows. In a much-moderated tone he said, "We can all have another adventure!"

"Nay, laddie," Smelt told his friend. "You need to stay here and sing your songs, start that career of yours. It seems like a good place for that."

"I agree," Verity said, when Devent looked disappointed. "I may have need of your skills soon. I need time here to poke around, to look into who is behind this lovely Fair and what they really mean to accomplish with it."

"I can go alone, lad," Smelt said. "I once knew these hills better than I know the color of steel at any given heat. My wings have been healing as we've traveled, and I can fly a bit now. I fancy I can sail over yon wall with no problem and be back by tomorrow night at the latest so her can start schoolin' the young'uns."

Earlier in the evening they had found the feast laid out for the dragon guests in front of a low stone building, so all had enjoyed helpings of fresh meat. Verity made do with a chicken pasty she'd bought from a food cart set up by some enterprising soul. It had cost her three coppers, but she hadn't eaten for some time and even the cold pie stuffed with what tasted like stringy old rooster was worth it.

Smelt soon blended with the night. As she and Devent continued cleaning, she realized that the erratic little fires no longer burned where they had been before. In fact, though she could make out a depression in the ground where the mother dragon had lain, neither she nor her young were there any longer.

"I was too loud," Devent said remorsefully. "I scared them away."

"I just got a twinge when you said that," Verity told him. "So it's not true."

"Where did they go?" Devent asked.

"I don't know," Verity said. "So now it's one of the things we need to learn about this event."

The next morning the dragons wakened to a chime calling them to feed again before lining up for the Hiring Fair. While Devent did that, Verity took the opportunity to visit the human side of the grounds.

Even in the drowsy morning, the Fair had life as people in various bits of garb probably gleaned from their grandparents' attics and storage chests swaggered about attempting to pose and speak as they imagined people might have done in 'ye olde tymes'.

She heard a familiar clacking and peered under the awning of one booth to see Mistress Marsha at her sewing machine, pedaling away, stitching a white garment. A rack of similar gowns hung from one of the walls of the booth. Marsha was absorbed in her sewing and did not look up until Verity stood beside her and said, loudly enough to be heard over the sewing machine. "It's good to see you here," Verity said. "Please don't give me away. I'm incognito. Not a majesty or anything. In fact, I'm a humble groundskeeper and sweeper of dragon dung, or so the organizers think."

"Yes," Marsha said, her foot releasing the pedal. "So I can smell."

"Who else is here? Have you seen anyone you know from the city? Did Toby help organize this? Do you know where he and Taz are?"

"I've seen them flying from time to time, but I wasn't paying attention really."

"Why are you making only white dresses today?"

"Oh, these are damsel dresses. All of the girls are wanting them for one of the activities advertised, the game of

Damsels and Dragons. When damsels were once sacrificed to dragons, they seemed to always be wearing a flowing white gown that was impractical in almost every way, with a lot of flowers woven into their hair, and bare feet."

"I'm quite sure the dragons would have preferred a side of beef," Verity said. "So many maidens are underweight. They can't compete with a nice elk or moose."

"I'm sure you're right. I think the white dresses are emblematic of the image the maidens are supposed to present. Pure and virginal and all that sort of thing."

"I hope the fabric is inexpensive, anyway," Verity said.

"It is because it's not supposed to matter. I don't even bother with pockets or any sort of styling on a lot of these. They're just supposed to burn up when the girl dies."

"Except she won't, of course," Verity said. "Die, I mean."

"Of course not. It's just for show. A tableau depicting an era in dragon lore."

"That hardly seems helpful to bring up when the dragons are trying to better themselves. I'd think the aim would be to present them in a more trustworthy and benign light."

"You'd think. I suppose the organizers feel that presenting them as one-time powerful monsters that could devour women in one bite unless deterred by some man in armor is more appealing to the general public."

Verity sighed. "If you see Toby, please tell him I'm looking for him."

"Of course," said Mistress Marsha, her foot poised above the pedal.

Verity didn't notice until she began walking away that one of the beads on her necklace was jigging against her skin, clicking on the adjacent beads. She'd been around Mistress Marsha several times since she sorted the beads, but she had never noticed their reaction to Marsha. She hadn't noticed this time until she stepped away from the stall. The clatter of the sewing machine masked the bead's noise. She turned around and returned to the stall. Mistress Marsha looked up with a smile that was a little hollow. "Yes?"

"I was wondering if you had any magical ancestry... wizards or witches, that sort of people in your family tree?"

"Oh yes, as a matter of fact, since you mention it. My great-great-grandmother Gladys was a fairly well-known

Stitch Witch. Invisible cloaks were a specialty of hers. Seven League dance slippers, bottomless reticules in a wide variety of stylish shapes, colors, and currencies. My mother had no use for magic, but says it skipped a generation and came to me instead, along with the family business. I just make beautiful dresses, but they are enchanting if I do say so myself. Fancy you bringing that up!"

"I have something for you," Verity said, untying her necklace and slipping off beads until she came to the active one.

"Oh no, not one of your special beads! I couldn't really, Verity. Those things everyone thought were so magical don't even work! They're nothing but vintage clothing with some entertaining stories attached."

"So, do you still have some of them?"

"Only one old cloak. I use it to wrap some of my new things in, to keep the rain and dirt out of them."

"I'd like to see it, if you don't mind. But please do accept the bead. It's not my idea, you know. It's the magic in the beads."

Mistress Marsha gave her a slightly skeptical look and a somewhat put-upon sigh but duly dug through her things and finally unwrapped a bundle of white fabric and pressed the dingy old cloak in which it was wrapped into Verity's hands.

Verity shook it out and wrapped it around herself.

"My word," Mistress Marsha said. "It's never done that before! If it had, I'd never have been able to find anything I wrapped in it."

"Mmm," Verity said, looking down at herself and seeing that she did not, in fact, actually appear to be there. "This could come in very handy. Do you suppose I might borrow it?"

"Well, yes, certainly. Be my guest."

"Thanks," Verity said and started to add something about when she would return it, except she didn't know yet. "I'll need something to wrap it in that's not invisible, so I can find it again."

"That's easy enough," Mistress Marsha said. "Take one of the damsel dresses. I think this one is large enough for someone your height."

"It might make a nice nightdress. It's not anything like what I wore when I was being sacrificed to the Dragon Vitia. Thank goodness I had on heavier clothing and a stout coat and boots when that happened, or I'd never have survived winter in the lair."

"Shhh," Marsha said, pretending to whisper. "It's the popular conception of what a dragon's damsel ought to wear. Mustn't disappoint the punters, as Captain Lewis might say. If you wear it with nothing else, it's nearly transparent and I suppose that's the attraction. Other than that it is wildly impractical and would make it very difficult for anyone wearing it to hide from the dragon in question, if one had slipped whatever bonds or restraints were involved."

"Thanks again," Verity told her, and tucking the damsel dress-wrapped cloak of invisibility beneath her arm, set off to continue observing the morning's activity.

Almost as if mentioning Captain Lewis had invoked her, she appeared, dressed in her best, dandified piratical gear, surrounded by her shipmates and a number of the ladies from Aunt Erotica's, dressed in their most festive work clothes. It would take more than a flimsy white dress to make many of them appear pure, but they seemed to be in a playful mood. Verity had no doubt some attendees would be glad to see them.

The crew carried the poles and canvas for two structures, a stage with sails in the background for the cabaret artists of the *Belle's Shell*, and a pavilion for the ladies. It started as a plain item in natural hempen color but before the gates to the grounds open, it was swagged with colorful veils and scarves tied with tasseled ropes.

Verity started in that direction but stopped when she saw the pottery display Clodagh had erected, with Kiln concealed behind the back panel of the stall and stacks of plates, cups and bowls glazed with red and bright blue advertising themselves beneath the front awning. Clodagh was bent over a table, hand forming snakes of clay and coiling them into the shapes of vessels she quickly patted and smoothed into shapes of more cups, bowls, plates, pitchers and vases before ducking behind the curtain long enough to take them to Kiln.

The golem girl was intent on her work and Verity didn't interrupt her.

A murmur rapidly building to a crowd-generated cacophony broke into the relative silence of the morning, as a river of people flooded in. The gates had opened, and the Fair had begun.

The foremost feature was supposed to be the Hiring Fair, she understood, where dragons would be offered the kind of food they required now that they had been released from their former employment. At the top of the grounds, the area backed by the mountains, a long row of booths had been erected. The area in front of it was a precisely laid out charred field, free of trees or structures. Verity counted twenty dragons waiting to be summoned.

She saw a few she recognized from the streets and roofs of Queenston.

"You, there, lad," a male voice called from behind her. "You're the one who speaks dragon?"

"Aye, sir," Verity said, deepening her voice just a little. Her head throbbed a bit from not correcting the man's assumption that she was a boy. The commanding voice was familiar and when she got a look at him, she realized her was one of Malady's uncles on the council. She hoped she could learn more about what this Fair was for before Malady arrived. Verity had no illusions about being able to fool her old school 'friend.'

The councilman handed her a clipboard such as she'd seen in some of her classes. "Here. For each applicant, get his name, previous employment, and desired future occupation. Find out how much each of them can eat and if they were happy at their former job. Then escort them to the employers waiting to hire them."

"Aye, sir," she said again, but she missed Toby and Taz. They were the ones who should be doing the translating. They had a much better idea about the problems dragons had than she did. But she saw neither dragon nor wrangler in the crowd, or among the applicants. Approaching the stagecoach-sized beast at the head of the line, she said, "Erm. Name?"

"Petunia," the beast replied. Her eyes were the size of Verity's boot prints. She was less like an actual petunia than like an old rose in coloring.

"That's a pretty name. What work did you do before, Petunia?"

"I heated the glass houses where out of season plants were grown."

"Did you like it?"

Petunia blew sparks through her nose. "I'd have preferred something that gave me more creative leeway, if you must know. But—say, how did you come to speak Dragonish? Your accent is not bad, for a human."

"I worked for a dragon one winter, doing childcare," she said.

"You, a human, worked for a dragon? What did she pay you?"

"My life."

"That was a good price, but I didn't know it ever worked that way."

"Yes, that and some beads I helped her twin babies make."

"Bead making. I might like to try that myself."

From a table with a pennant declaring it to be 'Dragon Resources,' someone beckoned her, calling out, "You there, the job creators are waiting. Bring the beast over and let's see what it's suited for."

Verity introduced Petunia. A rather severe looking woman sat in the first booth. "She's quite a large beast. It would be expensive to feed her. What can she do?"

"She says she provided the heat for a huge glass house in the city where many of the vegetables and flowers are grown for the markets."

"All we need is someone to create fire to drive our engines," the lady said. "We make gardening tools. Next."

"What sort of appetite does she have?" the next potential employer asked.

"That would be hard to say, wouldn't it, sir, when she's only been fed kibble until recently?"

"Well, we only are prepared to pay in chickens."

"Do you like chickens, Petunia?" Verity asked.

"I don't know. Do they taste like Kibble?"

Verity shrugged.

"I'll try it," Petunia said, looking as shy as a dragon's face could look. "And—yes, I would like the job—but for part of my pay I want someone to show me how the tools are used so I can start my own garden."

"That certainly sounds fair to me," Verity said, half to the dragon and half to the people conducting the interview.

"What?" the interviewers asked.

"Well, she wants to grow food and flowers, too," Verity said. "That might help with the expense of feeding her if she grew some food. Don't you think?"

"That might figure into the bargain, especially if she is actually willing to eat some of what she grows. I've never heard of a vegetarian dragon before though."

"Kibble is made from grains..." Verity began.

The man she thought of as the dragon foreman took her arm and led her away from Petunia while another man led the horticulturally inclined beast in the opposite direction. "Wait, did she get the job?" Verity asked.

"That's not your concern," he told her. "You have more translating to do before you clean the grounds this evening."

She translated for ten more interviews. Petunia was one of the cleverest of the applicants. Many of the dragons were either much dimmer or more damaged by their former working conditions than she was and had no idea what they wanted to do beyond 'get food' and 'make fire.' She wondered if they would be more forthcoming for Toby with Taz to help him. They might communicate more openly with another dragon.

She was going to suggest it to the foreman—surely Toby would be one of the organizers of an event like this. She couldn't imagine that it could have been produced without his help.

Before she mucked the grounds that night, she tried to find him. Campfires blossomed in front of the vendor stalls and in the campgrounds, and in both areas, new pavilions and stalls continued being erected, which seemed timely since the skies at dusk boiled with navy blue and steel gray clouds. Anyone not under canvas when the rains began would be drenched.

Some of the people frantically raising poles, pounding stakes and lashing down ropes looked familiar, although she couldn't recall where she'd seen particular individuals before. From the look of them though, they seemed to be Gypsies, and this was the sort of enterprise, because of the transitory nature of the work, where she thought one might expect to find them. Could they be her mother's people? Probably.

She was starting to ask when two men dragged out a pair of hefty wooden boxes. Casimir climbed onto one, accompanied by none other than Devent.

The dragon saw her. Her beads began to rattle and the ghost cats, who had been missing since they appeared in Mistress Marsha's stall earlier in the morning, materialized, twining around Casimir's legs.

Since Verity had been traveling with the bard for several days without so much as a click from the beads, she considered their timing in announcing their selection in the wizard's legacy lottery somewhat whimsical. Nevertheless, it seemed that Devent's human tutor was chosen, if somewhat belatedly. Perhaps the beads inventoried the surrounding populace for possible matches before choosing the most likely candidates?

Casimir breathed experimental tootles on his flute and Devent performed some rather terrifying vocal warmup exercises.

The ghost cats twined around the minstrel's feet. One sat on his head, causing his flat cap to slip sideways, while a number of others perched on the dragon's head and back.

Devent lashed his tail and one particularly fearless ghost cat clung to it, allowing itself to be whipped back and forth. If cats could have said 'Whee!' it would have.

"May I have a word, Casimir?" she asked, interrupting him as he tuned his instrument. "I have it on good authority that you are from one of Argonia's old magical families."

Devent grumbled, glowing slightly in the dental area, impatient at the interruption of his informal debut.

"I'm sorry," she apologized to the dragon. "It really is important. I think."

She fumbled with her necklace and the beads bounced into the dusty path, fortunately free of dragon dung, thanks to her own efforts.

The minstrel replaced his flute in its case and hopped down to help her herd beads and shells.

The one she had been about to pass on to him was not difficult to locate but it was tricky to capture. It kept jumping up and down, rolling over to turn somersaults and she thought, squeaking. "Hmm," she said. "Never knew one to do that before."

Casimir walked up to it, and it rolled to him and stopped at his toe, inanimate once more as he stooped to pick it up.

"None of them have done that before either," she said. "Did you realize you had a magical ancestor who was killed at the end of the Great War?"

He turned it over with his forefinger, rolling it in his palm. "No, I don't believe I did. Perhaps—" he looked up and met her eyes, "Perhaps a descendant?"

"I don't..."

"There are a few things I should probably explain to you," he said, and popped the bead in his waistcoat watch pocket. "Later."

He stepped back up on the box-stage, leaving her to gather the rest of the beads.

She picked them up, pleased at how few were left.

Devent stopped his impatient tail twitching and said, "Feel free to join us if you like."

"Thanks, but I must get to work now. Dung to shovel since my assistant has found better things to do."

"I'm sure Auld Smelt will help you," Devent said. "If you happen to see that pretty pinkish-mauve hothouse dragon Petunia, would you let her know I have composed an air in her honor?"

"I just met her today," Verity said. "She seemed lovely."

Devent sighed sparks.

She returned to what she thought of as the 'broom tent' where the tools and wheelbarrows were stored. Also brooms. According to the seashell archives she had read regarding her family, some of her ancestresses knew how to use such implements for transportation. She tried to imagine that. Sounded uncomfortable and precarious.

She wheeled her barrow over to the dragon side of the Fairgrounds. There were mountains of dung to shovel unless she could find Smelt. Perhaps Petunia would help for a little while, before or after the florally-inclined dragon saw Devent.

However, after searching half of the dragon encampment, she failed to find Petunia, and was starting to despair. It began to look as if she might actually have to shovel the piles and piles of fewmets.

A bolt of flame shot past her, incinerating the nearest dung heap, and Smelt fell in beside her. She drove the wheelbarrow for show and told the old beast about her activities that day.

"That's all well for the young ones who've never known another life, Lady, but I have, and I'm done working for men.

"My hoard's been pillaged so there goes my retirement, but I meant to retire. I reckon as soon as the snow flies I'll crawl back into my cave and sleep on that pile of rusty armor that was all the looters left me. Maybe when I wake again, the world will have changed for the better."

He sizzled another pile. She said, "Devent and Casimir are singing over on the human side of things. Do you want to go see them?"

Smelt snorted ashes and sparks, which she guessed passed for a chuckle. "I can hear them from here, can't you?"

She listened closely and realized she'd been hearing them the entire time, the minstrel's lute and voice enveloped by the young dragon's voice, underlying the chatter and the slide of belly scales through the dirt while dragons grumbled.

"Devent seems to have struck up a friendship with a female named Petunia. Have you seen her?"

"Not lately. I met her with the lad this morning after we helped you on your rounds, but I haven't seen her since then."

"She was led away after the interview, so I imagined she got the job. Perhaps she went back to Queenston with her new employer?"

"Doubt it," Smelt said. "There's been no southbound train today."

Of course the old fellow was right. The new employers and dragon employees might have found some other way to return to the city, but what? Especially with a dragon in tow, horseback would have been awkward.

She did not see Petunia, or the mother and young they'd glimpsed the night before, as they continued their rounds on the dragon side.

Back on the human side, the music changed to one of the tunes Verity recognized from the Changelings Cabaret.

A crowd gathered in front of the stage to hear the crew of the *Belle's Shell*, now in their alternate personas, performing one of their saucier numbers with Madame Louisa, or Captain Lewis, taking center stage. With no bar to tend, Legs was now playing several stacked keyboards at once in a complicated contraption of an instrument.

Verity saw one of the women from Aunt Erotica's strike up an acquaintance with a man wearing the distinctive blue waistcoat with the dragon over the left breast she now recognized as a uniform sported by the Fair's organizers. After a brief business discussion, the woman pulled him into the pavilion assembled earlier in the day to house the women's commercial activities.

The Fairgoers, about to retire for the evening, and the vendors, about to settle down, instead crowded around the stage or began dancing in front of it.

The minstrel and the dragon had surrendered the stage and now Casimir executed a simple box-style dance step, encouraging Devent to imitate him. The dragon, elated by the music and the approval of the crowd, gleefully did so.

Devent's attempt at dancing was a bit much for Smelt, who puffed tiny candle-size flames of disgust.

"They're making a fool of the lad," he said. "Dragons don't do such tricks."

"Dragons have done a lot of things they didn't used to do," Verity said. "He's enjoying himself."

"It ain't becomin'," Smelt grumbled.

Verity shrugged and wheeled her barrow up the path away from the crowd.

Smelt stalked after her, still grumbling ashes and sulfur.

They finished patrolling the most heavily travelled byways of the Fair when a tall man emerged from beyond the barrier wall in the back, carrying a large package in his arms.

Verity stepped aside to let the man pass and Smelt gave way a little. By the light glowing around his muzzle, Verity saw that the package had rust colored spots on its butcher-paper wrappings.

Its odor was strong and familiar. She had smelled it among the decapitated dragon corpses scattered across the fields beside the railroad tracks.

Now she followed the track that looped around the upper camp, and by moonlight saw a trail that was little more than a deer path running back to the wall. Part of the barrier was recently erected brick and mortar, built onto an old stacked stone fence. The path led to a gate in the fence, well concealed behind the edifice at the back of the human section of the Fair.

Behind the fence was what seemed to be the ruins of an old farmstead, shored up and hastily repaired. Lights shown within it and three men waited on the dilapidated porch for entrance. This was where the smell came from—blood, decay, and odors she recognized from the chemistry labs in her various schools—chiefly formaldehyde, a preservative, acetone, and others she could not identify. People inside the building made no attempt to moderate their voices so she could hear every word.

The proprietor was saying, "You did pre-order, didn't you?"

"No," the customer replied. "Was that necessary?"

"Stock is limited to supply on hand, and the items were extremely hard to come by." The proprietor told him. "Only fifty specimens were suitably intact for preservation."

"But I must have one! It will look smashing in my den. I have just the place for it, to balance out the unicorn head and the griffin."

"Unicorn head?" the proprietor asked sharply. "Where did you get that? Isn't it illegal to have one of those?"

"I inherited it from an ancestor. I'm sure it died of natural causes. The horn is still in situ. You know if it had been hunted that would have been the first thing to go."

One of the men on the porch grunted, sounding remarkably like Smelt except no sparks and ashes came out of his mouth. "You can make wager on that!" he answered the customer's remark, although that person wouldn't hear his. His two companions did though.

"Hunters know how to make the best use of their kills," said another of the men on the porch.

The third occupant of the porch said, "I really want one of those dragon trophies. It would look very smart over our leather Chesterfield sofa. I'd like to have it re-covered in dragon hide. Wouldn't that be splendid? But I doubt the authorities would allow it."

The customer who had been inside left, the proprietor following him to the door. Overhearing the remarks this time, he said to the man with the sofa, "Now, now, cheer up, friend, I wouldn't be too sure about what's allowed and what's not. If you miss the heads currently available, there'll be a fresh crop once the real fun begins."

What real fun would that be? Verity considered asking but had a feeling this particular sale was by invitation only and her presence would be unappreciated.

She crept away, pushing the wheelbarrow and carrying her broom. Most people wouldn't know she had not been asked to clean up in this area, so her equipment was her camouflage. If that didn't work out, there was always the cloak of invisibility, although it only covered her to her knees. Maybe when they had a bit more time, Madame Marsha could let the hem out.

She continued on the path away from the wall and beyond the lights from the booth. The path was lit from lamps placed at intervals just close enough to keep walkers from stumbling in the dark. It had been cut through tall shrubbery and weeds. Wide wild eyes blinked out at her from both sides.

A ruined farmhouse with a barn and smaller outbuildings nestled into a low ridge of foothills and it too was lit, but appeared to be unoccupied. The house was patched with wooden planks and affixed to them all across the front were posters. Above the door, a painted wooden pub sign swung. 'Dragon's Lair' said the sign. 'Hoard Hunt Treasure Quest Begins Here,' said one of the posters. 'Damsels and Dragons Battle to the Death Demo,' said another, 'Dueling Dragons Demo,' said a third. Then, on the door itself, a plastered poster gave her the chills. 'Book Your Personal Hunt Here: Stalking the Wild Wyrm!' Below in smaller letters it said, 'Must be twenty-one to apply. Swords, Spears and Armor available to rent or bring your own ancestral kit! For Booking and Prices Inquire Within,' was written in elegant script above the door handle.

Whatever the real purpose of this event was, it was no Hiring Fair! The path led onward, but now unlit, to the barn. She picked up one of the lamps from the ones leading to the ticket office and set it in her wheelbarrow, then trundled on.

On the Barn door was painted:

'Dragon Aptitude Tests. Line Forms Here,' and a downward pointing arrow indicated that the 'applicant' had arrived. She ought to have known something was wrong with this setup. If it was really a Hiring Fair, it ought to have been in Queenston, where both dragons and employers were located, but it had been arranged to look like a holiday event.

The Barn was locked with a heavy padlock. She was about to move on when she saw smoke curling from under the door.

Chapter 18: Malady in Chains!

At least the floor had stopped moving, but Malady was still not sure what hit her or how she came to be in a dank and chilly room wearing a simple but chic white gown and no jewels at all. She was pretty sure she was no longer in the palace and also pretty sure her uncles were behind her predicament, whatever it might specifically be. Any illusions she might have had about family loyalty were finally totally shattered. Apparently, her history instructors at Our Lady of Perpetual Locomotion had not been making up all of those tales of brother killing brother to acquire a throne.

Actually, she was not entirely on the floor—just her lower legs and heels. The rest of her was chained by the waist to a stone wall.

How was it that she had gone her entire life without seeing the inside of a cave and in the space of—what? —a week? —had been imprisoned in two of them? At least, she didn't think this cave was the one in the castle. Durance's hoard, also known as the royal treasury, had contained rich fur-lined, jewel-embellished robes to slip into for warmth. This cave was cold and the white shift thing she wore showed the damp and dirt and if she didn't get away from here and into something warmer soon, she'd catch her death.

The place was dark as a dungeon—darker really. She had seen the dungeon and there was at least enough light for the guards to make sure the prisoners were all accounted for as well as the rather horrible fire with the irons and torture implements heating in it and the teapot on the rack across the top of the firepit.

When she paused her own sobbing, choking, coughing and sniffling, she became aware of others doing the same. Also, there were smells. Human smells like gas and urine and unwashed bits, but also perfumes of different types.

"Hello? Who's there? Is anyone else less constrained than by a chain to the wall?"

"I have leg ironth," a little-girl voice lisped.

"Shackles," another voice said.

When she considered, Malady really didn't know what to do with the information. She wasn't really interested in freeing the others so much as finding a way to help herself.

"You sound small," she told the lisper. "Can't you pull your foot out?"

"I already scraped a sore on it."

"Don't be such a coward. I've heard of animals that chew off their feet to get out of a trap. Show a little back-bone!"

A huskier voice said, "If you think that's the thing to do, sweetie, then chew off your own foot."

"That would be useless," Malady replied, irked at the suggestion. "I'm not shackled by my feet, you bossy cow. I believe I mentioned previously that my waist is chained to the wall."

Malady felt that both of the other women had insufficient respect for her leadership position.

The husky voiced woman continued, "Doesn't matter anyway, I suppose. The dragons will roast us with or without chains."

"What are you talking about?" Malady asked.

"Didn't you read the signage on the way in, dearie? In the game of Damsels and Dragons, guess who we get to be? Unless there are some unadvertised gallant knights equipped with bucket brigades of squires to save us, I fear chains will be the least of our worries."

"I have no idea what you're talking about. They wouldn't dare. There are laws against that sort of thing."

"It was right there on the building. They'd drugged me with a little somethin', but I could still read the poster. That whole Hiring Fair thing is just a cover for the real entertainment—dragon/damsel snuff shows and other fatal sports involving slithery things. I don't suppose you brought a hacksaw with you did you, sweetie?"

"Of course not. And there are no pockets in these stupid white gowns. Anyway, we're more likely to die of pneumonia than because of dragons. I have it on very good authority that they haven't eaten anybody for years and years."

Dragons and Dastardly Deeds

"So how do you want to present this? Damsels and dragons first—or the treasure hunt?"

"Damsels and dragons. And not one at a time as we were talking about earlier. All of the girls and the biggest, hungriest dragons so there'll be blood and girly bits all over the arena. That should motivate the hunters to go after the savage beasts with gusto."

"So—what? Do we wait until the tourists are cleared out and only the serious investors remain, the ones who will kill off the excess beasts and pay handsomely for it, while throwing such a fright into the others that they'll do as they're bloody well told and accept that they are the lower order of beasts and can expect no say in the judgement of men about their role in our society?"

"Something like that. I say we feed Malady to them right away. That will solve an additional problem and make the punters hate the dragons for good. But we wait for night at any rate. The flames make a more dramatic display that way."

"Makes the color of the blood harder to see though," another uncle said in a tone of mild disagreement.

His relatives gave him an annoyed look and, lest he be considered problematical, he quickly added, "But I suppose it will look quite stunningly scarlet in the flare of dragon flame, what?"

"An amazing spectacle indeed."

"Now then, how about the hoards? Not all the dragons will have them, of course."

"That's what will make it such a lovely treasure hunt. The treasure seekers will help us locate the real loot hoarded by the elder dragons—the rest of the hoards will contain basically junk."

Beneath the floor of stone flags over solid stone, a wise old wyrm, made testy by the long trip through secret tunnels leading from the city, listened and hissed quietly, barely restraining his lashing tail. He had warned the princess of the treachery of her kin, although, truly, perfidiousness toward princesses was to be expected. But that these people sought to subdue dragonkind once more, and loot their lairs of treasure, that could not be tolerated. Durance the

Vile had spent centuries guarding dungeons, and he knew much of what occurred there. He would make sure these men lived almost as long as dragons and would grow to loathe every tormented breath he'd allow them to draw.

"What if the dragons don't attack the girls? They don't make dragons like they used to."

"Perhaps not, but currently, circumstances have made these dragons hungry ones who will no doubt eat anything with a blood supply. Once the audience sees what they do to the sacrifices, they won't care about anything but exterminating the bloodthirsty beasts."

There was a knock on the door of their erstwhile conference room. Eustus Siek undid all of the locks and bolts and admitted the Minister of Defense, his brother-in-law Brutus Hyde. "It was a mistake putting Malady in with the others," Brutus said.

"How's that?" Marquette asked.

"She's stirring them up, is why. That one is a born trouble-maker, or hadn't you noticed?"

"If you think it's a problem, take care of it," Marquette said.

"Already did. I put a bag over her head, gave her a little tap on the noggin, and threw her in the chamber across the corridor where we stashed that hag of a head doctor. She hadn't come to from the last time we knocked her out. So I swapped them out, including their chains, so Malady is all alone."

"The old woman might make worse trouble than she did."

"She'll have to regain consciousness first."

Undercover Underground

Durance, a level beneath the conspirators, was irritated that these nobodies thought they were experts on dragon dietary customs. It had been ages—back before the Great War, before the first king sat on the first throne of Argonia—since he had eaten humans. Gave him heartburn, as he recollected. Being a law-and-order-adjacent dragon, if not actually an authorized enforcement officer himself, Durance had developed an appetite for seeing miscreants suffer, especially those who threatened his hoard, other dragons, and the one princess he had taken a fancy to. Whether or not he chose to devour her was entirely his own business. It was the principle of the thing. They had no right to go around trying to feed her to just anyone.

Verity Invisible

Verity always carried the little pouch with her jeweler's tools inside. She wore it on a sash around her waist inside her shirt, so enterprising pickpockets wouldn't mistake it for money or jewels. It included a variety of metal rods with a differently shaped implement on each end, for cutting, shaping, and polishing stones and precious metal. In the past, she'd found dragon flame, carefully controlled, worked well for shaping glass into beads, and had added a few items helpful in that process as well. Now she needed something far less specialized. A lock pick. Her reputation as a troublemaker in the various schools she'd been expelled from had on three separate occasions caused groups of criminally troublesome girls (of good birth and bad inclinations) to befriend her. This lasted until her inability to lie became a liability such cliques could not tolerate, but meanwhile, she had learned a few simple skills that had served her far better than Home Economics.

Fortunately, lock picking required more from her fingers and ears and much less from her eyes—severely limited in the dim light emitted by the lanterns.

She returned the tools to her kit and hid the kit beneath her clothing, straightened the outer garments, pulled and propped open the barn door, then drove her wheelbarrow inside, carrying the lantern aloft, and pulled the door shut behind her.

The odor was a familiar one. Great stores of dragon kibble had until recently filled bins and barrels near where the dragons (once) worked and the aroma filled the barn, though it had to compete with the stench of smoke leaking around the trap.

Straw had once covered the floor, but had been flung aside so that now the trap door, outlined by the emissions, lay clearly visible among the farm implements and bales of containers of kibble.

She half expected the ring set into the door to be hot, but it was very cold. Taking it in her fingers, she yanked, fell back onto her rear and coughed convulsively while waving her arm in the air to clear the choking fumes of sulfur-laced smoke. Of one thing she could be certain. There were dragons down there.

Scooting back and standing, she wheeled her barrow between two stacks of kibble bags, while keeping the lantern, before returning to the hole in the floor. The smoke had cleared enough by then that by holding the lantern so it targeted the middle of the opening, she spotted the ladder leading down into the hole and lowered herself onto it.

The descent led to the floor of what seemed to be a root cellar of some sort, but another hole in the floor of that was cut into layers of ice. A permafrost cave perhaps?

It felt cold enough. Verity pulled the sleeves of her jacket down over her hands, since the circular iron staircase that descended in a wobbly fashion into the space below was rimed with frost and freezing cold.

At the top of the staircase, in spite of the darkness and smoke-filled air, she had the impression of vastness. The icy ceiling wept constantly.

Steam met smoke down here and she almost reached ground level before she could see the dragons clearly, although sporadically one or another would leap as high as it could go, only to be brought back to the floor again by something—chains. They jingled like carriage harnesses in a more civilized setting and clanked like dropping anchors.

Carefully, she stepped down onto the cavern floor.

Her beads and shells rattled against her neck until she thought she'd be strangled to death by her own jewelry. She reached up to loosen them. A dragon rushed her. Startled, she fell over backward. She wasn't afraid, she told herself. Just surprised. A reflexive reaction.

She tried to rise, but a clawed foot on her chest pushed her back down. A smoking countenance with holographic eyes loomed over her.

"Wrong one!" the dragon shrieked to the cavern at large, though fortunately it didn't shriek with fiery emphasis. "You're not the boy! Where's the boy? But—I know you. Lair girl, swamp girl, why are you here? Where is my boy? What did they do with him?"

229

"Taz!" Verity responded with all of the dragon-friendly goodwill she could muster. "I haven't seen Toby. I wondered where you and he were. Some of the other dragons mentioned you, but when I didn't see you, I thought you were just lost in the crowd."

"He went to meet other men. He did not return, but other men did. They motioned me to follow. I went with them, seeking him, but they brought me here. They tried to feed me the slave food, but I spewed it."

"Good." Verity said. "If we're to get out of here, can't have you all compliant." She started to ask how many others were there, but she didn't know if dragons understood counting. "May I get up please? Your foot?"

"Sorry," Taz said, and stepped back.

"Ahh, better."

Taz's foot remained shackled to a chain that tried to pull her back. She jerked at it again and again, and Verity feared she would injure herself. Pulling out her lock pick, she pointed to Taz's cruel bracelet. They could converse—barely—but with the noise and other distractions, Verity was skeptical about their capacity for involved interspecies communications.

"First the chain. Then we find Toby."

With so much hot dragon breath in the ice cave, the walls spouted waterfalls and a stream rapidly turning into a river flowed briskly down the middle of the cave.

The melting warmth did not extend to Verity's fingers, which felt like jointed icicles as she tried to pick the lock by touch alone. The fantasy she imagined of freeing the dragons with her criminal skills quickly fled.

Just as she at last heard the click of the lock—in about the time it would have taken her to saw through it with a hacksaw, human voices babbled in incoherent waves from some distant part of the cavern she couldn't see.

Dragon voices stilled, as did dragons, who crouched, waiting, nothing moving but the occasional tail tip and large glowing eyes.

The approaching men did not exactly move into the light—they carried it with them—a couple of the lanterns from the grounds. Raising the lanterns, they pushed someone forward—Toby!

Taz growled, but Verity hushed her, curious about what the men intended.

"You speak their bestial jabber, boy," one of the men growled to Toby. "Get them to tell you. Anyone who helps us find treasure will find life goes much better for him from now on."

Toby stumbled forward. He had a collar with a chain attached to his neck, the other end held by one of his captors, and was also encumbered by a ghost cat that had attached itself by all four sets of claws to his trouser leg. He might have been aware of its presence, but it wasn't like the incorporeal creature could be of any use.

The cat shone like a lantern, white and glowing. Then as if streetlights had been lit, other cats popped into view illuminating the dragons upon whose heads the phantom felines had chosen to perch.

The ghostly forms glowed without actually lighting the features of the dragons hosting them, but Verity's eyes had adjusted to the gloom to a degree and the lanterns were drawing closer.

Petunia had not gone off with her new floral employers as Verity had been led to believe. She was one dragon down from Taz, and her cat-chapeau-ed head hung low.

"Use your influence with these beasts to learn where their hoards are," one of the men behind Toby reiterated. "Or else you and your animal will be the first in the arena."

"Taz would never harm me," Toby said firmly.

"Perhaps not, but others among our fire-breathing guests might not be so particular. They're becoming hungrier all the time."

"Why are you doing this?" Toby asked. "They've not harmed anyone. They've come in good faith to try to find Fair employment and food. I can help you reason with them. There's no need to wage all of these barbaric contests."

"Of course, there's need," his captor replied. "They've given up their place in our society and have been made redundant. So many loose dragons are a threat to humans and most people are sensible enough to be properly afraid of them."

"Dragons were our allies even before your lot subdued them with the kibble and virtually enslaved them. They

231

have no interest in harming people, and they're perfectly willing to work for food and a fair wage."

"Surely you mean food as a fair wage? Producing fresh food for so many dragons will be expensive and hazardous."

"Their labor is very valuable, as present circumstances should show you. The city shuts down without them."

"Convincing one and all of the folly of using capricious beasts to do the work of men. In Frostingdung these days, they have alternative energy sources that don't require beasts to get their nourishment."

"I've heard about those. They say their fumes blacken the sky and you can smell the reek of them for miles around."

"People will get used to it. They'll adapt, as they always do when something has so many other advantages."

"Such as?"

"No dragons, for one thing."

Verity recognized this as a circular argument, but Toby just made a rude noise. But right around the time Toby's captor said the thing about 'adapting' knives stabbed into her lie-averse brain and kept stabbing until Toby asked, "And what, pray, is wrong with that? My best friend happens to be a dragon."

"Yes, we know. It will be waiting to eat you in the arena."

"Nonsense," Toby said stoutly.

"We gave these beasts the benefit of our scientific knowledge and the advantages of selective breeding and have they shown appreciation? No. The moment our chemical restraint is removed from their diet, they become aggressive and demanding."

"Just because they've been worked day and night for years on end?" Toby asked. "How ungrateful of them! You're too right they're aggressive and demanding and I'm amazed you've been foolish enough to hold them all in this room beneath your so-called Fairgrounds. You people are literally sitting on a powder keg. Without the powder, but to the same effect. I suggest you release each of these creatures with profound apologies, for all the good it will do you, and fresh food as compensation for their inconvenience. You lied to them to get them to come..."

"Well, no," said Lord Lickspittal, "Actually you lied to them. You and your pet dragon. I don't think you'll last very long if we offer you up as a between-meal snack."

"You misled us," Toby said.

"I grieve for our misunderstanding but never fear, I'll get over it."

"Shove him in there," said one of his companions, hidden in shadow. "Let them eat him."

"For free? When people have paid good money to watch? You've no head for business, brother. Remind me not to appoint you finance minister. If he's not going to talk to any of them, he's useless. Chain him up with the rest of the fodder."

Toby was jerked backwards.

Taz reared, roaring, and spouting flame, but her leg was not yet free of the chain and she fell back, still roaring, as the men manhandled her friend back the way he and his captors had come.

Taz cried piteously, unable to help him.

"Keep your scales on, Miss," Verity said. She pulled open the lock with her hands and gave Taz an encouraging pat on the flank.

Once freed, Taz flew to the far end of the cavern, where the men had brought Toby. Verity, half concealed by the invisibility cloak, was right behind her.

Malady in Solitary—Practically

She wanted her coat and her fur-lined cape, her mittens and muff, and her hat with the flaps that tied under her chin with a pretty ribbon. Instead, looking down, she saw she was still wearing the same sack-like garment rumpled with rope bindings to whatever was behind her. An actual sack was tangled in her silken golden curls.

"What happened? Did everybody else get a sack too?" she asked aloud. No one answered. "Little girl? Slutty-sounding woman? Where are you?" Again, no answer. What if they had taken the others already? Were they saving her for dessert or what?

Angry hissing broke in on her chaotic thoughts.

"Duplisssssssssity! Perfidy! Treachery!" a familiar voice said, making even the s-less words somehow part of the hiss.

"Who, me?" she asked, twisting to try to see where Durance the Vile was. No more sweet cajoling tone. The dungeon dragon sounded extremely cross, maybe even fatally so. Fatal for her, she feared. "Don't blame me! I didn't do anything."

The dragon didn't respond. Perhaps he hadn't been speaking to her at all? She heard the dragon without actual words being exchanged. But when another voice spoke from within the room, a human voice, it very definitely spoke human words, saying, "That's just it, sweetie. You never did anything."

"Uncle Marq? Is that you? It's very dark in here. Help me, please. All is forgiven!" she added, crossing her fingers behind her back. "Get a lantern and untie me. There's a dragon who is not best pleased with me, through no fault of my own, I swear."

"I can't imagine, dear," he said, making no move to grant any of her requests. "And I don't know really why I or any of your other guardians should care. Here you've been moaning about not having access to the treasury and the maid reported finding all sorts of what turned out to be historical treasures among your smallclothes."

"Well, yes, the dragon brought them. He wanted to make friends."

"And you didn't think to mention it?"

"I was going to but..."

"That won't do, Malady. It simply won't. We thought with you as regent we could implement our plans for development, but you've been worse than a naughty girl. You've been a useless girl."

"So what?" she asked, feeling more petulant than ever.

"I'm afraid there are no wealthy men with treasuries to loot of their own beating down the door, asking for your hand. Fortunately, we do have a surfeit of hungry dragons."

"I never realized what a horrid man you really are, Uncle."

"I never realized until recently what a whiny, insufferable, spoiled little bitch you are, Niece."

"Durance told me you said that sort of thing, but I thought you meant it affectionately." Durance hadn't put the uncles' poor opinions of her in such blunt words and cruel tones. She knew from the tone of his voice that there was nothing affectionate about Marquette's opinion. "At least I found the treasury, which is more than you lot were able to do."

"And that would be, where?"

"Wouldn't you like to know?"

"Oh yes, and I will find out," her formerly favorite uncle said, his expression hardening and darkening into one she had seen before, just not directed at her.

Malady realized she might have been a bit premature in her assumption that personal dragon, plus knowledge of treasure location, equaled power. Her head had been turned. She had always known how to get what she wanted, but her tactics had been subtler, more indirect, and when all else failed, sneaky.

"But of course, I could help you get it if I wanted to. He likes me. He'll probably be glad to show you where the treasure is if you release me." She kept herself from smiling at the thought that while Durance was showing the uncles where the treasure was, he might dispatch them. That would be good. Obviously though they were family, the uncles had never been that fond of her and after the little incident with the dungeon, she would have no regrets about their deaths either. She might actually look quite lovely in black. She wondered briefly where her therapist had gone. Malady was, after all, experiencing considerable trauma and alienation and lots of other things therapists were concerned about.

Dear Uncle Marq had to cut through her thoughts. "I wonder if he'd like you better with sugar and spice and everything nice, or barbecue sauce?"

Chapter 19: Carnival Hall (Devent)

Devent's singing, sad to say, had thus far been more appreciated by his fellow dragons and true musicians like Casimir than by the average Fairgoer. Or so he began to think as the night wore on and his audience dwindled, until no more dragons were listening, and only a few of the ladies from the 'hotel' tent next to the stage remained.

His spirits picked up a bit as two men wearing the special dragon-emblazoned waistcoats joined the three ladies lounging lasciviously (had Devent realized that's what their poses suggested) nearby. But as his tale of dragon derring-do drew to a close, the men approached Casimir and said something to him that made the bard's face light with joy.

"Devent, I told you your chance would come!" the dragon's mentor cried. "You've been discovered! These gentlemen are here to offer you a gig at Carnival Hall. Most prestigious, my friend. Most prestigious indeed! Besides, of course, there's real pay involved, not just tips." Tips had been proffered during the evening, but they consisted mostly of rodents, which were tasty enough, but not very filling.

"Er, where is Carnival Hall, exactly?" Devent asked.

"You'll see. It's not far," one of the vested men replied.

"I must practice then," he said and began running up and down his scales. In his case he had actual scales to remind him of the notes. Casimir was pleased for him, though baffled about how the dragon, who had performed in public for the first time only that night, had spread his fame so quickly as to receive such an invitation.

Their guides led them to the back of the Fairgrounds, beyond the walls, to what appeared to be a maintenance area. Devent sang so joyously that from his hidden place lurking among the brush and boulders beyond the wall,

Auld Smelt heard and followed the guides, Casimir and Devent into a hole in the hillside.

Smelt wondered how far this particular cave went, for he knew better than the men or even the younger dragons how interconnected the labyrinthine system of tunnels, caves, caverns, and mineshafts were.

More and more of Argonia's inner geography was coming back to him since his brief slumber in the bowels of the castle that once harbored his hoard. Forgotten passages invaded his dreams and with the dreams came the lore of the land he had learned long before the Great War. Songs returned to him, songs whose choruses he had once imparted to a frightened fledgling who now sang them full-throated, accompanied by instruments played by a human!

The song penetrated the interwoven underworld realm, under streams and through hills, startling captives both dragon and human and amazing one particular ancient wyrm a long way from the dungeon he guarded.

The Lady in the Knowe

The song resonated through the subterranean corridors until it reached the ears of the Lady in the Knowe.

From the Knowes, the portals to all that had happened, was currently happening or would happen in Argonia, the renegade princess, Romany, also known as the Rani, the Lady of the Knowe, sought to correct the course of events. She had the aid of the Argonian Gypsies among whom she'd been raised. Survivors, they were strong enough and wily enough to escape notice as they came and went from one mission to the next.

Time was extremely slippery and the history ahead of where and when she happened to be at any moment was written in invisible ink, the whens she had occupied at other times clouded and dream like. It was just as well. It kept her from being omnipotent and she really didn't want any more responsibility than she already had.

Such reluctance seemed to run in the family since her daughter had buggered off from being a queen before her bottom ever had warmed a throne.

The young dragon Devent actually held more promise as a leader than her daughter. He had a beautiful voice, if one liked dragon voices, as she did, and thanks to her glamor, he had the power to persuade others of his kind.

She knew where to find him, not because she knew everything, but because advertising for the Dragon Hiring Fair had been extensive, even pervasive. Devent's song told her the time had come to investigate.

The Lady had no sooner vacated the Knowe near the old dragon's lair and appeared in one interconnected with the caves and tunnels used by the Fair organizers, when someone else appeared in the Knowe she'd just left.

Scratching his red furred chin with his slender hind foot, the family lawyer wondered where Romany had taken herself off to this time.

An Affinity for Dragons

Verity dodged bursts of frustrated flame from the captive dragons as she ran a gauntlet between them and Taz. Twice she had to smack out flames that singed the invisibility cloak. The lantern clearly showed holes that from the outside would no doubt show patches of herself seemingly bobbing around in mid-air.

That presented another problem, if and when she encountered other people. A seemingly disembodied lantern floating through the air with a pair of worn boots walking beside it rather negated the effect of the invisibility cloak, although it might frighten any dragon snatchers who were afraid of ghosts.

The moment she blew out the light and set the lantern down beside the cave wall, a blur of white luminescence streaked past her and bounced ahead a few steps before returning to twine through her ankles and sit weightlessly on her shoulders. They provided enough illumination to prevent her from stumbling or running into something.

The Fair organizers were nowhere to be seen, but Taz blocked the far end of the passage, hissing and trumpeting at the top of her voice, scratching and tearing at a door, desperate to get to Toby. Verity rushed forward to offer her services.

"Calm yourself, Taz," she whispered, gingerly stroking the top of the wing nearest the dragon's body. "If you'll let me pass, I'll pick the lock. Excuse me," she said to the distraught dragon, pushing her aside.

From within the room, someone said, "Call off your beast, boy, or I'll shoot you."

Verity pulled out her tools and knelt at the door, hoping that if the villains in the room decided to shoot anything or anyone she would make a smaller target.

"Do you hear that? Your dragon has given up. Probably gone to sample the menu in the arena."

"Taz would never eat someone," Toby said. "Except maybe you. She might make an exception in your case."

Taz roared, and Verity flinched. The extra movement was all it took to click the lock. Motioning Taz to stand back, she flung open the door, which swung out into the corridor. Before Toby's guards could react, Taz snaked her long neck into the room and plucked Toby out by his shirtfront. He ducked under her body, and she ignited a firewall between them and their enemies. Toby didn't stop to ask how the door opened or who was behind it. He vaulted himself up onto Taz's neck and the two of them swooped away down the passage. Sulfurous wind and dim light blinked into view before Taz was silhouetted against the brighter light. A babble of voices rose and was silenced abruptly as the opening closed.

"Come on," said one of Toby's former captors. "The women are out there already. We don't want to miss the fun. I've got a bet on how long it takes to find a dragon that will eat one of them and how long it will take him to do it."

Warmup Act

Verity backtracked through the cavern, past the dragons, and up the winding staircase to the barn, where she retrieved her wheelbarrow and wheeled it down the path as if she were supposed to be there. Smelt slithered out of the brush to join her.

"I saw no more of my kind around here," he said, "so I felt stand-out-ish."

"You didn't see any of your kind here because our enemies have most of them locked away," she said.

The ghost cats reappeared at her ankles and riding on Smelt's spinal ridges. The festival site was defined by torches burning a light semi-obscured by the resulting smoke, weaving ribbons through the camp. Now, though, a new area was delineated, four channels of torches along previously hidden paths leading into a sunken circular area between the dragon camp and the human camp.

Devent's voice rose over the other sounds, including the fiddle keening through the lament he sang of the 'Great War and the Battle of Blazing Bog.' Smelt puffed himself up.

"That's from the story I told him when we left the mine," he told her. "The lad's in good voice tonight."

Devent was surrounded by attentive listeners. He paused to allow the fiddle to escalate into a series of short, staccato trills biting into the night.

When the fiddler danced forward and back again, Verity was surprised to see her mother, her skin dyed brown and her hair stained black as it was when she traveled with her Gypsy band.

Surrounding them and Casimir, who seemed to be sitting out on the current number, Captain Lewis and the *Belle's Shell* crew all played along on instruments they used in their cabaret act at the Changelings Club.

For a few moments, the Dragon Fair seemed to be as advertised—a happy gathering of dragons and people who knew their value, despite the degradation they had undergone in recent years.

But suddenly, from 'backstage,' two of the festival crew took over, sweeping Verity's mother up with Devent before Verity had the chance to apprise her of the true nature of the Fair. They herded both performers toward the back of the Fairgrounds. Deserting her wheelbarrow and breaking into a run, Verity followed the procession until she made out what her mother was saying, "Looks like your career is commencing with a bang, Devent. Carnival Hall indeed!"

Surely they realized that something was amiss and the public face of the Fair masked a more sinister purpose? Why would Mother be here otherwise? She was not the sort to take holidays, from what Verity knew of her.

Before she could decide her next step, she found herself surrounded. Captain Lewis took one arm and Mr. Grey the other and prevented her from following.

"It's dangerous back there, dearie. We've been watching and have yet to see an un-uniformed soul cross over that wall and come out again."

"Oh, so you have noticed! I thought you were too busy performing," Verity told them. "They are plotting something quite horrible. But I can't put a stop to it from here."

"Likely you alone can't put a stop to it period, dearie," Captain Lewis said, patting her arm. "Come along now and never you fret. Your crewmates are here to help. But we must be careful."

She didn't need the captain to tell her that. Dropping her voice to a whisper, she told them what she had witnessed.

"I don't understand why these people have turned this from a Hiring Fair into something apparently much more sinister," Verity said. "The dragons were restless, but considering the circumstances, they were very patient. Why in the world do these stupid men want them to start eating people again, if indeed they ever did before?"

"I suppose so they can make money off the show. For some blokes, making a mess of beautiful girls is not only fun, but a good business opportunity." The feminine side of Captain Lewis was slit-eyed angry.

"That can't be all of it," she said.

Mr. Grey hazarded an opinion with a soft, seal-like cough discreetly concealed by his fist. "The girls at the rock say big shipments of smelly stuff have been crossing the channel to Argonia. Smells like that coal stuff they dig out of the ground in Frostingdung that makes it reek so. Perhaps they'd rather sell what they control than leave it to dragons they can't, and this is a good opportunity to get rid of them?"

Verity groaned. It sounded likely enough to her. "Good of you lot to show up to help," she told them. "I know it's a grand crowd for the cabaret act, but..."

"Naught to do with that, dearie," Captain Lewis said. "We was looking for you. Before you got here, we had a wee word with your mum. You still have that treasure cask we brought up? Did you open it?"

"Not yet," she said. "But it doesn't rattle like coins or jewels, so it didn't seem valuable enough to worry about amid all the other goings-on."

"I think the crew should be the judge of that, Brown," Legs said. Verity liked Legs, or maybe was mostly amused by the shifter octopus/bartender/rigger, but now it seemed that Legs didn't trust her much. Oh well, it had been weeks, so perhaps she'd have started to become impatient—or at least curious—also about a sunken treasure that someone else absconded with.

Verity unslung the pack she had carried so long it felt like part of her, pulled it open and felt toward the bottom for the cask. It was tarred wood bound with iron bands.

"You've not opened it yet?"

"It didn't seem important and I knew you'd want to see, too," she said. "I was going to wait until I saw you again in Queenston."

"Do 'er now," Mr. Grey said.

"But my mother..."

"There's more to that one than meets the eye," Grey told her. "She'll be grand."

"Go on," Legs prodded.

The lock was extremely tricky, but after a quarter of an hour, she gave her picks one final wiggle and the top of the cask sprang open.

A parcel wrapped in what looked like dragon hide lay within.

She unrolled it, and it unrolled and unrolled and unrolled. It was covered with rows of drawings of tiny cattle, pigs, deer, and other creatures, overlaid on a crude map of Argonia, with lines collecting each of the drawings to what seemed to be a specific area.

"Aha!" Captain Lewis said.

"Aha what?" Verity said.

"Them's ledger drawings is what they be," he said, lapsing into pirate-speak. "For keeping tallies of accounts and such."

"Accounts? But there be no numbers," Chips the carpenter said, puzzled.

"Count the critters," Doc told him.

"It's worthless," Legs said, waving three of her legs at the scroll.

Verity felt a twinge that told her that was not true.

Captain Lewis shrugged. "Sorry to trouble you, love. Wasn't worth the bother, was it? We could have left it at the bottom of the sea."

"Will you help me protect the dragons and the ladies?" Verity asked. "I don't think introducing dragons to a diet of human flesh is going to be a good thing for anyone, least of all the humans whose flesh it is."

Smelt, who had somehow made himself inconspicuous behind a tent, poked his head in among them. "Nevertheless, Lady. These people are right about one thing. We do need to eat. The good old days of plentiful meat everywhere you look are gone forever." He sighed a deep dragonly sigh full of sparks and ash.

Verity stood holding the scroll and felt a familiar twinge. "Are they? The days are gone but... blast. If only they hadn't taken my mother."

"Don't worry," Casimir said, squeezing her shoulder. "She's very resourceful, your mother. I'm sure she'll be fine."

"No doubt," Verity said. "But I need to ask her something and she's inconveniently unavailable. As usual."

"She'll be back," Casimir said. "I've never known her not to come back."

"Being eaten by a dragon might make it a bit difficult," Verity told him.

Auld Smelt lashed his tail. "Maybe in the heat of battle, we might have nibbled an enemy or two for strength, but..."

"I'm relieved to hear it," Casimir said.

"For them as took your mother, lass, I might could make an exception," Smelt said. "Even if they're nasty."

Casimir cleared his throat and said, "I'm more inclined to fret for Devent. He's an innocent and the Rani Romany is a woman of resources."

Verity's curse agreed with him and gave her not so much as a throb at his assessment of the situation.

"You may be right," she said.

"Come with me, lass. I'll show you her lair," Smelt said.

"You won't find it alone," Casimir said. "She keeps the entrances to the Knowes secret."

"Secret from men, maybe," Auld Smelt said. "Nothing a dragon can't sort out. We has our ways, has we."

"Nevertheless, I'll come with you," Casimir said. "I was the author of the ledger after all." That would have made him a tax collector, from what Verity could tell.

"You were? But you're a minstrel!" she said.

"Day job," Casimir said. "I was between jobs and I had to get my lute out of the pawn shop."

Verity wavered, nonetheless. "I can't just go scooting around in Faerie Knowes. I have responsibilities to the others. I must find Toby and Taz."

"Oh that!" Casimir laughed. "We should be able to return to this very time and place without losing a moment. Just remember it well."

Taking a deep breath, Verity looked around her. Even in the gloom of night, with the lanterns lighting the paths and the tents, it was not a place that her memory would easily confuse with any other in Argonia.

Captain Lewis gave her a brief salute, and he and the crew melted into the night.

When she had fixed their location in her mind, she nodded and followed Smelt, who also melted into the night. For an elderly dragon, he could slither with surprising stealth and speed and he did so, turning his head every so often so they could see where he was by the gleam reflected on his great golden eyes.

She had not noticed how large they actually were before.

She was watching the old dragon's progress instead of where they were going when she bumped into someone.

"Oh, sorry, pardon," she said.

"You!" the man said. It was Sir Whatshisname, the minister of finance. "You're no boy. You're that pesky person who thinks she's queen."

"The very morsel to tempt a dragon's palate," said his companion, aka Lord Lickspittal. "Nice large helping."

She glared at them. "Let us pass. We've urgent business to attend to."

"Oho! I think not, Your Majesty. We have even more urgent business for which your attendance is required."

"I decline," she said, and pushed past them.

"That's right," Casimir said. "Let the lady pass, or you'll have me to deal with."

Not having eyes in the back of her head, she couldn't see if they were properly intimidated or not.

Smelt had led them beyond the gate and into the hills before they heard shouts of pursuit.

The ghost cats popped into view briefly, before crowding into what appeared to be the sheer face of a cliff backing the Fairgrounds.

Well, they were ghosts and able to walk through solid things. On the other hand, they had often given her clues to what she sought. Without blinking, she thrust her boot forward and when she stepped down, was within the entrance to another cave.

She was a bit startled when Casimir took her hand, but he said, "I've been there." Smelt wrapped his tail around their legs. And....

"We should be good now, Casimir said after what seemed only a moment later.

When Dragons Were Brave and Cattle Were Many

Smelt nudged the wall and it opened. They stepped out again. There was an incredible stench in the air, worse even than the pong in The Dragon Vitia's lair. Cattle milled about where tents and people had been what seemed like moments before.

The sun was up. Auld Smelt was the first to walk forward into the crisp chilly morning. But there was nothing Auld about the senior dragon now. It seemed his clipped wings were able to grow after all and he unfurled them to display magnificent wingspread. His scales shown all shades of green from aqua through the new green of the tenderest shoots through fern and grass and all of the greens of the forest. Verity had never noticed how beautiful he was before.

"Have you grown young again, Master Dragon?" Casimir asked him.

"I have returned to the age I was when first I was here," Smelt told him.

"You seem—larger," Verity said. She was sure he was. The Smelt she knew was larger than a warhorse and a bear put together, but this Smelt was no smaller than the Dragon Vitia and his head alone was now the size of a buggy.

"A life in the mines do reduce a body," he said. "Now hurry, hop onto my back. Not that I'm in the habit of offerin' rides for humans, but a queen and the teacher of my foster lad are worth their weight to carry, particularly in the service of my kin and country. Do know, though, that if we come near the Battle of Blazing Bog at the battle's hour, I'll take ye anywhere else but there."

"Very wise," Casimir said. "Otherwise, your former self might claim yourself of our time and this time you might not survive the battle." Verity gave him a hard look. He might have warned them. She could hardly be expected to know such things, having never previously lollygagged around in history.

"It's happened," the bard said with a shrug.

"Hold on," Smelt told them, and with a blast of fire and a drum of his ribbed and webbed wings he lofted over the highest hills before sailing out over the trees.

Casimir mounted behind her, yelled into her ear, "See there?" and released the spinal ridge with one hand to point.

Beneath them, the forest canopy was sparse enough that she could see that it teemed with animals scurrying from the sight of the dragon looming above them. The moose that had been standing in each pond suddenly bolted and churned out of their pools onto the forest floor. A sounder of wild pigs dove deep into the brush, and deer froze in place until the flurry of the other beasts caused them to run in ones and twos, and family groups of three and five.

Changing course, Smelt flew over tundra and pasture, where cattle and sheep looked up from their grazing and horses galloped madly to escape the shadow of dragon wings.

Casimir tapped Verity's shoulder and pointed again, this time at a lone figure sitting uphill from the herds, pointing with his finger as he counted before returning to the scroll on his lap. The man doing the counting looked oddly familiar and she realized this was another, earlier version of Casimir, dressed in old style traveling clothes and making notations that became the scroll she had found in the casket. Casimir gave an ironic little wave to his former self as they passed.

The country was teeming with animals of all varieties—including human, soldiers marching down roads while townspeople fled ahead of them, some on roads and others on deer paths and trails through bogs and forests.

At length Smelt circled back the way he'd come and set himself and his passengers down smoothly on the field. Verity pulled out the scroll and spread it before Casimir.

"It seems to me we saw far more animals than you recorded."

"Well, yes, I did this before Blazing Bog, of course, but the dragons were active in many parts of the country, patrolling the perimeters with an eye to the invading forces."

"At the battle the dragons would have been fighting—will be fighting—not eating, unless there was a victory feast?"

"The battle whetted the appetites of some of them other flamers," Smelt said, "but me, I was tired of it all and returned to my lair. When I awakened and sailed out to slake my thirst and break my fast, seemed to be nary a beast about and though I slept for half a year, I smelled smoke still."

"Can we choose another time?" Verity asked.

The minstrel screwed his face up into a tortured expression and wobbled his flattened fingers back and forth, "It's possible," he said, "but I know where and when we are now because I was here the first time. Another would be less accurate."

"The battle is near," Smelt said, patting his belly with a front foot. "I feel it in my oven."

All through the night, miles from the battlefield, they trembled, not with cold as Smelt's body was warmer than most stoves, but from the strobes of fire, the roars of battle and the anguished cries of the dying. In the morning, Verity found she could not stop her hands from shaking. Casimir sang under his breath. At first Smelt had tried to tell them what was happening in the battle, but that made Casimir sing louder, and Verity shake harder.

By dawn it was all but over. Two dragons sailed by them at a short distance.

"Now we wait," Casimir said, "and find out what happened while Smelt hibernated."

The battle must have been decisive, Verity thought, because on their next flight, well after Smelt recalled returning to his lair, they saw no enemy activity at first.

Smelt flew and flew, stopping only for his passengers to warm their noses and fingers. He made a circuit of the entire country, which was still heavily populated with both game and domestic animals. Verity had understood that the invaders had sacked the farms and towns and killed and eaten the livestock, but there was rather a lot of it left.

But on the third day after the battle, she finally saw the uniforms of the invaders as they, along with people whose uniforms identified them as Frostingdung allies, got to work on the pastures and forests near the place where the so-called 'Hiring Fair' was being held. The livestock they herded into pens then methodically slaughtered and butchered every single farm animal. Musket shots rang from the forest. It was more frightening than the sounds of the battle. As they watched over the next week, the carcasses of more wild animals than a castle full of people could consume in a year were dragged from the woods as well.

"So that's what happened to them," Casimir said with a low whistle, while they listened to the slaughter. "They always said it was the dragons decimated the wildlife population, that and the invading troops—they are, but not while on the move fighting. And I thought the people of Frostingdung were our allies. What are they doing colluding with enemies?"

"A very good question," Verity said. And that day, the pasturage that had fed the livestock burned in a deliberate and controlled way, while what had been forest was cut down, the branches piled, and the trunks cut into logs and hauled away by the wagonload. Then there was a huge fire and the smell of roasting meat. "Why don't we ask them?"

Casimir sauntered down to the fire where the men celebrated with food and drink. Meanwhile Verity huddled against Smelt.

Casimir did not ask if the workers would care to be entertained, he just started in on a medium-bawdy ballad. The truly bawdy ones were a bit too rough, in his judgement, for Lady Verity's ears, but all listeners of this particular era were well-versed in certain phrases and metaphors with sexual comparisons inherent in their utterance within the context of the song.

As he had been fairly certain they would, the men stopped their own chatter to listen to the story of his song and included him in their circle. Between songs, he was included in the general conversation.

One was saying, "It's a tall order in a short time, but I reckon we're up to it. We start planting as soon as the beasts are destroyed and the burning's done."

"So this is the last meat anybody tastes in the land?" asked another.

"It will drive the price up for the humans, but there won't be much left for predators, so they have to eat what they're given, the bosses figure, and that only if they work as they're told."

Laughter and jokes followed as the men tried to imagine what kind of work dragons might do to earn their keep and after awhile, when they were all becoming drowsy, Casimir made his way back to Smelt and Verity, and woke them to tell them what he'd learned.

"Have they done this all over the country?" Verity wondered aloud.

"Perhaps not, farthest from the cities and main roads," Casimir said.

Smelt rolled to his feet and knelt so they could mount, unfurled his wings and soared. This time he flew in wide circles and they were rewarded with sightings of many more animals both in forest and field.

So, they'd all been lied to about the food supply being so far diminished by the ravages of war and dragon depredation. The destruction of the herds occurred, was occurring, after the war was essentially over, to create a shortage that would eventually force the growth and consumption of the grain-based kibble.

Smelt landed where the Mountains of Morn met the Troutroute River. Verity had seen this terrain while traveling from her last school, Our Lady of Perpetual Locomotion, back to Queenston. It was odd to see the country without the railroad stitching it together as it once had. It also provided a logistical problem.

"Now that we know there are animals here, how do we get them to the time and place where they're needed?"

"That will be trickier. Both because the Rani Romany is otherwise occupied, or was when last we saw her, and cannot open the nearest Knowe for us, but also simply herding all of these beasts inside will be no easy task."

"Smelt, can you herd them?"

"I can stampede them," he said. "But that's all. They're not bound to want to go where a dragon directs 'em."

"Oh. Yes. I can understand how that might be," she said.

"I don't suppose we can explain to them that they are to be slaughtered anyway and they may as well let their deaths serve a good purpose?" Casimir suggested.

"I don't suppose so," Verity agreed. "You and I might try driving them ourselves."

"Fancy being trampled, do you?"

"Hmmm. No. They didn't cover droving and shepherding at Our Lady of Locomotion."

"In my time everyone could do it, so it can't be that hard."

"I'm not from your time. Perhaps if we had mounts..."

A dog barked, and a cat mewed somewhere below them, and a voice said, "Do you think we are safe to come out now?"

Casimir scrambled down the rocks to greet them. "Timoteo, Marja, good to see you here. Are you camped nearby?"

"Casimir!" The male voice lowered then. "Are you alone?"

"No," he said. "I came through a Knowe with the Rani's daughter and our mutual friend, Smelt, a dragon of this region."

The woman walked away from the overhanging ledge and waved up both arms at Verity. "Come down, come down. You look frozen."

Verity did, more from curiosity than chilliness.

Smelt fluttered his wings in greeting. He was very proud of having new wings. How had he managed without them? He hoped he wouldn't lose them again when he returned. Perhaps he wouldn't. But then, he'd have to go through the long years in chains at the mine. And the lad would need him. But he hoped he could keep his wings this time.

Devent's Debut

Devent of course recognized the Gypsy Lady brilliantly accompanying his songs—she was the Lady from inside the hill where Casimir went to hide that time. He had no idea she was such a good fiddler, the best he had ever heard. Of course, she was the only one he had ever heard, but still, the effect was very pleasing, and he judged it enhanced his performance. He was so caught up in how they sounded together that he scarcely noticed where the men were leading them, into the trees and through a pair of doors he could step through without having to stoop. The floor sloped downward into a tunnel, which, to his professional eye, had been hastily constructed and perhaps wasn't as safe as it ought to be.

He put a protective wing behind the fiddler Lady, prepared to shield her in case of a collapse. When he looked around for Casimir to shield him too, he was disappointed not to see his mentor anywhere near. More surprising, Smelt had not followed either.

But he was once more reminded of the day he and Casimir had been attacked when he saw Grudge, the warrior maiden who had battled so valiantly to protect them. She wore an orange ribbon across her torso with a badge similar to those of the other festival officials.

She stepped in front of them, staff held horizontally to block the entrance to a broad circular field surrounded by people.

"Halt. Who goes there?" She demanded. "Password now or die."

"Stand aside, Troll. We are your bosses," said one of the men escorting him and the Lady.

"Why didn't you say so?" she grumbled, withdrawing her staff to let them pass. Then the Lady stepped out of the tunnel's shadow, with Devent following her.

"Well, hello there, hot shot," Grudge greeted him with an almost friendly scowl.

"Maiden," Devent said, inclining his head.

"Come along," said the man who had invited him. "You stand there, between those two doors, and the others will enter while you sing."

"You will introduce us?" the Gypsy Lady asked with a lifted eyebrow that said, 'you'd better.'

"Not necessary," the man said. "How many dragon and violin combos do you suppose there are in this country or even the world?"

The Lady shrugged, but glanced sideways at Devent, signaling him that all was not as it should be. But what could be wrong? This was Carnival Hall. Casimir had said it like it was famous and nothing bad happened in famous places to famous people—did it?

He and the Lady stood where the man directed. Meanwhile other people entered the field from the tunnel he'd just come from and took their places among the rows of benches stacked from the floor to the top of the structure surrounding the great field. So that was what had separated the dragon area from the human area of the Fair! Apparently, it was only used for special performances.

The man nodded, the Lady raised her bow and played the same note that Casimir usually played on his lute, and Devent sang the first long note of his new song, the cautionary tale he had composed from the story Mistress Verity told him about her adventures rescuing the Dragon Vitia and her twins. How the valiant Vitia had awakened in time to rise and lead the men away from her lair wherein her most precious treasures, her hoard and her children, lay.

The audience, to whom he looked for reaction, appeared startled, but not especially appreciative. This might have been because of the language barrier. It might have been because of the distraction as a column of white clad ladies entered from the right and were prodded, some of them weeping, to stand to one side while dragons of many sizes and colors, chained, as were the ladies, entered through the larger left-hand entrance.

Devent didn't know what to make of this and looked to the fiddler. Both of her eyebrows were raised, and her eyes darted from maidens to dragons and gave him a warning look, while continuing to play as if nothing untoward had happened.

He came to the part in the song when the men shot Vitia as Verity looked on. It was very dramatic and very frightening and sad. He was proud of it. It was hard to find rhymes for some of the events he'd wished to depict.

He glanced at the other dragons to see if they got the point about the guns the men used on Vitia, which was when he noticed that their faces looked odd. Now that he wasn't singing anymore, he also heard the clanking of chains from both the dragons and the ladies. Devent's night vision was better than average, but with the flickering of the torches around the edges of the arena, and the distortion of the shadows cast, it took him a second hard look to see that the dragons were muzzled. He had mixed feelings about the fact that the men who muzzled the other dragons (however they had managed it) had not tried to muzzle him. Didn't they think he was dangerous? He might have liked to be considered a little dangerous. On the other hand, they would know he couldn't sing while muzzled. When his song finished, he started another one right away and the fiddling Lady increased the tempo, volume and intensity of her performance, which the human audience would understand even if his dragon song was beyond them.

Halfway through, however, the man who seemed to be the boss, pointed at the fiddler and at the scared looking ladies in white. Other men forcibly escorted her to stand with the ladies. Devent did not like that. Men headed toward him with chains, and a heavy net and he tried to bolt. The boss unholstered a pistol he wore beneath the fine blue jacket he wore over his waistcoat.

Grudge hurried forward, saying, "I'll show this big blow-hot who's in charge here, sir." She grabbed the chains and the net from the man and approached Devent. He was puzzled. He thought she was a friend, but she said in a very mean tone, "Come on, you noisy brute, over where you belong." But when she was close enough he could see her face clearly, he saw that her very thick brow was twitching this way and that and her eyes were pleading—as much as a troll's eyes could plead, he supposed, signaling him to go peacefully. She had a plan. At least it seemed to be a plan to keep him out of chains and muzzle because she ordered him around and brandished the net at him but never even tried to throw it, and when she led him over to the other dragons, she dropped the chains at his feet and stood beside him without forcing the muzzle on him. He felt like weeping. This was not how his big debut was supposed to go.

Recruiting Cattle

Casimir and Smelt, as well as Verity, were learning the robust art of animal herding. The Gypsy family who had taken refuge in the cave had the traditional Gypsy understanding of animals.

"We don't tell them what you said that dragons might eat them in the new place and time we're going."

"It's that or men will slaughter them here for nothing," Casimir said. "They are doomed to meet a tragic end, so it may as well be to serve as food for the hungry."

Verity scratched her head. She didn't have a headache over Casimir's logic, but it made her rather twitchy nonetheless. "I don't know..."

Casimir shrugged, both annoyed and troubled by her sudden attack of scruples.

Verity turned to the Gypsy woman, "Marja, what do you think?"

Marja raised her eyebrows and spread her arms wide, a broader version of Casimir's shrug. "What you really want to know is what the animals think, yes?"

"Yes."

"Ask them yourself."

"How?"

"With your power, of course."

"I speak a little dragon. I've never tried cow or sheep before."

"What are you, a snob?"

Timoteo laughed. "She's a queen, luv. Of course she's a snob, too grand for the likes of farm animals."

Verity glared at him. "That's not it. I just don't know if I can."

"It's up to you."

Matilda the ghost cat appeared between the horns of a bull. Verity got the message that this was probably the leader of the herd. "Er, excuse me, sir," she said politely.

He snorted and stamped his foot, and in her head, she heard a voice demand, "Whut?"

"If I were to tell you that in a matter of hours, men will come and slaughter you and all your kin as well as the sheep and pigs and goats, but that we could save you from

254

them, only to lead you to a time where you would almost certainly be devoured by dragons, what would you say?"

"Run!' he replied, to her, not as an order to the herd.

"Very sensible, but what if there is nowhere to run to really? And all of the grass has been burned away and you face starvation? In the new place, although there are dragons, the men will care for most of you and make sure those not taken by dragons have food and water and room to roam."

The bull stamped his foot and shook his horns, as Verity believed, in horror.

A very old cow, one with swaying udders that marked her as one whose career had involved providing milk rather than as one marked for her meat. She'd been standing chewing her cud so placidly that Verity hadn't seen her before.

"Not so hasty, Durham," she said to the young bull.

"But, Ma," he said, mooing. "Dragons!"

"Exactly," she said. "Starvation and slaughter anyway, of use to none, that's a terrible fright but a dragon, now that's another matter. Dragons are very big and very hot, and they end you very quickly and then, you know, you're part of a dragon."

"Part of a dragon?"

"Of course. Humans like to say, 'We are what we eat,' but with the rest of us, more accurately, We are what eats us. We become something larger than ourselves."

"I'd become—him?" the bull asked, looking up at the ledge where Smelt had seemed to be sleeping until he winked back.

"Only if he was the one who ate you and he doesn't look hungry," the old milker said consideringly. "When are the men coming to kill us?" she asked Verity.

Marja said, "Soon."

Durham mooed sadly then bellowed at the herd. "Herd, to me! Follow!" And with a bellow that was something of a war cry, he galloped into the Knowe, followed by the old cow who was his mother and the other cows, bulls, and calves. The sheep did not even need to be spoken to. They followed the cattle.

The goats followed more cautiously. They were not convinced, and they were also not trusting. Somewhere along the way both they and the pigs became separated from the sheep and cattle and by the time the humans and Smelt arrived at the place and time from which they'd left, they were goatless and pigless.

Verity stuck her head out of the opening to the Knowe, expecting to see her mother. Instead, she was all but knocked over by a long slurp of an unfamiliar dragon slithering inside and startling the cattle into a bellowing chorus.

Smelt confronted the newcomer casually, smoking a little around his teeth, outlined in orange from banked fire. "Who might you be, Stranger?"

"Out of my way," Durance the Vile snarled. "The girl is on her own. I must quit this vile place and return to my treasure before the men find it and carry it off."

"Are you sure this treasure of yours is still valuable and not a metal scrap heap?" Smelt asked him.

"What a horrible thing to say!" Durance huffed a puff of smoke.

"It can happen," Smelt said. Only a handful of ashes sifted down from his mouth.

"Mine is there. It was there when I left. If it is not still there on my return, these men shall learn what it is that dragons eat."

"Fair enough," Smelt said. "Just beware of their steel and shot."

"They're coming!" Timoteo warned. Durance sucked his tail into the cave and gave no mind to how he stampeded the cattle as he fled down the ceiling of the passageway, dodging stalactites as he slithered.

Verity made little sense of what followed, for the battle cries of the men, the screams of the women, and the bellows of cattle and bleating of sheep created a cacophony her truth seeking could not penetrate.

Sacrifice

Malady's former favorite uncle controlled the crowd as if he had fed them all the placidity-inducing dragon kibble. Maybe he had.

"Dragons, eh? We've been told we can't live without them, but the truth is, we can't live with them, either. Am I right?"

Half the audience laughed and cheered, and the other half clapped uncertainly.

"Ladies and gentlemen, we now come to the exciting portion of the festival. Many of you have been forced for lo these many years to work beside the smelly and dangerous beasts in order to make a living. You have been frightened and alarmed by their recent rebellion. You have been told by those who would control you that the scaly brutes will become docile again once their food source, destroyed by those who seek to overthrow the government, is restored.

"But history tells us otherwise. Before the Great War, dragons ravaged the land. It was only with the coming of the Allies that they were brought to heel and the crippling strictures of superstition and witchery were banished." He went on at some length, about the evils of a world where anything that didn't make money within a few minutes was a false ideology. His charm (which had vanished for Malady about the time he threw her in the dungeon) slipped away as he grew more and more passionate on the topic. Malady had not previously noticed how much he seemed to love to hear himself talk. The audience, most of which did not seem to share his enthusiasm, grew restive. Finally he must have sensed their unease or perhaps he was ready to see some blood shed at last. "Dragons often demanded the sacrifice of beauteous maidens and tonight we reenact the bad old days for your entertainment in this program, starting with the Game of Dragons and Damsels."

Malady would have been shaking in her boots if she still had any. They'd been left out of her sacrificial ensemble, along with any item of warm or protective clothing.

"How dare he!" she growled to her closest fellow incipient sacrifices. "He may think it's a game but I for one am not game and I decline to be treated like it!"

She was further outraged when the burly men Uncle Marq ordered to 'prepare the sacrificial maiden' took one look at her angry face and veered away to grab a young girl, the one who had been trying to escape her shackles back in the cave, Malady was sure of it. The silly chit shrieked so piercingly you'd have sworn she was descended from banshees.

"What's the matter with you, girl?" Malady demanded. "Rip their faces off!"

"You're next, girly," said the heavier of the two men, the one with the shaved head and a scar that looked as if an axe had cleaved his head in two at one point and the head had been clumsily reassembled.

Malady shrieked louder than the girl who was actually being attacked and in fury stamped her bare feet on the ground. Which hurt, and she stumbled. Someone braced her up from the back. The thugs manhandled the younger girl forward, and one of them bent to unlock her shackles.

As he stood, the Gypsy fiddler fumbled and fell against him. He pushed her back into Dr. Hexenbraun, and she too fell, in a domino effect.

Marquette took one look at the terrified youngster and pointed at his henchmen to return her to the group. Then he pointed at Malady.

"Her," he said clearly.

The henchmen closed on Malady. The Gypsy woman, Romany—Verity's mother, supposed to be the hereditary queen—brained him with her fiddle, which oddly enough did not break, so she smashed it into the face of the other assailant. Malady, whose shackles had mysteriously fallen away shortly after Dr. Hexenbraun fell across her feet, broke and ran for the closest tunnel. All eyes followed her, so most people did not notice the trio of dragons that flew into the arena until they swooped after her.

They were too big to squeeze into the tunnel and looked at each other in frustration until the singing dragon, Devent, who could not simply pretend to be tethered in the face of his old enemies, sang out to them.

"Three of you against one young lady! Have you no honor?"

"Uhh—nope," said Chainy, rattling his tail.

"What's honor?" demanded Spike Tail, turning his back to the tunnel mouth to confront Devent, who was halfway across the arena by then. "Is it tasty?"

Bobbinears dove on Devent, who easily snaked around him.

The audience went wild, trying to escape from the unplanned and unsupervised dragon dispute. They scrambled over each other dismounting from the stands, stepping on those who remained seated. The cries of those stepped on by panicked dragons rent the air.

Malady picked the moment when the attacking dragons were halfway between her cave and Devent to make her reappearance—this time with several coils of dragon encircling her.

From the air, Bobbinears had turned from pursuing Malady to confront Devent, circling him, while Devent turned to face his opponent directly. But Devent was no more a warrior now than he had been when he met the three fierce dragons before. Fortunately, Grudge was the same as well. A rock the size of a dinner plate seemed to catapult from her hands to hit the attacking dragon on the wing, crippling him.

Bobbinears screamed and fell, then flapped back to his feet and charged Devent, only to receive a face-full of troll.

"Hello, creep. You want a piece of this maiden, come and get it!" she said, crouching as she hopped from side to side to confuse his attack moves, tossing a stone the size of a man's head from hand to hand.

"You!" Bobbinears said.

"You noticed," Grudge said. "It's your lucky day, hot and bothered. Pick on someone who fights back, you bullying sack of burning poop." She threw her rock and it hit him squarely in the right eye this time. He went down like a—well, a rock.

Spike Tail and Chainy concentrated on menacing Malady until Spike Tail's concentration wavered and he suddenly thought, why go after the loose one when there were so many others to pick off.

Flaming, he flew at the swoon of chained and restrained maidens, some of whom seemed distinctly less than maidenly. He didn't care as long as they had flesh to sear and blood to spill. Two of them who were old and stringy-looking stepped out in front of the others and fixed him with stares that ought not to have been as compelling as they were. "Dragon, I bid you, flee while there's still time!" the one who looked to be older said. She said it in the tongue of humans, which he did not understand.

"Ooh," he responded in his own tongue. "You're threatening me, old woman. I am very frightened, but I cannot run away fast enough so how about I just roast you where you stand instead?"

At the same time, Chainy swooped toward their prima-
ry target, but just as he was about to snatch her up, the
tunnel seemed to fill with fire and a spikey old head poked
out of it. It whipped toward him on its long flexible neck
until he was face to face with it.

"Death to any who attacks my pretty, pretty princess!"

Chainy blasted a bolt of flame into his smug old face.
The elder dragon dodged the blast and snaked his head
up to meet his attacker, but most of him remained on the
ground, wrapped protectively around the prey the gang of
three had been specifically directed to barbecue.

Marquette stood in the stands now, addressing a group
of armed people. "Any of you who came hoping to bag a
dragon, now is your chance. They aren't performing as
they're supposed to. Put them down."

"We don't get to question them about their lairs at all?
Pity."

"Perhaps when things are less hectic."

Six men and one woman, all in hunting clothes, stepped
into the field with rifles held at the ready, aimed into the
dragons clustered along the side. They raised their weapons. Something sailed through the air and knocked three of
their weapons from their hands and onto the ground.

In a recently vacated section of the stands, a mud-
brown girl stood beside a large stack of pottery plates. She
skimmed one into the air with dead aim, and it took out
another firearm. The small dragon beside her launched into
the air on the periphery of the aerial battle, also carrying
plates, several in its mouth and some in each set of talons.
A gentleman dressed in a fern and heather colored hunting
costume raised a musket to his shoulder and three plates
smashed onto his head, toppling him before he could fire a
shot. One of his armed companions took aim at the dragon and the girl picked up three plates and flung them in a
burst so rapid it defied the eye's ability to track. The musket flew from the man's hands.

One of his companions took aim at the girl and he fired.
With unusual accuracy for a musket, the round struck
her. She looked down at the hole in her chest, which did
not bleed, and stooped, scooping up a little dirt from the
ground, spat on it, and slapped it over the hole. Madame
Erotica and her girls saw their chance and ran in among

the women distributing vials of love potion, before all concerned sprinted to the dragon side of the arena and began pelting dragons with the potion, which spattered in a huff of enchanted scent and ran pink as dilute blood down the scales it hit.

A gang of trolls from the audience tromped over other spectators to reach Grudge.

"You're not doing this right," her brother said. "Dummy."

"If you can do it better, you take out a few," Grudge said, feeling the old resentment flair within her, even though she knew this was the troll way of taking an interest.

"I should just let you die," he said. "You were always worthless anyway."

Grudge grinned. "You say the sweetest things."

Her family covered for her standing stonily between the attacking men and the dragons while Grudge unlocked shackles.

When she ducked in among the other dragons to work, Devent, on an impulse, took to the sky, singing his heart out, singing of peace and freedom and gold and jewels and how nasty people tasted compared to other delicious dietary items a dragon might consider. The main thing about his song was that the tune was soothing as a lullaby and soon nerves began to be less twitchy, trigger fingers grew less itchy, and Chainy, still menacing Malady, stepped back, shaking his head as if confused.

Durance the Vile's head struck like a snake's at the attacking dragon, then suddenly retracted, his body slipping out of position, knocking down the girl.

"Fat lot of protection you are!" Malady complained, but just then the ground shook itself like a wet dog.

"Earthquake!" yelled one of the older women, "I think."

Bringing Home the Bacon

The cattle didn't care for the underworld. The icy stone surrounding them was not to their taste, with neither grass nor grain to tempt them. They lowed, bellowed, stamped and snorted. They exploded from the Knowe, for even though they had agreed in theory that to be eaten by a dragon and thus become a part of one would be a great honor, none were anxious for the honor immediately.

Verity had no experience with stampedes, but Smelt chivvied and shepherded them in the direction of the chute-tunnels leading into the arena. They were more inclined to go anywhere else until Casimir began humming and 'ooo-ing' an intriguing tune that caused them to slow, look at the ground for some errant hank of grass and, finding none, investigate the tunnel toward which they, along with the sheep, goats, and pigs that followed, ambled.

Wild things sprang from the Knowe too: bear, lynx, moose, caribou, foxes, squirrels, ptarmigan, beaver, otters, and others that had not been seen in Argonia with any frequency in over a century. These creatures, however, spread out, leaving the compound to look for their familiar habitat in the woods, meadows, streams and mountains.

The dragons in the arena, newly freed by Grudge and pacified to a degree by Madame Erotica's love potion, fell immediately in love with the feast galloping before them and fell upon the beasts, some to devour them and others, slightly confused, to court them, or attempt to.

The humans they totally forgot or ignored.

Storm clouds that had been gathering in the night sky, blotting out stars, were suddenly upstaged by a glorious multi-colored balloon, a huge one, big enough that Taz could perch at the mouth of it and gently heat the gas that filled it.

The gondola was huge, big enough to carry at least two dozen people. Toby set it down outside the arena and, after noting that their ankles were free of restraint, the captive 'maidens' made a beeline for the exits and an airborne escape from a holiday that had become a nightmare.

An unfamiliar lady who bore a striking family resemblance to Aunt Ephemera, Madame Erotica and the upper half of Aunt Eulalia led a frightened youngster up through the tunnel, sternly making a path through the other women, "Excuse me, children first." "What is the matter with you? This kid is frightened and battered." "You should be ashamed of yourself, pushing like that. You're okay, I'm okay, we're all okay and will soon be out of this place if you exercise a bit of patience and calm."

Devent landed beside Smelt, and they were roundly hissed at by an unfamiliar dragon with a coil wrapped proprietarily around Malady. Of course, Malady. Who else but that trouble-maker? To Verity's surprise, her mother, Romany, had remained as well instead of disappearing into a tree or a hill somewhere as she usually seemed to do. She was clad in her customary disguise of black dyed hair and walnut stained skin, her colorful skirts pushing out the white garment hastily thrown over her head by her captors so that she resembled nothing so much as a peeled potato adorned with ruffles for a festive touch.

"What did you do?" Romany demanded, boggling at the bones piling up beside sleeping dragons.

Beside her stood no brave knight, but the foxy family lawyer, N. Tod Belgaire.

"You mean to say you didn't know everything already?" Verity asked. "How refreshing." She briefly recounted their journey through the Knowe, to meeting with Marja and Timoteo and the decision the cattle had made regarding their upcoming demise.

When the first balloon load took its load of ladies away from the Fairgrounds, Devent lit the pile of timber gathered from dismantled pavilions. Most of the dragons slept. The Fair organizers had mysteriously disappeared, which at least meant nobody had to listen to them. Verity, Romany, Malady, and Casimir surrounded by the tails and coils of the drowsy Devent, Durance and Smelt, warmed themselves. While the 'game' was going on, everyone was more than warm enough, but this night the weather grew cold and made it plain that winter was about to descend upon the land once and for all.

"This Fair promoted the idea that dragons were to be feared and exterminated," Verity said. "But it turns out the most fearsome creatures we have to face are the so-called allies and former government ministers seeking to destroy the reputations of the dragons as workers and have them all killed so they can bring in what in their own country passes for power."

"We'll see about that," Mr. Belgaire said.

"I had nothing to do with all of this," Malady protested. "The uncles—I mean, the ministers—tried to kill me too!"

"We know, dear," Dr. Hexenbraun said, patting the arm the girl did not have across Durance, as if afraid to lose contact with the wily old dragon. "Your family is not your fault."

Verity frowned at the other girl. "You didn't do much to help me, however."

"I don't like you," Malady said honestly, to Verity's relief. "I knew all along that I was supposed to rule. Even Durance says I am a princess and he is the oldest dragon ever and has lived in Queenston Castle practically before there was one. He showed me the treasury, not you."

"Well, I wasn't there because your uncles had me shanghaied."

"Girls, girls," said Romany. "I had hoped you might get along better, once you both learned of the jeopardy to our kingdom from those men."

"But you made me queen," Verity said. "I had to wear that bloody tiara and everything."

"I knew that you would hate it. Except for your stature, you have always taken after your father's side of the family, my dear."

"Maybe so. Or maybe I was just more like him because he was there." Verity snapped. She was weary and sore and a bit loopy from the step-missing disorientation of time travel. She did not feel like being tolerant, or even fair. "Malady isn't related to either one of you though. So why her? Why not someone else."

"She is a pretty, pretty princess. My fairy princess," Durance said, laying his chin on Malady's knee.

"I never told him that," Malady said, holding up her hands as if to defend herself from accusations.

But to Verity's puzzlement, the dragon's statement did not trigger a headache for her. She narrowed her eyes at her mother. "There's something else you're not telling us, isn't there? Is she my sister from another timeline? Did you leave Dad for some other man?"

Her mother rolled her eyes. "No, dear, I did not. Isn't being a time traveling witch princess/Gypsy queen complicated enough? You don't need to think me a slut as well. No, Malady is not my daughter. She is our relative though. She is descended from my older brother, Rupert, and like me is directly from the line of King Roari Rowan and Queen Amberwine, who was indeed of Faerie lineage."

"But, she's a Dungie!" Verity protested, and was immediately upset with herself for using the pejorative for the Frostingdungians, even if the ones who had been in power were responsible for the recent trouble.

"Half," Romany said. "She is my niece and your cousin. On his way home from the quest to rescue me, Rupert was sed—claims he was seduced—by a Frostingdungian merchant's daughter. He says his heart had already been taken by the dragon Grippeldice, daughter of Grizel and Grimley, who were friends of the family."

Durance opened one eye and a noise vibrated from his throat that was very like a cat's purr. "I knew it," he said. "I knew there was a whiff of dragon kin about this fairy princess."

"Well, I'll be damned," Malady said. "I had no idea."

"I discovered it in a recording Rupert made that had been buried in the Seashell Archives. But I knew nothing of you, so I thought it best if you girls sorted it out among yourselves. It seemed to me that between Verity's visions of the truth and your emphasis on being a vision of glamor and beauty, your qualities might complement each other."

"It all sounds very complicated," Verity groaned. Malady, on the other hand, sat straight up and leaned forward eagerly.

"Yes," she said. "Complicated. But..."

"That," said N. Tod Belgaire, the family lawyer, "Is where I come in. We are going to need new counselors and functionaries... I will have to reread the law books from before the Great War and try to determine which modifications from current times to keep and which are out-moded or rooted in the self-interest of the larcenous lordships and murderous ministers, who, if I may be so bold as to suggest, should either be banished back to Frostingdung or continue to enjoy our hospitality from the dungeon."

Verity looked around, at the seats where other weary people sat listening, and found she was staring at the individuals distinguished by a ghost cat on their heads, in their laps, or draped across their shoulders. Madame Marsha, Clodagh, Grudge, Zeli, Mr. Bowen, Captain Lewis and several of the others she had not yet given dragon beads to served as perches for the ghost cats, informing her of the whereabouts of some of the remaining magical heirs.

"I think we might consider choosing from a broader pool of people to govern than before," she said. "And perhaps Casimir and Auld Smelt can advise us more of how things used to run, since you chose not to participate in politics before, Mother."

Durance raised his head and Malady said, "Durance the Vile knows where a lot of bodies are buried—literally as well as metaphorically, and who has whose skeletons in their closets, quite aside from the uncles. We actually might be able to work this out." She sounded not at all sarcastic, but hopeful.

"I'm going to go invite the people the cats seem to be favoring to come to the castle," Verity said. "I am not sure the country needs a queen or royals at all, Mother. Not in these modern days. But we have a lot of different species and races to consider. What with Faeries, trolls, merfolk, the heirs to wizards, and dragons, they will all have different needs and also different skills they can contribute."

A few months later, the first full council convened in a totally transformed throne room/council chamber/ballroom. Seating for fifty circled the room for the newly appointed regional representatives. A balcony strong enough to accommodate one or more dragons had been built outside of the windows where Durance used to peer in at Malady. From the minstrel's gallery, another outcropping was designed to hold Devent. Smelt was a roving ambassador for the dragons who wished to return to their former jobs or new ones—or go into business for themselves. Fiona and Zeli represented working women, Clodagh tradespeople and Grudge provided the loyal opposition to almost every debate and decision.

Malady, due to her influence with the keeper of the royal treasury, was the new finance minister, a job which Casimir suggested must require the person to travel around the country not only to explain the need for taxes, but also to dispense aid where it was needed and become acquainted with the needs of the citizen/subjects.

The system was by no means perfect, but on the anniversary of the ill-fated Hiring Fair, people celebrated anyway.

Verity addressed the crowd while Malady posed in her most glamorous gown and jewels on loan from the treasury. She waved to the populace while Verity spoke, trying to sound a bit like the kings and queens of old, not autocratic but formal, respectful and hoping to inspire respect and trust in return. The trust part, at least, was something that was becoming easier for her to gain as her reputation for compulsive honesty became more widespread and more deeply entrenched in the peoples' regard.

She downplayed her role as queen but was well-known as a judge and dispenser of justice in all disputes. It gave her alarming headaches some days, but by fixing a little shelf for the crown to sit on above her head, she was relieved of the literal burden of it at least.

"Argonians, human and non, we have survived the year and with any luck we'll survive another. My Aunt Epiphany tells me it is entirely likely, and she knows these things. It is our hope that we as a nation are learning to utilize all our skills and powers, magical and non-magical, to make our land prosperous, healthy, and as happy as humans can reasonably be expected to be. But for now, we will make merry, celebrate, and otherwise party and live happily ever after. You know it's true, because I say so."

She left Malady waving and blowing kisses, the most beloved tax collector ever, and joined Toby on the dance floor.

She did not see when another couple slipped into a side alley from which they would access what would soon be the sewage system that now was an underground passage leading to the Faerie Knowe and another time.

"Devent's songs of this time and the adventures of your good daughter queen will be sung and embellished upon for generations to come," Casimir said.

"But not during her lifetime," the Rani Romany said with a smile. "For her lifetime, they are confined to the truth, the whole truth, and nothing but the truth."

"Huzzah," Casimir said softly.

About the Author

Elizabeth Ann Scarborough is the author of more than 25 solo fantasy and science fiction novels, including the 1989 Nebula award winning *Healer's War,* loosely based on her service as an Army Nurse in Vietnam during the Vietnam War. She has collaborated on 16 novels with Anne McCaffrey, six in the bestselling Petaybee series and eight in the YA bestselling Acorna series, and most recently, the Tales of the Barque Cat series, *Catalyst* and *Catacombs* (from Del Rey). Recently she has converted all of her previously published solo novels to eBooks with the assistance of Gypsy Shadow Publishing, under her own Fortune imprint. *Spam Vs. the Vampire* was her first exclusive novel for eBook and print on demand publication, followed by *Father Christmas* (a Spam the Cat Christmas novella) and *The Tour Bus of Doom. Redundant Dragons* is her newest exclusive novel in The Seashell Archives series and follows *The Dragon, the Witch, and the Railroad.*

WEBSITE: http://www. eascarborough.com
DEDICATED BOOK SITE:
 http://scarbor9.wix.com/beadtime-stories
BLOG: http://spamslitterature.wordpress.com/
TWITTER: https://twitter.com/KBDundee
FACEBOOK: http://www.facebook.com/elizabeth.a.scarborough
OTHER: http://www.goodreads.com/author/show/4811383.K_

CPSIA information can be obtained
at www.ICGtesting.com
Printed in the USA
FSHW011102050121
77428FS